Colliding Forces

Constance
O'Day-Flannery

tor romance

A TOM DOHERTY ASSOCIATES BOOK
NEW YORK

This is a work of fiction. All the characters and events portrayed in this book are either products of the author's imagination or are used fictitiously.

COLLIDING FORCES

Copyright © 2005 by Constance O'Day-Flannery

Edited by Anna Genoese

A Tor Book
Published by Tom Doherty Associates, LLC
175 Fifth Avenue
New York, NY 10010

www.tor.com

Tor® is a registered trademark of Tom Doherty Associates, LLC.

ISBN 0-765-35102-1
EAN 978-0-765-35102-9

First edition: October 2005

Printed in the United States of America

0 9 8 7 6 5 4 3 2 1

For my mother, AnnMarie O'Day, one of the
strongest women I know.

ACKNOWLEDGMENTS

Anna Genoese . . . thank you for your patience and your faith in me.

Richard Curtis . . . thank you for guiding me with a gentle hand.

William Rivers Pitt . . . thank you for your tireless efforts to report the news responsibly. Your words and ideas inspired me and made it into this book.

Miko, Kristen, Ryan, Vic, Don . . . thank you for being there.

Vernon Edwards . . . thank you for being you and calling the night I asked for a miracle.

Lady Laidlaw . . . thank you for the laughter. The smoke is still rising from the chimney!

PROLOGUE

*I*t was like the ending of a fairy tale, Deborah Stark thought while watching her friend Maggie sail off into the glorious Bermuda sunset with the love of her life. She was stunned to find that her eyes were burning with embarrassing tears and she blinked furiously to stop such a display of emotions.

Good God, what was she becoming? Soft?

D., as she was called by friends, having long ago dropped cutesy nicknames, straightened her shoulders and took a deep breath of salty sea air. Okay, so the whole wedding show had an effect on her. How many times does a person witness a friend find out her long lost father is a United States senator, capture the love of one of the most eligible men in the northeastern United States, marry him at his exotic island estate and then, literally, sail off into the sunset? She felt as if she were an extra in a movie and what galled her, really galled her, was that she couldn't report a word of it until next week.

Here she was, an accomplished and respected newswoman, the six o'clock anchor in Philadelphia, and she had to sit on this story which had already gained national attention when Senator Gabriel Burke had announced Maggie O'Shea was his daughter, and this, coming out of a hospital news conference where Burke was recuperating from surgery after an assassination attempt.

C'mon . . .

But a promise was a promise. And she did promise Maggie to sit on the story.

She turned her head slightly and glanced at the cliffs leading down to the sea. If any of the paparazzi got word of this wedding and were lying in the tall grass snapping pictures she would spit nails at being scooped.

The devil and the angel immediately sat on her shoulders, shoulders that were draped in a sexy, pale yellow Versace material that barely skimmed over the rest of her body. The devil, unfortunately the voice she was all too familiar with, whispered that she could fly back to Philly in a little over an hour and make the eleven o'clock news. She'd scoop them all, the networks, the cable stations . . . maybe she would even be featured on *Entertainment Tonight* or a live feed in to CNN. Her face would be plastered across the nation. Think of what an opportunity it would be . . . getting the network brass in New York City to not only notice her, but remember her. She could leave Philly behind, return to the Big Apple victorious, and this time sit in the chair she had been working for since she was a teenager. It was destiny. Think of the money, the recognition, the prestige. . . .

Hold it.

The angel seemed to kick sand into the voice of the devil, carrying it away on a soft tropical breeze. She had promised a friend. How many friends did she have? Sadly, Maggie was the only one she could bare her soul to and tell the truth. The truth . . . dear God, she was so far from the truth even she had trouble remembering it all. In her past was too much that she'd had to bury with hard work and illusion in order to survive. And survival had led her to success. Still, her stomach muscles clenched when she thought of betraying Maggie. A promise is a promise, D. thought, quickly shrugging her shoulders as if to get rid of that angel too.

Damn, she wasn't becoming nice, was she? Just thinking the word made her actually shiver in distaste. Nice people didn't stand up for themselves or get ahead of the pack. For the sake of niceness, they put up with all kinds of shit she would never in her life—

"Are you cold?"

It was that voice, *his* voice.

Marcus Bocelli.

Gorgeous. Italian. And so *hot* that she immediately broke out into a dewy sweat like some fifty-year-old woman in menopause. Which, at thirty-six, she was nowhere near. What the hell was wrong with her body? She glanced at her side and up to his beautiful Roman profile. "No, not cold," she whispered, staring out to the sea again with the rest of the guests as Maggie and Julian McDonald reached his yacht. "Perhaps a little envious," she added with a grin. "I was just thinking this was like the ending to a fairy tale or a romantic movie."

"You like fairy tales?" he asked in his sexy accented voice, turning his attention away from the happy couple and onto her.

She wasn't even looking at him and she could *feel* him. It was like nothing she had ever experienced, this bizarre drawing of her body, this yearning to be closer, to touch him. She turned her head and smiled. "I don't believe in fairy tales."

Good God, she could feel the intensity of his eyes at he gazed into hers and had to force herself not to look away. Something witty was called for here to break this absurd attraction. "Any princess worth her tiara will tell you it never lasts. Why do you think the fairy tale or movie ends with them riding off together into the sunset? Happily ever after?" She chuckled and shook her head. "Nobody wants to read the after, of the happily ever after."

His eyes narrowed slightly, along with his smile. "I'm sorry. I don't understand. My English, I thought, was fairly good, but your statement confuses me."

She laughed. "Oh, Mr. Bocelli, your English is perfect. Probably better than mine. What I was trying to say is that nobody wants to read about real life . . . after the happily ever after part is over."

"Ah . . . yes. Now I understand. You prefer to deal in reality, yes?"

No man had the right to be so gorgeous. His eyelashes were actually longer than hers. Doesn't he know he intimidates women with his natural beauty? "Yes. Reality. It's my business. The news."

"Yes, yes, Magdalene said you are on television, a news reporter."

"Actually, I read the news that's given to me."

"And reality tells you that Magdalene and Julian will not be happily ever after?"

She delicately shrugged. "I don't know the future. I sincerely wish them the best, but reality has shown me that marriage isn't an easy institution."

"You have been married?"

Throwing her head back with laughter, she added, "Absolutely not! The only institution I've been in is one of learning. And college wasn't that easy."

"I see," Marcus murmured, smiling gently into her eyes.

All right. This was progressing well. Time to wrench it up a notch. "And what do you see, Mr. Bocelli?" She hoped her voice was as sexy as she felt, now that her body temperature had regulated back to almost normal.

"First, please call me Marcus. We have been formally introduced months ago and have been in each other's presence before."

Hmm, so formal. "Okay, what do you see . . . Marcus?" she hesitated only a moment before using his first name.

His smile remained gentle. "I see a lovely woman who has turned her back on fairy tales and romance. Such a shame."

"Hold on. I didn't say I didn't believe in romance. I'm all for it. Just that it doesn't last." She paused, letting out her breath. "But I'm all grown up now and know how the game is played" She paused again for effect. "Any time you want to play Marcus, just call." There. That was more like it. She was back, no simpering little female at the feet of a Roman god.

Smiling as her gaze slowly left his chest and traveled up to his eyes, she added, "I'm easy to reach." And with that parting shot, she started to walk back to the party. That was better. Let him do the chasing. Oh, she'd read *The Rules* and, as much as it irritated the hell out of her, they were probably right. The male animal wants to stalk, to be the aggressor in order to fully savor surrender.

"Deborah . . ."

She stopped and turned around. Against her will, her breath caught in her throat as she took in the sight of his tall frame against the sunset, the breeze playing with his dark curls. Curls her fingers were itching to touch. Swallowing, she asked, "Yes?"

"I just called."

1

Residents of Center City were certainly out in full force today as everyone took advantage of the unexpected summer-like weather this close to Thanksgiving. Should we be defrosting our turkeys, Jim, or pulling out our barbeques again?"

"I'm afraid, Deborah, this has only been a tease," Jim Carter answered, picking up his cue as he stood in front of the blue weather screen and faced the camera. "The warm weather is already on the way out . . ."

As Philadelphia's top-rated weatherman began his report, D. leaned back in her chair at the anchor desk and tried to concentrate on the pages in front of her, the same lines that were on the teleprompter over the camera. Another soft story. This must be the tenth in two weeks. She found that her back teeth were grinding in annoyance and relaxed her jaw. They were feeding all these tug-your-heart stories to her because of that last *focus group*. Just thinking about them had the ability to raise her blood pressure.

This time they said she wasn't feminine enough. Too tough. She didn't have any softness. One of them even had the balls to say he couldn't imagine her being affectionate! If they wanted the Pillsbury Dough Boy to read hard news then they should have hired him. Affectionate! She'd exploded in her boss' office two weeks ago when Dan, along with the station manager, tried to tell her she needed to soften the edges a little. Why were they brainwashed by a group of obvious morons who had completely missed the point that she reported hard news . . . politics, wars, murders, hit-and-runs, kidnappings, robberies. What was she supposed to do? Dab at her eyes with Grannie's lace handkerchief while telling the tri-state their news in order to please a handful of people they had pulled off the street?

But it was the affectionate remark that seemed to linger in her back teeth, like an irritating kernel of popcorn that couldn't be dislodged. Immediately, her brain ran over the last time she'd been *affectionate*. Hah! They should have seen her then . . .

The encounter with Marcus Bocelli still had the ability to warm her body whenever she thought of it . . . the two of them walking on the beach, how he casually took her hand, wooed her with his voice, his sensuous eyes, until she was actually preening just being in his presence. A kiss had led to being held in his arms, pulled against his lean hard body and, for the first time in a very, very long time, she had lost control.

It played back in lightening flashes . . . her pulling him into a cove, her back against a stone wall as his mouth explored her and her hands tore at his clothes. She couldn't remember the last time she'd made love with such abandon. She could picture Marcus' hands sliding up the skirt of her Versace dress as she clung to him, became one with him. It had seemed as though nothing existed in that space of time except a man and a woman doing the most primal thing in the world . . . humping each other like wild monkeys. It was only days later that she wondered if they'd reacted so crazily because they each seemed to have lost something at that wedding. Maggie. D. knew Marcus loved Maggie, or had loved her at some point. And Maggie would no longer be in Philadelphia after she married Julian. Not having many friends, D. hated to lose Maggie, even if it was to love and marriage. Still, the whole encounter with Marcus had left her stunned and craving more. So far, she hadn't heard from him and—

"Deborah?"

"Deborah!" she heard in her earpiece, the floor director jerking her back from a magical tropical love fest to the dark television studio in Center City, Philadelphia.

"Sorry, Matt," she breathed with a smile to her co-anchor. Squaring her shoulders, she looked into the camera and tried to soften her facial expression. "We all know dogs are man's best friend, but what happens when your precious, furry friend disappears without any warning? When we come back we'll find one woman's answer, and we'll tell you how she fought city hall to reclaim her best buddy."

They went to commercial and Matt Jordan laughed. "Now that's the first time I've caught you lost. Where were you, D.?"

She grinned. "If I told you, Matt, the rest of your hair would turn gray with shock."

"Good or bad?" he asked as the makeup crew came up to the desk and blotted sweat off his forehead.

"Neither," she answered, waving off the hair stylist who wanted to make her brown wisps even more defined. Having no desire to appear as a talking whisk broom, she said, "Thanks, Sheila, but the hair is fine as it is." And she had no intention of telling anyone about her personal life, or why she'd lost her focus. "Sorry, Alan," she called out to the floor director. "Won't happen again."

Alan nodded as he stretched out his hand to the news desk with his fingers splayed. Everyone waited in silence as they came back from a short commercial. One by one, Alan's fingers curled into his palm, until he was pointing at her. Picking up her cue, she tried to appear sympathetic. "And now we'll go to Andrea Miller, for the story of one woman's struggle to reunite her canine family, a story of persistence and love."

"Thanks, Deborah. Judith Zink's best friend had recently given birth to triplets, no easy feat for human or animal, and Judith couldn't have been more happy to welcome the adorable West Highland Terriers into her family. That is, until Junibelle went missing. Was it merely a question of a mother needing a break, or something more sinister?"

D. hated the cutesy copy, was grateful she didn't have to read it, and she truly attempted to pay attention to the feature reporter, a young fresh-faced woman who seemed to ooze softness and sympathy and probably was as affectionate as one of the puppies whose footage was being telecast out to the viewing audience. Despite the image, D. knew Andrea would stop just short of murder to sit at the six o'clock anchor desk. D. knew about ambition and acknowledged it came with the job description. She'd watch her back and the pretty blonde, who wouldn't hesitate to stick her high heels into D.'s shoulder blades to climb the corporate news ladder.

Her mind wasn't on job security or even on the reuniting of Junibelle and her puppies as Andrea's piece continued. Instead, it flirted with daydreaming as her thoughts took her back to that beach in Bermuda and to a great looking Italian who had apologized to her on the walk back to the party, telling her he hadn't meant for things to get out of hand. She had still been buzzing with electricity, feeling like she could walk on water, and had thanked him for getting out of hand and had told him anytime he wanted another play date to give her a call. She'd meant it to be casual, maybe even flippant, but secretly she wanted him to take her hand again, to walk her back to the wedding party, stay at her side, and fly with her to Philly, instead of New York, so they could continue exploring each other. It had been a long time since she'd felt that need. And that's what burned inside of her now. Need. She didn't just want to see him again. It was as if her body had a need, a hot flaming condition, an itch that required relief.

God, she was becoming pathetic.

Forcing herself through the rest of the newscast, she unplugged her mic and walked back to her office. She simply had to forget Marcus Bocelli, she thought as she sat down at her desk and began to log onto her computer. It was simply a crazy fling, not her first unfortunately, and could be filed away. Should be filed away, she mentally added, and yet her brain could easily conjure him up . . . flashing his face across the screen of her mind. She could see those dark, probing brown eyes, staring into her own as if he had some special pass beyond them into her soul. Even now she could actually feel a shiver of electricity pass over her skin as desire welled up within her again. Before she'd left Bermuda, she'd handed him her business card with all her phone numbers and her email address. The ball was in his court. She couldn't even talk to anyone about her ridiculous obsession with Marcus. The only person would have been Maggie, but Maggie was out of the question. Maggie had warned her off Marcus numerous times, telling her she'd only wind up heartbroken. Well, her heart wasn't broken. Her heart wasn't even involved. It was her body. That Roman god had put a spell on her.

It was up to her, alone, to find a way to remove it, she determined as her phone rang. No man, no matter how gorgeous, was worth becoming pathetic and jeopardizing her focus at work was out of the question.

"Deborah Stark," she automatically answered.

"Debbie, hon? This is Aunt Tina."

Immediately, she sat up straighter as all her internal

alarms began buzzing. "Hi, Aunt Tina," she answered in a surprised and cautious voice. No one from her family had ever called her at work. "How are you?"

"Oh, honey . . . I'm so sorry. I don't know how to tell you this. It's your mom. She . . . she's passed, Debbie. About an hour ago. They say it was an embolism in her brain. She was talking to Anna Devers about Thanksgiving, her turkey, how excited she was that you were coming home for the holiday and . . . and then she just stopped speaking and went down. It was that quick, the doctors said, and . . . I'm so sorry to tell you like this over the phone, but I didn't know what else to do." Her paternal aunt began crying.

Numbness descended over D.'s body like an invisible shield as she tried to find her voice. Her mother. Dead. An embolism. She felt like her whole world was tilting at a dangerous angle and she gripped the edge of her desk to stay centered and not fall into a chasm of guilt. "You did the right thing," she whispered as she looked at her Gucci purse and envisioned her cars keys inside. "I was planning on driving up tomorrow morning, but I'll leave tonight. I'll be there tonight."

"Come to my house, honey. Stay with us."

She had to focus. "Yes," she murmured, running over in her head everything she'd have to do. Dan would give her the time off. Go back to the apartment and pack different clothes. Something black. "I might not be there until really late. Maybe it's best if I just go . . ." she found she had to force the word from her lips. ". . . home."

"Nonsense. You come as late as you like. We'll be up."

"Okay, then . . . I'll see you tonight. I should get started here and . . ." her words trailed off.

"I'm so sorry, Debbie. Even though your mother was my sister-in-law, she was like a real sister to me."

"I know," D. answered, picturing her father's sister staying in their lives, trying to make up for the fact that her brother had abandoned his wife and child. "And mom knew that too. She loved you, Aunt Tina."

"You be careful driving, Debbie. All that holiday traffic."

Debbie. No one, not even her mother, had called her that in decades. "Right. I should get going. I have to speak to my boss about getting some time off."

"I love you."

She felt the first stirring of emotion as tears welled up in her throat and burned her eyes. "I love you too," she answered, watching her hand as she hung up the phone.

Her mother. Dead. Gone . . .

She sat for a moment out of time, stunned by the news delivered by her aunt. Her body didn't feel capable of moving as years of regret and guilt swept over her. How fucking ironic that this was the first Thanksgiving in three years that she had arranged to spend with her mother. Within seconds her brain fired off reasons, good reasons, for not seeing more of the woman who had given her life . . . but deep down, in a place she wasn't ready to explore, Deborah Stark knew she had relegated her mother to the past, a place she rarely wanted to visit.

It hit her with the force of a bat to the back of her knees, bringing her down to reality. It was time to be the adult. There was no one ahead of her any longer being sensible and grown up. All her life other people took care of things like this. Births, deaths, weddings . . . when her mother had informed her of family news she'd called a florist and sent a huge arrangement of flowers, but her lifestyle and work had kept her from anything more personal, like showing up in person.

She couldn't back out of this one or expect anyone else to take care of it. Now it was up to her. She wished for a moment that she believed in a Supreme Being, someone to call upon for assistance, but in truth she only believed in herself. Long ago she had learned the lesson of depending on another for answers or help. She was too intelligent to blindly place her faith in anyone's dogma, but for a moment—a split second—she wished she was a religious person who could lay their troubles at the feet of a savior.

That wasn't her. She had already laid the foundation for her life and now she had to walk her talk. She had to be strong, push away the pain and also the guilt. She had to pretend to be what everyone expected, what she had worked so damn hard to make them believe.

And now . . . now she truly was alone.

Marcus Bocelli closed the lid of his wireless phone, disconnecting his call, while looking out the window of his apartment and watching a squirrel deftly climb the delicate limbs of an maple tree, moving quickly, only stopping momentarily to test the strength of the next link on his journey. For a moment he thought that's what his own life has been like, moving quickly, only stopping briefly as he tested his next course of action. He placed the tiny phone back into his trouser pocket and knew he'd made the right decision. The last place he'd wanted to be was Senator Burke's farm in Maryland.

Maggie would be there. And so would her new husband. It would be a family Thanksgiving dinner and, even though Gabriel's invitation had been sincere, Marcus knew he wasn't family. Not really, and not anymore. Not with Maggie discovering Gabriel was her father. This Thanksgiving should be a private celebration for them.

He liked the American tradition of taking one day to be grateful. It was at times like this he yearned for his own family. His mother and sisters and all his nieces and nephews crowding the family home in northern Italy for holidays, creating noise, laughter and love to bounce off the old plaster walls. He missed his home, his family.

At thirty-seven, he'd seen enough of the world to realize how blessed he had been to have been born to his parents for he had grown up surrounded in love. This American holiday was a time to take stock and to be grateful. And he was, very, very grateful.

He was the only son in a family of four sisters, along with eight aunts and more female cousins than he could count. His father, an international banker, had spoiled him and was gentle with his discipline, leaving him to the females in the family to raise . . . and Marcus, being cherished by all those around him, came into manhood with a great fondness for the feminine gender. His early life had been a great influence, for he'd matured loving the way women smelled, the softness of their skin, the sound of their voices, the miracle of their bodies to create, sustain and nourish life. At eleven he found out about the pleasure and joy they could bring him. From that time on he had spent his time devising ways to be in their presence. By seventeen he'd had multiple affairs at the same time, in Italy and across the border in Monte Carlo. It hadn't mattered to him if the women were married or single, young or older, rich or poor. He had loved them all. And he had especially loved to see how they would blossom into fragile, fragrant flowers, offering up their unique, innate beauty under his expert hands. His skill with women had come naturally and he'd perfected it with each encounter. Romance had been his natural high, pleasurable and powerful. He'd been, to put it simply, a ladies man and life had been gloriously sweet until the summer he'd left for university.

Even now, twenty years later, just thinking about his father caused his body to tense with grief and regret. Returning home from his bank, Emilio Bocelli had been cruelly assassinated by remnants of the Red Brigade, an extreme leftist terrorist organization that had been intent on destructuralization of the capitalist economy by kidnapping and killing scions of Italian government and business.

Marcus' idyllic life had been shattered the moment he'd heard his mother's scream of horror upon being given the news. The house of grieving females had nearly stifled him. Hell-bent on revenge, he'd gone to university and joined a student movement whose undercover motives were to separate Italy from the western alliance and promote its withdrawal from NATO. He had thought if he could infiltrate the group he would find his father's murderers and exact justice. And visions of that justice was what had kept him sane while he sank deeper and deeper into the underbelly of a fanatical political movement.

It was hard for him to now remember being that young man, bitter and secretive, so bitter that his mother had contacted her husband's good friend in the United States. She had begged Gabriel Burke to save her son's life, to take Marcus away from Italy.

And Gabriel had saved his life, and his sanity.

He'd brought Marcus into his home and began tutoring him in the ways of the world, showing Marcus that answering violence with violence only creates more violence and there was another way, besides killing, to gain justice. Through the influence of Senator Burke, members of the Red Brigade were captured in a severe crack down of the organization and imprisoned, including the killers of Emilio Bocelli. Many of them turned informant, leading security forces to other members and hastening the group's slide into obscurity.

Under Gabriel's tutelage, Marcus gradually regained his personality and finally, thankfully, his love of life. He'd had been an excellent student and was soon learning about the mysterious foundation that helped to balance light against the darkness of the world. He had attended college with

Gabriel's son and was welcomed into the Burke family while being schooled in the traditions of the foundation. He learned about power, real power to bring about change. And, since he was fascinated with the sciences, he eventually learned about the structure of life . . . pure energy. The ability to shape shift came easily to him and he later learned his grandmother had also possessed that gift. He learned of the power of love in a much different way than he had used it in his youthful days. When he graduated from college he came into his inheritance and through Gabriel's guidance invested it wisely. He then began working for the foundation full time, using his ability to help heal damaged hearts and facilitate change in the world, one soul at a time.

He never questioned his purpose in life or his place within the foundation. Not until Maggie had married last month. Somehow, perhaps foolishly, he had believed he and Maggie were two of a kind, that they would grow old together, each serving in their own way, meeting up and enjoying each other for however long the pleasure lasted. They had understood each other, taking their leave before the pleasure led to possession and ruined a great relationship. But she had married another and he had witnessed her great love for Julian McDonald. He had made a mistake with Maggie, never realizing how much she'd wanted a husband and family, and he had lost the only women he had let into his soul.

Turning away from the window, he looked down to his desk and saw the business card of Maggie's friend. His finger traced the engraved printing. That had been another mistake. Deborah Stark. He never should have weakened and used her to wipe out the image of Maggie and Julian leaving the wedding reception. Never mind that she had been more than willing. She was Maggie's friend. He pictured her in his mind . . . tall, lovely, short dark hair, brown eyes that burned with ambition and a smart biting humor.

He closed his eyes and could almost sense her again . . .

her breasts crushed against his chest, her mouth deliciously mating with his, her hips meeting each thrust with a challenge for more. Even now, he could feel his body become aroused by the memory of her passion.

How long since he'd had a fling?

His new assignment would begin in two weeks. That left this holiday weekend free.

Grinning, he wondered what Deborah Stark's plans were for Thanksgiving. It had been so long since he'd had fun for just the sake of it. No strings attached, no assignment. Just pleasure. Deborah Stark was the kind of woman who could appreciate exactly what he wanted.

Giving in, he took his phone out from his pocket and picked up her business card.

2

In the daylight, once you passed Exit 9 on the New Jersey Turnpike, the landscape slowly went downhill, D. reminded herself as she prepared to drive by a city of refineries and manufacturing plants. At night, if you didn't look too close, it appeared almost futuristic with all the lights twinkling in the distance. Driving north from Philly, she could see why New Jersey was the Garden State, but hit north Jersey and she understood all the jokes about the state. North Jersey was really like another borough of New York City. Something happened at Exit 9. The closer you came to the city, the drivers became more impatient, even rude. That mentality of "move or I'll mow you down" usually resonated with her, but tonight she was driving in the slow lane, actually doing fifty-five miles an hour, being passed by every other vehicle on the road, save an old station wagon that had settled behind her as though she were its leader in this madness of speeders jockeying for position.

For once in her life there was no need to hurry.

In fact, she wished she could stay in the slow lane and drive through the night, passing her exit and everything that awaited her. Just keep driving away from it all, she thought with longing, knowing soon she would pay her toll and arrive at her aunt's home and the ordeal of burying her mother would begin. God, she so wanted to exit onto the Parkway and make her way down the shore, sit on the sand and stare at the ocean and pretend none of it was real. Emily Stark would be waiting for her in the kitchen of the old house, her robe zippered up to her chin, her hair in rollers, making a pumpkin pie or stuffing for the turkey. That's how it had been ever since she'd gone away to college . . . well, every year she'd made it home for Thanksgiving. Her mother would be waiting.

She'd done a lot of waiting, D. realized, mentally picturing a pretty woman who got old waiting . . . for her husband to reappear, for her paycheck to arrive in time to keep the water or electricity in service, for her daughter to come home for a visit. In her mind, she saw her mother as a ghost of a woman even when she was alive. She must have had some dreams, some goals, some hopes. Not all of them could have centered around a man who married her, got her pregnant and then fought with her until one day he went out and never came back. If there was such a thing as an afterlife, was her mother reviewing a life not really lived?

She paid her toll and turned toward Hadley, her stomach now tightening with dread each mile she drove.

Hadley.

What a name for a town, but then when it's named after the man who brought jobs with the refining of oil into gasoline it fit the place where working families raised their kids and hoped for a better life for them. She came to the entrance to the town and was surprised that Rizzi's Pizza was still there and business looked as good as when she'd been a teenager. Kids were crowded outside, gathering just like their parents had done to avoid going home. That is, if you were part of the 'in' crowd, which D. never was.

She slowed her BMW and looked at the teenagers laughing and talking, until one girl whose hair was twisted and resembled wild spiked turkey feathers noticed her and quickly gave her the finger in a defiant show of superiority. Even as she pressed her foot to the gas pedal, D. felt she had time traveled back to her own youth and was being shown her presence still wasn't wanted. Damn, she was glad to be out of this place, a feeling she'd had for as long as she could remember. If she hadn't been planning on getting out when she was younger, she'd been planning to stay away from visiting for as long as she could. Only now there was no escaping the place. She was back, but she vowed it would be for the last time. She would put this godforsaken town behind her where it belonged. She would bury it with her mother. Her past would be gone and she could finally walk away without any ties.

She pulled onto her aunt's street and parked the car close enough to the row house so it would be under a street light. She didn't trust that some punk in the neighborhood might think taking the Beemer out for a joyride would make his Thanksgiving holiday. She'd have to keep checking on it until the morning. She grabbed her overnight case from the back seat and locked the car. The street was beginning to look run down, not the same place she had envied as a child. Staring at her aunt's house, the porch light still lit, D. took a deep breath and squared her shoulders.

This was not going to be easy. Not any of it.

She dragged the suitcase up the steps and pressed the doorbell, feeling completely overdressed in her gabardine slacks and cashmere sweater set as she looked to the neighbor's porch littered with plastic furniture and toys. Her only jewelry was a pearl necklace her mother had given her at college graduation. D. didn't know if they were real pearls, but they looked real, and she'd worn them tonight for sentimental reasons—guilty reasons was more like it, she thought as she heard someone unlock the front door.

"Oh, Debbie . . . !"

Her aunt Tina immediately began crying and D.'s smile was tight as she closed the distance between them and allowed herself to be wrapped in the woman's arms. Her aunt looked older, though not a strand of gray could be found in the dark brown hair that probably was done every Friday at the same beauty parlor she'd been going to since she was twenty. Tina Cabroletti was one of those women that dared you to tell her to look her age and grow old gracefully. She would wear the same hairstyle for the rest of her life. She still applied eyeliner and mascara and iridescent eye shadow in the creases of her lids. She probably still sat on the sand at Long Beach and got her deep tan because that's just what you did in the summer to stay attractive. Aunt Tina would speak her mind without much censure and be the first to admit she was certainly a character, but one with a good heart.

D. found herself patting her aunt's back in sympathy and realized Tina had shrunk, for she stood a good five inches above her. Maybe it was because D. was wearing heels or her aunt was wearing a silky caftan, but whatever it was, Aunt Tina was no longer a woman of stature, the way she had always thought of her. "I hope I didn't keep you up waiting for me," she whispered, not knowing if her uncle was awake.

Tina sniffled and pulled back. "Goodness, no. Come in, come in."

D. walked into the living room, thinking it hadn't changed since the last time she was here, which had to have been when she was high school. Her mother had insisted that every Christmas they would drive over and make the obligatory visit to the only family that cared if they were alive or dead. Well, her mother had been right. It did seem that Aunt

Tina was the glue that had kept them if not together, at least informed.

D. placed her suitcase on the pile rug and looked at the furniture and its plastic coverings a bit yellowed with age. She never understood that, even as a kid. What was the point of having furniture if you never actually sat on it? Shaking those thoughts out of her head, she again smiled at her aunt. "Is Uncle Joe awake?" she whispered.

Tina closed the front door and waved her hand in dismissal. "You ever know your Uncle Joe to be up at this hour, even if he no longer works the swing shift? I guess a man gets settled in his ways and my Joe is one settled man. He went to bed hours ago." She pointed to the back of the house. "Leave that suitcase and let's get us a cup of tea."

Nodding, D. followed her aunt through the living room, the small dining room with its artificial yellow and rust arrangement of Thanksgiving mums on the table, and into the smaller kitchen. She sank into a chair, again covered in plastic only this time fake leather, and watched her aunt put the kettle on the stove to boil. "Thanks for waiting up for me," D. said and meant it. Right then it was somehow comforting to be sitting at Aunt Tina's kitchen table at eleven o'clock and watching her putter around her kitchen.

"How you doin,' Debbie? I mean, really," she asked, as she took out the same cups and saucers with tiny blue flowers on them that D. remembered once thinking were so pretty, not like the chipped and mismatched ones in her childhood home.

"Pretty good," D. answered, reminding herself not to fall back into her aunt's accent that was just like a New Yorker's, one that had taken quite some time to lose. "Traffic was a little heavy," she added to make up for her lateness.

"That's not what I'm talking about," Tina answered, putting a Lipton's tea bag into each cup. Bringing them to the table, she looked right into D.'s eyes and said, "I'm askin' how are *you*. Your mother just died."

D. found she couldn't tear her gaze away from her aunt's penetrating stare. She wanted to plead with her . . . *don't pry and don't be nice. I don't deserve nice. Right now nice will rip away at my heart and the cracks will appear and God knows what will spill out and follow.* Instead, she simply blinked and said, "I'm in shock, I guess. I always thought she'd just be there, you know?"

Tina nodded and went to her cupboard, bringing out the sugar bowl and creamer.

D. watched as her aunt opened the refrigerator, filled the creamer with milk, and then brought them to the table.

"Always a shock when you lose a parent. But that's life, Debbie. Each generation has their time, and then time's passed on to the next. Your momma ran out of time. But the way she passed was a blessing. Fast."

D. nodded in the following silence that seemed to last for a full minute, feeling like the baton of time was just passed on to her. A sensation of panic started to suddenly bubble up in her belly, as though there was now a running meter on her life. *Tick. Tick. Tick* . . .

The whistle of the teapot interrupted what might have become a real panic attack and D. sat up straighter, desperately trying to regain her composure. Maybe she should have just gone back to the old house and dealt with the guilt and her mother's ghost tonight. All of a sudden sitting here in this kitchen wasn't helping to quell what felt like a gathering of terror that had begun in her office with Tina's phone call.

Her aunt brought the kettle to the table and poured out the boiling water into each cup. D. quickly moved an arm away as the water sputtered, barely missing her. When both cups were full, Tina placed the stainless steel kettle onto a cool burner on the stove and then shuffled back to sit down opposite D.

"Now, what are your plans?" she asked, scooping out two teaspoonfuls of sugar and putting them into the water that was already turning the mahogany color of tea. She slid the sugar bowl in D.'s direction.

D. wanted to ask for artificial sweetener, but didn't want her aunt to get up again, so she put two teaspoonfuls of sugar into her cup and added some milk to cool it off. She hadn't had tea like this in years and it too reminded her of old times. Realizing her aunt was waiting for her to speak, she said, "Well, I was hoping you could help me there, Aunt Tina. It's been so long since I was familiar with Hadley and—"

"I know how long it's been since you were here," her aunt interrupted in a far off voice as she stared into her teacup and swirled her spoon around in it.

She didn't say it as a condemnation, but D. could feel a heat rushing up her cheeks that had nothing to do with the temperature of the tea. "Yes," D. murmured, not pretending to misunderstand her aunt's statement. "I just meant that I don't know the names of any funeral homes. I can look in the phone book or—"

"Lombari's good. Emily would have liked that. Nicest one in town. Only the rich get laid out there."

"Did mom have . . ." God, how could she ask the next question? It was something a daughter ought to know. ". . . an insurance policy, or a will, or anything to tell us what she wanted?"

"I don't know, Debbie," Tina answered with a sigh, before sipping her tea. "You'll have to go home tomorrow and look into it."

As far as D. was concerned when her time came to pass on the baton, she wanted to be cremated. No fuss, no viewing, no morbid funeral. But her mother was of a different generation. She was Methodist. This would have to be the whole nine yards . . . viewing, mass, funeral and then reception. Her mother hadn't gotten much out of life that she'd wanted, but D. was determined in death she'd get the best. "Okay, I'll call Lombari in the morning."

"We're all real proud of you, Debbie. I want you to know that."

Surprised, D. looked up from the table. "Thanks, Aunt Tina."

"Especially your momma. You know she got a VCR and a satellite dish just so she could get the Philadelphia stations."

"I didn't know that," she said, as a mixture of pleasure and guilt swirled together. There was a lot she should have known.

"Did you eat? I have some leftover lasagna I can heat up in the microwave."

Shaking her head, D. answered, "I'm not hungry, but thanks. I remember your lasagna. When we visited on Christmas we always took some home for the day after. It was a treat."

"I wish I could have done more for Emily and you. She didn't have an easy life."

"No, she didn't."

"Debbie, I have to ask you something," her aunt began, holding her teacup in both hands as though to warm them. Her voice was hesitant.

A feeling of alarm filled D., but she knew she had respond. "What? What is it?"

"It's your dad. Your father. I called him about your mother passing and he wants to know if he should come to the funeral."

Suddenly, D.'s body became rigid with outrage. "Why *should* he come? Why should he come *now?* It's a little late to show his respect for my mother or me."

Tina nodded sadly. "I know. I just thought maybe by now . . ." her words trailed off.

"By now what?" D. demanded. "I would forget the hell he put my mother through? That he could walk away from his responsibilities and never look back? That he could abandon her and me? That he never sent us money to help out?"

"That maybe you could find a way to forgive him," her aunt murmured.

"Well, that hasn't happened," D. snapped back and then reined in her anger. "I'm sorry, Aunt Tina. I know he's your brother and you did care about us and tried to make up for him, but I refuse to even think about him, especially now. I have enough to deal with and get through without *Danny Stark* reappearing in my life." She knew she said his name like a curse and wished her words didn't hurt her aunt, but really . . . how could the woman even think about asking? She should have told her brother to take his respects and shove them where the sun don't shine!

"Tomorrow's going to be a long day, sweetie," her aunt announced, pushing back her chair. "I'll help you however you want. We'll get through this."

Taking her cue, D. rose and realized she didn't even sip her tea. She picked up her cup and Tina said, "Bring it with you. You'll be sleeping in Rosemary's old room. The grandkids stay in there when they spend the night, so don't be alarmed at all the stuffed animals."

"I'm glad to be here. Thanks and . . . and I'm sorry for blowing up like that."

Tina nodded and placed her cup in the sink. She then took the saucer out of D.'s hand and said, "No need to apologize. Now, I'll carry your cup if you'll carry your bag. Threw my lower back out last month carrying around those grandbabies so I'm not chancin' anything heavier than my purse for awhile."

"No problem," D. answered, walking through the dining room back out to where she'd placed her overnight bag. She picked it up and followed her aunt up the flight of stairs, wishing she hadn't lost her temper in the kitchen. She wouldn't think about her father. He had nothing to do with her or her mother. As she climbed the last stair D. realized how tired she was and gratefully followed her aunt down the hallway to her cousin's old room.

"I put fresh sheets on the bed. You should sleep in. I'll wake you around nine and then after breakfast we can get started."

Still holding her bag, she leaned down and kissed her aunt's cheek. "Thanks for everything. I know this isn't easy for you either."

"Glad I can be of help. It's the least I can do. Get a good night's rest, Debbie."

She smiled, hearing her aunt's use of an old nickname, and nodded. "Good night."

Alone, she closed the bedroom door and dropped her bag while staring at the room. How could all these years have passed and it looked almost the same? How did her aunt keep everything as though frozen in time? Save for the stuffed animals piled onto a rocker in the corner, the long narrow room was just as she remembered it . . . a pink ruffled satin bedspread with sheer pink curtains on the windows, a fluffy white rug by the bedside, crisp white cotton runners on the long dresser and a big wooden jewelry box on top.

Rosemary's room.

How many times had her aunt instructed her older cousin to bring her up here so the adults could talk in private? It wasn't Rosemary's fault that D. wore the girl's old hand-me-downs, including shoes. It wasn't Rosemary's fault that she would love to show off her collection of jewelry, especially when she got her ears pierced, something D. had desperately wanted to have done but wasn't permitted. It wasn't Rosemary's fault each Christmas evening she would show D. every single present, raving about the newest music tape she'd received while D. had to settle for Rosemary's old eight track tape player that no one made tapes for any longer, so she was supposed to be happy with Donnie and Marie, instead of Madonna. It certainly wasn't Rosemary's fault that she resented being told to entertain a younger cousin she had nothing in common with.

Rosemary had been popular. Debbie Stark had been a true geek.

And she had envied Rosemary with a child's passion, wondering why it had been written by God that Rosemary got everything and she only got the leftovers.

Now, sitting on the bed she had envied, she felt the springs of the mattress. Aunt Tina hadn't thrown out the old bed either. She looked at the dresser, to the array of pictures covering every spare inch of display space. The faces of young children and babies smiled back at her. Rosemary's children. Cute, with their mother's eyes and smile.

That was another thing Rosemary had.

A husband and children.

Marriage.

It didn't matter that if you had asked her at lunchtime, D. would have said a husband and children weren't even on her priority list at the present. Tonight, surrounded by her past, she wondered for the first time if maybe, just maybe, she'd taken the wrong fast track.

Forget it, she told herself, shaking the ridiculous notion out of her head. No, it was an absurd notion. Did she really want to live in north Jersey, married to a construction worker and spit out kids every other year? She quickly rose and picked up her suitcase. Heaving it onto the bed, she unzipped it and found her nightgown.

It was time to turn off the past and get some rest.

Aunt Tina had been right. Tomorrow was going to be a very long day.

The next morning she awakened and stared for a moment

out of time, wondering what the hell she was doing in Rosemary's bedroom. And then it hit her, like the sunlight on her face.

Her mother.

Moaning, D. rolled over and wished she could stay in bed and pretend none of it was real. Unfortunately, she could hear the shower running down the hall, the scent of bacon wafting upstairs, and knew she had to assume for the day that she was an adult and capable of making the decisions required of her.

She waited in bed until whoever was in the bathroom finished their shower and then she dragged her tired and aching body off the mattress, pulled on her robe and vowed to spend the night at her mother's house. She'd bought her mother new furniture, so at least the mattress would be more comfortable.

After brushing her teeth, she left the bathroom and made her way downstairs. She needed a cup of coffee before showering, something to give her a jolt of energy. As she walked into the kitchen she saw her Uncle Joe at the stove, a plate of bacon on a greasy paper plate next to him. "Good morning, Uncle Joe."

He looked up, a grin on his face. "Morning to you, Debbie. Good to see you again. Get a good night rest?"

"Yes, yes I did," she lied, not mentioning that she'd lain awake last night for hours, turning and turning, trying to find a comfortable position, to claim sleep so it would wipe out the thoughts that haunted her.

"Well, good. How about some bacon? I make a good breakfast."

Not wanting to appear ungrateful for the offer, D. came to the countertop and lifted a piece of bacon from the pile, one that was cool. "I didn't know you cooked, Uncle Joe."

"Started when I retired a few years ago," he answered, flipping the sizzling meat in the frying pan. "Your Aunt Tina been cookin' for me for years. Guess it's my turn to help out. Used to bring home the bacon and now I fry it up."

D. grinned. "Tastes great," she commented. "I haven't had bacon in a long time and this is delicious."

"Went on that Lipitor for the cholesterol, so I guess I can have my bacon every once in awhile as a treat. How 'bout another? There's plenty here for the three of us."

"Actually, I'd love a cup of coffee."

"Sure 'nough, kid. You remember where the cups are?"

Nodding, D. opened the same cabinet her aunt had last night and took out a cup and saucer. She poured herself a cup of black coffee from the Mr. Coffee maker and took the cup to the kitchen table. "This is good," she murmured, savoring the taste and waiting for that jolt of caffeine to enter her system.

Uncle Joe had gotten older looking too, and wider, she thought, watching him from the side and seeing how his belly hung down over his jeans. His T-shirt seemed to be straining to cover the bulk. Once she had thought him to be so impressive. It was only natural for the difference be noticeable. Almost twenty years had passed. She felt like he was a stranger or, more accurately, she was the stranger. The last time she'd seen him was the summer of her graduation from high school. He'd been a cop, big and a little scary, and yet he had always been decent to her.

"You're looking good, Debbie," he said, not taking his attention away from his morning chore. "Sure am sorry about your mother. She was a good woman, that Emily."

"Yes, she was," D. answered. "I'm sorry I didn't see more of her in these last years." She figured she might as well say it, before he did.

Uncle Joe nodded. "Person's got to do what a person's got to do. You're something of a celebrity around here, you know."

"Me? I just read the news."

"Television. When they got these reality shows makin' celebrities out of nobody, you've been around and made a good career of it for yourself."

"Well, thanks," she replied, feeling better. She *had* been around television for a long time and she *had* made a good career of it.

"Be prepared, now that you're back."

"For what?"

"Oh . . . betcha some people show up just to get a look at you."

"Show up?"

"Sure. For the viewing and the reception after the funeral. You figure out when that'll be yet?"

D. wasn't all that pleased to learn she was a curiosity. "Not yet. This morning we're going to contact Lombari's."

"Good place," Uncle Joe remarked, turning off the heat under the frying pan and picking up his cup to join her at the table. "I liked your momma a lot. A good woman who got a raw deal in life, but she never got bitter. Says a lot about a person, that does."

D. picked up her cup and took another sip, not knowing how to answer that.

"I remember the first time your daddy brought her around. Me 'n Tina liked her right away. She had the best laugh, a giggle you could say. And pretty . . ." Uncle Joe grinned while remembering. "Don't you tell your Aunt Tina, but had myself a little crush on Emily even though I was a married man with a little daughter starting to walk. Just something about her. She had that thing the movie stars have . . . what'd they call it? Kinda like a light around her. She sparkled. That's it. Emily sparkled."

D. stared at him, thinking old age was getting the best of his memory. Her mother *sparkled*? The only aura that D.

could remember around her mother had been constant worrying.

"Oh, I know you find it hard to believe, but take my word on it, girl. In her day, your mother sparkled like a fine Tiffany diamond. Hated to see that disappear over the years."

"She worried a lot," D. murmured, trying to picture her mother vivacious and sparkling like a Tiffany diamond.

Uncle Joe nodded. "Don't surprise me none that she went the way she did. Guess her poor brain had enough."

D. was stunned for a moment. "You think my mom worried herself to death?"

"Happens. Glad she went quick though. Maybe she finally got her reward. One moment talking over the fence to Anna Devers and in the next you're standing before your maker. Don't think your momma had to answer for much. Think they opened the gates to heaven wide for her to march right on it."

"You really admired my mother," she said, a little in awe by Uncle Joe's words and the fact that his brown eyes were filling with a sheen of moisture.

The older man grinned and D. could see that in his own day, Joe Cabroletti must have been a charmer. "Shh . . . you keep that under your hat, young lady. Your aunt gets wind of that and I'll never hear the end of it."

She simply smiled, glad that someone, some male, saw something special in her mother and held that image of her.

"Well, I'd better get upstairs and into the shower. It's going to be a long day."

Uncle Joe nodded, showing his bald spot. "You go on up, Debbie. Good to see you again."

She brought her cup to the sink and then impulsively kissed the top of his head. "Good to see you too, Uncle Joe. Thanks for telling me that about my mom."

Walking up the stairs, she tried to adjust her thinking to take in the revelations.

Her mother had once sparkled and she'd had a secret admirer.

Fascinating.

3

It was a little rancher, painted white with black shutters and, except for the color, looked exactly like every other house on the block. Grandlake Estates. First, there was no lake and the tiny subdivision wasn't exactly grand. It had been, in fact, low income housing so everyone knew your status as soon as they knew your address. D. noticed that some of the neighbors had put on additions, extending the space, but mostly it was just as she'd remembered . . . except now her mother wouldn't be inside the house.

She'd never realized how many decisions had to be made when someone dies. She'd hated the two hours she'd spent at Lombari's, especially picking out a casket and learning that her mother's body was still at the County Hospital morgue, waiting for permission to be moved. Shaking her head as she parked the car, she vowed to wipe out those memories and concentrate on finding the documentation the undertaker had requested. Insurance papers. Social security number. Will. She'd felt like such a lousy child, not having any answers. Plus, because of the holiday, the viewing couldn't be held until the weekend.

Locking the car, she sighed as she squared her shoulders and prepared to enter her mother's home. It already looked deserted with the fallen leaves littering the little square of grass by the front door. Her mother's mums were the only bright color that said somebody once lived here and took care of the place. And a squirrel, a big fat gray squirrel, seemed to be sitting on the front walk as though waiting for her.

The thing continued to stare are her as she came up the walk. She stopped and sighed deeply with frustration since it stood between her and the front door.

"Okay beat it, Rocky," she called out. "The last thing I need right now is some crazy rodent."

It didn't run away as she'd hoped, but now stood up on its haunches and began chattering.

D. stopped dead in her tracks and had the weird feeling that it was trying to communicate with her. "I don't speak squirrel, my friend, so why don't you just run up a tree or something." Not willing to give it any more of her time, she stepped onto the grass, making a wide circle around it, and then headed for the front door.

I am so sorry.

She was about to insert the key her mother had given her years ago, when she heard those words. Not sure if they were in her head, she slowly peered over her shoulder to the squirrel. It was gone.

Okay, you are not hearing things, she mentally commanded, a little freaked by what she'd obviously made up in her head. *Animals are not talking to you.*

She turned the key in the lock. Time to face it, she thought. She couldn't put this off any longer.

The first thing she noticed as she stepped over the mail on the floor was that the house smelled like her mother. She'd developed a fondness for honeydew melon candles in the last five years and had housewarming oil plug-ins in every available socket. Honeydew melon . . . she supposed for the rest of her life whenever she smelled it, she would think of her mother. Closing the door behind her, she dropped her overnight bag on the floor and placed her suit bag carefully over the back of the an armchair. Then she flipped the light switch by the door.

For a moment, she was stunned.

The new living room set her mother had picked out was surprisingly stylish. A cream colored sofa with a delicate floral pattern was contemporary and inviting. Silk pillows in shades of moss and sage green seemed artlessly tossed onto the cushions. The wooden tables looked to be mahogany, deep and rich. Couldn't be. There was even a fake fireplace surround that appeared to be marble and on the mantle were tall brass candlesticks along with a very nice brass pendulum clock. D. knew her own decorating skills were lacking, yet if she could forget the house that enclosed it, her mother's living room might well have appeared in a magazine. It reminded her of old money. Tasteful and understated. There were even brass picture lights over the paintings on the walls.

She'd arranged a line of credit for her mother at Macy's, but she never expected this. It looked like a designer showroom. Even the old tile flooring had been removed and replaced with a warm, deep brown wood. The rug under her feet seemed Turkish, picking up the aubergine in the floral pattern of the sofa. It couldn't be a real Turkish rug. Who knew her mother had such taste? She remembered her mom fighting her on the gift, until D. said it was time to get rid of the second hand furniture that others had cast aside. D. had established the line of credit and told her mom that the money was non-returnable and she'd waste it if she didn't use it. But this . . . ?

She walked into the small square dining room and her jaw dropped. Again, tasteful and appropriate for the space. Five thousand dollars couldn't have bought all this. What about the bedroom?

She went down the hallway and stood at her mother's bedroom door.

Who would have thought Emily Stark slept under a multicolored silk canopy, twisted and looped to the tall four posters of the bed?

D. felt disoriented, as though she'd stepped into the wrong house. Yet the pictures of her on her mother's dresser confirmed she was in the right place. She remembered her mother's excitement when she'd tried to describe the rooms and D. had promised to see them as soon as she could . . . but that hadn't been soon enough to share her mother's pleasure. Guilt flooded over her for not visiting before, to praise her mother's choices, to see her mother's face as she showed her around. That's what a good daughter would have done.

Face it, she told herself, *you are not a good daughter and haven't been for years.* There was no use pretending to herself or anyone else. Facts were facts.

She stepped lightly into the room, almost reverently, as though not to disturb anything, until she stood in front of a secretary desk, also new. On the top was a list of chores, half of them crossed off.

Her mother had always been one for lists.

Clean floor
Change sheets in guest room
Defrost Turkey
The ones not crossed off were:
Make stuffing
Pumpkin pie
Buy heavy cream
Flowers
Set table

She had always been organized, D. thought, picking up the pencil her mother had been using and rolling it around in her fingers. She had also been a good cook with whatever she had been able to pull together. Their house had always been clean, no matter how it had been decorated. Her mother never seemed to have minded that they lived in a low income neighborhood. She had been grateful for everything, but constantly worried over the money to keep it all going.

A sudden thought came to her, totally unexpected. What if she finished the list? Thanksgiving was tomorrow. What if she tried to make dinner for herself? That would have made her mother proud. And she desperately wanted to keep busy until after the holiday. She'd already told Aunt Tina she wanted the time alone, without company. It seemed like a plan.

She rushed back into the living room, picked up her bags, and took them to her old room. Stopping short at the doorway, she simply stared. Her bedroom had been turned into a library and television room. Bookshelves lined three walls and a sofa took up the last. It was oddest sensation, to feel like a stranger in her mother's house. She supposed the sofa pulled out into a bed, but since her back still smarted from the old mattress at Aunt Tina's she wondered if she had the guts to sleep in her mother's bed.

For God's sake, she was a thirty-six year old woman.

She might even feel comforted. It wasn't like her mother died in this house.

Making a decision, D. turned around and placed her things in her mother's room, just as the doorbell rang. Must be one of the neighbors. Anna Devers probably.

She opened the door to see their neighbor standing before her, her arms holding a long casserole dish.

"Oh, Deborah, I'm so sorry for your loss!"

D. smiled tightly, trying not to show how tired she was. "Thank you, Mrs. Devers. Won't you come in? I just arrived." She stooped to pick up the mail in front of the door.

The older woman whose face was the color of dark coffee

crinkled up her brown eyes as though to hold back tears as she crossed the threshold. "I just saw you pull up. Don't want to bother you none, but I thought maybe you could use a hot meal tonight." She held out the dish.

"Well, thanks. That's sweet of you." She knew she should accept it, even if she didn't eat it. Besides, she owed this kind woman who had been a good neighbor for the last twenty years. Tucking the few envelopes under her arm, she took the casserole and walked into the kitchen. At least here, everything appeared the same. The old wooden cabinets and Formica countertop seemed oddly reassuring. Opening up the refrigerator, she saw a huge uncooked turkey on the top shelf. There was no room for the casserole. D. placed it on the cold stove top. "I'll heat it up later."

"It was so sudden, Deborah," Mrs. Devers said from behind her. "I want you to know that. I was there. Did your Aunt Tina tell you that?"

She closed the frig, put the mail on the counter and turned around. "Yes, she did. Thank you, Mrs. Devers, for being there for my mother. You were always a good neighbor."

"Well, your momma and me were good friends. Talked about a lot of things, shared a lot. She was a good woman."

D. nodded as another wave of guilt washed over her. Everyone said that about her mother. A good woman.

"I knew to call your Aunt Tina. She was the only family your momma talked about. She called me back to say she got in touch with you and that you'd be spending the night with her."

Again, D. simply nodded, not knowing what else to say. This woman knew her mother better than she did. She should be asking lots of questions, but guilt kept her silent.

"Well, I best be starting dinner for my brood. You know yet when the funeral will be? I'd like to send flowers. Emily liked flowers. She said they made her happy."

"I made the arrangements today. Sunday night at Lombari's, and the burial will be Monday. The Methodist church. Ten o'clock," she answered, rattling off the details she had spent the day organizing. "And then a reception lunch at Maxwells."

"You going to your Aunt Tina's tomorrow for dinner?"

She shook her head and smiled. "Not up to company, I'm afraid. I was thinking about finishing mom's turkey. I'll bring you the leftovers for your family, if it turns out edible. Is that okay?"

Anna Devers grinned. "None of my boys or their tribe will ever turn down leftovers. Seven grandchildren and six of them are males." She sighed. "I cherish them all, but I have a special fondness for little Emily."

"Emily?" D. asked, surprised by the name.

"Oh yes . . . didn't your momma ever tell you? My daughter-in-law went into labor early and it was your momma who rushed all of us to the hospital. She stayed till my James could get there from work. Did that Lamaze with Juanita and had us all laughing in between the contractions when she almost hyperventilated. Juanita says your momma saved her sanity and maybe even her baby girl. Besides," she added with a sad smile, "she liked the name Emily. Said it was a retro name, or something like that. Old fashioned and now back in fashion."

D. had to swallow hard, to get her words past the lump in her throat. "Thanks for telling me, Mrs. Devers. I keep hearing all these stories about my mother and—"

"Now, child, you aren't the first not to really know your parents," Mrs. Devers said to fill in the silence. "You keep thinking about them as they raised you and forget they had a whole life before you ever showed up, and they get that life back when you take off on your own."

"I guess you're right." D. nodded to the dining room. "She

certainly did a good job on redecorating. It's really . . . lovely."

"That it is," Mrs. Devers agreed, as she walked back into the living room. "Oh, you should have seen her, Deborah. She was like Martha Stewart in this house. Found almost everything on sale or clearance. She spent days making those drapes, staying up nights sewing until it was just right, just as she wanted. She had a gift, didn't she?"

"You're right. She had a gift. I didn't know . . ."

Mrs. Devers patted her arm. "Well, thanks to you, it was brought out and shared with the rest of us. She was so proud of you."

D. simply nodded, wondering what other gifts her mother had been born with, but never got the chance to use.

"Well, you need anything, anything at all, you just give me a call."

Again, D. nodded.

At the front door, Mrs. Devers eyes welled up. "I'm gonna miss her something terrible. She was a good neighbor and a good friend."

A good woman, D. mentally added. Seems everyone held the same opinion.

"She thought the same of you, Mrs. Devers. Thank you for coming over tonight. Maybe I'll see you tomorrow evening with those leftovers."

"You ever make a turkey, Deborah?"

D. shook her head and chuckled. "This will be my first. It can't be that hard."

Mrs. Devers hesitated for a moment, as though she might have something to add to D.'s last statement, but thought better of it. "Well, you just yell if you need help, okay?"

"I will. And . . . thank you again."

"Good night, Deborah."

D. closed the front door and walked back into the kitchen.

She lifted the aluminum foil from the corner of the casserole and a delicious scent traveled up to her nose. Chicken and rice. Her stomach clenched painfully, like a cocaine addict that hadn't had a fix in days, and she suddenly realized how hungry she was. Maybe she would heat up some after she unpacked. Or, maybe, she would just taste it now to feed her craving.

She pulled open a drawer, took out a fork, and dug into the corner, picking up some rice and tender white chicken that fell apart. "Oh, God . . ." she mumbled, tasting the fabulous, down-home comfort food. Anna Devers had always been a great cook. Swallowing, she threw the fork into the sink and took out a big tablespoon. She stood at the counter, stuffing her face, feeling the tightness in her belly ease, when the doorbell rang again.

D. dropped the spoon onto the casserole and wiped her mouth with the back of her hand as she chewed to swallow the last of the chicken. It was probably Mrs. Devers again, feeling sorry for her and bringing instructions for cooking a turkey.

She opened the door and froze in shock.

He stood there in the fading sunlight looking like a bronzed god dressed in jeans and a tan cashmere turtleneck sweater, his curly dark hair swept back off his face as he gazed into her eyes with such deep kindness that she felt a burning behind her lids.

"Marcus . . ." She said his name in a whisper of disbelief, not quite sure he could be standing in front of her. Here. In Grandlake Estates. The place she had vowed no one would ever know about, let alone see. "How . . . ?"

"I am so sorry, Deborah. I called your office and was told about your mother."

She blinked. He finally called?

"Thanks," she murmured, still unsettled, and spotted the bouquet of white roses in his hand. "How did you know where I was?"

He smiled slightly. "I have my ways. I hope you don't mind me coming here like this." Hesitating for a moment, he actually looked unsure of himself. "I . . . I was alone and wondering what you'd be doing for Thanksgiving when I called your office. Forgive me for intruding, but I just wanted to see you and tell you how very sorry I am to hear about your mother."

Scared he might just hand her the flowers and walk away, she opened the door wider. "Come in, Marcus. I'm really, really glad to see you." And she was. It was too late to worry about what he thought of her childhood neighborhood. He'd seen it. But bless her mother's heart for making the house into a welcoming home.

He came into the living room and turned as she closed the front door. "I hope I didn't interrupt anything. I know you must be busy with family and . . . and details."

She shook her head. "Nothing really. I took care of all the details this afternoon."

"I don't want to intrude."

"You're not intruding." She was *so* glad to see him that she hurried to add, "Really, Marcus. I'm all alone tonight. By choice. I could have stayed at my aunt's again, but thought it was time I came home. I was about to get something to eat if you'd like to join me."

His smile increased. "You're sure you don't mind? I just wanted to give you these," and he held out the roses, "and to offer my condolences. It was sudden, I heard."

She nodded and took the flowers. "Yes. A brain embolism. Thankfully, very quick I'm told."

"You must be devastated."

Clutching the flowers to her chest, she said, "I think I'm in shock. Devastated might come later."

"Yes, yes . . ." He seemed to be thinking about something and then his face brightened. "Is there anything I can do to help you? I am entirely at your disposal."

He sounded so formal, so old-world charming, and D. was ashamed that the first thing coming to her mind was being held in his arms again. "Well, do you know anything about making stuffing?"

"Stuffing?"

She chuckled, feeling relieved to have his company. "For the Thanksgiving turkey. Bread stuffing."

"Ah, yes. Bread stuffing." His grin was sheepish. "Actually, no, I don't. Surely, two fairly intelligent people can figure it out."

She grinned. For the first time in what seemed days, she found her smile was genuine. "Then come on back into the kitchen. The neighbor brought over chicken and rice and if you haven't eaten I can highly recommend it."

It wasn't awkward as she'd thought it might be, after all the last time they'd seen each other they'd been screwing like rabbits. Instead, Marcus helped her serve the chicken and rice, finding a bottle of white wine in the refrigerator that D. figured her mother had bought for Thanksgiving. They were seated at the dining room table and neither one spoke while they ate. It was funny, because even the silence was comforting. She didn't feel like she had to fill it with meaningless conversation. The only thing she'd been talking about for the last twenty-four hours was depressing, so she welcomed the companionable quiet.

"You were right. It's very good."

D. nodded. "I know. Mrs. Devers has four boys, big hungry boys. She learned how to make meals that stick to your ribs."

"Your neighbor?"

"Yes," she said, sitting back when she was finally filled. "She and my mother were close. Mrs. Devers was talking to my mother when . . . when it happened," she added, still not able to say out loud her mother had died.

His hand reached across the table and caught her fingers.

She looked down, seeing his long, tanned fingers wrapped around her pale ones. "I lost a parent suddenly too, Deborah. I know how terrifying it is to have them one moment and discover in the next they are forever gone from you."

As much as she enjoyed his touch, *really* enjoyed it, she gently pulled her fingers away from his hold and picked up her wine glass. "I'm okay." She took a long sip of the Chardonnay.

"Are you really?"

She couldn't look at him, was afraid to see his eyes. This time she didn't want him peering into her soul, for she was terrified he would know just how rotten a daughter she had become. Nodding, she answered, "I think we should try and find a cookbook for that stuffing . . . that is if you're still willing to help out."

He smiled sadly, as though knowing she didn't want to talk about herself, and pushed his chair back. "A promise is a promise. Together we shall tackle this turkey stuffing."

"Good," she answered, picking up her plate and bringing it to the kitchen. She stood at the sink and squirted liquid onto a sponge, then turned on the hot water. "It's really silly. I came across this list my mother had made in preparation of Thanksgiving dinner and I had this crazy thought I could finish it. That's she'd like me to try." She felt his presence before she saw him put his dish on the counter.

"I can do those, you know," he said, standing just slightly to her side. "You could find the cookbook and then we can get started."

She just couldn't picture Marcus Bocelli washing her mother's dishes. She wondered if he wanted to get going so he could leave after fulfilling his promise, or if he was just being helpful. Turning sideways, she stared at him and said, "Look, Marcus, I'll release you from your promise, okay? There's no need to stay. I can make the stuffing, or not. It was a harebrained idea anyway."

He lifted his eyebrows in surprise. "Are you asking me to leave?"

"I'm saying, stay if want, leave if you want. You don't owe me anything."

He reached around her and shut off the hot water. "What do you want, Deborah?"

His body brushed hers and she had to stop herself from inhaling and then moaning at his nearness. He must know what an effect he had on her and probably every other woman who'd ever met him. "It doesn't matter what I want," she murmured, staring at the cashmere material at his neck because she didn't dare look into his eyes.

"You are angry because I didn't call you?"

Was he reading her mind? She shrugged. "It was a moment of madness in Bermuda."

"I agree."

Her gaze jumped from his neck to his face, feeling insulted that he so quickly agreed with her. What she had wanted was his denial. "Well, you've done your good deed for the day, Mr. Bocelli. Thank you for your condolences and the roses. You can go back to New York, or wherever you came from, because I'm just fine."

His hand reached out and cupped the side of her face, slowly running his thumb across her cheekbone. "Ah, *bella mia*, you don't have to be so defensive with me. I wanted to come to you when I heard of your mother, because I know what you are going through. The sudden loss of a loved one can be a shattering experience." He paused and sighed. "What happened in Bermuda was a moment of madness, a fine madness to be sure, but inappropriate nonetheless. I came here tonight because I'd like to be your friend."

Her hand pushed at his shoulder as her chest began to ache and her eyes began to fill. "Don't be nice to me, Marcus," she demanded, as she turned back to the sink. "I can't take nice right now."

"I am sorry? What do you mean, you can't take nice right now? If not now, for heaven's sake, when?"

"Never," she answered in a rough voice, letting the hot water run over the sponge and turn it to bubbles. "I don't like that word. Nice people aren't good survivors, and I have to survive this."

"You equate nice with being weak? Perhaps, I am not translating well."

"Nice," she emphasized, "to me is a phony way of living. People say, 'oh isn't she nice?' and what they don't know is that person takes all kinds of crap so others will like her. She's never herself, just lives her life trying to please others. I'd rather be truthful than nice any day of the week. At least I'm trying to be real."

She stopped scrubbing a fork when she felt his touch on her back, slow and comforting.

"What about kind?" he asked in a low voice. "Will you allow someone to be kind to you, Deborah?"

She shoulders dropped for a moment, feeling every place he touched beginning to relax. It was as if the muscles in her back were like rubber bands he was untwisting merely with his touch. "I can't take kind either, Marcus," she whispered, closing her eyes and savoring the feeling of peace, even if just for a moment. "Right now kind will tear away my defenses and I'm terrified of what will happen next."

His arms came around her, his chest against her back, and he turned off the water. "You don't have to be terrified," he whispered right behind her ear. "Go find your mother's cookbook and I will finish the dishes. We have to stuff this Thanksgiving turkey."

Oh, if he didn't stop being nice to her she might just burst into tears and then she would become a slobbering, guilt-ridden mess. "It's not like I'm begging you, you know?" She gave over the sink to him. "I can do it myself."

Glancing at her, he grinned, causing his dark brown eyes

to twinkle. "I have a feeling, Deborah, underneath that tough exterior you are . . . how would you say it . . . ?"

"Don't you dare say a softie. I am not soft."

"Oh, you are soft. I have felt your softness."

Okay, that pleased her since it meant he remembered how she felt under his touch. "I am a strong, independent woman. I appreciate your help, but that doesn't mean I need it."

Marcus chuckled as he continued washing the last few dishes. "Are you always this argumentative when someone is trying to be . . . kind . . . to you?" He emphasized the word kind, as though showing her he wasn't being nice.

"I just don't want you to think I'm a softie, because I'm not."

"I was going to say underneath that tough exterior, Deborah Stark, I believe you will find a good person, with a good heart."

She blew out her breath in a rush of derision. "And that statement proves you don't know me. That's not me."

"You're heart isn't good?" he asked with surprise, picking up a towel and beginning to wipe the dishes. "Why would you say that?"

"For too many reasons I don't want to talk about," she answered, becoming unsettled by the direction of the conversation and also by seeing this elegant Italian with his elegant clothes and his elegant manners wiping the same dishes she had used as a teenager. "I can't find any cookbooks in here. They must be in the other room. Be right back."

She was actually glad to get away from him for a few minutes. It gave her time to compose herself. She'd have to be very careful not to allow Marcus Bocelli to get under her skin, at least not now. Strength. That's what she needed to get through this weekend. One tiny bit of Italian *niceness* combined with his charm and he might just tear down the dam that was holding everything back. Control. More control. That's what she needed. She had been on autopilot since Aunt Tina's phone call. She simply couldn't allow her emotions to come forward. Not now, she thought, walking into the library and flipping on the lights.

This room still rattled her. She knew her mother would devour second hand novels from friends or neighbors. It had been her treat to herself at night in bed. Instead of in the arms of a man, her mother had fallen asleep with Robert Ludlum, Mary Higgins Clark, Morgan Lewellyn and *Rosemary Altea?* D. picked up the book on the small coffee table and turned it over. A few years ago in New York, she'd been in the studio when this author was being interviewed and thought the staff was crazy for being so thrilled. Some actually wanted to make appointments with the woman.

She opened the front cover and read the words:

Do you long to communicate with your loved ones in the spirit world? You own the power. You were born with it.

"Oh my God," D. muttered and slammed the book closed. Her mother had been reading *this* book? Totally bizarre, she thought, turning to the shelves of books. She wouldn't think about it right now. Maybe not ever. Typical of her mother, the books were organized into categories and she soon found the cookbooks. Seeing one that looked well used, she pulled it out and thumbed through the index until she found poultry and then stuffing. She flipped to the page and stared at her mother's handwriting in the margin.

Add diced apples, raisins. Deb loves it! Must teach her one day to cook.

She stood for a moment of out time, staring at her mother's script, in her mind envisioning other Thanksgivings and how much she had loved the day when food seemed plentiful and her mother had appeared happy for the two of them to give thanks for their many blessings. Again, D. remembered being selfish, impatient to dig into the feast, and thinking her mother foolish for thanking a God for blessings in a life that was a constant struggle.

What did you have, Mom, to be so thankful for all those years ago? Why didn't you rail at a Supreme Being that seemed to test your courage every month as the bills came due? Your hair turned white almost overnight after dad left us. You worked day and night to keep it all together by a shoestring and God let you down lots of times. Why didn't you ever lose your faith? Was your religion your opiate, was it what got you through, that God loves suffering? You loved a cruel God, and—

"Deborah?"

Startled, she slammed the book shut and spun around. "I . . . I found it. The cookbook," she said, feeling guilty at talking to her mother's spirit when she didn't believe in any of that bizarro stuff and had ridiculed others who were weak enough to be so gullible.

"Good," Marcus said with a grin. "Shall we get started?"

"Right. Let's get started," she answered, walking past him into the hallway.

"Interesting."

She heard Marcus' word and turned back to see him surveying the room.

"Your mother was an avid reader."

"She was," D. said, wishing he would just follow her and not . . . *no, no . . . stay away from the coffee table*, she mentally called out. It was too late. He picked up the book and opened the front cover.

His face seemed serene as he looked up at her. "Did you see this? Does this not seem remarkable that your mother was reading this before she died?"

"I can't talk about it, Marcus. Please, let's go back to the kitchen and make the stuffing."

"Deborah, this is not something you have to be frightened of. You know that, don't you?"

"Frightened? I'm not frightened," she lied, pulling back her shoulders. "I just don't believe in that mumbo jumbo."

Marcus laughed. "Mumbo jumbo . . . you Americans are so young. I find it fascinating to watch as one by one you are given opportunities to mature."

"Can we postpone debating international cultures and simply make the damn stuffing?" D. demanded, her hand on her hip.

Marcus gently put the book back onto the coffee table and nodded. "Just don't miss recognizing the opportunities, Deborah," he said meaningfully.

She marched down the hallway and tried to get her emotions back under control. Right. Like just because her mother was reading about communicating with spirits meant she should entertain such a ridiculous notion? She reported hard news. Facts. Her brain wasn't wired to accept the supernatural. Besides, everyone with half an ounce of rational thought knew it was . . . well . . . mumbo jumbo.

Right?

4

"It's stuck. I swear I'm going to be sick if this doesn't work!" D. complained, pursing her lips together as a barrier should her stomach rebel even more. "It's still partly frozen!"

Marcus tried not to laugh as she shuddered while attempting to pull out a bag of giblets. "Oh, come now, Deborah. Surely, you have cooked before this!" he chided good-naturedly. He found himself having a amusing time, watching this highly attractive woman battle with a dead turkey. Who would have thought when he'd come to pay his respects that he'd stay and become involved in a cooking lesson?

"Not like this!" she retorted, getting red in the face with her efforts. "I've thrown together a few meals, but I tend to order out. This . . . it's *disgusting!*"

"Well, someone's got to do it," he answered, then bit the inside of his lower lip to hide his amusement. He knew she would not be pleased if he laughed. Deborah Stark was one stubborn woman. He'd offered to get the giblets out himself, but she'd puffed up as though he'd insulted her and insisted she could do it. Watching her expression of disgust as she tugged on the bag inside the cavity of the large bird with long tongs, Marcus shook his head and crossed his arms over his chest. "Perhaps it would be easier if you grabbed it with your hand."

She looked up at him and her jaw dropped. "Put my hand inside it?"

"Well, if you don't, I will."

She puffed up again and used her forearm to wipe away the wisps of brown hair that were sticking to her face. "It's supposed to come right out."

"It's supposed to be completely defrosted. The inside isn't yet."

"I could put it in the oven for a little while, or pour boiling water inside," she said in a hopeful voice, as though anything was better than sticking her hand inside the bird.

Uncrossing his arms, he came forward. "Just let me try, all right? Besides, I don't think you should partly cook it now, do you? I know enough about cooking to realize you might get sick when you eat it tomorrow."

"You think I can possibly eat this thing after giving it a rectal exam?" she demanded.

"Then why are you doing it?" Marcus asked gently.

"Because . . . I told you," she answered in a voice that sounded like a young girl's. "I wanted to finish what my mother had started. See how she wrote in the cookbook that she wanted to teach me to cook? Well, she didn't, because I never had any interest in it." Her voice became stronger, determined. "I want to complete this, even if it means I just give the whole thing to the Dever family next door."

"Then, my dear, it appears we are on a mission. Either stick your hand in there and get those giblets, or I will." He knew, somehow, that D. didn't just want to prepare this meal herself, she needed to do it and would take up his challenge because the very last thing she wanted to show anyone was weakness. Especially a man.

"Oh, so now you think you're Wolfgang Puck just because—"

"Wolfgang Puck?" he interrupted, no longer trying to hide his smile.

She shook her head as though it didn't matter. "Just because you chopped the onions, the apples and the celery doesn't make you the better chef. I'll do this," she announced and threw down the tongs, stuck her hand inside the bird and tugged with intention.

She shut her eyes as if she couldn't bare to watch herself and Marcus quickly held the legs of the turkey as D. pushed against the chest to counterbalance the pressure as she pulled on the bag. Suddenly, without any warning, her hand came loose with the booty bag of giblets and Marcus watched in disbelief as the thing tore apart and frozen organs hit D.'s cheek and shoulder like red rocks of ice.

"*Augh!*" she screamed. "Get it off me! Get it *off!*" She was dancing frantically around the small kitchen.

He couldn't help himself as his laughter erupted. "It's not on you," he said in between chuckles. Bending, he picked up a heart, a liver, and threw them into the sink.

D. was standing with her hands out, as though frozen in shock. "Are you sure it's not on me?" she demanded, looking ready to cry. "I can *feel it!*"

Marcus quickly picked up a towel and ran it under the water. He wrung it out and came to her. "I'm just going to wipe your face," he whispered, truly struggling to keep his laughter under control.

"*My face!*" she nearly screamed. "Get it off my face!"

"Shh," he murmured, dabbing at her cheek. "You were very brave, Deborah. I know you didn't want to do it."

"Brave!" she muttered, closing her eyes, as though she

couldn't stand to think of giblets touching her skin. "You made me stick my hand inside that bird. It's your fault!"

He forgot about controlling his laughter. "It's *my* fault the bag broke?"

She opened one eyelid and glared at him. "You practically dared me."

"And do you take up every challenge offered to you? I said I would do it."

Grabbing the towel, she scrubbed at her face. "I have to take a shower," she insisted with another shudder. "Dear God, what exactly are giblets anyway? Are they what I think they are?"

"I'm afraid so," he answered with sympathy. "I seem to remember they are boiled and used to make gravy, at least in chickens. I imagine it's the same with turkeys."

She lowered the towel and stared at him. "How do you know, Mr. *GQ*? Where did someone like you learn that?"

"Someone like me?"

"Like you . . . ," she nodded, sweeping her gaze over him from his shoes to his head. "All continental, suave, charming, impeccably dressed. You must have read it in the cookbook."

"From my childhood," he replied, taking a small pot and filling it with water from the faucet. "We had a wonderful kitchen, overflowing with wondrous scents. I would at times sit at the table as my mother and my aunts prepared dinner and fed me treats."

"Giblets?" she asked with dread.

He chuckled. "Cookies, you would call them. Almond cookies. Covered in powdered sugar. They were heavenly."

"Well, I'll take baking cookies any day over shoving my hand up a damn turkey."

He washed off the organ meat and stuck them into the pot of water. Placing the pot onto the stove, he turned on the gas and said, "Perhaps another day we can tackle cookies. Why don't you take your shower?" He turned to her and smiled. "I know you won't feel clean until you do."

"You don't mind?" she asked, placing the wet dishtowel on the counter. "It was thoroughly disgusting." And she shuddered again at the thought.

Glad she had calmed down, he nodded. "Go on. I'll watch the giblets and make sure they don't boil over. We've had enough accidents for one night. Why don't you pamper yourself a little."

She seemed to melt before him. Her shoulders sagged. Her expression softened and her eyes filled with a sheen a tears. "Thanks for being here," she whispered, wringing her hands together at her waist as though uncomfortable by the admission of her next words. "I didn't realize just how much I didn't want to be alone tonight."

Instinctively, he reached out and pulled her into his arms. "I'm glad to be here," he whispered back, feeling her body stiffen with a resolve to be strong.

"I . . . I'm so scared," she mumbled, trying so hard to control her tears that her gulping was audible. "I don't know what to do or say to people and . . . and I was a terrible daughter, Marcus. I should have been here more."

"Don't have any regrets, Deborah," he whispered into her hair. "Don't look back with negativity. Try and remember the positive times you had with your mother. Your guilt isn't going to change anything, except give you added stress . . . which you don't need to carry now. Your mother wouldn't want you to bear such a burden, would she?"

She shook her head and sniffled. "No, she was a good woman. Everybody says so. I just wasn't a good daughter."

"Stop saying that."

"But it's true, Marcus," she insisted, pulling away from him, her eyes red with tears and something else . . . fear. "You don't know me," she declared, staring at him, defying him to challenge her. "You think because we screwed on the beach in Bermuda that you can come here and give me clichés about remembering positive times? There weren't many positive times, okay? You want the truth? My mother led a lousy life, always worrying about money. Do you know what it's like to live without running water or electricity?"

He shook his head in sympathy, watching her buried fears rise to the surface of her mind.

"Well, I do and so did my mother," she stated in a passionate voice. "I know what it's like to try and hide from everyone what's happening at home, to have to wear the same clothes to school. For two weeks there was no running water in this house because there wasn't the money to pay the water bill. And it didn't happen just once either, and I had to—"

"Deborah stop it," he commanded as gently as he could. "None of that matters now."

She stared at him, her brown eyes wide and defiant. "Of course it matters. It *has* to matter. My whole life revolved around it. I made important life decisions because of it. It *must* matter."

"Is it real now?"

"What do you mean, is it real now?"

He shrugged. "Today, in this moment. There's electricity and water here."

"So? That doesn't wipe out what happened in the past."

"Who says you have to carry around the past like a badge of courage or, worse yet, a suitcase of regret?"

She blinked, staring at him with her mouth slightly opened and he knew she was trying to think of a comeback that would silence him.

"You think you are your past, Deborah," he added before she could retort. "But you're not. You think you are your memories, but you're not. They may have influenced your decisions, but they aren't you. Not anymore. Do you know that the cells of your body are created, destroyed and replaced many, many times during your life? Nature is constantly remaking you, yet you hold onto old energy through your emotions. Your mind, your thoughts, aren't physical and nature can't heal them or recycle them. Only you can do that . . . when you're willing to let go of them."

She didn't say anything, just continued to stare at him. He took a deeper breath. "Let me ask you something. Do you believe your mother loved you?"

"Yes, she loved me."

"Did you love your mother?"

"Of course."

"Then that is all that matters now. Love is the only energy we take with us when we leave this dimension."

Her eyes narrowed. "This *dimension?*"

He felt his lips moving into a smile. "That's right, Deborah. The non-physical part of your mother has moved into another dimension. Your guilt and anger and resentment and even your negative memories are meaningless now. The only thing they will accomplish is to punish you. But realize, it is *you* punishing *you.* Your mother is so beyond that."

"Yeah? Well, when I go to the funeral home on Friday I'll be sure to tell her that." Her voice was angry, sarcastic, defensive.

He'd been in this position too many times to count and her anger passed right through him. She wasn't really angry with him. She was angry with herself. "Surely you are too intelligent to believe that the body you will bury is your mother."

"Really?" She shook her head, as though not believing she was even having this conversation. "I suppose you're going to tell me who I am burying then."

"You're not burying anyone. It's merely symbolic. Your mother's body was simply the vehicle she was using while traveling in this dimension."

She stared at him as if he'd lost his mind.

He smiled gently, knowing what he was saying sounded incredulous to her. If it were not for the negative emotions surrounding the death of her mother he probably never would have brought it up. He now knew that his choice this holiday weekend had led him to be in this kitchen, in this position, to try to bring light into a dark situation. "Can you at least try to imagine the body as simply a vehicle? Think of it like a space suit that kept your mother grounded against the force of gravity. Your mother, the non-physical part of your mother, her mind, her thoughts, her emotions, her soul if you will, used that space suit during her lifetime on this planet. When she left this dimension, when the vehicle she was using no longer worked, she simply dropped her space suit and became what she always was and always will be . . . a being of light and of love."

Her breath left her in a rush of frustration. "You actually believe in all that mumbo jumbo?" she demanded, appearing agitated as she again began wringing her hands.

"I believe in what I just told you, yes. And so do you, Deborah. Down deep, it resonates with you, the real you who isn't afraid, who knows your consciousness goes on, who knows that the eternal spark within you is not of this world. It's been ridiculed so much that most of humanity has pushed it to a far corner of the mind for, you see, so many of us have bought into the irrational fear of the unknown."

"Who *are* you?" she insisted, with a nervous laugh. "What's coming out of your mouth isn't exactly the charming repartee of the Italian playboy."

"I'm not a playboy as you call it," he stated in a serious voice. "Do I enjoy the company of women? Absolutely. I have since I was a young boy, surrounded by my aunts and cousins. I adore females. Young. Old. Each one is a miracle to me. A masterpiece in the making. Some are DaVinci's. Some are Monet's, Gaughan's, Picasso's or Waterhouse's.

And some, perhaps like you, Deborah, have yet to be recognized and adored."

She grabbed the edge of the counter, as if she needed support, and then laughed again, though the sound of it was shaky. "Oh, you're good, Bocelli. Very good."

"You ask who I am." He tried to let her see who he was by dropping all invisible barriers so she could know she had nothing to fear from him, no reason to argue with him. "I'd like to be your friend. And all I'm telling you is that you don't have to be afraid anymore. Grieve for the loss of your mother's physical presence around you, but don't grieve for her. And, whatever else you might think right now, at least consider that she isn't lost to you forever. You carry her in your heart, and in your mind, in that eternal spark we all share that can never be extinguished. Your mother is in your soul. It's the place where you can exist with her anytime you wish, because you aren't separate from her where it's real."

"Real?" she countered, shoving back the hair from her forehead as her defensiveness seemed to swell once again. "You want to talk real? I report hard news, pal, based on facts, *rational* facts, not some pie in the sky wish that we're all *eternal* and united in some metaphysical or supernatural spark. *That's* mumbo jumbo, and I ain't buyin' it."

He smiled. Even though he knew from his little experience with this woman that it would only fuel her indignation, he couldn't help feeling a bit amused. "What if I told you that science, and I'm sure you'd agree that scientists are most rational, what if science has come to the realization that the true nature of reality is all things, visible and invisible, are not separate but interrelated? *All things,* Deborah. At a quantum level of existence everything consists of information and energy. You can't touch it or feel it or smell it. It can't be perceived by any of your senses that would tell you it's real, but you know your mind is real, your thoughts are real. You know an atom is real. When you were in school did not someone teach you that everything solid is made up of molecules and those molecules are made up of something smaller called atoms, and then we come to learn that atoms are made up of subatomic particles which have no solidity at all . . . they are packages of information and energy. That counter your hand is on, at a subatomic level, is not solid at all. It's mostly space."

She lifted her hand and stared at the counter. "Not solid?" Smacking her palm down hard upon the Formica, she declared, "Seems pretty damn solid to me."

"You perceive it as solid because what is happening is at the speed of light."

"You're losing me, I'm afraid. What does *any* of this bizarre conversation have to do with my mother?"

"It has everything to do with your mother and your state of mind. You want rational, Deborah? How about Albert Einstein? If energy equals mass times the speed of light squared, then that countertop, matter, and energy are the same thing only in different forms. Energy equals mass. Energy waves contain different kinds of information and that is determined by the frequency or vibration of those energy waves. Our senses simply can't process what is occurring at the speed of light. What you perceive of as reality is blinking in and out so quickly your brain *sees* it as solid. Like those decks of cards with pictures on them. Flip them quick enough and it appears that something is real, solid, moving. You tune in on the radio to one station, perhaps one that plays opera. Turn the frequency and you'll tune into and pick up on another station playing country western music. Your mother, the consciousness that always was your mother, her energy is simply at another frequency . . . one you believe you are unable to reach. Science will tell you energy cannot be destroyed, only transformed. Your mother is transformed, but she is not destroyed."

She simply stared at him, blinking, not moving, as if she'd lost the ability to speak.

"Go take your shower, my dear. Our giblets are beginning to boil."

And with that, he turned away from her to the stove, turning down the heat under the pot. He sensed her leaving the kitchen and wondered if he'd overwhelmed her by too much information. Shrugging, Marcus sighed deeply.

Who knew his desire for a weekend fling would turn into an assignment?

D. turned on the hot water, staring at the gush coming from the faucet. Reaching out she rotated the right handle and added some cold, all the while attempting to behave normally. Taking a shower seemed normal, and she so wanted normal after that conversation.

Who the hell was that man in her mother's kitchen?

She thought of Maggie warning her off Marcus several times, saying he would only break her heart. And now she knew why. Not only was Marcus Bocelli too damn handsome for any male to be, he also possessed a charm that could leave a woman helpless. His charm wasn't just his continental, old European grace. Marcus' charisma was that he could not only sell ice to Eskimos, he could actually make a person, an intelligent rational person, believe that death was simply a transition into something extraordinary. If she believed Marcus, her mother was just fine, was maybe even blessed that her transition had happened quickly. One moment she was talking to her friend and in the next, she'd simply dropped her space suit and was one with . . . what? Everything?

Shaking her head to wipe out the silly thought, D. began undressing, dropping her designer clothes onto the bathroom floor. How many times had she done this growing up? Then, the clothes hadn't been designer, and most of them not even hers, but hand-me-downs. She stared at the old tile around the sink. It wasn't even real tile, but some kind of plastic with sparkly dust baked into it. Her mother's remodeling hadn't touched this room, save for new paint and towels. A part of her was ashamed of herself for being ashamed of this place, but she couldn't help it. Too many bad and humiliating memories were associated with this house.

She stepped into the shower and quickly began lathering herself with a bar of soap. Suddenly, she stared at the soap in her hand. Her mother's soap. The last person to touch this had been her mother, probably the morning she had died. Was that just yesterday? It seemed like a week ago. Bringing the soap to her nose she inhaled the scent of Dove and, without any warning, she began to cry. Really cry. The wall around her heart felt like it was cracking open with sorrow and regret. If she could just touch her mother again, feel her skin, wrap her arms around her like she should have done more often. She just wanted to hear her voice, listen to her and not be impatient this time . . .

"I am so sorry," she mumbled, clutching the little chrome bar over the soap holder to steady herself as the hot water rained down on her. *I wasn't a good daughter, Mom, I was always complaining and I know you did the best you could under the circumstances. And I'm just so sorry I wasn't here more . . .*

And then, in her mind, she heard her mother's voice.

Seriously.

D. stopped crying, blinking away the water, staring at the tile she had once hated as a shiver of recognition and shock swept through her.

You are my sunshine, my only sunshine. You make me happy when times are gray. You'll never know, dear, how much I love you. Please don't take my sunshine away.

She had to remind herself to breathe.

Her mother had always sang that song to her when she was sick.

5

She was dressed in pajama bottoms and a silky pale yellow sweatshirt with the sleeves rolled up. Okay, she didn't want to appear to be trying to impress Marcus, but she also didn't want to look like a slob either. D. knew she needed to get her act together, and beginning physically was a good start. After hearing her mother sing to her in the shower, coming from out of nowhere, her composure wasn't exactly on strong ground.

She'd tried to tell herself it had been her imagination because of Marcus' conversation, or that somewhere in her subconscious she had dredged up the memory of her mother singing that song to her as a sick child, but there was a part of her that didn't quite believe either explanation . . . too many coincidences . . . that squirrel on the walk, that book her mother had been reading, the speech Marcus had given her about death and space suits and communicating with the essence of her mother.

It scared her.

And, truth be told, even if just to herself, the possibility he might be right was playing around in her head when she should have been laughing at herself and this gorgeous man who was stirring around the stuffing with a large wooden spoon.

"Now, it says we should refrigerate it overnight and then stuff the turkey in the morning."

D. nodded, moving away from the counter and opening a drawer, glad to be given something to do so she wouldn't have to think anymore. "How about a big plastic storage bag?" she asked, pulling out a box. "These have zippers on them, so it should keep it fresh."

Marcus grinned. "Sounds good to me. Do you want to hold it open and I'll try to get this into it?"

"Okay," D. answered, standing next to him, very close to him, and holding the big plastic bag open. She could inhale the scent of him, expensive cologne and onions. Quite a combination, she thought. Dashing Marcus Bocelli smelling like the onions he had diced earlier. She hated to admit that endeared him to her. This gorgeous Italian had given no mind to his appearance as he had worked in her mother's kitchen pulling together a Thanksgiving dinner neither one of them would probably eat. And all because she had said she'd wanted to do it. She waited as he scooped the last of the stuffing into the bag, squeezed the air out of it and zippered it closed.

"There," Marcus proclaimed with a pleased voice. "We're done, Deborah. Turkey stuffing."

She couldn't help grinning at him. "You did most of the work," she admitted.

"Well, now we both know something we didn't know this afternoon."

"What's that?" she asked, picking up the bag with both hands.

"We've been enlightened about this very good holiday you Americans have."

"We know how to make stuffing?" she asked with a laugh as she placed the plastic bag onto a shelf in the refrigerator.

"We both have a better understanding about Thanksgiving and gratitude. I thank you for this opportunity, my dear. To-night was very illuminating." He was washing his hands at the sink.

She leaned against the fridge and sighed. He sounded so formal. "Thanks for all your help, Marcus. I guess you'll have to get going now." She looked at the kitchen clock. It was after eleven. "It's getting late."

Why did her heart feel heavy at the thought of him leaving? Was it just her fear of being alone in this house, or was there something more? She knew it would be beyond stupid if it were something more. Maggie had been right. Marcus Bocelli would break her heart and she couldn't afford any more assaults on her heart now.

Picking up a dishtowel, he wiped his hands and glanced at the clock. "It is late. I hadn't realized. What is that saying I've heard? Time takes wing when you're having fun?"

"Flies. Time *flies* when you're having fun," she repeated.

"Ah, yes. Well, it had surely flown, has it not? You must be exhausted, Deborah."

For some insane reason, she actually liked the way her name sounded coming from his lips. *Deborah*. He said it like an exotic endearment. For years she had avoided being called by it, save for business, and now she looked forward to hearing it spoken again by him. Part of the reason she disliked her name was that it meant honey bee. Long ago she had made up her mind that if she'd had a choice between being sweet like honey or stinging like a bee, she would chose stinging for the respect over sweet which was simply another word for nice.

"You are tired, aren't you?" he asked.

She blinked, forcing herself back into the present. "I am," she admitted. "You must be too."

"A bit," he confessed with a grin as he folded the dish-towel and placed it by the sink. "It has been a full day."

She nodded. "You'll get back to the city late. You live in Manhattan, don't you?"

It was his turn to nod. "On the West Side, by the park."

"I know very little about you," she answered with a shy smile. "Here you've come into my life and saved the day and it seems . . ." Her voice trailed off, not knowing how to say what she wanted.

He stepped forward and gently brushed her bangs back from her forehead. "And it seems after what took place in Bermuda we should have known more?"

Embarrassed, she nodded. "That's the inappropriate part you were talking about earlier, huh?"

"Yes. I don't know what you think of me, but I would like you to know I don't normally behave like that."

D. inhaled deeply and just said it as she stared into his warm brown eyes. "You love her, don't you? Maggie. I was convenient. Right there. Throwing myself at you as she was sailing away with another man."

His eyes darkened and he looked away. "I will always love her, Deborah, but I truly am happy for her. She deserves a happiness I couldn't give her. She made the right choice."

"Do you still love her?" The question popped out of her mouth before she could censure it.

His head jerked up and he now gazed her directly. "I just said I will always love her."

She was already in this and she might as well finish it. Be-sides, she really wanted to know the truth. "But are you in love with her, Marcus?"

He slowly shook his head. "I don't know if that can be an-swered. If you are asking if I hold any hope that Maggie will leave Julian McDonald for me, then the answer is no."

She let his words settle around her for a moment. "You see, I love her too, Marcus," she stated, wanting him to know her questions weren't just an invasion of his privacy. "Maggie was the first friend I had that I could tell the truth to and not be judged. I was happy for her and Julian, but I miss her, really miss her. I almost called her today, but didn't want to ruin her first Thanksgiving with Julian and Senator Burke."

Marcus smiled with sympathy. "She would want to know about your mother."

"I know. I'll tell her after the funeral."

He sighed deeply. "I might as well admit I turned down an invitation for Thanksgiving dinner with Gabriel Burke for almost the same reasons. I didn't want to spoil this holiday for Maggie and her new family. My presence would only remind her of her past. She deserves a fresh start."

"I don't think Julian McDonald would appreciate you showing up either," D. added with a grin. "You make that man nervous."

The tension left Marcus' face and he grinned. "He has nothing to worry about."

"You underestimate yourself, Mr. Bocelli. If I were Julian McDonald, I'd do everything in my power to keep my wife away from you."

He laughed. "Your flattery is unwarranted, Deborah. Maggie and I have been friends for years, not lovers. She is deeply in love with Julian and I've accepted that. I am happy for her."

D. nodded and sighed, letting her shoulders drop with the release of tension. "So it seems the two of us, two of Maggie's good friends, are feeling the same thing. What are you doing tomorrow? Want to help me stuff that bird and then cook it? At least it will keep us busy until the holiday is over."

He didn't say anything and his silence stung like a rejection. "Okay," she added. "It was just a thought. I wasn't trying to put you on the spot. You've already done your good deed and I'm extremely grateful for your help today. I can do this tomorrow and—"

"Are you that uncomfortable with silence?" he interrupted. "You don't even give a man a chance to answer. I was trying to think how long it would take me to get back here."

She brightened. "Then you'll come?"

"Yes, Deborah, I'll come for Thanksgiving preparations and dinner."

"I don't know if I can eat that bird after everything tonight," she complained.

"We'll eat it," he declared. "And two friends will give thanks. We earned it."

"I'll attempt it," she whispered, trying hard not to show him how grateful she was that he'd come back tomorrow. "You know it's going to take hours for it to cook. It has to be in the oven in the morning."

"So I'll be back in time." He kissed her forehead. "Now, go to sleep."

She watched him walk to the door and knew she wouldn't sleep tonight.

And she didn't . . . at least not for hours.

After Marcus left, D. had felt like Goldilocks in her mother's home. She wasn't comfortable using her mother's bedroom, so she tried the pull-out sofa in what used to be her old room. When she spied that book about connecting to dead people, she gave up and dragged a pillow and a blanket out to the living room sofa. She turned on the television set and tried to find anything interesting, but she could swear she felt her mother's presence all around her and was way too scared to close her eyes. What truly frightened her was that right at her shoulder was grief, standing like a silent sentry, waiting to be recognized. And she couldn't do that, not yet, for she feared she might lose her tender grasp on reality if she acknowledged what was tearing at the edges of her heart. Somehow she had to get through the next few days like a normal human being. She had to get through a holiday and find some kind of gratitude for her mother's sake. Then would come the real test. She had to bury her mother and close up this house.

Of course she was scared.

She had tried to rationalize everything, telling herself it was only natural since she was in her mother's home to be spooked. Most of the time she was good at rationalizing and could talk herself out of almost anything by being a smart ass, but this time her smart-ass attitude wasn't working. A smart ass couldn't explain hearing her mother singing *you are my sunshine* in the shower. Finally she had decided that her mother loved her, despite being a terrible daughter, so there was nothing to fear . . . still she knew she'd jump right out of her skin if anything else weird happened. And so she waited for the weird stuff to continue. And waited. Somewhere around four in the morning, when she couldn't possibly keep her eyelids open any longer, sleep claimed her and pulled her into the comfort of darkness.

No dreams. No childhood songs. Just exhausted sleep.

It was with resentment that D. heard the chirping of a bird right outside the window. *Go away,* she thought, pulling the pillow around her ears. She could still hear it and it's bloody cheerfulness was getting annoying. "Shut up," she muttered, refusing to be drawn into wakefulness. Then came a persistent noise. A pounding. She tried to shut it out too, but it was getting louder. Moaning, she buried her face into the pillow and tried to reclaim the wonderful oblivion of sleep. It was no use. Pulling herself up from the sofa, she felt half drunk and stumbled to the door.

"Okay," she called out in a aggrieved voice, trying to wake up as she flung the door open.

Her jaw dropped as she blinked herself into awareness and tried desperately to make sense out of her situation. She wasn't in her apartment in Philly. This was her mother's house. With a terrible crash inside her brain it all fell into place. Death. Funeral preparations. It was Thanksgiving and Marcus Bocelli looked so clean and handsome and awake, he hurt her eyes more than the sunshine that drenched Grandlake Estates.

"Deborah? Have you just awakened?"

"What time is it?" she mumbled, pushing the hair back from her eyes and licking her lips, hoping dried dribble wasn't on her chin.

He glanced at his watch and grinned. "Ten-twenty, time to finish our preparations for our feast."

How could he possibly be so formal and cheerful when she simply wanted to crawl back to the sofa and sleep through the day? Realizing she had to do something, D. held the door open wider and allowed him to pass before her into the living room. "Are you always this cheerful so early? Surely the traffic out of the city should have put a damper on that sunny Italian disposition."

Marcus laughed as he came into the house and turned back to her while she shoved the door, closing out Grandlake Estates and that blinding sun. At least he didn't seem to mind her morning surliness, which had in the past put off more than a few men and had ended several going-nowhere dating cycles. "You're actually more cheerful than that bird who, I do believe, was trying to break in through the window."

"You can be so humorous, Deborah, even when I know your heart is breaking. Someone once told me that a sense of humor can be our most valuable asset on this adventure of life." He dropped his soft leather jacket on the back of the chair by the door and smiled at her. "Besides, I'm sure that bird was simply trying to nudge you gently awake to join the day." He was dressed in autumnal shades of tan and olive green and his smile was endearing.

Okay, she couldn't let him past her barriers. She didn't need nice today. Nice would shatter her reserve of strength to get her through the funeral. "Oh, yeah?" she asked in a sarcastic voice as she headed back to the sofa. "And what mindless moron gave you that piece of advice?" She plopped down and dragged the comforter back over her shoulder.

He slowly sat down in the chair and she would swear he had pity in his eyes . . . or something close to it. He would probably call it compassion, but it felt like pity from where she sat, or laid, or whatever. And she didn't like it.

"Mindless moron . . . what an interesting phrase," he remarked, not seeming to be offended in the least. "Though if I understand English correctly, that term, moron, would imply a state of mindlessness, therefore would it not be redundant?"

She opened one eye and glared at him. "Are we going to debate this, or are we just going to have an English lesson . . . for me?"

Again, he chuckled, not taking the bait. "Ah, Deborah . . . you are a treasure. If only you knew that. Perhaps then you would not be so hard on everyone, particularly yourself."

"I'm a treasure all right . . . the kind Wiley Coyote would open and it would explode."

He didn't laugh and silence filled the room for more than a few seconds. "You must explain this. Who is Willy Coyote?"

She couldn't help it as her lips started to curl into a smile. "Listen, Marcus, you can't claim to be informed about Americans unless you know about Wiley Coyote. He's a cartoon and his life's passion is to catch the Road Runner and he will go to any length to get him, only everything he tries fails miserably, usually blowing Wiley right out of the water or the sky or whatever cliff he happens to be hanging from with one paw. He's like our national symbol. Even though the Road Runner is this nice character, we're all secretly cheering for Wiley Coyote. We don't want the Road Runner dead, or anything like that . . . we just want the loser to finally win. We love underdogs because most of us identify with them."

"Underdogs?"

She sighed. How could he possibly understand her point if he didn't know basic jargon? "Underdog . . . someone who tries like hell to get ahead and fails."

"You're not an underdog, Deborah. You have succeeded, have you not?"

"We're not talking about me," she said with a sigh of weariness.

"I thought we were. You said you were the kind of treasure Wiley Coyote would open and it would explode."

"It was joke, Marcus. It's called self-deprecating humor." Sheesh, this was basic stuff.

"And you enjoy that? Self deprecation?"

It took her a full thirty seconds to answer as she attempted to rein in her impatience. "You take everything too literally. Self deprecating humor is just easy, that's all. And if you really knew me, you'd realize I very seldom put myself down publicly."

"Only in private then?"

"Rarely in private." She wasn't about to tell him the truth.

"Good. It is not a healthy thing to depreciate one's self."

"Well, I don't." White lie.

"Very good."

He sounded like he was her teacher and she didn't care for his approval, especially since she'd lied to him. "So who said it . . . about a sense of humor being a valuable asset on life's adventures."

Marcus leaned back in the chair and grinned. "Gabriel Burke. He taught me many things. I lived with him, you know."

She leaned up on her elbow. "No, I didn't know. Is he like a relative, or something?"

"No, not a blood relative. He was very good friends with my father. After his death, my mother sent me to Gabriel. He is my godfather and he fulfilled his role." He looked from the living room toward the dining area. "Would you, by any chance, have coffee?"

She threw back the cover and sat up fully, running her fingers through her hair. "I truly am a lousy host," she muttered, remembering how thrilled she had been last night when he'd announced he would come back this morning to help her.

"Stay," Marcus softly commanded while rising. "It is obvious I awakened you. Allow me to make the coffee. I know where everything is."

She watched him smoothly walk into her mother's kitchen, as though he had done it a hundred times, and then heard him open cabinets. He would know where everything was, for he had done more work in the kitchen yesterday than she had. Grabbing up the pillow and comforter, she left the living room and was determined to make more of an effort in being pleasant. He had, after all, come back as he'd promised. Pleasant, she could do. Nice was out of the question.

Twenty minutes later she was sipping a cup of delicious coffee and watching one of the most handsome men she had ever met spoon soggy seasoned bread up the arse of a turkey and feeling . . . grateful. Especially for his presence, cheerful though it was, for she didn't know how she would have gotten through this day in this house alone. All over America families were gathering together to cook, watch television parades, play ball or just reunite for a day of thanksgiving, of appreciating each other and the blessings they had been given during the year. Last year she'd had to work. Volunteered to work was the truth. She could rationalize it as everyone else had family dinners to attend, but the plain ugly truth was that she didn't want to come back to Grandlake Estates. If her mother would have come to Philly, she would have taken her to dinner at the Four Seasons, but Emily Stark had never come to visit her in Philadelphia as she'd done in New York City. It wasn't just the extra distance. For some reason her mother always had a ready excuse not to travel to the City of Brotherly Love. And so this year was supposed to make up for the last few Thanksgivings she had missed.

Wasn't meant to be, she thought with a sigh. But maybe, just maybe, if all that mumbo jumbo Marcus talked about was even a tiny bit true . . . maybe her mother knew she was here, making the holiday dinner, in her own silly way paying tribute to all the years her mother had prepared the meal for them both.

"Deborah, I'm afraid I have a very unpleasant task for you."

His words brought her back to the present. "And now I'm afraid to ask what," she mumbled, pushing herself closer to him.

"Well, you see you have a choice. Now that the turkey is stuffed, you either have to hold this together while I put these long skewers into it, or I'll hold . . . this . . . closed," he said, indicating the flapping skin, "and you can pierce it and sew it together."

The distaste rose in her mouth, generating saliva that she gulped down. "I never really appreciated what women go through to pull off this meal," she muttered, opening the cabinet under the sink and taking out yellow rubber gloves. "I'll hold it together and you can do the sewing," she declared while holding her hands up before her like a surgeon going in for an operation.

"Someday, Deborah," he answered with a grin, "you will have to get used to distasteful things."

"I will?" she asked, gingerly placing her hands over his and keeping the skin together. "Why, when there's always take-out?"

"Life is full of distasteful things, is it not? Someday you may have children. Do you intend to hire a nanny to perform chores? Or, perhaps, will your love of that child overcome your distaste and you will do things you never thought you possibly could?"

"I don't know," she answered, turning her face away as Marcus began piercing the turkey skin. "I never thought about it."

"You never thought about motherhood?"

Sensing he was still working, she didn't look back just yet. "Why is that so surprising? I mean, I've thought I'm not ready to even think about it. Kids don't fit into my equation."

"One day you must tell me about your equation. And, I'm finished so you can take your hands away."

"Very neat work," she observed, turning on the water at the sink and rinsing the gloves. "Thank God we're done with this bird. Let's stick it in the oven and forget it for a few hours."

"Good idea," Marcus said, picking up the bird and placing it in the disposable aluminum baking pan her mother had bought. "The recipe said we should cover it in the beginning."

D. glanced at the book on the counter. "With foil, but first we need to put butter all over it and sprinkle it with salt and pepper and sifted flour. Did we sift flour yet?"

"You sift the flour and I'll butter the bird. I can't see you touching it again until it's served." He opened the refrigerator and took out the butter. "I should soften this, I think."

She nodded, barely paying attention while she tried to figure out how to sift flour. She didn't want to admit she had never done such a domestic thing. It was bad enough he thought her a wimp when it came to touching carcasses. This sounded more like baking, something basic she should know. She found the flour and was looking through the bottom cabinets, searching for some kind of utensil to use. She spied a dented aluminum thing in the back of one shelf and pulled it out. There was a handle on it that turned a blade at the bottom. It must be a sifter.

Feeling very good about herself and her discovery, she poured some flour into it and gasped when most of it fell through the little holes onto the counter. "Damn," she muttered, holding her hand over the bottom and not knowing what to do except to suspend the thing over the sink. "This is all just too much work for one lousy day!"

He looked up from the pan where his butter was melting and smiled at her exclamation. "It's done for love, Deborah. Women are capable of such love that most men cannot even fathom. Is there any doubt why they are so admired?"

"Admired? What planet are you from?" she demanded. "Women have to work harder for everything. How many women all across this country at this moment are trying to pull this meal together with no help from anyone? And this after working a regular job, taking care of kids and homework and after-school activities and laundry, the in-laws are coming and the house isn't yet cleaned and the husband is planning what footballs games he's going to watch for the rest of the afternoon? No thanks. If that's being admired, I'd rather be out of favor with you and every other admiring male in the universe. And I'd rather go to a restaurant and be served, thank you."

He poured the butter over the turkey and then seasoned it with salt and pepper. He then looked at her by the sink and said, "I believe we are ready for the sifted flour now."

She could sense she had offended him and wished she could take back her rant, but it was out there, hanging between them like a naked fat man that couldn't be ignored. Great, she'd done it again. Driven off a man because of her mouth.

Holding her hand under the sifter, she brought it over to the turkey and began twisting the little knob at the top. To her amazement a fine dusting of flour fell onto the bird like soft snow.

"I think you should move it quickly all over," Marcus whispered.

"Right," she answered, regretting the heavy dusting in one spot. She tried to make up for it by smoothly moving the sifter all over. When the bird was covered, she put the thing into the sink. "That should do it," she declared.

Marcus nodded and tore off a long sheet of foil. The oven was already preheated and D. watched as he covered the top of the turkey with a tent of foil and then put it in the oven.

"There," he pronounced. "I believe we have done it."

D. poured the rest of the flour down the sink and ran the water. "Actually, you did most of the work, Marcus. I was your helper and not a very good one at that."

"Did you do the best you were capable of?"

Startled by his question, she nodded. "I think so," she murmured.

"Then you were a very good helper."

He walked over to the sink and she moved away as he poured dish liquid onto his palms and began washing his hands. D. had moved to give him room, but she was close enough to see his expression. Gone was his cheerfulness, and she now found herself wanting to bring it back, missing that optimism and even his mumbo jumbo theories about life.

Taking a deep breath, she began something that was never easy for her. "Look, I apologize for going on like that about women and men and admiration. I'm a smart ass, okay? That's who I am. Most people ignore me, or at least don't take me seriously. I'm just venting and I'm sorry for doing it with you. I think it's great you admire women and are so open about it. Really, I do."

He dried his hands and looked directly and deeply into her eyes. "Who was it, Deborah, that wounded you so? Was it a boyfriend, a lover . . . your father?"

She felt as though she'd been struck by an invisible force and actually moved a step back from him. "I don't know what you mean. Nobody wounded me. I told you, I'm just a smart ass and can go into a rant on any subject. Bring up the Middle East, the environment, or the current administration and I can do the same thing."

He simply nodded as he moved past her to the coffeemaker, but she knew he didn't believe her. He was letting her off the hook, but he'd made it clear he had her number. She didn't like that any man, especially him, had her by the short hairs, but was unsure of what to do. She could always revert back to her old way of baiting a male until he left, yet D. knew in her heart she didn't want Marcus to leave. His presence was the only thing making this day bearable.

"I'm sorry, okay?" she whispered, hating that her voice sounded almost pleading. She didn't think pleading was in her. Just goes to show you what she knew about herself when she felt desperate for company.

"I accept your apology, Deborah," Marcus said in a formal voice. "Now I think I would like to go for a drive on this splendid day. Will you accompany me?"

She felt as though she'd been given a reprieve and found her head bobbing up and down like an eager dog. Pathetic, she knew, but the thought of getting out of the house with gorgeous Marcus Bocelli in his sleek Italian sports car was just too tempting to be sedate. "I'd love it," she answered.

And it was the truth.

6

S he gazed at the interior of the black Porsche with admiration as she inhaled the expensive leather. "You do know," she said, as Marcus turned over the powerful engine, "what they say about men who drive these cars."

"What do they say, Deborah?" he asked, his hand on the gear shift between them, ready to throw the engine into first as he waited for her answer.

"You must have heard."

"Tell me."

"Well, it's said that men who own these cars are overcompensating for lack in . . . in other areas of their life." Since their encounter on the beach, she could attest that he wasn't overcompensating in *that* area.

"And what do you think?"

He might as well be reading her mind. At least he no longer appeared upset with her. She stared at her knees covered in her good chocolate gabardine trousers and grinned. "I think that any man who looks like you, acts like you, dresses like you *and* drives this car is definitely going for overkill." She glanced up to capture his reaction.

He chuckled and it was good to see his smile back again.

"And what if I told you that I simply admire the exquisite engineering of a car that was built in my country?"

She inhaled deeply, trying to get her composure back to normal. Seeing this man behind the wheel of a Porsche, so comfortable, so suitable, so damn attractive, was unnerving. "You know what, Marcus? I'd believe you. You definitely don't need this car. You just like it. But you will concede the whole package does border on too much of a good thing."

"Is there ever too much of a good thing?" he asked and then threw the car into first gear. They took off down the street to the roar of a magnificent engine, leaving Grandlake Estates behind them.

Dear God . . . he was a hedonist too. Definitely her kind of man. She had better be careful where her heart was concerned. She kept hearing Maggie's voice in her head, telling her that Marcus Bocelli would break her heart. D. knew if she were so supremely foolish as to fall in love with this man, Maggie's prediction would become true.

They left the small subdivision and were stopped in traffic before Main Street as the annual Thanksgiving parade made its way down a street that had lost whatever charm it had once possessed to draw shoppers. Kresge's was gone. So was LaRosa's Butcher shop and Foyle's Market. A large Dollar Store had replaced both Rosvold's Pharmacy and Keenan's Foot Fair. "It's changed so," she whispered to herself.

Marcus turned to her. "What has?"

"This town. I guess the superstores on Routes 1 and 9 took all the business. It seems even worse than I remembered it. And look at them . . ." she added, nodding to the chamber of commerce float carrying the high school's football team and the usual gaggle of pretty cheerleaders. "It's like this town has one last gasp left in it and they're going to go out with tradition."

"Well, good for them," Marcus answered, then sighed. "It is a very sad thing to see a town die, is it not?"

She shrugged. "Maybe not for this town."

"Why? In Europe, our towns stay alive through good times and bad. We hold on when it feels as though the last reserves of strength are squeezing our lifeblood and rebuild when that eases. I have never, myself, lived in a town that has died."

"Your culture is much older than ours. We Americans move on fast when it doesn't feel good. Haven't you heard? We're the disposable culture. If an iron breaks, we throw it out rather than get it fixed. And where would we get it fixed anymore? Kusack's Repair Shop shut down years ago when it was cheaper to go to the mega stores and buy an iron manufactured overseas than repair it."

Gazing at the closed stores with spray painted graffiti scrawled on the dirty windows, she shook her head. Who would have imagined she'd be sorry to see this decay taking over? Then she thought about what was happening, really happening. "Money rules," she murmured. "When the superstores opened up on the busy highways, mom-and-pop stores faded away. The middle class thought it was getting a break at Alphabet Marts, but what it really got was a potentially fatal wound to a main artery. What's happening here is happening all across the country. Cheap overseas labor is making big corporations mega bucks, but the money isn't trickling down to the workers. Not the overseas workers who are paid a pittance, nor the workers in this country. And we all thought we were getting that iron at a bargain. The real price isn't such a bargain after all. It's what we're looking at . . . loss of manufacturing, the squeeze on small business, dying towns, skyrocketing unemployment and a deficit of hope. We're heading toward the haves and the have nots. The rich and the poor. The middle class is fading away."

"Deborah . . ."

Blinking away her verbalized thoughts, she turned her attention from the street scene and looked at him. "What?"

"You could do a story on just what you've told me. The distribution of wealth has always been out of balance, but now it is enormously and dangerously one sided. Don't misinterpret me. There is nothing wrong with money. I have a goodly amount myself, but there has always been those wealthy who have known how to manipulate the poor, to keep them under control. Now the unscrupulous wealthy are turning their attention to the middle class, as you call them, finding a way to eliminate those who could be most vocal, who had always in your country stood up and blocked them from absolute power. Control the masses and you control the power. I'm not saying you can stop this, for it is out of your control, but you feel passionately about this issue and you must be a very good news reporter. It is a story that needs to be told."

She sighed. "It's been done, and by far better reporters. Nobody wants to listen anymore to the death rattle of the American dream, Marcus. Outsourcing is accepted. Do you know that our government has outsourced the security of guarding our borders to a foreign business? Now doesn't that sound like insanity? Don't hire Americans to secure American borders, right? When I wanted to do an in-depth report on that, I was told to let it go. *Let it go!* I report what I'm told. I'm a news reader, not a reporter. Not anymore."

The last of the parade was passing and the cop at the corner was waving the car in front of them to pass on. Marcus put the gear shift into first and said, "That doesn't sound very democratic . . . to be told what to read to the public."

"Welcome to the twenty-first century's version of a free press that's owned by huge corporations with agendas. We're supposed to be *entertaining* and have focus groups that tell us how to be just that. But it galls the shit out of me that some guy on the Internet can get it right and get it out there weeks before the American press is given the go ahead by their bosses. Maybe that's the free press now . . . the Internet."

"Then use the Internet."

She burst out laughing. "And give up television! I don't think so. I've worked too hard to get where I'm at now." She didn't mention the nose job ten years ago or the Botox injections to give her a fuller upper lip, something a focus group had pointed out.

Marcus nodded. "It was just a thought. That looks like a nice park. Shall we walk for a while? Fresh air would do you good."

She shrugged as Marcus turned the car into Rosemont Park. "I used to come here as a little child with my mother," she murmured, seeing the small man-made lake that had always been her favorite place when she was little. "Park down there," she said, pointing to the water where ducks were swimming. "I used to chase the ducks, but they always ran away from me."

"What did you want to do with the duck once you caught it?" he asked, pulling the car to the shoulder of the road.

"Do with it?" She shrugged. "I don't know . . . I guess I thought they were magical."

"And now?"

"Now what?"

"You no longer believe in magic?"

"Marcus, I was a child then. Now they're just ordinary ducks. No magic at all."

"Hm . . ." He unfastened his seatbelt. "I'll be right back."

"What?" She turned to see him opening the car door. "Where are you going? The car is still running."

He nodded and held up his hand. "One moment. You watch the car."

What the hell was he doing? Did he have to pee? How totally unlike the dashing Marcus Bocelli to completely throw cold water over his debonair image by doing something so common as urinating in public. Her brain seemed to be screeching to make the mental adjustment as he disappeared behind a wide bush. Leaning over, she turned off the car engine, pulled out the keys, and opened her door. She stood in the sunshine, her lower back against the car, breathing in the clear November air, and thought Marcus, aka Nature Boy, had been right to get her out of the house. She never would have thought about coming here, a place that held good memories. And they were good memories . . . her mother packing a picnic lunch for the two of them. If she closed her eyes she could still remember her mother's fingers gently stroking the hair back from her forehead as she laid her head in her mother's lap and stared out to graceful swimming of ducks. Her first tooth was loose and her mother promised not to pull it but to only work it gently back and forth . . . and she'd let her, mesmerized by the gliding birds on the water. She felt tears building up behind her lids as she remembered the tender scene.

"Quack!"

Startled, D. opened her eyes and was shocked to see a duck waddling up to her. It was big and fat and its feathers glistened in the sunlight in shades of green, purple and magenta. She had never seen anything so brilliant. "Hey you," she called out in admiration. Opening her hands, she added, "No food here, pal." They were probably trained to beg because so many people fed them bread or French fries from the fast-food joints on the highway.

The duck tilted its head to the side and seemed to be studying her.

"You're so friendly because today's a free ride for you, right? It's the turkeys who get the ax on Thanksgiving. Of course, in a month you'll have to hustle those pretty tail feathers outta town or you could wind up on someone's Christmas table." It might be dumb, talking to a wild duck, or any duck at all, but it did make her feel better, lighter . . . playful and—nah, innocent was going too far.

The duck actually waddled around in the circle and shook its tail feathers at her. She burst out laughing. "Well, look at you, so full of yourself. You'd think you understood my words." She glanced at the wide bush where Marcus was . . . doing whatever . . . and shrugged her shoulders. Turning her attention back to the duck, she couldn't help grinning at the memory of a little girl who would have been thrilled at this close proximity. "You're about as puffed up as that glorious man over there in the bushes. Both of you prancing about in your finery and . . ."

Her words trailed off as the duck came closer to her legs, tilting his head to one side as he stared up at her with wondering eyes. She leaned back even more against the car and wished she hadn't opened the door and gotten out as the thing actually stood right in front of her, inches from her feet, staring up at her as though expecting something.

"What? What do you want? I already told you I don't have any food."

It simply stood there, staring, waiting . . . for something. It was almost as though it were trying to . . . to communicate with her. And that was absurd. It just wanted food, or something. And then her gaze was suddenly captured by the sunlight reflecting off the lake water. For a moment, a timeless span, she was mesmerized by the magical twinkling of light as it came closer to her on soft waves lapping at the shoreline. She could lose herself in what looked like fairy lights dancing upon the surface. If she just stared at it, she could feel nothing—no pain or sorrow, no guilt or remorse—just peace, an awesome peace that seemed to flood through her body.

"Deborah?"

She had to pull her vision away and, blinking rapidly, was surprised to see Marcus at her side. She looked down and the duck was gone. "You should have seen this duck, Marcus," she exclaimed, searching the surrounding area for it. "I don't know how it could have walked away so fast, but you should have seen it. Gorgeous colors and—"

"And what?" he asked with a grin, as though pleased to see her excited.

"And it was just pretty," she finished, knowing anything else she might add about the lake and the lights and peace would only make her appear foolish.

"Tell me, Deborah . . . did the duck make you happy? Happy to see it?"

She shrugged, glancing around for it so he could see for himself. "I don't know about happy, but it was a really cool duck. Sorry you missed it." How *could* it have disappeared so quickly? "Oh, well."

"So you didn't have your moment of magic?"

"What are you talking about?"

"You said as a child you thought ducks were magical."

"I did, didn't I?"

He nodded.

She thought about it and decided to blurt it out. "Well, this might seem stupid, but I thought it was trying to communicate with me. I mean, just the way it kept looking at me, and then the sunlight on the water caught my eye and . . . and I felt this . . . peace, I guess. I don't know how to explain it."

"Good," Marcus declared, as though somehow he'd arranged it.

D. shook her head at him. He couldn't produce pretty ducks, nor order the sun and the water to combine in a magical moment while he hid behind a bush doing his business. He really was full of himself, she thought, watching as he opened the trunk and took out a navy blue throw.

"Why don't we sit by the water? It seems pleasant enough." He didn't wait for her, but began walking to the shore.

She moved away from the car and followed him, not quite pleased by his suggestion. It was too reminiscent of her memory of her mother. Blowing her breath out between pursed lips, she straightened her shoulders and watched as he spread out his navy Polo blanket on the grass.

Sitting down, he grinned up at her. "This is very nice, Deborah. Come join me."

Reluctantly, she sat down yet held her body rigid as though the tension in her muscles would be a barrier he couldn't penetrate.

"So you came here as a child."

"Yes." *Almost this exact spot,* she thought.

"Tell me about her."

"Who?

"Your mother, before she was worried. What was she like as a young girl? Did she ever tell you her hopes and dreams?"

"Oh, God, Marcus . . . I don't want to talk about my mother now." She felt her jaw clenching in resistance.

"No? I thought you would . . . since we are here where you came with her as a child. You must have good memories too, Deborah. They all can't be bad."

"I have good memories," she answered a bit too defensively.

"Then tell me one."

She bit her bottom lip.

"Just one," he said in a soft voice while staring out to the ducks on the water. "I am here because of her. I helped make a stuffed American Thanksgiving turkey because of her. I would like to know something of her, something besides her years of worrying."

He was right. He was here because of her mother. Trying to give him what he wanted, she said, "Well, two days ago I found out something about my mother."

"And that is . . . ?"

D. grinned, watching the ducks now too. "My mother had a secret admirer."

"Secret?"

She nodded, relaxing her muscles. This was safe to talk about. "My Aunt Tina's husband."

"Really?" His eyes held a hint of mischief.

"Nothing like what you're thinking," she scolded. "Secret, remember? I don't even know if she knew about . . . about how he felt. Uncle Joe told me when he first saw my mother she was radiant, had a glow about her. How did he put it? Like a Tiffany diamond. She sparkled. My mom *sparkled*," she murmured, still in awe by the statement. "I would have liked to have seen that."

"Did he meet her with your father?"

Nodding, she said, "Aunt Tina is my father's older sister. I guess my father brought her home to meet the family."

"She was in love," Marcus replied. "That's why she was sparkling like a diamond."

"Well, her sparkle didn't last long, that's for certain. And my father sure as hell didn't sparkle when he left the two of us alone. Love . . . what a crock. More like a cubic zirconium. Shiny and pretty at first, but then with time and wear it begins to turn gray and dull and well . . . shows itself for what it really is, a fake."

"Love isn't fake, Deborah."

"Yeah, right. Love's like a form of contagious madness. I'll love you for however long you make me forget how miserable I really am inside. I'll tell you what you what to hear and you tell me what I need to hear and then in a few years when you no longer make me forget my self doubts and my truly miserable state, I'll blame you because the love wore off."

He was grinning, still staring out to the water.

"Am I right?" she demanded.

"You're not talking about love. You're talking about romance. There's a big difference. Romance is the madness you speak of. And yes . . . it is like a drug, nothing manufactured can compare to it."

"You sound like you know what you're talking about. You're a romantic, right?"

He sighed. "Guilty, as charged. But I am also a lover."

He needn't remind her, she thought as a vivid picture of the two of them on that beach in Bermuda sprang to her mind.

"I am not speaking of our encounter, Deborah."

How did he know? What *was* it about this man that he could so easily read her?

He turned his head and smiled. "Don't bother to deny what you were thinking. How could you think anything else when you know so little about me? When I said I am a lover I wasn't just referring to women. Yes, I love women. But I also love so many things—the lines in an old man's hands that speak of his contributions to this world, the beauty of a flower as its head turns and follows the sun, even the magic in a girl's eyes when she encounters a duck. I love life, Deborah . . . all of it, every single piece that fits together to make the whole. The animating force behind that duck, that girl, that flower and that man is also in me. If I deny or judge any thing, I deny me. And I am not going to deny me, who I am. While I am here on this glorious planet I intend to live and also to love."

She waited for a moment, to digest his words. "You're one weird man, Marcus Bocelli," she finally breathed. "I don't think I've ever met anyone quite like you before."

He threw back his head and laughed. "I sincerely hope not. I am unique."

"That you are," she agreed, trying hard not to weaken before him. It was the first time she had seen him laugh like that. Spontaneous and from his gut. And the effect was immediate, traveling straight to her heart and winding down to her belly. Great, as if she needed another confirmation that she was attracted to him . . . *strongly* attracted. Dangerously attracted, in fact.

"We'd better get back to the house," she stated, standing and wrapping her arms around her chest. "We have to make the mashed potatoes and the sweet potato casserole. And we should be basting that turkey." Enough of this talk about love, especially when she knew she was vulnerable.

He stood up, grabbing the throw from the ground. "Someday, Deborah, you will love someone and you will know the difference between a real diamond and a cubic zirconium."

"Hey I already know," she said, watching him shake out the blanket. "One you get from Tiffany's and the other from a shopping channel on television. It's the price that—"

"No, Deborah," he interrupted before she could finish. "One is manufactured to satisfy a false need. The other is created through years of pressure and grows into something spectacular that takes our breath away when we view it. And when we do, we know we are seeing something rare. We all yearn for the real thing. It is in our nature."

He held open the car door for her and she looked into his eyes. "Do you, Marcus? Do you yearn for it?"

His smile was endearing, gentle and kind. "Every living thing on this planet yearns for it. It is, in my belief, that animating force behind all of creation."

She swallowed, trying to gulp down the surge of attraction that seemed to pull at her even more. "The diamond?" she asked in an innocent voice. "You believe it's behind all of creation?"

His eyes searched hers for a moment and then he grinned. "You really are a smart ass, aren't you? Get in the car, Deborah. We have a meal to prepare."

7

She looked up to the stars and blew her breath out in a rush as they walked back to her mother's house. "Well, those guys seemed to appreciate the leftovers. Mrs. Devers tasted the stuffing and said it was wonderful. How about that?"

He grinned, watching her pleasure. "How about that, indeed? We made a wonderful turkey dinner. I thought it was quite tasty myself."

"I didn't think I would be able to eat any of it, but it smelled so great and—" she turned her head. "Thanks, Marcus." There was sincerity in her voice. "It made me feel good to prepare Thanksgiving dinner and even better to give the leftovers away."

He nodded, following her lead to the front door. "I like the Devers' family. They remind me of my own. Loud and loving."

"Yeah. Great people. They moved in after I graduated from high school so I only really know Anna Devers, but her sons seemed friendly. And their wives." She paused. "They made me forget for a little while . . . about tomorrow and everything."

He sensed her grief coming to the surface and touched her

jacket arm. "This is a difficult time, Deborah. Losing a parent so quickly . . . I know how you feel."

She stared down to his hand and seemed to consider his words for a moment, but only a moment, then her happy face came back. "And what about that little Emily" She was a character, wasn't she? She's named after my mother, you know."

He transitioned with her easily, putting aside his own feelings along with hers. "I know. I think I heard the story five times tonight." Picturing the toddler who demanded attention from everyone as though it were her right, Marcus chuckled. "She is a wonder. I believe I enjoyed her the most."

"Well, I would think so, considering the love affair going on between you two. She didn't want to leave you alone."

He stood at the door, staring down at Deborah in the light from the lamp on the house. "Haven't you ever noticed something . . . special . . . about very young children? It's as though they haven't forgotten who they are. They still know they are precious."

"You mean precocious," she answered with a grin.

"No, I meant precious." He looked deeply into her eyes, seeing how far she had come from that state of knowing. "Just as you are, Deborah. Always have been and always will be. You've just forgotten."

She made a noise with her mouth and looked down as she fumbled in her jacket pocket for the house keys. "Listen, Marcus, if I was ever precious it's been replaced by precocious, which in my case is another was of saying I'm a smart ass. I'm more comfortable with that, okay? I'm definitely *not* precious. See, if you really knew me, you'd agree."

He felt such a depth of sadness that he knew he had to leave. He simply didn't have the energy tonight to be in her presence any longer. Guilt he could deal with, even anger, but such a negative self image would drain him. He didn't have the strength to fight against her well-built fortress of why she was so unworthy of love. And he knew, instinctively, that tomorrow and Saturday were going to be difficult not just for her but also for him. He had already made up his mind to stand by her and support her during the funeral. "Well, Deborah, it has been a most fulfilling day, but it is time for me to depart. I think the traffic will be heavy going back into the city tonight."

He watched her expression change and tighten with defensiveness. "Oh, sure. You don't want to come in for coffee or anything?"

He smiled. "No, but thank you for the offer. And thank you for today. I enjoyed myself."

She nodded, inserting her key into the lock. "Me, too. It took my mind off, well, everything I guess."

"And now you must prepare for tomorrow."

"Right." Her smile was tight and she was blinking rapidly to stop the moisture at her eyes from becoming tears.

Leaning down, he kissed her temple. "I will see you tomorrow. What time is the viewing?"

She sniffled as though angry with herself for showing any weakness. "You don't have to come back, Marcus. I'm sure even your polite European manners are telling you you've done enough."

"What time is the viewing?" he asked, ignoring her last words.

"Seven to nine."

"I will see you tomorrow. Good night, Deborah." He turned and walked to his car, wondering if she would call him back. He knew her pride wouldn't allow it and, for once, he was glad that pride was giving him some distance. When he reached the car, he waved to her at the door and then got inside. He didn't wait to warm the engine, but immediately put it into gear and left her presence. It was hard to admit that Deborah Stark was getting to him, not as an assignment, but as a woman, a troubled woman whose eyes seemed to reach into his soul and stir something he hadn't felt in years. A protectiveness that bordered on unreasonable. He knew she would laugh at the idea of anyone thinking they had to protect her, for she had spent so many years building a barrier, convincing herself to believe she needed no one. But the truth was he wanted distance tonight. He had to get his emotions into alignment. He had an assignment coming up and Deborah Stark couldn't jeopardize that. He would help her get through this weekend and then his attention would have to turn to his assignment. It was what he did. He woke up people.

And, sometimes, he was very tired of walking among the sleepwalkers.

She closed the door on the sight of him driving away. It was too painful to realize she would be spending another night alone in this house. She turned to the living room and thought she might as well make up the sofa for she knew she couldn't sleep elsewhere. Slipping her arms out of her jacket, D. dropped it onto the chair and walked into the kitchen to get a glass of wine. The room sparkled with orderliness. No waiting dishes or leftovers. One would never know a huge and difficult meal had been prepared. Marcus had insisted they wash up before taking the leftovers to the Devers.

Marcus.

What should she make of a man she hardly knew who shows up on her doorstep when she most needs a friend, helps her make a feast, charms the neighbors and then kisses her on her temple and walks away? Well, he was definitely a nut case, she thought as she poured the remaining wine into a glass. All that stuff he talks about, like tonight, right before he left. He had taken a minor remark about little Emily and turned it into some kind of emotional contest.

Precious.

Ha! If he only knew her better.

But then as she wandered into what had once been her bedroom, D. tried to remember a time when she'd felt like that. The image at the lake with her mother flashed through her mind. She'd felt loved then. And trusting. And—maybe— precious.

She sat at her mother's desk and placed her glass on a botanical print coaster. Time to find out the information the undertaker wanted. Tomorrow morning she had to go to Lombari's with her mother's social security card, insurance info and the dress her mother would be buried in. She'd tackle the dress later. Right now searching through her mother's papers was bad enough, rummaging through her mother's clothes would be too damn painful. Best to put that off for as long as possible.

Who knew her mother had been so organized? Which only served to remind her of how little she knew her mother, a woman who rarely talked about herself yet insisted that even if they were alone in the world and trying to keep everything going, they still had their dignity. No one could take that away. Well, it hadn't felt very dignified to have lost the water and electricity, to have the neighborhood kids make fun of her when it was obvious that she and her mother were using candles to see at night until her mother got paid on Friday. Damn, she had to stop thinking about all that. It was this house. It brought up all those dark memories.

Shaking away those thoughts, D. pulled out the bottom drawer. As she opened a folder entitled insurance, she found everything she wanted . . . including an envelope. An empty envelope addressed to Emily Stark in a formal, old fashioned, yet shaky handwriting. There was no return address so D. simply placed it back in the folder she would bring with her tomorrow. She looked around the room and it suddenly hit her that it would be up to her to dispose of everything, all her mother's things. She would have to spend time here going through everything, getting rid of furniture, putting the house up for sale.

Tears welled up in her eyes and her throat burned with constriction.

Stop it, she mentally commanded. *Do not go there!*

How could she sell her mother's furniture, after her mother finally got what she wanted? Determined to go about business, she took a deep settling breath while sitting back in the comfortable chair and looking at the pretty mahogany desk.

She didn't have a desk. She didn't have much of anything, truthfully. Not good furniture, just some stuff she'd quickly bought when she'd gotten the job in Philly and had less than a weekend to find necessities. Decorating was never high on her list of priorities. Running her finger over the polished dark wood, she realized she could bring some of her mother's furniture to her apartment in Philly. It really was very tasteful and, well, maybe it would be another way of honoring the woman who gave her life. Her mother would like that. With a sigh she realized she'd procrastinated long enough. It was time to go into her mother's bedroom and find the burial clothes.

D. felt as if a dark stone were attached to her heart. This was it. This was the moment when she had to admit she was the grownup, the one with responsibilities. No one was going to do this. Even if she called Aunt Tina and asked for help, she knew she'd always feel like a coward and a failure. *Just get it over with*, she thought. *It's just you. Alone.*

As she left the library, in the back of her mind, a thought flashed. She would have welcomed Marcus spending the night. Not as a lover. Just a friend.

The only real friend she could claim was Maggie and Maggie was wrapped in the arms of her new family this weekend. She was making a new life for herself and Julian in New York City. Soon, she'd have her baby and Julian would probably win a seat in the Senate and then maybe they'd send Christmas cards every year as way of remembering each other.

She needed a new friend.

Too bad the only one to have appeared also was the best lover she'd ever known. And everybody knew you can't have both . . . can you?

The first ones to show up Friday night were Aunt Tina and Uncle Joe. She waited patiently and tried to appear full of adult responsibility as she watched her aunt and uncle sign the guest book. But she didn't feel adult. She felt childish, unsure, scared to have been left alone with that coffin containing her mother's body and, if truth be told, on the verge of losing it. Aunt Tina's somber black dress and Uncle Joe's black suit made the couple look like official mourners at a *Soprano's* funeral. In fact, D. was beginning to think the whole thing might be turning out to be a bit too Mediterranean for her mother's Dutch and English taste. Lombari's was like a mini version of Trump's Taj Mahal in Atlantic City. Glamorous to some people, but she didn't think her mother would have liked all the gilt and marble. Even her own dress, a simple navy blue sheath with long sleeves seemed like some kind of dreary funeral costume. Her mother's pearls were the only relief. It was like a show, not for the dead, but for the living. All the ritual, the somber tone of everything. Maybe the Irish had a good idea, throwing a party and celebrating a person's life. Not to mention, she really could use a drink right now. But then, what would everyone celebrate? A life filled with abandonment, worry and loneliness?

The thought of a drink sounded even better.

Grateful for company, D. held out her arms to her relatives in true welcome. "Thanks for coming," she whispered, though there was no one alive who would have minded a raised voice. Still, this place seemed to demand hushed tones.

She simply couldn't think about what her mother looked

like, frozen in death, her once so busy hands crossed at her
abdomen, wearing the simple beige suit D. had brought earlier in the day. Marcus had been right. That wasn't her
mother in that coffin, surrounded by flowers. It couldn't be!

D. was wrapped in her aunt's embrace. "Where else
would we be tonight, if not right here with you." Aunt Tina
took a handkerchief from her purse and dabbed each nostril.
"She was such a good woman."

D. started to nod when Uncle Joe hugged her tightly. "I'm
sorry for your loss, Debbie. Tina's right. Emily was a good
woman. A damn good woman," he added in a rough, emotional voice.

"Yes," D. whispered, starting to feel even shakier when
she looked into Uncle Joe's eyes. He missed her mother and
really was grieving her loss. *Oh, don't do this to me, Uncle
Joe. Not tonight. I have to keep it together. She would not
want a blubbering daughter greeting her friends.*

"I'll say my prayer now," Aunt Tina whispered, patting
D.'s arm.

D. nodded as her aunt slowly walked past the baskets of
flowers and stepped up to the casket, lowering herself to the
kneeler before it. D. looked away and smiled at her uncle.
"They've been very nice here," she whispered stupidly, not
knowing what to say to him or to anyone else who might show
up. She had nothing to fall back on, since the majority of her
life had been spent thinking up wise cracks, not niceties.

"Lombari's a good place. You've done right by your
mother, Debbie. She deserved no less."

D. nodded, thinking maybe her mother deserved a daughter who might have known her real wishes. What if her
mother really wanted to be cremated and her ashes cast into
the sea or someplace better than a Hadley cemetery? What if
her mother had a special place? What if she didn't want to
spend eternity in Hadley, New Jersey? *Who would, for God's
sake?* The shakiness increased and she started to panic,

thinking she'd made all the wrong decisions. Her palms were beginning to sweat and she could feel a rush of blood sweeping up to her face and rushing back to her feet. She grabbed her uncle's arm when she thought her knees might not support her.

"Are you all right, honey?" Uncle Joe asked, wrapping his arm around her waist. "You want to sit down?"

"I don't know what's—" she stopped speaking as Marcus seemed to fill the entrance to the room with his presence. Dressed in an impeccably fitted suit, he was signing the guest book. "I'm—I'm fine, Uncle Joe," she said in a stronger voice, never feeling more grateful to see anyone in her life.

"Oh, Debbie," her aunt moaned as she came back from the coffin. "You're mom looks wonderful, doesn't she?"

She felt it bubbling inside her throat, demanding release. D. wanted to scream that wasn't her mother with that mask of death painted on. And it wasn't wonderful, at all. None of it was wonderful! Instead, she simply said, "Excuse me," and hurried up to Marcus.

"I have to talk to you!" she blurted out, knowing her voice sounded high and almost shrill.

He appeared startled. "What is wrong?"

She grabbed his arm and dragged him into the adjoining room. "Listen, Marcus, I made a terrible mistake here and I've gotta fix it."

"What are you talking about?" he demanded, concern showing in his expression.

"I think my mother would have wanted to be cremated, or something . . . anything but this! And now I've got this Goodfellas funeral going and . . . and I have to stop it. *We* have to stop it."

"We do?"

She nodded, desperately searching his eyes for understanding. "Look, I may not know everything a daughter should know about her mother, but this I do know. Emily

Stark spent her life worrying how to survive in Hadley, New Jersey and she ain't gonna spend eternity in this dump of a town. I won't allow it," she stated, knowing her voice was sounding—well, a little hysterical now. And that North Jersey accent was creeping right back into it.

"Deborah," he began gently, "we discussed this. It isn't your mother in there. It is merely the body she was using and—"

"And that body is not spending forever in this little town of horrors," she interrupted hotly. "I want her cremated and I want to spread her ashes at the lake, the one we went to yesterday. She was happy there once and . . ."

"Deborah, do calm down," Marcus murmured, stroking her upper arm. "You look pale and not at all well."

"I am not at all well!" she insisted. "I feel like I'm going to throw up or faint or just scream if I don't stop this madness. Look at this place! You saw my mother's house. Do you really think she would want all this?"

He stared at her intently. "What do you want to do?"

"I want to talk to the funeral director and cancel the burial."

"You don't think you might be . . . a little . . . hysterical right now?"

She stared right back. "No, I'm not a little hysterical. I'm a *lot* hysterical. And you've got to help me with this. You're the only friend I've got and . . . well, that's what happens when you show up on a girl's doorstep with flowers and sympathy. You get to ride shotgun."

"Ride shotgun? What exactly are you planning to do, Deborah?"

"Don't worry, I'm not about to steal my mother's body at gunpoint," she said, looking around the overly furnished room. "We need to find the funeral guy and change everything."

"The funeral guy?" Marcus repeated stupidly.

She looked back to him and held out her hands with exasperation. "Mr. Lombari? The undertaker? Only he's not undertaking anything more with my mother. My aunt Tina said my mother looked wonderful. She looks dead and Aunt Tina thinks that's wonderful. There's something very wrong about that, you know?"

"People say those things at funerals, Deborah. They don't mean anything by it. Don't become hysterical now. You were doing such a fine job until this time holding yourself together and—"

"*That's* because it didn't even dawn on me until this point that I was just going along with what everyone *else* thought I should do. But my mother wasn't born here in Hadley. She was dumped here by her husband who then abandoned her here. Can you even imagine how she'd feel to know she has to spend forever in this place? I might have been a lousy daughter, but I'm going to do this one thing right for her."

Marcus was shaking his head with sympathy. "Your mother isn't going to spend eternity here in Hadley. She is so beyond Hadley or anything else in this dimension. We talked about this, remember?."

D. pulled him into a corner as more mourners began arriving. "Look, Marcus, I don't care about dimensions or any of your other bizarre theories right now. I made a mistake here and I need you to support me as I try to fix it. Now, are you with me, or not?"

There was a few moments of silence as he studied her face. "This is riding shotgun?"

She kept his gaze level, not even blinking. "You got it, partner."

He blew his breath out in a rush and looked around the room beginning to fill with strangers. "How do we find this Mr. Lombari?"

For the first time in days she felt she really was doing the right thing and the tension miraculously left her body. "We find one of his associates and demand to be taken to the boss."

She watched as Marcus Bocelli straightened his expensive gray and white silk tie that blended so well with his dark gray pinstriped designer suit and then held the crook of his arm out to her. "Perhaps this young man might be able to help us," he said, covering her hand on his arm with his own as he led her to a man directing people into the next room.

"I beg your pardon," he began, getting the man's attention.

"Are you here for the Stark funeral?"

"Yes, we are," Marcus answered. "This is Deborah Stark, the deceased's daughter. She would like to discuss some changes to the proceedings with Mr. Lombari. Would you mind finding him?"

"Changes?" the man inquired politely. "I'm sorry, I don't understand. Everything has been arranged and—"

"And they are the wrong arrangements. Please," Marcus added in his most polite voice. "Find Mr. Lombari and we can conclude our discussion. Miss Stark really should be greeting her guests, no?"

Rattled, the man quickly walked away.

"And so, does this make me a good shotgun rider?"

D. grinned with relief. "Marcus, you should have been born in the wild west."

Fifteen minutes later, D. was standing by the coffin, greeting the line of people who had come to pay their respects. She had insisted that Marcus stay at her side for support and so even Aunt Tina and Uncle Joe were assuming that Marcus Bocelli was more than a friend. She let them, and so did Marcus . . . who had been spectacular with Mr. Lombari, resorting to speaking Italian when the undertaker started to argue about the last minute changes. In the end, it was decided that her mother would be cremated tonight and her ashes would be in a jar that would be at the church in the morning.

"I'm sorry for your loss, Debbie," a woman said, shaking her hand.

D. brought her attention back to the present and smiled at the stranger. "Thank you," she said automatically, ready to hand her off to Marcus.

"You don't recognize me, do you?"

"I'm sorry?" D. searched her face, wondering if she were some distant cousin in her father's family. The woman with teased hair was dressed in a black coat and looked tired, overweight and a bit frazzled.

"Marie Pereggi. We went to school together."

For a moment, D. stared at the woman in disbelief, trying to reconcile the person who stood before her with the pretty and popular girl who had been her chief tormentor in high school. A surge of dislike and resentment spiked through her body and then, curiously, mingled with something else. Maybe compassion.

Marie smiled with embarrassment. "Three children changes you. I—I just wanted to come tonight to say how sorry I am . . . for everything," she murmured awkwardly. "For your mother's passing and . . . well, for the past."

D. knew she had to say something. For years she had wanted to confront this person, to show her that she had been wrong. When she'd wanted to escape from Hadley and make something of herself, Marie's face had always come to mind. With each success, each A on a college term paper, each job promotion, each transformation she had wanted to stuff it into Marie's face and watch the pretty and popular bully squirm. It suddenly dawned on her that Marie had been an important person in her life. Not a nice one, but one who had been instrumental in her climb up the ladder of success. How odd, how very, very odd.

Even Marcus was looking at her, waiting for her to speak. Something important was taking place and D. didn't have the time to digest it. Instead, she swallowed deeply and said,

"Thank you for coming, Marie. May I introduce Marcus Bo-celli?" And she handed the woman over as she turned her at-tention to the next person. She couldn't think about it right now. Later, tonight, she'd try to figure out this curious feeling.

Greeting a man who said he knew her mother, D. was con-scious of Marcus holding Marie's hand, speaking to her in a very soft voice. Sneaking a peek, she saw Marie's eyes wide and brimming with tears as she gazed up at Marcus as though he had descended to earth on wings. D. tried to listen to the man's words of sympathy, yet a small part of her brain, okay a shameful part of her brain, was taking satisfaction that Marie Pereggi seemed in awe of the man at her side.

Bizarre and maybe even wrong . . . but D. had a moment out of time. It was as if she were standing outside herself, observing everything. In a timeless span, so quick it couldn't even be measured, she saw how the tables had changed. How Marie was now getting to experience what it felt like not to be pretty or popular. What it was like to feel trapped and only dream of another way of life.

"Your mother was such a lovely woman. We . . . we en-joyed many hours together and I will miss her more than I can say."

She finally focused on the person in front of her, a distin-guished man in his sixties dressed in a dark suit with tears in his eyes. "I'm so sorry, I missed your name," she mumbled stupidly as she finally gave the man her full attention.

"Alex Finney. I met your mother many years and we were reunited some months ago when she was purchasing furni-ture. We both were attracted to the same piece, a desk."

"My mother's new desk," D. added with a nod.

Mr. Finney smiled sadly. "Yes. I . . . I just wanted to come tonight to pay my respects to a woman I had come to know as extraordinary. She truly loved you and was very proud of you."

D.'s brain was spinning. "You were friends with my

mother?" she asked, knowing there was a line of people, but desperate to hear anything more this man had to say.

"I would hope that Emily considered me a good friend."

"Mr. Finney, I would love to speak with you about my mother."

He glanced to those waiting. "Perhaps tomorrow, after the funeral?"

"She's going to be cremated. I changed the plans. It's going to be announced at the church tomorrow morning. I'm going to scatter her ashes at Rosemont Park, by the lake."

The man's shoulders seemed to fall inches lower and he pinched the bridge of his nose. "We . . . we had picnics there. I think she would like that very much, Deborah."

Okay, so even though she was the grieving daughter and, well, slightly wacky at the moment with trying to find some kind of balance within an ocean of emotions, the well developed reporter side of her was sending up intuitive signals there was more to the story. And she desperately wanted to hear it. *They had picnics together?*

"We'll talk tomorrow?"

"Yes, of course," the man answered. "If it won't be an intrusion."

D. turned to Marcus and gave him a look, one she hoped he could read, considering he seemed to do that so well for the past few days. "Marcus, this is Mr. Alex Finney, a friend of my mother's." Her mind was yelling *find out everything you can about him.*

Marcus' smile was as charming as always as he took the man's hand and asked him how he knew Emily.

Satisfied, D. turned to the next person in line.

Ann Devers.

As the older woman held out her arms, D. looked into Anna's dark sorrow-filled eyes and felt the burning at the bridge of her nose increase while her lids refused to stop the tears from falling down her cheeks.

"C'mere, child," Anna whispered.

And in that instant, D. found she no longer had the strength to hold it back. Here was her mother's good friend, the one who had been with her when she'd died. The grief and sorrow and guilt and regret seemed to gather like a huge wave and sweep her under. Leaning forward she buried her face into Anna's neck, inhaling the comforting scent of the woman as D. tried to choke back what felt like a whirlpool of emotions that would surely take her under.

"I—I can't," D. muttered. "Oh, Anna, if I lose it now I'll never be able to get through the rest of it."

Anna turned her head and whispered into D. ear, "You listen to me. Your mother loved you somethin' fierce. And that's all you need to remember right now."

D. nodded, sniffled and gulped, determined to regain some measure of calm as she moved away from Anna and stood upright again. She accepted the crisp white handkerchief that Marcus offered her and wiped her eyes and her nose and Anna squeezed her hand and turned her attention to Marcus.

"And now do I get a hug from you too?"

His smile for Anna was so genuine and dazzling that it hurt D. to look at him as he gathered the older woman into his arms and said, "It is I, Mrs. Devers, who am honored to share your presence with an embrace."

Anna turned her head to D. and winked. "He's a charmer, Debbie. And a keeper."

In the midst of everything surrounding her, D. had another realization in that moment. She really wanted Marcus Bocelli, but he would never be a keeper. It simply wasn't in his nature. Maggie had been right. As if her abused heart hadn't taken enough hits in the lasts few days, it was going to take another eventually. He was going to break her heart. Even if she never saw him after tonight, she knew there would always be a part of her that yearned for something more between them. She would compare all other men to him. In a few short encounters his charm, his compassion, his ability to read her so well, even his bizarre theories had ruined her for anyone else.

And the totally weird part was, she didn't care.

Marcus followed her home after the viewing and was finishing his glass of wine when D. just said it. "Listen, do you think you could spend the night?" When he looked at her with a thoughtful expression, she hastened to add, "Just as a friend. You could sleep in my old bedroom on the pull-out sofa, or even in my mother's bed."

"Do you think it's wise?" he asked, gently putting his wineglass on the coffee table.

She shrugged. "I'm beyond knowing what's wise, Marcus. Besides, it would save you the drive to and from the city tomorrow. There's an extra toothbrush in the bathroom, clean, never used. And your clothes . . . well, we could put everything washable in the washer. I'll even try to iron your shirt, though I can't promise it won't have a few wrinkles and—" she stopped before she sounded totally pathetic. "I just don't want to be alone again tonight. Not tonight," she said truthfully, clutching the thin stem of her mother's wineglass as she rose.

He didn't say anything and she realized she had sounded truly pitiable and he was trying to find a polite way of refusing. She'd save him the effort.

"Look, it was just a thought. A stupid one. Put it down to a woman acting like a scared kid."

"Now, see, Deborah, I would stay to ease the fears of a scared kid."

"You would?"

He nodded.

"Even though I'm only acting like a scared kid?"

"Deborah, you *are* that scared kid. You carry that kid with you day and night. At least you are acknowledging she's still with you. So many refuse."

She stood for a few moments, staring at him, wondering about this feeling inside of her that was clawing to come to the surface. She didn't want to be a scared kid. She'd spent too many years as that scared kid. And the heartache that she carried was way too much to take on now. "Well, then that kid thanks you for your company. I know it's stupid, Marcus, but so many things happened tonight, so many emotions . . ."

He nodded again. "I know. It's to be expected."

"So . . . if you're really going to stay then I have to ask you to get undressed. Only," she held up her hand, "so we can throw your shirt and underwear into the washer. It's already late and we'll be up all night waiting for it to dry."

He was grinning and she took that as a good sign.

"Well, what if I told you that you don't have to wash anything?"

She raised her eyebrows. "Really? I'd heard Europeans weren't particular about hygiene, but I'd thought you were different."

She saw he noted her teasing tone, but chose to ignore her words.

"I have a bag in the car. I have reservations at a hotel by Newark airport. Thought it would save me time in the morning if I just stayed there."

"And you let me go on and on about washing and ironing your shirt?"

"It was a very nice gesture, Deborah. I appreciated how . . . scared you were to have offered to do something so . . ."

"Menial?" she interrupted, cringing as she saw herself nearly pleading with him. Wash and iron a man's shirt? Cha'right. Thank God he had his own.

He shook his head. "Never menial. It would have been

something very generous, very different for you . . . to serve another."

"So I'm not generous?"

"I'm not taking the bait, as you Americans say. Instead," and he rose from the sofa, "I shall go out to my car and get my luggage."

He picked up his suit jacket and slipped his arms into it. At the door, she called out to him.

"Marcus?"

He turned, probably waiting for her to say something smart. Instead, she said what was in her heart. "I don't have any friends right now. Thank you for being one during all this."

He smiled, nodded, and left the house.

Yep, someday, hopefully later than sooner, she was going to have her heart broken by this man when he disappears from her life for good.

Four hours later, D. was staring out to the darkness of the living room. She'd turned off the TV two hours ago when she thought she was nodding off, but as soon as the silence enveloped her she became wide awake. She would have turned it back on, but she didn't want to awaken Marcus, who was sleeping in her mother's bed. He'd chosen that room, saying he would prefer the comfort of a bed if she wasn't going to use it.

Marcus Bocelli asleep in her mother's bed.

Her mother would have liked him. Everybody liked him. How could anyone resist him? He was formally polite, yet a mischievous gleam could enter his eyes with lightening speed. His body spoke of strength, though his touch seemed to calm frayed nerves. He was intelligent, almost too intelligent with his crazy theories, but could giggle with a toddler over simple things. And D. remembered how it had felt to be held in his arms, to be the recipient of a passion that had left her breathless.

She shook the thought out of her head and prayed for sleep. Tomorrow was going to be another tough day. She would scatter her mother's ashes at the lake and then close up this house. For some reason, the thought of returning to Philadelphia and her job didn't seem as important now. That would have to change, and quickly. She couldn't lose her edge or she'd be out the door and on her way to a news desk in Ohio faster than Andrea Miller could squeeze her perky little arse into the anchor chair. Her bosses might give her some slack because of her mother dying, but in television news you were only as good as your last telecast. She was just going to have to put all this behind her and—

You are my sunshine, my only sunshine. You make me happy when skies are gray. You'll never know dear, how much I love you. Please don't take my sunshine away . . .

Okay, she didn't just hear that! Her heart was pounding inside her chest like a jackhammer. From the corner of her eye, she saw something—like sparkling fairy dust swirling in the corner of the living room, moving toward her.

She would never know how long it lasted, that feeling of total awe as she stared at it, once more experiencing that feeling of complete peace, no worries, no regrets, nothing, save . . . joy. And then from a back corner of her brain came a shout that it wasn't real, that she was hearing things, seeing things that were not normal and fear raced through her with the speed of light, obliterating her sense of peace and replacing it with terror.

And it disappeared. Just like that. Gone.

Without further thought, D. raced from the living room sofa into her mother's bedroom. "Marcus!" She grabbed his shoulder and shook him. "Marcus! Wake up!"

8

"Deborah?" His voice was deep and sleepy, yet quickly became alert. "What's wrong?"

Her body was shaking and she could barely speak because of the hammering of her heart against her rib cage. "Something's out there . . . Marcus, I'm scared."

He pushed himself into a sitting position and stared at her in the darkness. "What are you talking about? What happened?"

Okay, she knew she was teetering on the edge of reason because she wasn't even moved by the moonlit vision of the sheet falling to his waist revealing the outline of a well defined bare chest. "There were lights . . . some kind of weird lights swirling around and . . . and I heard my mother singing again."

"Singing? Again?"

"I didn't tell you, but the first night you were here and I took a shower. I heard her singing then. *You Are My Sunshine.* That was the song she sang to me when I was sick or scared and I'm hearing it again. I'm not making it up. I swear. I heard my mother singing! And now I'm seeing crazy lights! I can't go back there . . ." her voice trailed off as tears welled up in her eyes.

There was a moment of silence and then Marcus moved the sheet. "Come and share this bed. Nothing will happen to you here, Deborah."

So grateful, D. scrambled under the sheets and pulled them up to her neck, staring about the dark room nervously.

"Nothing would have happened to you if you had stayed where you were, you know."

"No, I don't know," she muttered, only relaxing slightly now that there was another person around her. "That's why I'm here, shaking like the cowardly lion."

"This is a reference to the *Wizard of Oz*, yes?"

"Yes. What do think that was? Those lights? Was it my mother?"

"What do you think it was?"

"You sound like a psychologist, answering a question with a question." Her voice was beginning to sound shrill.

"You saw them, not I."

She then allowed herself to think about it, feeling safer now that she was in bed with Marcus . . . which if she actually contemplated the situation, she might just burst out into hysterical laughter. Here she was fulfilling a fantasy she had harbored since before Bermuda and the very last thing on her mind was sex. "When it appeared, the lights, I didn't have time to think about them. I was in awe, I guess. And filled with . . . well, a peaceful feeling. And then, then I thought I must be crazy. This kind of stuff just doesn't happen to people. Normal people. And I was suddenly filled with fear and it all disappeared." She swallowed deeply. "And then I ran in here."

She heard him sigh and wondered if he was losing patience with her and her childish performances. It wasn't as though she'd been the picture of maturity around him.

"So you were filled with awe and peace, until you attempted to name what you were experiencing?"

She nodded and then realized he might not be able to see

her. "Yes," she murmured, wishing she could cuddle up next to him instead of keeping her body rigid and a good six inches away.

"Well, it sounds to me you were blessed with something extraordinary that once your mind insisted on defining, disappeared. You can't define or label the extraordinary. To do so puts limits on the unlimited. It simply couldn't co-exist with the state of your mind any longer."

"You mean I scared it away?"

"I don't know, perhaps your fear did. At least you know it was intelligent."

"I do?"

"It made a choice."

"It did?"

He sighed. Again. "What is the opposite of fear?"

"Bravery? Courage?"

"Anyone who was truly brave or courageous would also tell you they were fearful, but proceeded anyway. The opposite of fear is love. Whatever visited you, Deborah, was of love and could not exist with your fear. It chose love over fear."

She thought about that. She did feel a kind of love in that awe and peace. "But what *was* it? My mother?"

"I can't answer that, Deborah. Would it be so impossible to even imagine the energy that was and always will be your mother paid you a visitation when you were grieving her loss? You know, you wouldn't be the first to have claimed such."

"And you know what people say about that, don't you? I wouldn't want word of this insanity to get around. I'm supposed to be a reporter. Facts. Reality. That's my bread and butter. Not swirling lights and ghosts and—"

"The supernatural?"

She could hear the amusement in his voice. "I'm serious, Marcus. People would think I'm crazy."

"Deborah, for such an intelligent woman, sometimes you can be very naïve. Don't you realize the most effective way to degrade anything is to ridicule it? Our egos are so fragile we cannot bear to think of ourselves as anything ridiculous, so we accept what we have been taught, that there is no such thing as the supernatural. What do you think would happen if more and more people came to realize there is only a very thin veil between the seen and unseen worlds, that it can be accessed by ordinary human beings, that you don't need intermediaries who might claim to have more knowledge?"

She didn't answer, trying to envision what he was asking.

"Can you not see the loss of power to such institutions as governments and churches, whose business is to tell you what to think and how to act? You may believe my theories are bizarre, as you put it, but do take this one piece of advice under counsel. If anything is ridiculed down through the ages, pay attention to it. There is something to it. There are simply those in power who do not want you to know about it."

She thought about that too. Anything was better than thinking about what had just happened to her in the living room. "You mean like aliens? Like how there have been over fifty thousand reportings of sightings, even from airline pilots, and the government says fifty thousand people from all over the world are wacko?"

He chuckled. "Exactly. They publicize the more outlandish and we all laugh, but I think every single one of us has had something unexplainable happen to us, that can't be cast aside as mere coincidence. Down deep in our very nature, there is a belief that there is more to existence. That we each have a purpose for being here."

"Do you have a purpose, Marcus?" She paused, and then asked, "Do you know what it is?"

He was silent and D. glanced at him in the darkness. She could make out his exquisite Roman profile and see the hard line of his jaw. He didn't want to answer her.

"It's okay," she murmured, leaning back against the headboard and sighing. "I don't know what mine is either."

"I know what my purpose is . . . at least for now."

She looked at him again. "Yeah?"

He nodded and turned on his side, reaching out his arm and bringing her down to her side. He pulled on her waist and wrapped his arm around her, resting his hand on the sheet by her belly. She could feel his breath on the back of her shoulder as he spooned her, and her body was vibrating with nervousness. She didn't want him to make love to her. Not now. Not tonight.

"Right now my purpose is to be your friend, to protect that scared little kid inside of you so you can sleep. So we both can sleep," he added.

Dear God in heaven, she was spooning with Marcus Bocelli in her mother's bed!

"So . . . I guess we'll just go to sleep then," she muttered, hoping he couldn't feel her heart pounding and how the nerve endings on her back were almost singing out the Alleluia chorus against his chest.

"A very good idea," he muttered, already sounding sleepy.

She simply nodded, biting her bottom lip to keep from talking. She had already disturbed his sleep and he was making it clear he wanted to return to it. Still, how was she supposed to sleep when the very act of him breathing was tickling her neck? And she was in her mother's bed! Shit, having thoughts of sex in her mother's bed seemed sacrilegious, at the very least. She really was a shallow person and could only be thankful she was wearing a pair of cotton pajama bottoms because if she felt his skin next to hers she would have had to bolt from the bed, scary lights or not.

But they hadn't been scary at first, she thought, trying to take her mind away from the man behind her. Until she did just what Marcus said, tried to analyze what they were.

When she couldn't find a rational answer, her mind became fearful.

The lights, whatever they were, were intelligent.

Something intelligent had come to visit her.

The more she thought about it, the more she felt as though her belief system was engaged in a tug of war, stretched to the limits. She didn't believe in such stuff. She had been trained to seek the facts, follow the paper trail and find the clues. But there was no accountable paper trail here, save for the tabloid claims of people who really did sound like nut cases. This wasn't like that. There was no alien, no shape at all. There was no abduction, no terror. There was awe . . . and peace.

Considering the agitated state of her mind now, D. suddenly felt as if she had ruined something rare by her fear. What if it was her mother? Like Marcus had talked about . . . her energy. She had heard the singing. That had been real. It wasn't in her head.

Or, maybe she was cracking up.

"Okay, let's talk about it."

"What?" She was startled by his words so close to her ear.

"I said, let's talk about it. You are not going to sleep and your energy is so scattered it's keeping me awake."

"My energy?"

"Deborah, I can feel you. Don't ask me how, because buried under all your programming you can do the same thing. You've just stifled it over the years. You are ready to jump out of your skin and you're not going to calm down until you've settled it in your mind."

Truthfully she was thrilled he was still awake and wanted to talk to her, but she thought she ought to throw out some apology. "I'm sorry to keep you awake. It's just so weird, Marcus. Nothing like this has ever happened to me before."

"Really? Nothing extraordinary has ever happened to you before?"

She shook her head. "I lived a pretty normal life."

"Nothing in your childhood?"

"It was normal too, save for the worry about money, but that's normal for the majority of people in the world, isn't it?"

"Who was Maria Pereggi?"

"What do you mean? She was somebody I went to school with, that's all."

"That's all? It didn't seem that way to me. She was very upset."

D. was silent for a moment, picturing her old classmate as the grown woman who had stood before her at the viewing. "Guilt," she muttered through clenched teeth.

"Yes, it seemed that way to me," he answered.

She found that her body tightened with apprehension. "Why? What did she say to you?"

"Not much, simply that she wanted to tell you how sorry she was for the way she had treated you."

D. snorted in derision. "Yeah, too little, too late."

"You would not forgive her when she asked?"

Just *how much* had Marie told him? "I really don't want to talk about it."

"You would rather talk about the lights and the singing?"

Well, she really didn't want to talk about that either. "I just meant there isn't that much to talk about. High school stuff, that's all."

"Really? That's all? It seemed much more than that to Marie."

"Why? What did she say to you?"

"I already told you. What I'd like to hear is why you couldn't forgive her if it's just high school stuff, as you claim."

She was silent, trying very hard to keep her mind from wandering back to Jefferson High, to walking those crowded halls with her shoulders hunched over, trying to blend in and become invisible. To not be a target.

"Deborah?"

She blinked away the memory and sighed. "Kids. They can be cruel little monsters."

"You or Marie?"

She snorted. "I guess, considering how I've acted around you, you would first think of me."

"Then it was Marie who was a monster to you?"

"Why do you want to talk about this? For God's sake, it happened years ago."

"Then why can't you forgive her?"

"Look, I was just startled when she came up to me at the viewing, okay? She used to be . . . so pretty. Beautiful, I thought."

"And she wasn't tonight?"

"You saw her. She certainly wasn't the way I remembered."

"You didn't see the beauty of her sincerity?"

Closing her eyes, she sighed loudly. "All I saw, Marcus, was a woman who looked tired, overweight and guilty about being a real bitch when she'd had it all her way. I guess like the old cliché, she had to walk a mile in another's shoes to realize what it's like."

"Are you saying she's walking in your shoes now?"

"What used to be my shoes," she murmured, picturing herself as a teenager . . . pimply, frizzy hair, big nose and baby fat that clung to her like a doughy three inch padding against the cruelties of the world.

Weebols wobble but they don't fall down.

She cringed as those words played out in her head. It had become a chant as Marie and her posse of tormentors had passed her in the hallway.

"What were you just thinking?"

"Nothing," she lied, refusing to be led into a conversation where she revealed just how miserable she had been as a kid. That kind of whining and victimhood belonged to the weak. She had learned long ago not to be weak.

"All right, Deborah, just remember forgiveness is more about you than the other person. It's gift to yourself."

"I have nothing to forgive," she muttered . . . again, another lie. But then there were so many.

The minister didn't come to the park after mass, but enough people were present that when D. released her mother's ashes she felt she had done the right thing. The sun was shining and a light breeze seemed to take the ashes on wings of air to the lake. They had stood afterward and had spoken of her mother. Anna Devers, Aunt Tina and Uncle Joe, members of her church remembered Emily Stark with admiration and love. Instead of grief, it had seemed almost bittersweet, releasing her mother back to the earth. There were tears, but they weren't tears of mourning. Little by little the small crowd made their way back to their cars and it was only D. and Marcus and Aunt Tina and Uncle Joe who remained.

"You know what Anna Devers told me?" Aunt Tina asked, linking her arm through D.'s as they stared out to the lake.

"Hmm?"

"She said in her church they call funerals homecomings. Isn't that a great way to look at it? She said they had happy music and celebrated the person. Doesn't that seem like good thing?"

"It does," D. murmured, staring out to the sun playing on the surface of the water. Why was it she was so attracted to light now?

"I might as well tell you I wasn't exactly pleased when I heard you'd canceled the burial, but you know, Debbie, I think you might have been right. You mom would have liked this far better."

D. smiled. "And you're not upset I also canceled the luncheon?"

"Well, I still think it's only right to have something for the mourners afterward. I mean, you can still have some of the old traditions."

"You're probably right, Aunt Tina. I just thought when it's over, it's over and there's no point sitting down to a meal with people I hardly know. I tried to thank everyone here before—"

"I know," her aunt said, patting her arm. "That was a beautiful little speech you gave about your mother and how you appreciated everyone who had come to honor her. You did real good, Debbie. Your mom would be proud of you."

"You think?"

"Oh yes, you handled yourself just like her. She was always a lady, even when she didn't have a pot to . . . well, you know what I mean. Even when she was struggling, she did it with grace. That's what everybody liked about her, I think. She was different, but in a good way."

D. nodded, pleased that she was compared to her mother, though having *grace* was not something anyone else had ever applied to her. She usually bulldozed her way into getting what she wanted. Suddenly she looked around her to the departing guests, trying to find one in particular. "Aunt Tina, did you know my mother had a friend? Alex Finney?" She couldn't see him. Disappointed, she looked at her aunt.

Aunt Tina waved her hand out to the cars now leaving Rosemont Park. "Your mother had lots of friends. I didn't know most of the people here."

"No, this was something different, I think. Alex Finney, nice looking older man?"

Tina shook her head. "I knew nothing about it. That's strange. Emily had an admirer?"

"I don't know. I wanted to talk to him, but either he didn't come or he's left already."

"Well, she was pretty enough. I often asked her why she didn't remarry and she said she had no interest."

Nodding, D. remembered her mother turning down offers of dates from coworkers or men she had met at church. "She never seemed interested. Ever. But this man, Mr. Finney, said they had picnics here at the park. Isn't that odd?"

"Well, I hope she had a great big old grand affair with the man. She certainly deserved it."

D. laughed. "Me, too, though I can't even begin to picture it."

"Of course you can't," Aunt Tina replied with a sly grin as she led her away from the lake and toward the waiting men. "You young people seem to think you invented sex when you wouldn't even be here without us bein' pretty good at it in the first place."

Grinning, D. shook her head. "Please, let's change the subject."

"Okay, are you and that gorgeous man an item?"

"No. I told you, we're just friends."

"So you say, and what a shame. Well, how would you and your friend like to come back to my house for somethin' to eat?"

D. smiled down to her aunt. "Thanks, but I really should get back to Philly. I have some things to do at . . . at the house and then I need to get on the road."

"I understand." She stopped and D. stopped with her.

Aunt Tina looked up at her with a serious expression. "We're your family, Debbie. I don't want you to ever forget that, okay? Don't be a stranger."

Knowing that was exactly what she'd done in the past, D. nodded. "I'll keep in touch. I promise."

"Good, now go kiss your Uncle Joe goodbye and take your handsome friend away with you. Take my advice, Debbie. Marry that one. He'll make you happy."

D. sighed. "I don't think Marcus is the marrying kind, Aunt Tina." She paused. "And maybe neither am I."

The older woman patted the top of her niece's hand. "You'll change your mind, honey. We all do."

And that was what scared her . . . wanting someone, needing someone, loving someone you could never have, who would one day walk away from her. Better not to even entertain the idea.

"Well, that seems to be it. At least for now. I'll have to come back and decided what to do with the house and . . . and everything." She turned her attention away from her packed car and trunk and gazed up to the man who had helped her, not just with loading some boxes but with getting through the most difficult time of her life. "I don't know how to thank you," she said, already feeling the tears building.

He looked down into her eyes and smiled. "You are most welcome, Deborah. It was . . . an extraordinary time."

Why did he have to look so damn handsome? Why was his smile so damn endearing that she wanted to throw herself against his chest and weep like a little kid? Instead, she tightened her grip on her keys and tried to ignore the burning at the bridge of her nose. "You were . . ." she attempted to get the words out.

"A friend?"

She nodded. "A very good friend, Marcus. I can't imagine getting through everything without you there to keep me from falling apart like a child."

"I stayed for that child, remember?"

Having to sniffle revealed her emotions, but she was helpless to stop now and had to blink away the moisture at her eyes. She had wanted him to stay for the woman. "I have acted pretty childish around you, but you should see me at work. All adult. I promise."

"Now how much fun could that be?" he asked with that killer grin while reaching out to wipe a tear from her cheekbone. "You are all right to drive?"

"Sure." She took a deep breath and straightened her shoulders. "Time to get my life back and for you to get yours back too." She leaned forward and kissed his cheek. "Thank you for everything. I mean that."

He simply nodded.

"I hate goodbyes, so I'll just say that you have my number in Philly and my email at work. Let's keep in touch. And if you ever need me, Marcus, I'm there, okay? As a friend, I mean. I'm there."

"Thank you, Deborah. I will remember that."

He smiled at her again and she knew he felt as awkward as she at leaving. He reached out and held her hand. Slowly, he brought it to his lips and brushed a soft kiss below her knuckles. "It has been my honor to have shared this time. Be well, my friend."

And then he turned and walked to his shiny car. He didn't look back, just got in and drove away. D. felt it brewing inside of her and got into her own car. She drove away from Grandlake Estates, without looking back. Not for the reasons she had thought when she'd entered this town days ago. It was because she couldn't bare to look back. Her heart felt raw and exposed.

She got onto the turnpike and was driving south, her foot to the pedal as she kept pace with the cars in front of her. Traffic wasn't too bad, considering it was still technically a holiday weekend, and she thought she might be able to get back to Philly in less than an hour. And then it hit her, like a thrown rock between her eyes.

Her mother was dead.

Gone.

She would never see her smiling face again.

She would never hear her voice.

She would never feel her touch, smell her skin.

The woman who had given her life, had given so many years of her own life to raise her, love her, encourage her, forgive her—was gone.

A powerful pain wrapped around her heart and stomach like a slow moving snake, constricting her ability to breathe. Desperate, D. maneuvered her car into the right lane and clutched the wheel as she read a green sign announcing a rest stop a mile ahead. She had to hold on, drag air into her lungs, fight the escalating panic and get the hell off the road.

She turned into the rest area, bypassing the restaurant and gas lines to park the BMW by the trees whose limbs were quickly losing their colorful display of leaves. She turned off the ignition and forced her cramped fingers to release the steering wheel.

For a few moments she simply stared beyond the windshield, not really seeing anything, and then she surrendered. No longer having to be strong and responsible, D.'s shoulders dropped and all the grief she had been holding at bay rose to the surface.

Sobs of loss rippled up from her throat and, on the Jersey Turnpike, Deborah Stark forgot about being a woman in control and wept like an abandoned little kid.

9

U nhooking her mic, she rolled her chair back from the news desk after reporting the nightly litany of robberies, car crashes, muggings and police chases that dominated local big city news. She remembered the old adage she had learned early in her career, *If it bleeds, it leads.* Tonight there had been footage of a six-car pile up on I-95. The wreckage was bad enough, along with the sheet-draped bodies on the road, but when Andrea Miller had interviewed the sister of one of the victims, D. had been forced to fight back her own tears, identifying with the woman who had lost a loved one without warning.

"Good job tonight, D.," Alan, the stage director, commented.

"Thanks," she answered and smiled, walking away from the set and intent on picking up her coat and purse and getting home early. She couldn't explain why she was so tired. It had been two weeks since she'd buried her mother and she should be snapping out of whatever was wrong with her, but it felt as though something vital was gone from her life and the shame was she hadn't recognized just how vital until it was too late.

She was passing the small makeup room when she heard their voices.

"Did you see her eyes after Andrea's piece? I swear she looked like she was going to burst into tears. What'd you think that was about? Her mother?"

The question stopped her and she barely breathed as she listened to Gregg's response.

"I don't know. Maybe. Or, it could be that she's heard just how good Andrea was while she was off."

"Yeah," Sheila, the hairdresser, agreed. "Andrea was good, but . . . well, I hate to say this . . . but doesn't it seem to you that after D. lost her mother she seems more . . . . I don't know . . . human?"

"You mean humane," Gregg answered. "Like she's not so picture-perfect and above the rest of us. I swear, I thought I actually saw sympathy in her eyes tonight."

"Right," Sheila agreed. "She should do that more often. Oh, by the way, I overheard Dan telling Mark and Alan he's thinking about giving Andrea the weekend news spot."

"Really?"

There was a pause. "I think Andrea Miller is going places fast. She's new blood and the lens loves her. She's such an accomplished actress it makes you wonder why she's in hard news. I watched her ripping her sound man a new ear drum and then when Mark walked by you would have thought honey was dripping from her mouth."

Gregg snorted. "Honey, that wasn't honey."

"Oh, you're bad. And that's just a rumor."

"Rumor my ass. I saw them together at lunch and she ate off his plate. You *know* that's proof she's having an affair."

Sheila giggled. "Maybe she was just hungry."

"Okay, now you're setting me up. Of course she's hungry, sweetie. Underneath all that blonde hair that you keep in place and the pancake makeup I apply with a spatula is a true carnivore that wouldn't hesitate to eat her young to get what she wants."

D. had heard enough. She didn't have the energy for more. She banged her hand on the wall as she passed the partially closed door. "Goodnight, people," she called out.

There was a pause and then she heard the gossiping duo call out after her.

"Good night, D."

"Have a good one, D."

Let them wonder if she'd overheard.

Still, penetrating the fog that had wrapped itself around her since her mother's death, D.'s brain had registered two very important facts. Andrea was so good replacing her that Mark, as station manager, was going to try her out on the weekend news desk. And it was very possible that Andrea was having an affair with Mark, the station's manager, a very married man and father of four. Very, very interesting.

She said good night to the guard at the desk, left the building and walked toward the parking lot. Standing by her car was a woman and, for an instant, her heart stopped then leapt with joy. "Maggie?" she squealed, hurrying to close the distance between them. "Is that really you?"

"Yes, it's me," Maggie O'Shea-McDonald pronounced wrapping D. into a tight embrace. "I should be slapping you instead of hugging you," she whispered close to D.'s ear. "I am so, so sorry about your mother."

D. nodded. "I know you are. And I'm sorry I didn't call."

Maggie broke away and stared into her eyes. "Why didn't you call, D.?"

She shrugged. "It was Thanksgiving weekend. I knew you had plans."

"For heaven's sake, D., I would have come to be with you."

Again, she nodded. "Your surrogate showed up and saved the day. Several days to be more accurate."

"He called me last night, asking if I'd heard from you. Then he told me."

"Don't be mad at me, Maggie. I couldn't bare that right now."

Maggie linked her arm through D.'s and led her the rest of the way to the parking lot. "I'm not mad at you," she said, tightening her grip in a show of affection. "I just wish I could have been there for you."

"I know. So what are you doing in Philly? The last we talked you and Julian were moving into a brownstone on the West Side."

"We moved. And I'm here because of you, silly woman. I thought I'd combine business with pleasure. I have an appointment with the lawyers about Soul Provisions and I'd really like to spend the night with you, if you'll have me." Maggie held her overnight case out. "Took a cab here from Thirtieth Street Station, hoping I'd catch you before you left."

D. felt as though a huge weight was lifted from her shoulders. "I'll have you, all right. Never did have a slumber party as I kid. Guess it's not too late to begin the nocturnal female bonding ritual. You can have the bed. I'll take the sofa."

"I'll sleep on the sofa."

Reaching her car, D. pushed the unlock button on her key chain and said, "You're the pregnant one. You get the bed."

"I'm perfectly fine with the sofa, D. and—"

"And shut up, Maggie," D. interrupted, opening her door and looking at her dear friend. "You will never know how grateful I am to see your face."

Maggie stared back at her over the roof of the car. "That bad?"

D. simply nodded and got into the driver's seat.

Twenty minutes later they stood together in D.'s living room, surveying the clutter of boxes, clothes and newspapers.

"Hey, I told you before. I'm no Martha Stewart."

Maggie gently placed her overnighter on the bare wooden floor. "It's not so bad."

"Liar," D. said and then laughed. "I'm just no good at this stuff. It still looks like I've just moved in."

Shoving some magazines over on the sleek leather sofa, Maggie sat down and sighed. "Face it, D. You're not a domestic goddess."

D. laughed again as she pulled off her coat and dropped her purse onto a chair that was littered with newspapers and clothes. "That I'm not, my friend. Seriously, though, it's worse than usual. I just don't have the energy to clean the place."

"So hire someone to clean it for you."

D. shrugged as she picked up the phone. "I don't want strangers in here. Okay, so I know you must be hungry, being with child and everything, and I'm literally starving. One cannot live on a cream doughnut and six cups of coffee. Let's be really bad and order something sinful, like a cheese steak and French fries. And before you give me some lecture on nutrition, I'm dialing the place down the street. C'mon, you're in Philly."

Maggie placed her hand on her abdomen, running it over the taupe sweater dress that covered her bump. "Oh, I don't know, D. All that grease and—"

"Yes, hi," D. said into the phone. "I'd like to order two cheese steaks with French fries. One with fried onions." She looked over to Maggie. "Anything else?"

Her friend gave a look of surrender and D. grinned. "No. That'll be all." She gave her address. "How long? That fast? Great. Okay, bye." She disconnected and grinned at Maggie. "You are so easy. Stick with me and you'll gain fifty pounds with that baby."

Laughing, Maggie stood up, pulled off the sweater duster that matched her dress, and asked, "So, do I just throw this anywhere? And how, I might inquire, are you planning on sleeping on this sofa with all this junk on it? What do you do when you get home? Implode?"

"Are you saying I'm a slob?"

"Yes, I am. Anyone can be forgiven a lack of decorating sense, but honestly, D.," and she picked up a newspaper and stared at the date, "this is two weeks old. You're going to become one of those old people who live in a hoarder's prison, where the police have to make their way through paths of junk to find you."

"It's not that bad," D. said, trying not to picture herself in the nightmare Maggie had just described. "So I let some stuff go. Big deal."

"C'mon, I'll help you clear some of this so we can indulge in our sin of gluttony without adding sloth to it." She pulled the turtleneck of her sweater dress away from her throat. "And do you have an old T-shirt I can wear and maybe a pair of shorts? I don't care if it is December, I'm melting."

D. couldn't resist it. "That's all the weight you're carrying."

Maggie froze. "Really? Does it look that bad? It's only sixteen pounds, but you're right, D. If I keep gaining weight at this rate I'll be over two hundred pounds before this baby is born."

"Ah, forget it," D. said with a wave of dismissal. "You don't look fat. You look adorable, I guess you would call it. I just said that to get back at you for calling me a slob. Together we can make a big fat slob, how's that?"

"But see I meant it. You are a slob and after we scarf down our forbidden fruits in the form of Philly cheese steaks, you and I are going to do something about this place."

D. sunk onto the chair, not caring she was sitting on her purse, newspapers and a weeks worth of washed but unfolded clothes. She looked out the long window, wondering if that red cardinal would reappear. A week ago the small bird had perched on her windowsill, capturing her attention. Every few days it would just show up after she came home from work. Kinda weird, but it had felt as though something had cared about her—and kinda pathetic too.

"So?" Maggie persisted, drawing D.'s attention back to the conversation. "What do you think about pulling this place together?"

"Puh-leeze, Maggie. You didn't come here to be my mother . . ." her words trailed off and a few moments of silence followed.

Maggie smiled sympathetically. "I know. Just give me the chance to practice for my own daughter, okay?" There was a pause. "Face it, Deborah. You need some help."

"You sound just like him."

Maggie stopped gathering up newspapers and magazines. She straightened and looked at D. "How come we aren't saying his name?"

D. shrugged. "Do we have to?"

"Okay, did you sleep with him? Is that what all this is about?"

"No, I . . . well, I did sleep with him, technically, but I didn't like *sleep* with him."

"What does that mean? Are we in high school? You didn't go all the way?"

D. decided now was not the time to spill her guts about what happened after Maggie had left her wedding in Bermuda. She'd work it in when the time was right, if ever. "What did he tell you?"

"Geez . . . this *is* like high school." Maggie kicked off her shoes, grabbed the bottom of her sweater dress and pulled it over her head. Standing in her underwear and dark panty hose, she asked, "Get me a T-shirt, will you? If I have to have this conversation, at least I'm going to be comfortable." She peeled off the panty hose.

D. couldn't help grinning at Maggie's new attitude and her new figure. She could see why some people said pregnant women glow. It was probably sweat. She reached under her, pulled her purse out and dropped it on the floor and then began digging in the clothes behind her back. "Here, it's clean, just not folded yet," she said, throwing a white cotton shirt to Maggie that had printed on the front *If ignorance is bliss, why aren't more people happy?*

Grabbing the wrinkled shirt, Maggie read the saying and laughed. "Good one, D."

"I bought it after I met you. It reminded me of those signs in your store." Seeing Maggie practically naked stirred up something in D. All that promise and expectation growing inside of her friend made her wonder what it was like. Did Maggie feel it moving? Wasn't it like an alien taking over her body? Maggie was going for the American dream, the husband and the kid. Hell, she'd probably be a senator's wife by this time next year. Some women get what they want, D. thought. And then there were those who didn't fall for dreams, but were wide awake and wandering alone in a world made for couples.

Maggie slipped the shirt over her head and walked over to the chair where D. was sitting. The shirt outlined the swelling of her belly. "Okay, I need some shorts or—what's this?" she demanded, pulling something out from behind D.

"It's a pair of pajama bottoms with a draw string waist. It should fit." She watched as Maggie pulled them up her legs and tied off the waist. D. shook her head. "If Julian could see you now, he'd definitely say I was a bad influence."

Maggie sat back on the sofa, folding her dress and sweater. "If Julian could see me in this getup and scarfing down a cheese steak, he'd forget about the influence and run for the hills."

"Julian's not a runner. Not anymore, anyway."

Maggie looked up and smiled. "No, he's not. Which brings us back to high school. Did you, or did you not sleep with Marcus? There. I've said his name and broken the spell."

D. sighed. "You still didn't tell me what he said."

"He said he called your office and was told your mother had passed away. And then he found your mother's house and helped you get through the funeral."

"That's it?"

"Just that you didn't want to tell me because I was with my father's family for Thanksgiving, but he thought I should know."

D. nodded. "Well, he showed up on my doorstep with flowers and sympathy and we made Thanksgiving dinner together and he stayed by me for the next few days. I'll always be grateful to him for that."

"And that's all?"

D. was saved answering by the ringing of the doorbell. "Gluttony!" she called out, grabbing her purse as she stood up and headed for the door. Just how much could she tell Maggie without seeming like an idiot?

Within minutes they were seated together on the cleared sofa, each with half of a fat cheese steak between their fingers. "My God," Maggie moaned through chewing. "For a woman whose diet has been mainly green, this is like an oral orgasm."

Afraid food would fly into the room, D. held her hand up to her mouth as she laughed. Swallowing, she managed to say, "See, stick with me, kid, and I'll totally corrupt you."

"That's why I'm only here overnight." Maggie lifted a French fry and bit into it. "Now, seriously, since we're officially pigging-out and in our jammies, at least I am, let's get back to our juvenile conversation. Did you or did you not go all the way with Marcus? And, what happened in Bermuda that he called you at work?"

"You're not going to let this drop, are you?"

"What? You think a little grease has clogged my brain?"

Grinning, D. said, "We made a . . . a connection at your reception, that's all. I didn't hear from him again and so when he showed up at my mother's house I was stunned. And he came as my friend, Maggie. That's all."

Maggie nodded. "If you think it can be anything more, D., you're in for a world of hurt."

"You sound just like me when I was trying to warn you off Julian. And look what happened."

"Julian is normal and . . ." her words trailed off as though she was about to let something slip and thought better of it.

"Just say it. Marcus isn't normal. I don't think anyone who spends time in his company would argue with you. He's . . . unusual, all right. It's like he's some guru, or something. He always has something to say to put you at ease. Like you. Not tonight, of course," she said with a grin as she watched Maggie take a huge bite of a dripping cheese steak, "but most of the time you can manage to make sense out of chaos too."

Maggie was nodding as she chewed. "Just don't fall under his spell," she mumbled. "Believe me, it's too hard to wake up from it."

"You're speaking from experience, I take it."

Maggie sighed, put what remained of her cheese steak back onto the foiled paper and fell back to the sofa cushion, holding her belly. "I'm speaking because I love you, D. and I don't want you to be hurt."

"But you loved him, right?"

"I still love him."

D. felt stab in her bloated belly as she stared at her friend who was looking very uncomfortable. "You do?"

"Of course. I'll always love him," she said and then a loud burp escaped her lips. Looking horrified, Maggie held her hand up to her mouth. "I am so sorry. I think my body is rebelling against grease."

D. laughed. "You are so funny. Here you are, married to one of the wealthiest men in America, probably a future senator, and you look and sound like the girl next door. Don't ever lose that, Maggie. Don't become a pretender. Stay real . . . at least for me."

"D., if you only knew how real I am becoming, you would realize you have nothing to worry about."

"Good, so what do you mean you'll always love him?" she asked, having no intention of letting Maggie get away without a follow up. She wasn't a reporter for nothing.

"He's like a member of my family now, but that doesn't mean I'm blind. Marcus is a very good man, but he isn't a man who will ever settle down with one woman for a lifetime. It simply isn't in his nature. If you can accept that, truly accept that you aren't going to change him, then you can enjoy him. Anything else will lead to heartache."

"All this sounds very familiar. Do you remember me saying the same thing to you about Julian? And look at you now. Married. Pregnant. Making a home."

Maggie shook her head. "Julian and Marcus are as different as night and day."

"How's that?"

"Julian was grieving the loss of his family and couldn't commit to anyone until he healed that. Marcus simply enjoys women, all women, wherever he finds them. It's like it's in his DNA, or something. There really is nothing to change. That's who he is. It would be like asking him to change the color of his eyes."

"So, he's a womanizer."

"No. He's a lover of women. He doesn't use them. He loves them. And then he leaves them when he's attracted to the next one."

"Maybe he just hasn't met the right one."

Maggie stared at her with a look of almost pity. "Don't fall for that one, D. If you choose to pursue this, at least do it with your eyes wide open. Have a spectacular affair. But know it probably isn't going to last forever."

"I'm so glad you came," D. muttered, losing all interest in her sinful dinner.

Maggie chuckled. "Oh, come on. Am I really telling you anything you didn't instinctively know?"

D. waited answering, not willing to surrender her false hopes so quickly. "Not really," she finally admitted. "Why is it that when I finally fall for someone, it has to be someone I can never have?"

"Don't be so hard on yourself," Maggie said with a soft smile. "I don't know any woman that could resist the Bocelli charm. And don't forget that he came to you when you were vulnerable and saved the day, so to speak. He supported you during a very difficult time. Naturally, he'd be wearing a white hat."

D. smiled in remembrance. "He did seem like a gorgeous knight in shining Armani standing there in my mother's house. You should have seen him stuffing a turkey. And he didn't leave my side during the viewing. I really appreciated how he quietly was there for me . . . even when I thought I was losing my mind."

"Why? What happened?"

D. shook her head, dismissing her words. "You know, the funeral and everything. It was good to have him there, that's all."

"And now you're dealing with the let down. Have you heard from him?"

"You know I haven't. He probably told you he's staying away from a lovesick puppy of a woman who cried when he finally left in his Porsche."

"No, he didn't D. He just said he thought I should know about your mother. That you might need a friend about now."

She shrugged. "Well, at least he was thinking about me.

God, I sound pathetic, don't I? Maybe I am mixing up emotions around my mother with him." She rolled the remaining half of her cheese steak back into the paper. "I'm just going to put that man out of my mind and focus on work. At least there I can have some control over what happens."

"How is work?"

"Okay. There's this walking Barbie doll who thinks she's a reporter and I believe she's after my chair at the news desk. They're trying her out on the weekends, so we'll see if I'm in for a fight, or not. Besides that, the gossip is that my mother's death has made me more human. No *humane*, was the corrected word. Do I come across as thinking I'm perfect? I mean, not here or in life,'cause we both know how false that would be, but on the air?"

She could see Maggie thinking about her answer, which wasn't a good sign. It should have been an immediate denial.

"Well, I would say that on the air you are very professional."

"But not perfect."

"Why would you want to be perfect?"

"What's so wrong with perfection? At least on-the-job perfection?"

"Because, D., if you're perfect, you're finished. There's no room for change. You're done. There's no movement. It's over."

"You make it sound like dead."

"Well, creatively, it is. And you are in a creative medium."

"Do I come across as cold?"

"Maybe detached is a better word. You're so witty and I've seen your compassion. I would think about showing more of those things." She paused. "Who do you look up to in television news?"

D. didn't even have to think about it. "Walter Cronkite. The old man of integrity."

Maggie grinned. "Why am I not surprised?"

"I used to watch him as a kid and my mother wouldn't listen to anyone else give her the news. She trusted him."

"He wasn't perfect, was he? He certainly didn't look like a movie star and he allowed his compassion to show through. I remember seeing clips of him when he reported the Kennedy assassination. He had to wipe his eyes."

D. stared at her friend. "So you're saying, as nicely as you can, that I need to lighten up?"

Smiling, Maggie said, "I know how you feel about that word, nice, but take this advice from someone who not only loves you but also was a viewer when I lived in this city. Don't be so afraid to allow yourself to show through. You said a few minutes ago that you hoped I never changed, that I wouldn't become a pretender. Isn't that what you've become, in a way? Pretending to be the female version of Walter Cronkite? There already is a Walter Cronkite, but there's only one Deborah Stark. She's intelligent, funny, compassionate, pretty, determined and one hell of a friend. I trust her, just the way she is. She doesn't have to pretend to be anyone else."

"Now see, you sound like him again."

"Can't help it, D. we're cut from the same cloth."

"And what cloth is that? And if you say something like the Shroud of Turin, I'm going to choke you, pregnant or not."

Maggie smiled, yet hesitated before speaking. "Okay, how can I put this? I think I can speak for Marcus when I say we both believe that all of us have a greater purpose on this planet than merely surviving. It's up to each one of us to find out what that purpose is, and it changes as we change. Marcus and I sometimes offer our help if we can. That's all I meant."

"What did you do?" Study together?"

"You could say that. Actually, he taught me that love is without possession. One of the most difficult things a person can do, I think."

"I didn't say I *loved* him, Maggie." She snorted with derision. "I'd be satisfied with a playmate."

"You're not falling in love with him?"

She shook her head. "See, I think you'd have to actually see the person once in a while to fall in love. I don't know if I'm ever going to see him again."

"Just be careful, D." Maggie paused. "Now let's talk about getting this place in order. You haven't even unpacked boxes yet."

"Those are from my mother's house. I put together some things I didn't want to leave and I just haven't had the energy to go through them."

Maggie rose from the sofa and stretched. "Then we have our work cut out for us tonight."

"Maggie, please. Not tonight."

"I'm only here tonight. When else are we going to create your sanctuary?"

"Sanctuary? Hell, I just want a place to throw my coat, wash off stage makeup and fall into bed."

Maggie rolled her gaze toward the chair. "I can see where you've thrown your coat, along with two weeks worth of laundry. Listen, you're never going to feel any better when your surrounded by chaos. You need a place that's at least peaceful and uncluttered until you can get your head together."

"You're not going to let up on this, are you?"

Smiling, Maggie said, "Honey, before the night is over we're going to create a space you can call home. This place has great possibilities. Why, if we move the sofa away from the wall, and put this table behind it we could take those lamps and . . ."

D. stopped listening when Maggie suggested they move the sofa. All she could think about was that Marcus had called Maggie because he was concerned about her. That meant he had been thinking about her, right? Just knowing that created a tickle in her stomach and she was ashamed of herself. To be so pleased because the Roman god thought enough to wonder if she was all right was . . . well, beyond pitiable.

Still, she couldn't help wondering what he was doing with himself . . . and if he ever intended to talk to her again. She hated to admit how much she wanted to hear that deep, sexy baritone Italian voice.

"Carry out. Three bags of shredded mulch."

The voice over the loudspeaker penetrated his brain and Marcus sighed as he headed outside to the garden area. His steps seemed on autopilot as he made his way to a flatbed trolley and pulled it to the stacks of bagged topsoil and mulch. He grunted as he picked up the first fifty pound bag of mulch and dropped it to the flatbed. If nothing else, he was getting a workout on this assignment, he thought. And it wasn't the first time his muscles let him know he wasn't used to such physical labor. One week into this job and his feet were killing him. How he yearned for his soft Italian shoes and silk shirts, instead of work boots, rough cotton shirts and khaki pants: his uniform for working at Mitchell's Nursery.

He took the three bags of mulch to the wrought iron gate where a Mercedes was parked with an opened trunk. Standing at the gate was a woman holding a carryout receipt.

"Right here," the woman said, pointing to her trunk as her diamond rings caught the rays of the fading sun. "Do you have some paper to put down first?"

Marcus suppressed a sigh as he dropped the first bag of mulch back onto the flatbed and walked over to a box. He pulled out a stack of newspaper and walked up to the car.

"I just don't want to soil the carpeting," the woman murmured, giving him a long appreciative look.

"Yes, ma'am," he answered automatically as he had been instructed to do when he'd been hired last week. The customer is always right and deserves the respect of being called sir and ma'am. The proper word, madam, he was told, could imply *dis*respect and ma'am was the preferred salutation. That was part of his orientation as the new employee at the nursery. He spread the newspapers and then turned to get the mulch.

The woman was blocking his way.

"Excuse me," he said, moving to one side.

She moved to again block him. "Do you ever . . . do private work on the side? I'm thinking about redoing my garden and I can use a new man."

Acutely aware of the pull of energy she was directing at him, he looked at her cashmere coat, her matching slacks and designer shoes. And then he looked back up to her eyes. In them he saw a very lonely woman, one that most probably married a man with power and assumed that power, when transferred to her, would bring her happiness. Now she knew differently.

"There is a list of landscape contractors inside the main building," he answered.

"What about you?" she persisted, trying to flirt. "You look strong enough."

"I, madam, am not available. Now, I'll get that mulch for you." He walked around her, back to the outside yard and picked up the first bag. He dropped it into her trunk and repeated the same routine two more times. Closing the trunk, he smiled and said, "Have a nice day, ma'am."

Watching the car pull away from the curb, he shook his head slightly, marveling at the audacity of the ego. In a way he felt compassion for the woman who assumed he would be interested. She was probably used to getting what she wanted and was right now mentally putting him down to make herself feel better. Not for the first time on this assignment, he had to remind himself not to be judgmental, yet it was quite an eye-opener for him to be in this subservient position, where people knowing nothing about him assumed he was below them in status because of the work he was doing.

A week ago he had decided the best way to make contact was to apply for a position at Mitchell's Nursery. After being told that he would be seasonal help for Christmas, he'd been hired immediately. He was to be a roving store associate, which meant he would help out the regular employees and take care of the outside yard that was quickly filling with Christmas trees. He'd swept out the warehouse, repaired two potting benches and used a forklift to unload two trucks filled with boxes. He also had met his assignment.

Carolyn Davies.

Thinking of the woman who was the floral designer, Marcus found himself smiling. She was certainly not making his job easy, for she treated him with polite distance, just like she did everyone else who worked at Mitchell's. She even ate her lunch alone. He glanced to his left and saw her under the crab apple tree. She always carried out a leftover from summer white plastic chair and it appeared everyone respected her wish for solitude.

Well, perhaps it was time that was challenged.

He went inside the nursery, marveling again at the splendid display of decorated trees, and approached his manager. "Would it be all right, MaryAnne, if I took my lunch now?"

The tired looking woman glanced at her watch and nodded. "Sure. Go ahead. I'll have Mike do any carryouts while you're gone."

"Thank you," he answered, walking up to the cash register by the office and punching in his employee number. He then hit the button for meal time.

Two minutes later, and glad that the day had turned

warmer, he was crossing the parking lot with another white plastic chair and a paper bag that contained a soda and sandwiches he had made himself that morning.

"May I join you?" he asked Carolyn, who was looking decidedly uncomfortable by his presence on her little turf of grass.

"Yes . . . of course. It's a free parking lot."

Marcus simply nodded and placed his chair far enough away from hers so she wouldn't bolt back into the nursery. "Lovely day," he remarked, sitting down and pulling a sandwich out of the bag. "The air smells clean."

He heard her inhale.

"Yes. It is lovely. Maybe the last gasp of Fall, before the first frost hits."

Nodding, Marcus unwrapped his ham sandwich and took a bite. He was getting better and better at this taking of a lunch, learning to pack two sandwiches. One for lunch and one for later in the afternoon when his energy level was nearing depletion. He didn't think, however, he would ever get used to being on his feet eight hours a day.

"You have the Mitchell's walk," Carolyn murmured, right before taking a drink from her thermos.

He swallowed and looked at her. "The Mitchell's walk?"

She nodded. "You're limping. Not used to being on your feet all day."

Marcus laughed. "You're right, I'm not. Does everyone get it, this walk?"

She smiled, something he had seen her only give customers. "Not the teenagers who stand at the cash registers, but the rest of us adults who walk around all day seem to develop it. Don't worry, it should ease in a few weeks. You'll get used to it."

"My feet don't think so."

"If you're lucky it will pass."

He glanced at her from the corner of his eye. She was

pretty for an older woman, with soft blond hair that framed her face. Her complexion was flawless and she wore little makeup, sometimes none at all, as though she hadn't time for such things. She was always immaculate and he could tell she ironed the green cotton shirts that all employees wore. He knew she was fifty-three years old, but she could appear much younger if you didn't catch the fear in her eyes when she thought no one was looking. Carolyn Davies had suffered much in the last three years and his mind ticked off the reasons . . . once the wife of a prominent attorney, she was a divorced woman who had lost everything she had thought was so important. Even her married children were embarrassed that their father had stripped their mother of a house and alimony, having diverted money into his mistress's accounts and then declaring bankruptcy. Her home was sold to pay off creditors. Her furniture was auctioned away. She was left with a few precious belongings and was starting all over again. Brave. Courageous. And disillusioned with life.

"You make beautiful floral arrangements," he said, popping open his can of soda. "The large Christmas door wreath with the brass horns is impressive. Were you formally trained?"

She smiled slightly. "No. Mitchells needed a floral designer and I'd done it for myself and friends for years. I asked if they'd give me a chance. I made them a few arrangements and they hired me."

"So you are naturally creative."

"I guess."

"Don't guess, Carolyn." He looked at her directly. "You are."

"Okay," she murmured, rolling the top of her paper bag.

"I just meant that you are a creative person. Surely, you must have known that about yourself."

She simply shrugged. Neither of them said anything for a

few moments and then Carolyn spoke. "That woman you helped with the mulch. She was flirting with you, wasn't she?"

Surprised by her question, Marcus figured it was his turn to shrug his shoulders.

"I could tell by how uncomfortable you looked."

"Perhaps we were both mistaken and she was merely being friendly."

And then it happened. He heard her laugh. Not just a polite titter, but a full bodied expression of amusement and he felt her defenses lower.

"Take my word for it, Marcus. I've known women like her and she was flirting."

"Really? You've known women like her? How could you tell from so far away?"

Carolyn paused for a moment, as though considering how much to tell him. "From the clothes, the car, the way she handled herself, blocking your way as if it were her right. You have to understand all the status symbols, the outward signs that are used to demand respect. We all make assumptions the moment we meet a person based on exterior things. Some people believe that those things are important."

"You speak as though you know something about that kind of life."

She nodded, bringing her thermos up to her lips. "In another lifetime," she murmured, before taking a sip of her coffee.

"Another lifetime . . ." He let the words ride the soft breeze that played with the dwindling leaves of the crab apple tree. "Reincarnation?" he asked, knowing it wasn't what she meant.

"No. It was just an expression. I forgot you take everything literally."

"Ah, so life has been playing with you too. Changing you without your consent."

She turned her head quickly and stared at him for a moment, startled. "Yes," she answered softly. "That's exactly it. Changing me without my consent." She looked away to the parking lot. "I couldn't have put it better myself."

Marcus smiled. "I know something about that, Carolyn. Do you know the Chinese have a word for chaos that also means opportunity? Sometimes when the chaos comes it is hard to see the opportunity." He paused. "Especially when I have developed the Mitchell's walk."

She smiled sympathetically. "It took three months for my feet to stop hurting."

"And by that time I will no longer be here at Mitchell's. Christmas will be over and a new year will have come. Who knows where life will take me?"

Neither of them said anything for a few minutes. Marcus finished his sandwich, thinking that it had been a good beginning. At least she was friendly and starting to reveal herself.

"You know, Marcus, I sit here almost every day eating my lunch and I look at all the people coming and going . . . the couples, the families, and I wonder how in the world I came to be sitting in a plastic chair under an apple tree. Sometimes, it seems surreal."

"You took this job because you needed it. You are not the first person to have change forced on them. I know that change isn't easy, but fighting it takes more energy than the courage to do what is necessary for survival, I think."

She looked at him and smiled. Marcus was struck by the sadness and fatigue in her eyes, making her seem older than she was.

"You sound like a wise man, Marcus, and perhaps more courageous than I."

He shook his head, crumbling the plastic wrap and tossing it into his lunch bag. "Not so, Carolyn. If I might say so, I think you are very courageous."

She blinked and a slight smile played at her lips. "So what have the gossips at Mitchell's told you?"

"Gossips?"

"Please, I am quite aware that certain people here think I am . . ." she seemed to search for the right word. "aloof. That isn't true, at least I hope it isn't true. I used to like being around people and I had quite a circle of friends at one time."

"And what happened?" he asked gently, hoping she would continue.

"Life happened, and many of those I thought of as friends turned out to be less friendly than I had realized. Just because I don't broadcast my personal life over the PA system at Mitchell's doesn't mean I am a snob." She rose from her chair and began gathering up her things.

"You're not a snob. You're afraid," Marcus whispered.

She seemed to freeze in motion, one hand reaching for the back of her chair. "Afraid?"

He nodded. "I understand, Carolyn. Life has treated you roughly and you are afraid to trust anyone or even any circumstance in your life right now." He watched as she broke their gaze and lowered her eyes. "I have known fear," he added. "and I can recognize it in another."

She laughed self-consciously as she picked up her chair. "You're getting way too deep for me, Marcus. And my half hour of lunch is over. I have to get back."

He automatically rose and they stared at each other with embarrassment as though their casual lunch under a crab apple tree had been in a fancy restaurant.

Carolyn broke the silence with a chuckle. "Well, someone raised you with good manners. Sit down and finish your lunch. All too soon you'll be back on your feet."

Sitting down, Marcus said to her back as she walked through the parking lot toward the nursery, "Thank you, Carolyn, for the conversation."

Since her hands were full, she simply raised her chair in acknowledgment of his words.

Well, it was a beginning, Marcus thought, watching her straight back. Now if he could only speed it along so he could quit this job. He glanced at his watch, an inexpensive one he had bought a week ago. Fifteen minutes and then he would be back on his feet. He swore from now on he would treat people who worked in retail with far more respect.

It wasn't an easy way to survive.

10

"Listen, D., I wonder if we could have lunch together."

She glanced up from her computer screen where she was polishing her close for that night's news. Tom Harris was leaning on the edge of her desk. He was a young, good-looking reporter with an ambitious gleam in his eyes who had worked his way up quickly from a researcher. He was also somewhat of a rebel in the newsroom, keeping everyone else on their toes.

"What's up?"

Tom shrugged. "Just want some private time to discuss something."

Her fingers stopped moving over her keyboard and she sat back. "What?"

"Now if I wanted to talk about it here, there wouldn't be the need for lunch. Don't worry, D., you aren't my type. I said private, not personal," he added, swatting away a slow moving fly that had landed on D.'s desk.

For some reason his remark struck deep in her gut. Not his type? Sure she was older, but did he have to be so blunt? "Okay, I'm not your type. Where do you want to go?"

"If it's okay with you, I'd just like to pick up something on the street and walk over to the park."

"This is some invitation, Tom. A burger at a roach coach and a walk in the park in December. I'm flattered."

At least he had the sense to look amused. "I promise it will be worth it."

"All right," she said, pushing herself back from her desk. "I'll meet you outside in ten minutes. You've got a half hour and then I'll be chugging a bottle of Pepto to get me through tonight's news. It had better be worth it."

Tom grinned and sailed out of her office with an air of confidence and youthful bravado. What was he, twenty-six, twenty-seven? She wasn't *that* much older than him. Still, he had something he wanted to discuss with her that sounded mysterious and she was a sucker for a mystery. Besides, she had spent a good part of the morning in editing and maybe some fresh air was just what she needed to clear out the cobwebs.

Fifteen minutes later, she accepted the greasy cheeseburger from Tom and turned toward the small park across the street, glad she was wearing her good cashmere swing coat as it came down to her ankles and cut the cool breeze from snaking up her legs. "Okay, so what's so important and mysterious we had come here to discuss it?"

Tom swallowed and nodded his head. "Listen, what I'm about to tell you is off-the-record, right?"

She shrugged, seeing a fat squirrel sit up on its haunches and watch her unwrap her lunch. "Go ahead."

"Okay, there's this building going up on at Second and Chestnut, condos with a view of the Delaware. And there's this construction company that's heading it up, with real close ties to city hall. I mean, *real* close. And the thing of it is there's this person in the mayor's office who was a force is the last national election and who, if you follow the paper trail, happens to have a vested interest in the company that's supplying the material for the job."

"So, conflict of interest?" She threw a piece of the roll to the squirrel, who nabbed it and began to greedily devour the tidbit.

Tom shook his head. "That's the tip of the iceberg, to use a cliché. For years this supplier has been getting away with substandard materials, barely passing code and paying off inspectors. That new office building on Market is a time bomb, waiting to implode, but what's really weird is that nobody wants to hear about it."

"What do you mean? Who's nobody?"

"I brought it up to Dan, thinking he was going to pounce on it and he said he'll get back to me. That was three weeks ago. And here's what's really bizarre. This morning he called me into his office and told me to forget about the story."

"Forget about it? Doesn't sound like Dan," she murmured, picturing her immediate boss, the news director. She took another bite of her cheeseburger, knowing she was going to pay for this indulgence in an hour, so she ripped off a bigger piece this time for the squirrel who seemed to have figured out she was his meal ticket as he followed her and Tom.

"I didn't think so either, until I remembered doing research for a story Matt was working on awhile ago, about the possibility that the mercury in children's inoculations might be causing such a drastic rise in autistic children around the world."

"I don't remember that. Must have been before I came to the station."

"Doesn't matter. It never got on the air." He then chomped down on his cheeseburger, swallowing a third in one bite.

D. turned her head and studied the younger man. Tom looked decidedly uncomfortable. "Why?"

"We were all told to leave it alone," he mumbled through chewing.

"Who told you that?" she asked, amazed that he was able

to finish eating so quickly, like it was simply the pretext to what he really wanted: her attention.

Crumbling the foiled paper from his cheeseburger, Tom made a perfect two-point throw into a nearby trash can. "First Dan, then Mark. He told us it came down the chain of command to drop it. Now see, at the time I figured it was because revenue was way up from all the pharmaceutical ads and nobody wanted to rock the boat."

"Don't bite the hand that feeds you." She spied the squirrel who was tailing her and threw him another piece of her lunch.

"Exactly. Not pretty, but that was the first time I realized I'm not in the business of researching and reporting news to the public. I'm in a business that makes money first and reports the news second."

D. smiled sadly. "And even that news is sanitized before it ever reaches the airwaves."

Neither of them said anything as they continued to walk amid the students and nannies with their charges in strollers. Her other lunch companion, the hungry squirrel, seemed to have disappeared.

It was Tom who broke the silence as he sat on an empty park bench. "Do you know who owns us, D.?"

"Sure," she answered, sitting next to him. "The network."

"But who owns the network, not the people who sit on the board in New York City, but the actual company?"

She named the huge conglomerate. "Nova Communications."

"And who's behind Nova?"

"Is this a test? Cause, I'm getting pretty cold out here. Can we please just get to the point?" Tom looked disappointed by her impatience, so she softened the tone of her voice. "I concede you're a fantastic researcher. What did you find out?"

"The real parent company of Nova Communications,

based in the Cayman Islands, is the Forsythe Group, consisting of some of the most influential people in the world. Americans, Europeans, even Saudis."

She turned her head. "And how does this connect to your waterfront condo story? Are you going to tell me that this Forsythe Group is actually the material supplier?"

"And the contractors, though they're buried pretty deep in the paper trail. They're doing it on the cheap and you know they'll sell those condos for a fortune. What's worse is that their connection in the mayor's office is part of it. He made quite a name for himself speaking at his party's convention and has aspirations for a national office. He's been hand picked, it appears, by this Forsythe Group, for bigger and better things if he can continue to pull off their construction efforts here in Philly."

"Look, Tom, I'm not a big believer of conspiracy theories, but I think you're trying to tell me the company I work for is concealing criminal acts and is willing to look the other way while putting peoples lives at risk."

Tom leaned in closer and stared right into her eyes. "What I'm trying to tell you, D., is that there is no real news anymore. It's about entertainment now. Ever since O.J. went down that California highway in that white Bronco, we've become more interested in celebrity news than the real thing. Day after day, for sixteen months, every television was filled round the clock with soap opera entertainment passing itself off as real news. Somehow, the public became used to it. Addicted to it. Deprived of real information about the world around them, their interest was fixed on celebrities. Then the media went crazy when the president had sex. Between that white Bronco and that blue dress and the high ratings, who wanted to hear that the Taliban was taking control of Afghanistan, or that a man named Osama bin Laden was preparing to attack anything American? How many people in this country could honestly say they knew UN-

SCOM's weapons inspectors were taking apart Iraq's chemical and biological warfare capabilities, literally brick by brick and the sanctions against that country, which were killing hundreds of thousands of civilians, were also reducing Saddam Hussein's conventional arsenal to a large collection of paperweights? Hell, that's boring compared to O.J. and Monica."

She sighed. "Okay, I agree with you. Hard news is a tough sell in this country now. Don't you think I grit my teeth when I have to do the puff pieces? But we're run by a corporation, Tom. This isn't a cable station. This is a network affiliate."

Tom looked out to the park and shook his head. "The decision by mainstream media to get into bed with the very entities they are supposed to stand watchdog against has been a mortal one. We, and every other news organization, are owned by corporations who have no real interest any longer in the common Joe who's trying like hell to keep his head above the security waterline. NBC, MSNBC and CNBC are owned by General Electric, one of the largest defense contractors in America. They get paid every time we go to war. You think they're going to tell the truth when it goes against their profit margin? AOL/Time Warner owns CNN. This company lives and dies by the outsourcing of American technological jobs overseas where labor is cheaper. Do you think they will tell a straight story about the economy? Never mind their largest investor is a Saudi. Something fundamental has happened to American news. I don't care if it sounds like a conspiracy theory. There used to be a time when journalism challenged the powerful and tried to keep them if not honest, then at least close to the center of the road. Now the wolves are in the hen house and God help any of us that fights back. You're either with them, or against them. There is no middle of the road any longer. Not in anything. Look what they did to Arron Weiss."

D. thought about the Pulitzer Prize-winning journalist

from Washington, D.C., who was found hanging in his apartment, not two weeks after he'd done an explosive exposé on the decades-long failure of the war on drugs. And he named names. She stared at the bare limbs of the trees and a shiver ran down her back that had nothing to do with the weather. "He'd just won the Pulitzer, his wife just gave birth to twins. It never made sense . . ."

"Of course it didn't. But then Fox broke a story about him having a mistress, even produced the woman, and every other network picked up on it. Repeat a lie often enough and America begins to believe it."

"Why are you telling me all this, Tom? What exactly do you think I can do about it?"

"You've got guts," he said with a twinkle in his eyes as he jammed his hands into the pockets of his navy pea coat. "And you've got some pull here at the station. Talk to Mark. I could tell he wasn't happy to give me the news and that means he's still got a conscience. Maybe he'd listen to you."

Her eyes widened. "You think I'm going to march into the station manger's office and confront him with the Forsythe Group? Look, I like my job and worked like hell to get here."

"D., if all of us are scared then we all lose. They win."

"Who's *they?*" she demanded. "A bunch of rich fat cats who want to squelch anything that might interfere with their profit margin? Including me? I don't think so, Tom. The average Joe is going to have to fight for himself on this one. Why don't you just give it to another station or the print media?"

"Because I don't trust any of them to do the job. This is big time, D. These are some of the same families that supplied munitions to Hitler, for God's sake, and they're still pulling the strings and—"

"And that's why you'd be insane to go up against them," she interrupted, holding her purse closer to her chest, as if for protection. "Look, I don't like to admit I'm a coward. In fact, it nauseates me. But I'm just not willing to find myself hanging from a light fixture, okay? Mark was doing you a favor when he told you to drop it."

A profound sadness seemed to come over Tom. "Guess I made a mistake with you."

"Look, I'm sorry I'm not Lois Lane. That's fantasy, Tom. There is no Superman to save me from the clutches of the bad guys. Or you either. Is this worth your life?" she whispered, hoping to talk some sense into him.

"What if we all looked away, D.? What if nobody spoke up? They now own our airwaves. They tell us what to think, how to think. They shape the world as they like it. And maybe I could swallow it if America didn't have a worse birth rate than a third world country, or people weren't becoming homeless again because they lost their jobs overseas or so in debt to credit cards companies that there's no way out. I'm a researcher at heart and if you want to talk about nauseating, how about this fact? Twenty-two percent of U.S. children grow up in poverty, which means that America ranks twenty-two out of twenty-three industrialized nations, only ahead of Mexico. And yet people aren't going to the voting booth and casting their votes for their best interests. Their minds have been taken hostage by politicians who answer to corporate America and we deliver the messages. Can't you see how we're all being played? Stressed out about bills? Second mortgage your home and, oh-by-the-way how about a little pill, an antidepressant, to make all your troubles bearable? Nobody gives a shit anymore about the truth. We're all just trying to survive this new world order of theirs."

D. swallowed deeply. He sounded like her when she was trying to explain to Marcus why her hometown was dying.

"You may think I'm some conspiracy nut, but there was another country that took over the newspapers and the radios, fed the people fear propaganda and told them what to think and how to act. Got rid of the middle class, attacked and ridiculed the intellectuals or anybody else who thought for themselves. They persecuted homosexuals, violated human rights, set up concentration camps in other countries to hold the undesirables without trial, or habeas corpus, and became fixated on their own moral values, believing they were ordained by God to cleanse the earth. And then they tried to do just that." Tom took a deep breath and added, "I can't turn my back when I see it beginning to happen in my own country."

"Tom, your story points to criminal activity on the part of a government official, not a prelude to Nazi Germany."

"And where does unchecked corruption lead, but to more corruption. This is a major government official with national ambitions who is willing to risk the lives of ordinary people to gain favor with the ruling class and put more millions into their pockets. I'm not naïve, D. I know there could be trouble. I was asking for your help. Not just for the city, but for the country, the *idea* that was America—what's left of it anyway."

"Now you're scaring me. I am not a patriot, Tom. I'm just trying to survive with the rest of humanity. And now I'm cold, so I'm going back to the station." She stood up and took a deep breath, as if the cold air might wash away Tom's words.

"Sorry I misjudged you, D," he answered, standing with her.

She couldn't look him in the eye. Nodding, she said, "Let's just forget we had this conversation." She patted his shoulder and turned away from him.

Walking quickly, she kept her gaze straight in front of her, feeling Tom watching her put distance between them. Really! What did he expect? That she'd grasp the opportunity to put herself out of a job and her life in danger? She dumped what remained of her cheeseburger into a trash can.

Tom was young and, despite his protestations, naïve. There was no way to win this one . . . but somewhere, in the recess of her brain, she did feel like a coward and very unpatriotic. If anything Tom said was true, then America, what she perceived as America, was on the downward slide from glory. Like the fall of the Roman Empire. Corruption, greed and arrogance were going to kill it.

Her conscience kept bothering her as she automatically smiled at the guard, the fresh-faced assistant in the elevator and her own P.A., who handed her a stack of messages. She flipped through them as she walked toward her office and then stopped dead in her tracks when she read the third one.

She spun around to Pam. "How long ago did you get this call from Marcus Bocelli? There's no time here."

Her heart began pounding as she waited for her assistant to answer.

"Oh, about ten minutes ago. Had the nicest voice. Accented."

D. inhaled deeply through her nose, fighting the urge to dance the rest of the way down the hallway. "Okay, thanks, Pam." She turned and walked into her office, noticing a cell phone number to return the call. "Yesssssssssss!" she whispered, tearing off her coat and closing the door with her foot.

Her conversation in the park was filed into a corner of her brain as she savored the delicious anticipation of hearing his voice again.

Marcus sat on a park bench, watching the public rushing to their destinations. No one even paid attention to a man who had transformed himself into a rodent and then back into a man. If anyone had actually observed him shifting, they would have blinked to clear their vision and then dismissed the idea as simply their imagination. It always amazed him how people sometimes couldn't see what was right in front of them because their brains had closed off the possibility of the extraordinary. Still, humanity's preoccupation with itself had served him in this open space. Originally, it had been his intention to invite Deborah to lunch. After talking with Maggie a few days ago, his conscience had been bothering him. Maggie had said Deborah was still attached to him. He thought he owed Deborah an explanation of why nothing could happen between them, rather than leave her in silence, wondering if she'd ever hear from him. And that was why he was using his day off from Mitchell's Nursery to come to Philadelphia again. Truthfully, he was more than happy to go back to his apartment in New York and to leave behind his role at the nursery.

He looked down to his feet, encased in soft leather and wiggled his toes. His feet still pained him, his arms still ached and his lower back felt abused. Yet, putting on his own clothes he'd found himself wondering how much he had taken for granted. And it wasn't just apparel. The hour and a half drive in his Porsche had been wonderful. He realized how much in his life he hadn't truly appreciated. Perhaps because of his advantages he was becoming soft and the Universe had decided it was time to build his muscles again. It wasn't easy to build muscles, he thought with a grin. Muscles need resistance to expand, to strengthen, and he was put into the perfect situation to do that, both physically and mentally.

He'd learned not to fight against the winds of change, but to surrender to the direction and flow of the energy around him, knowing, trusting, that a force greater than himself was directing his course. Still, he couldn't deny that his body felt the effects of two weeks of menial labor. And so did his ego. Had he been getting too full of himself?

And was this impromptu visit to Deborah a subconscious need to reinforce his once held self image? Truly, he hoped not, for he knew how destructive the ego could be, and when he'd visited Deborah's office out of curiosity it had been his plan to transform back into himself and, later, simply ask her to lunch. But that was before her encounter with another who preempted his invitation. And he had to admit his curiosity had been deepened. What was the fellow so secretive about? Even shifting into the most innocuous of insects, Marcus had felt the man's urgency and Deborah's intrigue. He'd decided as he had waited for them to appear in the park that he could call her later and a dinner invitation might be even better. He could use the excuse of driving back to New York City to make it an early night. And he had to admit, even to himself, that he didn't want to get himself into a position of making a choice where Deborah was concerned. Never one to lie to himself, Marcus knew that he could easily mix his desire for the carnal with good intentions. And the memory of Deborah's carnal desires hadn't waned since Bermuda.

It would be very easy to fall into . . . what had she called it? Playmates?

Deborah would have been the perfect playmate, had he not stayed with her during her mother's funeral. Now they had that bond between them, and she would never just see him as a casual lover . . . which was exactly what he wanted. What he needed, he realized, thinking of his assignment. Carolyn was progressing, opening up to him little by little, but he wasn't thrilled with spending every night in his rented room, watching television as he had no energy left after work to do much else. His muscles might be getting stronger, but his mind was becoming more and more dull each week that passed.

Which was why Deborah's conversation with the young man in the park had intrigued him. He had heard most of it as he'd trailed them, accepting bits of food from Deborah.

The Forsythe Group.

His jaw clenched in another form of resistance. Gabriel

Burke had been the first one to explain the delicate balance between light and darkness many years ago, and he'd used several organizations as examples through history. The present challenge in his lifetime and facing humanity, Gabriel had taught him, was centered around this one . . . a complex web of international families and political figures that, for centuries, profited by organized chaos. Now they were taking root in America.

His phone rang and he exhaled the tension he had been holding before answering it.

"Marcus Bocelli."

There was a pause.

"Deborah Stark here," she replied in the same matter of fact tone. "Returning your call."

He grinned. "Good to hear your voice again, Deborah."

"And it's good to hear yours, Marcus." Her tone became much more friendly. "Where are you?"

"Actually, I'm in Philadelphia," he answered, looking up to her work building. "And I was going to invite you to join me at dinner tonight, if you're free."

Another pause. And he knew she was trying to figure out his intentions.

"If you're busy, I understand," he offered.

"No, it's not that."

"Then you are not busy?"

"Where do you want to meet?" she asked.

Marcus smiled, picturing the lovely Deborah Stark across from him while enjoying a leisurely dinner. "I will pick you up at eight o'clock, if that is acceptable."

"You mean at my apartment?"

"That is where you live, is it not?"

"Well, of course, but I thought we'd just meet at a restaurant."

It was his turn to pause.

"Is that what you would prefer?"

Moments of silence. "Fine. I'll be ready at eight."

"Wonderful."

"You have my address?"

"Yes, you did give me a business card some time ago." Immediately he knew he'd made a mistake, bringing up thoughts of Bermuda and their irrational coupling.

"Right," she replied in a whisper, letting him know she remembered. "Then I'll see you at eight."

"Till then, Deborah. Ciao."

He clicked his phone shut and ended the connection.

He would have to be very careful this evening and make sure he steered the conversation in the direction that would best serve them both.

D. stared at her computer screen, yet didn't see a word she had typed before lunch. Her mind was swirling with thoughts that had nothing to with that night's news broadcast. His image dominated her thought process. She was going to have to play this very carefully tonight. Get through the six o'clock news. Get home. Get a shower and dressed and thank God Maggie had turned her disaster of an apartment into some semblance of order. And then she would see him again. On her own turf.

With any luck she would turn dinner into an overnight success story.

Suddenly, she remembered talking to Maggie about Marcus. All Maggie's warnings seemed silly now. Besides, Maggie didn't listen to her when she'd warned her off Julian and now they were living the happily ever after part. Maggie had played it right. She had told her that on their first date, she had made dinner for Julian at her apartment and that had created the atmosphere where the two of them could relax and connect more intimately.

Her cooking skills couldn't match Maggie's, but she knew

of a great caterer in the city. In fact, she even had their info somewhere . . . what was it called? Global Warming or . . . no, no . . . She punched a line on her desk phone.

"Pam, what was the name of that caterer about a month ago who appeared on AM Philly and we all got to eat the leftovers? Global something . . ."

"Hold on. Take me a minute to get it up on the computer."

D. tapped her nail against her desk, waiting and wondering how she should dress tonight? Sexy? Casual? More formal? A dress? Slacks? A see-though blouse?

"Here it is. The Global Dish. Want the number?"

"Please."

She wrote down the telephone number and thanked her assistant.

"Are you having a party, D. and not telling me?" Pam teased.

"No, no party. This is for a friend."

"Okay."

"Thanks again," D. said and then hung up the phone.

Well, it wasn't a complete lie. Marcus was a friend. And a party? Time would tell if it turned into that, but a girl could still hope and in the meantime use every advantage in her deck to influence the decision.

11

Okay, even in jail, Martha Stewart had probably set a better table.

Standing back, D. observed her efforts and sighed. This shouldn't be so damn hard. Did the bread plate go on the left or the right? She tried to think back to dining in good restaurants, but the only thing she could remember was using her right hand to pick up her wineglass. Hah, at least she got that right, she thought as she once more tasted the Chardonnay they would be having with dinner. Excellent. She glanced to the half empty bottle on the kitchen counter. All right, so they'd be having the extra bottle of Chardonnay in the frig with dinner.

D. knew she should slow down, not drink any more wine, yet it was as if she had this incredible thirst that couldn't be put down to a simple case of nerves. She felt like so much hung on how this dinner played out. Never before had she even given this much thought to any dinner, especially not a night of entertaining in her apartment. Hell, entertainment in the past had inevitably led to the bedroom.

It wasn't like she did that very often either. Despite what

others might think, she was very choosy in her playmates. And there hadn't been one since . . . well, before Bermuda there hadn't been one since last year when she had first come to Philly and had celebrated her new job with a three week play fest that involved a very discreet investment banker she had picked up in a bar. It was embarrassing that it took her more than thirty seconds to remember his last name. Bradley Something.

She shrugged, as if the action might make the whole thing disappear from her mind. Why dwell on the impulsiveness of the past? Tonight she was entertaining *the* Marcus Bocelli who she had lusted after ever since she'd met him at lunch with Maggie. And that one time on the beach had only increased her lust. And yes, it was lust, with a capital L-you'd only have to meet the man-st. The muscles of her inner thighs began to tingle, dancing upward at just the thought of having him to herself again. This time she wasn't going to ruin it with hysteria, spooky things or a crying jag.

Tonight she was a woman on a mission.

She tried again to rearrange the flowers she had bought, white Casablanca lilies, then gave up and walked away from the table. It would just have to do. She really wasn't any good with girly things and trying her hand at it had made her even more nervous. Thank God Maggie had cleaned the place with her last week. The living room looked pretty great thanks to her friend. She entered her bedroom, not exactly a love shack, and surveyed it again. Not girly here, either. She really should get up to north Jersey and bring back her mother's things. No. No . . . do *not* think about your mother, she mentally commanded. Not tonight.

Instead, she looked around the large room, imagining what Marcus might think. It did seem like a warehouse. A large king-sized bed dominated the room. No rugs. No furniture, save two night stands. All her clothes fit into the walk-in closet. A huge six-foot mirror leaned up against one wall, away from the bed. It was the perfect mirror to get dressed in front of . . . very unforgiving, showing head to toe.

Standing in front of it, she stared at her reflection.

She'd opted for black slacks and a white cowl neck cashmere sweater that casually fell off one shoulder given the right moves. And she'd practiced them a half hour ago. Her mother's pearls were her only jewelry. She thought she looked casually chic. Not fussy. Just a stay at home evening of entertaining . . .

Right.

When she thought of Marcus appearing at her door, her stomach actually fluttered with excitement. "You are one pathetic woman, Deborah Stark," she said, looking into her eyes. "Get your act together." She knew Marcus was used to women falling at his feet in surrender and she couldn't, simply couldn't, be just another conquest. She had to be different.

Staring at her reflection, she tried to be dispassionate as she took inventory of herself.

She was smart, ambitious, pretty enough, witty when she should, perhaps, shut up, but she was a decent package, maybe even better than decent. So what if she hadn't mastered the feminine arts of hearth and home? She had a phone book for that.

She was a catch.

"That's right, Deborah," and she said her name like Marcus, drawn out with an accent. "And don't you forget it tonight."

She sipped her wine and worried for a moment that she was talking to herself, but shrugged her shoulders as she left the bedroom. Tonight she was relaxed, calm, unperturbed, maybe even tranquil—

When the phone rang, she nearly jumped out of her skin. She rushed to the kitchen wall and grabbed the receiver.

"Miss Stark, you have a visitor. Marcus Bocelli."

Her breath left her body in a rush of excitement. "That's right, Joe. Let him up."

She hung up the phone, grateful for the high security of the building which gave her a few moments to collect herself. The table was set. The dinner warming. She looked casually chic after showering, shampooing, shaving, buffing, creaming and trying on more outfits than a Miss America contestant. Casual chic wasn't an easy look for someone with a closet full of business suits.

Standing in front of the door, she heard the elevator down the hall and took a deep breath to calm her nerves. She opened the door a few more inches and hurried into the kitchen. Pouring the wine into another glass, she heard a soft knock.

"Deborah?"

His voice. His wonderful sexy voice.

"In here," she called out, and was replacing the cork into the bottle when he appeared at the kitchen doorway. He looked marvelous in a long black cashmere coat, opened to show a dark suit, a crisp white shirt and a colorful silk tie. "Hi," she breathed in appreciation as she held out the wineglass. He sparkled, or something . . . some kind of light entered the room with him. "Welcome to my home, such as it is."

"Hello to you, Deborah," he answered with a smile, accepting the glass of wine. "You look lovely."

Good start. Oh, wait . . . she should have taken his coat. "I'm sorry. I should have taken your coat."

He seemed amused as he handed her back the wineglass and slipped his arms out of his coat sleeves. "Where shall I put it?"

Standing with a wineglass in each hand, she couldn't help him. "Just put it on a chair, for the time being."

He did as she instructed and then came back to reclaim his wineglass.

"To an evening of relaxation," she stated, clinking the edge of her glass to his.

"An excellent toast," Marcus answered, lifting his glass. And then he looked around her kitchen and into the dining room area. "Was I mistaken, Deborah? I had thought we would be going out to dinner."

"I know, I know," she said, putting her glass on the counter and checking the oven to keep busy. "It's a woman's prerogative to change her mind. I made an executive decision and decided to stay in and relax." She turned to face him. "Do you mind?"

He took a moment longer than necessary to respond. "Not at all. What can I do to help?"

She grinned, glad that was over. "Nothing. Really."

"You cooked?" he asked with a grin.

She could lie, but he already knew how disastrous she was in the kitchen. "Let's just say, I ordered and heated. And I decided on Italian. Fettuccini with grilled shrimp for starters and then Chicken Marsala. How does that sound to you?"

"It sounds delicious . . . and unexpected." He was leaning on the counter, sipping his wine, staring at her.

She felt . . . nervous, silly, maybe even manipulative. Reminding herself that she was in charge, that he was now on her home turf, she closed the oven and waved her hand out to her living room. "Good. Now let's sit for a few minutes and catch up. What have you been doing since I saw you last?"

She waited for her answer as he followed her out of the kitchen and into her living room.

"I've been immersed in the art of landscaping, you might say."

Now that surprised her. "Landscaping? I thought you lived in New York City. Do you have a garden?" She sat on the sofa and he joined her, sitting back with his elbow casually resting on the arm, as though he was right at home.

"I do live in the city, but I'm doing some . . . research out of the city right now."

The way he said research made her reporter's nose itch. "What kind of research?"

"Hands-on research. It's very interesting. One might think because it's winter there isn't anything to do, but it is amazing how much preparation there is for spring."

He appeared serious.

"Why are you doing all this research, if you don't have a garden?"

"Because it's interesting. Haven't you ever just followed a lead and became immersed in your subject?"

"I suppose," she murmured, trying to picture perfect Marcus playing in the dirt.

"Now what about you? Any interesting leads you might be following? By the way, I saw you on the news tonight at my hotel. You're very good at your job."

Pleased by the compliment, she forgot his curious obsession with gardening. "Thank you. And it's just the regular news, depressing at best."

"You don't do investigative reporting any longer?"

His question brought her walk in the park with Tom to her mind. "Not really."

He looked so disappointed that she blurted out, "Well, one of my colleagues today brought up something interesting . . . but it probably won't go anywhere."

"Would it violate anything to tell me about it?"

Eager to please him, she sat back on the sofa and said, "He's young and impatient for a breakthrough story and thinks he has one. I'm afraid he's heading toward a conspiracy trap, though, and I tried to steer him away from it."

"You don't think he might be correct? Don't most conspiracy theories have a basis in truth somewhere along the trail?"

"I suppose so, but this one could . . ." she paused for a moment, trying to find the right words, ". . . well, he might put himself in danger if he followed that trail."

Marcus sat up straighter and put his glass of wine on the coffee table. "Now that sounds very interesting. Danger from whom?"

"I probably shouldn't say anymore. It's his story, not mine. But it seems today they're all about the same things: corruption and greed."

Marcus nodded. "It does seem greed has become the new religion, despite what the moral majority in this country chooses to believe."

"Oh, please. Don't get me started on that whole morality issue. I may be closer to a heathen than an evangelical, but if memory serves me wasn't the only time Jesus got angry was when he threw the money changers out of the temple? Same story today. Not much has changed when corrupt corporations and governments use religion to hoodwink the public The hypocrisy is enough to nauseate me."

"Your memory serves you well, Deborah. It makes one wonder if this rapture a certain element is so anxious to achieve might not surprise them. Who would Jesus be angry with today, do you think? By all accounts, he was a true rebel, encouraging progressive thinking and refusing to engage in the fearful practice of judging another, more comfortable in the company of a fisherman than a government official or a money changer. And yet, he is known as the Prince of Peace. To use a word that seems to have become insulting . . . Jesus, it would seem, was a liberal." Marcus smiled. "And it has always struck me as odd how the followers of the Prince of Peace could engage in warfare." He sighed deeply. "I am sorry to have imposed my thoughts upon you. Now, perhaps, we should change the subject. I wouldn't want you to lose your appetite tonight. The aroma coming from your oven smells heavenly."

Her smile was slow and appreciating. "You're very

smooth, Marcus. I'd like to see you in a debate with Jerry Falwell or James Dobson."

He seemed surprised by her last sentence. "That you would never see. I like being invisible."

It was her turn to look surprised. "You? Invisible?" She laughed at the absurdity of the very idea. "You are anything, Marcus, but invisible. You must be aware of that."

He leaned in closer to her to pick up his wineglass from the coffee table. At the same time he looked deeply into her eyes and asked, "What do you know, Deborah, about the power of your thoughts?"

Her mind seemed to have stopped functioning normally. A part of her was searching for an intelligent answer . . . it was important to appear intelligent with him . . . and yet another part seemed frozen like a deer in the headlights of his intense brown eyes—eyes that felt like they were probing the very core of her being. "My . . . my thoughts?" she finally mumbled, breaking the gaze as she looked down into the bottom of her near empty wine glass. She'd drank too much before he'd arrived. Stupid. She needed her wits about her now. "I don't know exactly what you mean."

"Of course you do," he answered easily, sitting back and unbuttoning his collar as his suit jacket fell away to his sides. "You know about imagination, picturing yourself where you want to be. At every step in your life, in your career, you had a thought and through your imagination you saw yourself there, intended it to happen and used your will to bring it into your life whether by education, jobs you sought, promotions you desired or this apartment we are sitting in tonight. Each time you used your will to bring about what you desired."

His smile had turned gentle, almost paternal, as though she were a young girl and not an intelligent and horny woman who only wanted to get dinner on the table and the man into bed. *That* had been her intention, right? She watched him sip his wine and admitted, "I suppose you're right."

He chuckled. "It wasn't a contest, Deborah. I'm just stating facts in order to explain myself. It is my strong intention that I remain invisible to those who might not . . . understand me, that's all."

"That's all?"

He swallowed his wine, then stated in a quiet voice, "What people don't understand, they fear. And that fear turns into prejudice. They pre-judge. I prefer being invisible to them."

It was time to shake the wine-induced fog from her brain and use her intelligence. D. sat up straighter. "But, Marcus, you can't be *invisible!*"

"Can't I?" He held his glass in his hand and twirled the thin stem. "Have you ever driven down a street a hundred, two hundred times? You know this street like the lines in your hand. And then one day, from out of nowhere, you notice a house or a building where you never saw it before. The house or building isn't new. It's been there for years. Your perception is what is new. You are seeing it with new eyes. My intention is to be like that house. I am here to those with the perception to see me."

"Believe me, Marcus, you are hard to miss," she stated with a laugh. "You're too good looking to miss, and I know I'm not the first person to have pointed out that fact."

"Thank you, Deborah, but that isn't what I'm talking about. I have learned to fly under the radar of a certain type of person. Please believe me, it isn't difficult to walk down a street unnoticed. Most people are too preoccupied with their own lives and what's going on inside their heads."

"I suppose you're right, but I would certainly have noticed you. In fact, I did. That day I first met you when Maggie and I were having lunch."

He grinned. "I wanted you to notice me. I knew I was intruding and I knew Maggie would be angry with me."

Okay, this was definitely getting off track. *Love you, Maggie*, she thought. *But tonight you are a banned subject.*

"Well, anyway, I'm glad we met and I'm really hungry. How about you?"

"Actually, yes, I am hungry."

She nodded. "Good. You looked relaxed, so just sit right there and I'll bring our starter out here."

"And I can't help?"

She grinned. "This I can manage, Marcus."

She left him in her living room, sipping wine, and made her way to her kitchen stove. The plates, already arranged by the caterer, were hot and she used a kitchen towel to transfer them to the thick, white ironstone chargers. She grabbed a fork and an extra cloth napkin on her way back. "Here we are," she announced, as though she did this every day. "Be careful, the inner plate is hot."

Carefully, she put the charger and the plate of food on the coffee table in front of him and then placed the folded napkin down with a pat and put the fork on top of it. "That should do it," she announced and stood up proudly to await his approval.

Marcus leaned in over the plate and inhaled. "Ah, the aroma is heavenly, Deborah. And the presentation is very attractive." His finger traced the edge of the embossed charger. "These remind me of Provence. Have you ever been there?"

"France? No," she answered, pleased that he was pleased. "Taste the shrimp."

"What about you, Deborah? Do we share this?"

"No, of course not. Mine's on the way. I just wanted to know what you thought."

He smiled up to her. "Then bring in yours and we will taste it together."

In a flash she realized he was too polite to eat before she did. Someone had taught him well. "Back in a flash," she promised, hurrying into the kitchen.

When they were once more seated together, D. took a

deep breath as she picked up her fork. "Okay, let's both try the shrimp."

Marcus stabbed his and brought it to his mouth, but he waited until D. had done the same. As if given permission when D. began chewing, Marcus finally tasted his shrimp. The flavor of the fettuccine sauce mixed with the seasoning of the grilled shrimp into a tasty combination. "Delicious," she murmured in appreciation.

"I agree. Very good choice, Deborah," he answered, already going back to his plate.

Neither of them said anything for a few minutes as they ate, content in the company and the food.

"Your apartment is very roomy," he said, swirling the long strands of fettuccine around his fork with an expertise D. admired.

She was having trouble finding a way to keep the noodles from sliding back onto the plate. Not exactly a polished look, she thought, putting her fork down and staring out to her living room. "I keep telling myself one day I'll get around to decorating, but I never seem to have the time. It's . . . functional, I guess is the best way to describe it."

Marcus nodded, watching her again attempt to twirl the strings of noodles around her fork. "Excuse me a moment, please."

Surprised, D. watched him rise and walk into her kitchen. She heard him open drawers and he came back into the room with two tablespoons.

"Allow an Italian to show you how to eat pasta," he said with a grin. Sitting beside her again, he handed her a spoon. "Now watch." He picked up some pasta with his fork and then used the spoon to twirl it. "See? Neat." He put the forkful into his mouth. "Now you try."

D. felt all thumbs as she tried to follow Marcus' directions. She twirled her fork into her spoon, just like he had shown her, and it was working with a few stray pieces hanging off the side. Just as she lifted it off the spoon, the whole thing fell apart and back onto her plate. "Damn," she muttered. "I thought I had it."

"Patience and practice," Marcus said.

"Easy for you to say. You're eating and I'm still hungry."

He laughed. "Okay, put more pressure on the spoon."

She did as he instructed and fettuccine nearly flew off her plate. She threw down her utensils with frustration. "I think I'll wait for the next course," she said, reminding herself never to order pasta, long flat pasta, if she ever wanted to impress anyone again. Obviously this was a talent she wasn't born with. Why did she have to pick fettuccine anyway? Because it was Italian and he was Italian and she thought he'd be impressed with Italian food. Instead she was proving how clumsy she was.

"Here, allow me to help. It's very good, Deborah. You should eat it," he added, reaching around her with one arm to hold her right hand.

She had to lean forward, but didn't protest as his face was very close to hers and she had to concentrate as he held her hands like she was a baby learning to eat with something besides her fingers. She didn't care. All she could do was inhale the delicious scent of him, a mixture of exotic spices, and try to keep the fork and spoon in her hands.

"There now, bring it to your mouth."

She did as she was told and softly moaned as he slipped away from her with a pleased expression.

"You did it. It was easy, no?"

She could only nod as she chewed the pasta, not really tasting it. If anything all it proved to her was that she was a woman on fire for a man. Every nerve ending in her body was screaming out to her to turn to him and tell him how she felt, to forget dinner and any other pretense and drag him into her bed. Crazy of course, but it was the truth. She was like a teenager with raging hormones.

"Try it again, Deborah. You can do it now."

She was having trouble breathing normally. "I think I'll see to the next course. We'll have at the table," she said, picking up her plate and standing. "Finish yours. It will take me a few minutes to get everything ready."

Lies. She just needed some time to cool down away from him. This evening wasn't turning out at all as she had imagined. Instead of being a siren, luring her man into her bedroom and eventually her body, she was feeling out of control and foolish. She had never in her entire life reacted to man like this. Standing at the kitchen counter, leaning her hands on it for balance, D. suddenly realized it went beyond his great looks, his intelligence, his impeccable manners, his kindness and compassion. With lightening speed another crazy thought washed over her mind . . . it was as if his parents conceived him for her, that he was born to be with her. She felt it in every nerve ending, still tingling for the loss of his nearness. But it wasn't just about lust anymore. She liked him. Really liked being around him, listening to him, watching him laugh at her jokes. Every cell in her body was telling her he was her mate. It was a primal and ancient knowing, an instinct she had never before experienced.

And, damn it . . . that meant she was falling in love.

12

Once they were seated at the table eating dinner everything took on an easy note. D. blocked from her mind the absurd revelation in her kitchen about falling in love. She couldn't be. She wouldn't. She didn't need that in her life right now, and Maggie had warned her too many times to ever forget. Marcus Bocelli would never settle down.

A lapse in sanity, that's all it was. It also occurred to her she was questioning her state of mind a lot around him.

D. told him funny stores about celebrities who came to the station to promote a movie or television show, how demanding some of them could be and how unimposing others were, comfortable in their fame. She related amusing stories about bloopers she'd made on air, a co-anchor who had fallen off his chair during a live broadcast and she couldn't stop giggling for five minutes of serious news. She became animated as she told him about being attacked filming a remote Thanksgiving spot at a turkey farm in upstate New York. She knew she was talking too much, but just couldn't shut up. If she did, she might think about falling in love with him and that was madness.

When she finally took a long drink of water, Marcus sat back and said, "What a delightfully entertaining dinner companion you are, Deborah. Thank you for sharing your glamorous life."

D. swallowed. "I talk too much, I'm afraid."

"No, not at all. Your face lights up when you speak of your work, and you are very humorous. I enjoyed it immensely."

"Good. Glad I didn't bore you."

"You have never bored me, Deborah. I don't usually have boring friends, do you?"

The way he said friends made her pay attention. "No. I certainly don't want to be bored."

He reached out and took her hand across the table. He held it gently, still, not running a thumb over her skin or any other sign of intimacy.

"I hope we can remain friends. How are you really, since your mother's funeral?"

Oh God, not that. "I'm fine," she stated, pulling her hand away from his and reaching for the remainder of her water.

"You seem fine. No more lights or singing?"

She cringed. "Please, Marcus, don't even bring that up. It must have been my state of mind, that's all. You were very kind not to haul me off to a mental health clinic."

"I am your friend, Deborah. I would never do anything like that."

She stared at him. "You keep bringing up the word friend, Marcus, as though you're emphasizing it. Why is that?"

"We are friends, are we not?"

She nodded. "But I'm a reporter at heart and I tend to listen to what's beneath the words. Are you trying to tell me there will never be anything between us except friendship?"

He actually looked embarrassed and she knew she was right. Damn him. For a moment she didn't know how to proceed. The man came here tonight for that very reason.

"Deborah, I value the time we spent together at your

mother's home. I feel honored that you included me as your family at her funeral. That is great friendship."

"And you don't screw friends?" It was out before she could take it back.

He didn't answer her and she cast her gaze to her near empty plate. "I'm sorry, I shouldn't have asked that. I did tell you about my mouth."

"You have a lovely mouth and—"

"But not lovely enough," she interrupted, and felt angry at herself for saying the words. "Look, I know I'm pretty—"

"You're beautiful."

She ignored him. "I know I'm intelligent, witty and all those things men value. I don't need you to tell me or to boost my ego. I know who I am."

"Do you really, Deborah?"

She stared right back at him. "Yes, I think I do. And do you want to know what else I think? You want to remain friends, but I don't think you could honestly deny there is an attraction between us that might just go a bit beyond friendship and, for some reason, you're are determined to stop it."

"I don't want to hurt you."

She reacted by laughing. "You hold a very high opinion of yourself, don't you? It would never occur to you that you might be hurt in the end?"

"Yes, I would be hurt if I lost your friendship."

Okay, she'd had too much wine, but since he was giving her the kiss off, without the kiss, she might as well let it all out. She had nothing to lose. "You know, Marcus, what I wanted from you was pure and simple. A playmate. A friend and a lover. I knew you'd be good at both, since I've experienced both. You think I want to possess you, make you settle down? Why? That wouldn't be you, the you I am attracted to. I just wanted to spend time with someone I could relax with . . . you know? Really relax. Be myself. You already know what a flake I can be and you don't seem to mind it.

And you know more about me than anyone else now that my mother is gone." She straightened her shoulders and stared across the table, right into his eyes. "And if you think I would be looking for a commitment, you're dead wrong. Commitment is the last thing on my agenda. I have a career that is my top priority. Men and relationships come in a far second. The truth is I would like to get laid every now and then by someone I trust."

She had warned him about her mouth. She wasn't diplomatic Maggie, nor had she been tutored in impeccable European manners. She was Deborah Stark from Hadley, New Jersey.

Lifting her napkin off her lap, she placed it on the table and smiled. "So, my friend, I enjoyed this evening, but I hope you understand that I'm a working girl and my alarm rings at six a.m."

"Deborah . . ."

She held up her hand to stop him. "You're a gentleman, Marcus. You said what you came here to say and I've responded. I'm not angry, believe me, but let's call it an evening, all right?"

He rose from the table and walked toward his coat, still laying on the back of a chair.

"May I call you? I don't like to leave like this."

"You can do whatever you want, Marcus. I imagine, like me, you do pretty much what you want anyway."

Marcus put on his coat and D. headed toward the door. Her hand was on the knob when he came up to her.

"Even though you say you are not angry, I sense it in you. I am sorry, Deborah."

She grinned up to his handsome face. "Hey, friend, don't you worry about me. There are a great many fish in the sea." She patted his shoulder. "Go and enjoy your landscaping, or whatever it is that keeps you busy. I have an early call in the morning."

"Thank you for tonight. I truly did enjoy myself." He bent his head to kiss her cheek, a friendly kiss, and D. allowed it. She even allowed a slight hug, one that went on a bit longer than was exactly friendly. Finally, she pulled away and opened the door.

He smiled and walked into the hallway.

"Marcus?"

Turning, he looked back at her with tenderness in his eyes. "Yes?"

"You're not a very good liar."

She closed the door on his stunned expression.

There, she thought, staring at the dining room table. Let him roll that around in his head for awhile. There was more than friendship there. When he'd wrapped his arm around her, she would have sworn she felt a slight tremor in his muscles.

Whatever.

He'd kissed her off and then she had kissed him off. They were even and she could hold her head up when she looked in the mirror.

What a totally bizarre night. Come to think of it, every night spent with Marcus had been bizarre. *He* was bizarre, that had to be it. And that stupidity in the kitchen . . . falling in love . . . well, she had admitted she could be a flake.

Shaking off the parting, D. looked at the dishes that needed to be washed and returned to the caterer. Tomorrow. She really didn't have an early call, so she could do them in the morning. All she wanted was to get undressed and fall into bed. She hadn't counted on it being alone, but she'd get through just like she always did. She'd concentrate her energies where there was a guaranteed return. Her work. She even started thinking about Tom's weird conspiracy theory. She could indulge herself for a few days and if it came to nothing at least she'd kept busy. That was the trick . . . keeping busy, she thought as she began turning off the lights.

She'd learned that one a long time ago. She pictured herself in high school, sitting in the cafeteria, her head lowered to a textbook, trying so hard not to react to Marie Pereggi and her friends.

Keep busy, she'd told herself over and over, and it had worked. *Don't think about it. Don't let them get to you. If they do, they win.*

They hadn't won. Here she was, almost on top of her game, and Marie was back in Hadley and—

A soft knock sounded at her door.

D. froze for a moment and then turned in that direction.

She opened the door, already knowing who it was.

He was leaning against the door frame, looking defeated. "You are right. I'm not a very good liar."

She simply reached out, grabbed his tie and, pulling him into her apartment and into her arms, she said, "Now will you *please* stop talking about it and kiss me?"

Somewhere in the recesses of D.'s mind as Marcus expertly unbuttoned her bra and dropped it to the floor, she thought it was like one of those movie scenes where the couple begin devouring each other with kisses, ripping off clothing and leaving it behind . . . a trail of a cashmere coat, a tie, a pair of heels, another cashmere sweater and an expensive white shirt . . . all taking place between hungry kisses and the frantic removal of clothing as she led him down the hallway into her bedroom. When he ripped off his undershirt and clasped her to his bare chest, D. moaned in exquisite pleasure as her breasts were crushed against him.

His hands came up and grabbed her hair, pulling her face up to his. Looking deeply into her eyes, he whispered, "I don't want either one of us to get hurt."

"Dear God, Marcus, will you shut up?" she pleaded. "I'm not hurt. I won't be hurt. I know what I'm doing."

"But . . ."

"Don't speak," she interrupted, right before she kissed him into silence.

That was all he needed. The hunger returned with even more intensity.

Marcus broke away from her to mutter, "Where's your bed?"

So shaken by the kiss, D. could only point to the end of the hallway. He then stunned her by picking her up like a child and carrying her the rest of the way. She was the one that couldn't speak. No one had ever carried her before. It wasn't part of her memory bank and she could only cling to him as he took her the rest of the way into her bedroom and gently, as though she were something precious, laid her down on top of her bed.

He stood at the edge of the mattress, staring at her as she tried to recover, and she silently prayed he wouldn't say anything to break the spell. For that was how she felt . . . as though something magical was happening. In the soft light coming from the dining room, she could see him unbuckling his belt, pulling it free and dropping it to the floor. When he started to unzip his trousers, she did the same to her slacks. It was going to happen. She knew they were crossing a line, deliberately, at least on her part, and she also knew there would be no going back. This would change them, both of them. She stopped thinking as she saw him naked, gloriously naked. Her breath caught in the back of her throat and she stopped trying to wriggle out of her pants.

Good God Almighty. He was beautiful.

Somewhere, back in far corner of her brain, the thought flashed through her mind that she really never considered the male body as beautiful, but Marcus was like those statues of Greek gods with finely chiseled muscles. He was male. All male. An exquisite creation.

He reached down and finished sliding her pants down her legs.

She still couldn't speak. Swallowing deeply as she laid naked before him, D. had a moment of insecurity. Was she really a match for this man? He was better than her in every way. Definitely in better shape, better looking, better educated, better—

"Stop thinking, Deborah," Marcus murmured as he bent down to place kisses on the inside of her knee, her thigh, her hip, her stomach.

All thoughts banished as she felt the flame of his tongue on her skin. His soft kisses seemed adoring as he left a trail up her body. He knelt on the bed, over her, stared into her eyes and began whispering, "*Ti desidero. Facciamo l'amore, bella mia . . .*"

Whatever he was saying sounded so sexy that D. moaned and wrapped her legs around his hips, gently pulling him down to her. He could have been reciting the ingredients for lasagne for all she knew. It just sounded so damn sexy. "Say that again," she pleaded, running her hands over his strong back. "Whatever it was."

"I said I want you desperately. Make love to me, my beautiful one," he whispered, his lips inches from hers.

"No, please, in Italian . . ."

He smiled. "Here is a word you can learn. *Baciami*. Kiss me."

"*Baciami*," she whispered. "*Baciami, baciami, baciami . . .*"

And he did. Over and over again as their hands explored each other, finding sensitive spots that made them inhale with pleasure or moan with passion. It was wild and frenzied and then slow and deliberate as Marcus placed himself between her inflamed thighs and began moving slowly, deliciously, not entering her but caressing her with himself, making D. raise her hips and slide in rhythm. All the while he stared into her eyes and spoke to her of his desire in a language that seemed made for love.

It was, in D.'s experience, the sexiest thing any man had ever done to her.

When the tension of his foreplay built to an exquisite mixture of pleasure and agony and she could no longer stand the waiting, when nothing in her existed save for him to enter her, she reached down between them and placed him where she wanted him. "Now, Marcus . . . *please* . . . *now!*"

He entered her easily, slowly, and when he filled her she cried out in pleasure and gratitude, as though nothing else mattered, existed, except that moment. He felt so right inside of her, fitting her securely, surely, like pieces of a puzzle that were made to be together.

It was then the ancient ritual began, lovers moving in perfect unison, the core of her exposed, waiting to meet and make contact with the thrust of him, over and over again, bringing her closer and closer to the edge. Her hands clasped the strong muscles of his back for an anchor. Her head was thrust back, her neck exposed to his mouth, her calves capturing his legs, pulling in deeper and deeper, making him a part of her. Never before had she felt this rightness. He knew exactly what pleased, when to go faster, to slow down and then bring her back again to the edge.

Marcus, sensing her passion, rose higher on her body, capturing her ear lobe with his teeth. "Come with me, *bella mia*," he breathed into her ear, sending even more shivers racing through her body, making her back arch with a need, a demand for fulfillment. "Let us ascend to the heavens, you and me. Come, *tesora mia*, come with me . . ."

"*Marcus!*" She felt the explosion of pleasure burst within her and rush through her limbs, out her fingers and toes, wave after wave of exquisite white-hot pleasure that pulsed through the top of her head . . . and then, when she heard Marcus' moan of orgasm, for a timeless space she was with him, clinging to him as together they left the boundaries of matter and time. Holding each other, simultaneously rigid as joy took them beyond their surroundings, beyond their bodies, they transcended the normal into the realm of the extraordinary.

Her heart was pounding in her chest and in her eardrums. She was clinging to Marcus as though he were her lifeline as aftershocks rolled over her body, squeezing him with her inner muscles and making him jolt with renewed pleasure.

Panting for breath, D. moaned. "My God, Marcus . . . I . . . never . . . in my life . . ."

"Hush," he breathed into her ear, his own breath ragged. "*e stato stupendo*," he added, shaking his head with wonder.

"What? What does that mean?" she demanded.

Grinning, he kissed her damp forehead. "It means that was amazing, yes?"

She let her breath out and giggled. "Oh yes . . . *stupendo. Mucho stupendo!*"

He leaned on his elbows, looked down at her and chuckled. "You're mixing languages, but I get your meaning."

"Good, because that was *macho mucho stupendo*," They both laughed as she wriggled her body beneath him, rubbing her breasts against his chest. Running her hands through his damp hair, she murmured, "What a man, what a man, what a mighty fine man. *Baciami*, Marcus."

He lowered his mouth to hers and gave her a long, tender kiss.

Her sigh of pleasure was long and breathless. "How about dessert?"

He grinned. "Is that an invitation?" he asked, moving inside of her, still hard.

She leaned her head to the side and smiled contentedly as she stretched her arms, causing her breasts to rise close to his mouth. "Actually, I was speaking about the cannoli I had ordered for dessert, but what you've got in mind sounds even better."

He laughed and kissed her nipple, gently sucking it into his mouth. "This is much tastier than cannoli."

"How admirable of you to say so," she replied, feeling aroused again. "But . . ."

He lifted his head. "But what?"

She stared at him in the dimly lit room. "Truth?"

His shoulders tightened beneath her hands. "Always the truth between us, *bella mia*."

"Okay, first what does *bella mia* mean?"

He kissed her other nipple. "It means my beautiful one. Now what were you going to say?"

Feeling very pleased by his endearment, D. almost didn't want to finish her thought.

"What I was going to say, and I should be calling you *bella mia* since you are *the* most beautiful man I have ever seen—"

"Stop delaying," he interrupted.

"Okay." She took a deep breath and just said it. "I think I would first like to use the bathroom."

He laughed as he withdrew and rolled off her, and D. suddenly felt sad at the loss of him inside her.

"Why didn't you just say so, silly woman? Americans can be very provincial about these things."

"I guess we can," she admitted, wondering why that was. With so much freedom regarding sexuality in movies and television, we still wanted to believe no one ever went to the bathroom. Weird. She sat on the edge of the mattress for a moment, willing her head to stop spinning.

Marcus reached out and stroked her back. "A little unsteady?"

She nodded. "You might say that. Whatever in the world did you do to me?"

She couldn't see his face, but she could hear the amusement in his voice. "It is what we did to each other, Deborah."

Again, she nodded. She then took a deep breath and rose to her feet. She resisted pulling something around her. She was okay with her body, especially now since he had adored it so wonderfully. Determined not to hold onto the wall for support, she slowly made her way into the bathroom and closed the door. She was still provincial enough for that.

Minutes later she heard him whistling. She stuck her head out of the bathroom and heard the sound coming from the kitchen. From her vantage point she could see him moving around. Marcus Bocelli was nude, gloriously nude, walking around her kitchen, whistling as he prepared their desserts and poured them each a glass of wine.

She blinked, praying she wasn't dreaming. He was here, with her, and he looked like he planned on staying the night. Or, at least she hoped so.

"Ah, there you are. I'm famished. Here, come take your plate and your wineglass."

Caught, D. could only walk up to him and do as he asked. How very odd to be standing naked with him in her kitchen, as though they did this all the time.

"We can just use the napkins from dinner, no?"

"Sure," she breathed, still rattled. She grabbed both napkins and walked toward the bedroom, hoping he hadn't meant for them to sit back at the table like this. That would be too much. In the bedroom, she placed the plate and the glass on a night table and sat cross-legged on the mussed sheets. Her down comforter had been kicked to the floor some time ago.

Marcus placed his things down on the other night table and said, "Be right back."

She watched him walk toward the bathroom. Given a few moments, she hopped off the bed, straightened the sheets and pulled the comforter over them. She wondered if she should put on a nightgown, or stay as she was.

Staying as she was, D. got under the blanket and picked up her glass of wine. *My, my my,* she thought, sipping the now warm Chardonnay as her head rested against the wall behind her. It had been better than she had anticipated. Far better. Way far better than any other man she had been with. The passion. The heat. And that thing he did, rubbing himself against her in foreplay until she thought she'd scream at him to put it in . . . no, never before. Not like that. Not that intense need. The hot, hard maleness of him stroking her over and over, urging her womanhood to come forth. Closing her eyes, she groaned with renewed desire. She'd had good lovers, a few, but this was something else. It was like he was making love to her, waiting for her to demand more . . . and she had demanded, pleading with him.

That was something new too. She had never pleaded with a man.

Instinct had told her it would be good. Bermuda had told her it would good. Nothing had prepared her for *stupendo!*

She heard the bathroom door opening, and sat up straighter while brushing the hair back from her face. When he appeared at the bedroom, she threw back his side of the cover and said, "Come, stay warm."

He slid under the cover, smelling of her almond soap and kissed her cheek. "I just remembered you have an early morning. It is after midnight now."

"Okay. The truth. I don't have an early call. I just said that to get you out the door."

"That one is forgiven. I also lied."

D. grinned. "Right. You did." She picked up the cannoli and bite into it. Licking the cream from her lip, she added, "What a great idea. Dessert in bed."

"That isn't the only dessert we'll be having here." He then bite into his own dessert.

She laughed with pleasure. "Really?"

"Really," he answered suggestively, licking his lips of the soft cream.

Not truly hungry for food, D. put her plate back on the night table. She then turned to him and took his plate. She swiped some cream from the flaky roll and held it in front of his mouth. "Are you really, really hungry, Marcus?"

He looked into her eyes and grinned sexily. "You should know better than to ask an Italian man that question, *piccolina*."

Her gaze remained fixed on his, refusing to even smile. "What does that mean?"

"*Piccolina* means pretty little one."

She could help it. She laughed. "You sound like the big bad wolf showing your teeth."

Marcus's grin remained steady. He took her finger into his mouth and sucked off the cream. "All the better to eat you? Are you asking?"

She giggled and shrugged her shoulders. "Could be . . ."

"Ah, woman, you truly are a good playmate," he growled, pushing her back onto the bed and proceeding to make good on his very welcomed threat.

13

He couldn't stop thinking about her.

Going through his day, Marcus realized she would pop into his mind and he'd find himself getting aroused. He would picture her in bed, the incredible way her body responded to his, the easy teasing and laughter, the morning after when he'd brought her breakfast and she'd looked so vulnerable he thought she might cry before a quick recovery and a witty remark covered her exposed emotions.

Deborah Stark was a remarkable woman and he felt he'd found an excellent playmate.

"Marcus to the Christmas aisle for assistance." The PA system ended his thoughts which were only stirring up desire as he swept out the large warehouse. He was actually grateful for the interruption.

Leaving his broom behind, he pushed open the double swinging doors that led to the main store and the twenty decorated Christmas trees on display. He saw Carolyn speaking with an older couple and walked toward them.

Carolyn turned when he approached. "Marcus, could you get tree number five seventy one for Mrs. Hailey?"

He nodded. "Be right back."

Once more in the warehouse, he looked at the rows upon rows of artificial trees and began searching for the number. After he carried the long box to a flatbed trolley, he wheeled it back out to the woman who was still in conversation with Carolyn.

"Oh, but I know you could do it," the older woman was saying. "I have no talent for those things and I only have tonight to transform a room in a sports restaurant into a last minute Christmas reunion for my family who are flying in from all over the country. I would help and I'd pay you and anyone else you bring to assist you."

"Thank you for your confidence," Carolyn said, looking flustered. "But I simply couldn't. I work until six o'clock tonight and I don't have the transportation to get there."

"I could drive you," Marcus interrupted, figuring the Universe just gave him an opportunity and he wasn't letting it pass.

Carolyn glanced at him with a hint of annoyance. "Really, Marcus, I don't think—"

"There," the woman interjected, seizing upon Marcus' statement. "He'll drive you. Young man, if you help Carolyn tonight I'll pay you fifty dollars. And you just name your fee, Carolyn." Seeing the hesitation in Carolyn's eyes, Mrs. Hailey added, "Please, dear. Everyone will be arriving and because it's so last minute the only place I could find was this room in a restaurant with sports banners on every wall. I can't imagine how to turn it into Christmas by tomorrow."

Carolyn's shoulders sagged in defeat. "Are you sure, Marcus?"

"I'm sure," he answered, not really sure of anything, save he would get some time with Carolyn outside the nursery.

"All right," Carolyn said, surrendering to the woman's pleas, "but you have to do some shopping before I arrive at seven."

Mrs. Hailey beamed. "I just knew you were the one who could do this."

"Please don't get too excited."

"Nonsense. You can do it. Look at your creations here. You're gifted."

"I don't know exactly what I'm doing," Carolyn said to bring the woman back to reality. "All I can say is I'll try to help you."

"Oh, you'll do a wonderful job, I'm sure. Now, what's on my shopping list?"

Marcus watch all this with amusement. He could sense Carolyn's fear, but it was more than balanced by Mrs. Hailey's confidence.

"All right, first we'll get things that are available here, like wreaths and banners and ornaments. And then you have to go to Kmart or Target or someplace like that and buy ten to twelve cheap white shower curtain liners."

"Shower curtain liners?" the woman asked with confusion.

Carolyn became more assertive. "Yes. You don't have time to buy fabric, but we can make do with the liners. We'll staple them in pleats to the ceiling molding to hide the team banners. Then we'll decorate them for Christmas."

The woman blinked for moment and beamed again. "Brilliant. I never would have thought of that. You see, I was right about you."

"We'll see about that tonight. Right now we have to pick out what we want to use for table arrangements, fabric ribbon with wire, lots of tiny white lights . . . how many did you say were coming?"

"Fifty, at least fifty, that's why I didn't want to have it in my home."

Carolyn nodded and began leading her customer away. "Let's get the white lights first. I think we'd be safe to get at least eight boxes."

"Carolyn?" Marcus called out.

She turned.

"What about this tree?"

"Oh." She stopped and thought about it. "Mrs. Hailey can pay for it this afternoon and then we'll bring it tonight. Do you have the room in your car?"

Thinking of the SUV he'd rented for this assignment, Marcus nodded. "I think I can manage."

"Good. Just leave it up front by the cashiers, okay?"

"Okay." Marcus grinned as Carolyn, now into it, turned back to Mrs. Hailey and began chattering about what was needed to pull off this impromptu Christmas family reunion.

How fortuitous to have walked into that conversation, he thought, taking the box to the front of the store. Tonight he would see where Carolyn lived. He would spend time with her in the car and who knew what other opportunities might come to light? Yes, despite the difficulties in her life and her lack of faith in herself, the Universe had a plan for her.

It was his assignment to help her find it.

The muscles in his shoulders were cramping from tacking the white curtain liners to the ceiling. They couldn't staple it, so Marcus had been given the job of using long steel tacks to keep it in place. He'd already tacked strings of white lights in front of the sports banners and now he had to cover the lights with the shower liners. It was a long, tedious assignment, certainly worth more than the fifty dollars promised. Though he'd made it clear to Carolyn after picking her up at her small apartment he only volunteered because he could use the extra money for Christmas presents. A small prevarication. He'd use the money for a gift. Someone's gift.

"It's looking good, Marcus."

"Thanks. Wonderful idea."

He glanced down at Carolyn from the top of the step stool. She was making large plaid Christmas bows that she planned to use in each corner of the room. Somehow, once she'd accepted her challenge, she had everything planned in her mind. He was simply following her instructions. Mrs. Hailey was of almost no use at all, becoming confused and flustered, making things more difficult. Carolyn had sat her down and made her roll the cutlery into white linen napkins provided by the restaurant. On the walls already done, he saw Carolyn had used some kind of tape to fix tiny red Christmas balls to the liners. The lighted Christmas tree was already set up in the far corner of the room and three lush wreaths on the long tables were waiting to be hung.

It took almost three hours to finish, for Carolyn to tie a plaid bow around each napkin and run the same wide ribbon down the center of each long table cloth. When the arrangements were placed, Mrs. Hailey clapped her hands in appreciation. It was only after Marcus had hung the wreaths in the center of each wall that Carolyn plugged in the lights behind the curtain liners. She turned off the main overhead light in the room and all three of them stood in awe.

What had once been a private room in a sports bar had turned into a winter wonderland with fresh greens on the walls and tables and a sense of magic from the lights behind the curtains.

"It's beautiful," Mrs. Hailey pronounced and sniffled as tears filled her eyes. "Who would believe we could do this in one night?"

"I did," Marcus said. "Congratulations, Carolyn. You are a gifted woman."

"Yes, yes," Mrs. Hailey added. "You performed magic in here." And she gave Carolyn a tight hug of gratitude. "You're so talented."

Carolyn seemed pleased, yet shy, as she shrugged her shoulders. "Well, I couldn't have done it without you two."

"It was your plan, we just followed orders," Marcus said, again looking around the room, seeing no trace of sports anywhere. It looked festive, yet tasteful.

Mrs. Hailey sighed. "I'm afraid I was more of a hindrance than help. I couldn't see it finished in my head and . . ."

"It's done now," Carolyn interrupted. "I hope your family has a wonderful reunion."

"Yes, and you two worked all day at your jobs and all night here. You went beyond the call to help an old woman." She picked up her purse from a table and brought out two envelopes. She handed each of them one. "Now, I'm exhausted and I have to get home, but these are for you and I've already talked to the manager here and paid for your dinners. Don't argue," she said as Carolyn opened her mouth to protest. "It's already done. You two go and relax. You've more than earned it."

"Thank you, Mrs. Hailey," Marcus said, putting the envelope into the pocket of his jeans.

"No, thanks to you, Marcus, this is happening. If you hadn't offered to drive Carolyn I don't know where I'd be right now." She reached up and pulled on his shoulder to give him a kiss on the cheek. "Now take this talented lady out to the dining room and feed her. My poor husband must think I've abandoned him."

"Merry Christmas, Mrs. Hailey," Marcus said, looking to Carolyn.

"Yes, Merry Christmas," Carolyn repeated, picking up her coat and purse. "Have a wonderful day tomorrow."

"We will, thanks to you both."

They left Mrs. Hailey in the room and walked into the main restaurant. "I don't know about you, but I'm famished," Marcus said, looking for the hostess. "I didn't eat dinner. Did you?"

Carolyn seemed uncomfortable. "No, there was no time, but you don't have to do this. You must be exhausted too."

Marcus grinned, holding up his hand for the attractive woman who seated patrons. "I'm more hungry than tired right now."

"May I seat you?" the woman asked, holding menus in her hands and smiling with approval to Marcus.

"That would be appreciated," he answered, waving his hand to Carolyn to proceed him.

"Follow me," the hostess said, leading them toward the bar. "These are the only ones available this late, I'm afraid."

"Carolyn, is this all right with you? It's a bit noisy."

"It's fine," she answered, sliding into a booth and putting her jacket and purse next to her.

"Thank you," Marcus said to the hostess as he slid onto the bench across the table.

"Can I get you something to drink before the waitress comes?"

Marcus looked at Carolyn. "Do you drink red wine?"

"Yes, but I don't think Mrs. Hailey had that in mind."

He glanced up to the hostess. "We'll each have a glass of Merlot, please."

The woman nodded and walked away.

"Marcus, Mrs. Hailey said dinner, not drinking."

"I will pay for the wine myself if it makes you more comfortable."

"You're supposed to be saving your money for Christmas presents, remember?"

He grinned. "I can afford two glasses of wine, Carolyn."

She sighed and looked around the bar area. "Fine."

"You are tired, aren't you?"

"Aren't you?"

"Yes, I am. But it's a good tired. We helped someone in need. That always makes me feel good."

Carolyn grinned. "It did turn out well, didn't it? And for relatively little money."

Catching her renewed enthusiasm, he nodded. "It is a wonderful transformation. You are very talented."

She brushed off the compliment. "Years of impromptu entertaining, that's all."

"Impromptu entertaining?"

Nodding, she said, "My husband . . . my ex husband would call at the last minute telling me he was bringing home a client for dinner. You learn to be creative and think on your feet after nearly thirty years of that."

"You certainly have developed a talent for it."

Shrugging, she said, "Well, this is the first time I've been paid for it, that's for certain."

The hostess brought their glasses of wine. After thanking her, Marcus held up his wine glass to Carolyn. "Here's to you, Carolyn Davies. May this be the first of such opportunities."

She raised her glass shyly and sipped the red wine. "It's not like people walk into Mitchell's and ask me to do this every day, you know. This was an exception. Like you said, a woman in need."

"No, they probably wouldn't come into Mitchell's looking for a party planner, but it is something, I believe, you could do easily. And make good money at it too."

"What? Planning parties for people?"

"Why not? You have thirty years experience at it. And you just proved you can make something from near nothing and get paid."

"But what about food? Liquor? I could never cook for a large crowd."

Marcus leaned his elbows on the table and looked directly into her eyes. "You wouldn't have to. Use a caterer. You organize it, Carolyn, like you did tonight. You're the director, the producer and the stage manager, for that's what a good party planner really is. You must have contacts from your past life, as you call it."

He could see her mind working with the possibilities.

"But it takes money to start a business."

"What did you spent tonight?"

"Not my money. Mrs. Hailey bought everything."

"Wouldn't a client have to retain your services? There's money up front."

"But advertising . . ."

"Get business cards made. It's unfortunate that you can't leave them here tonight. You know Mrs. Hailey is going to tell everyone tomorrow what magic you performed for her."

She sipped her wine, lost in her own thoughts.

"May I take your order?"

They both seemed surprised by the appearance of the waitress.

"I'm sorry. We haven't even looked at the menus yet."

The young woman smiled. "That's okay. It's kinda late for the kitchen, so you have a choice of burgers or our special tonight."

"And what is your special tonight?" Marcus asked, closing his menu.

"Talipa, stuffed with crabmeat, and a backed potato. It comes with coleslaw and applesauce."

"That sounds good to me. Carolyn?"

Carolyn nodded and handed over her menu. "Actually that does sound good."

When the waitress left them, Marcus looked at Carolyn and grinned. "So what do you think?"

Carolyn shook her head and chuckled. "I think it's a crazy idea."

"But crazy ideas can work out, no?"

"I guess. It's a lot to think about and—"

"Carolyn?"

Both she and Marcus turned their heads at the sound of her name.

A couple was walking toward their booth. They looked to be in their fifties and casually well dressed.

"Carolyn, I thought it was you," the woman announced, coming up to their table. "How are you? It's been . . . some time."

Carolyn looked decidedly uncomfortable as she forced a smile. "Hello, Ellen, Mark. I'm doing well, thank you. How are you both?"

"We're great, thanks," Ellen answered, eyeing Marcus with interest. "We were coming back from the city and I simply couldn't wait. This place looked decent enough for a quick stop."

Carolyn only nodded.

"I came out of the ladies room and . . . saw you. I told Mark it had to be you." Ellen again looked at Marcus, expecting to introduced.

There was a moment of awkwardness until Marcus extended his hand. "I am Marcus Bocelli. A . . ." he paused for effect, "a friend of Carolyn's. We just finished a lengthy evening and stopped for a bite to eat. Would you care to join us?"

He shook Mark's hand, who introduced himself, and took a moment longer than necessary to hold Ellen's diamond studded fingers. The slow flush of color on her cheeks increased as he let go.

"We don't want to intrude," Mark said.

"Actually," Carolyn murmured, looking now very uncomfortable, "we were just going to eat and run. It's late."

"Yes, it is late," Marcus repeated. "Carolyn just finished an incredible project. Perhaps another time?"

"Yes, of course," Mark stated, taking the hint.

"What project?" Ellen asked, not listening to her husband. "I didn't know you were working, Carolyn."

"She's a party planner," Marcus said before Carolyn could speak. "A very talented woman," he added, giving Carolyn a look of tender pride. "She fit this one into her schedule because her kind heart couldn't turn down a person in need." He looked up at Ellen. "A last minute family reunion for fifty guests. As you can tell, I am very proud of her."

"Yes," the older woman murmured, with a hint of surprised envy. "It's obvious."

"Well, it was good to see you both again. Have a wonderful holiday," Carolyn said in an attempt to stop the conversation.

"You know, Carolyn, just this evening, Mark and I were toying with the idea of a New Year's Eve party. I told him it was impossible at this late date to get anyone." She paused. "Do you think . . . ?"

"I'll call you, Ellen."

"Please don't forget. Maybe tomorrow evening we could get together and begin planning?"

"We'll see," Carolyn answered in a tight voice.

"It was a pleasure to meet you both," Marcus said.

Ellen extended her hand again to him. "And you, Mr. Bocelli."

Maybe he shouldn't have, but Marcus took the woman's hand and placed a light kiss above her knuckles. "Ciao, Ellen." He let go of her hand and extended his own to her husband. "Enjoy your holidays."

"Yes, you too," Mark answered, looking flustered by the entire encounter. He held his wife's elbow and steered her away from the table.

"You are a terrible flirt," Carolyn accused him. "And you know Ellen and Mark are going to think I'm with you."

Marcus grinned. "Of course. That was my intention."

"She'll be on the telephone the minute she gets home to spread that piece of juicy gossip."

"That also was my intention."

"Why?" Carolyn demanded. "You don't know me. You just gave them an earful and, I might add, an eyeful of rumors to spread. I moved away from those kind of people for a reason. Mark is a friend of my ex's."

"Is what I did so terrible? Really?" He sat back and took a sip of his wine. "The woman thinks I am your lover. So what? Is that so unreasonable?"

Carolyn almost spit out her wine. Swallowing, she laughed. "Yes! You're what . . . twenty years younger than I am?"

"Again, I repeat . . . so what? To me older women are succulent, and ripe. They have put mothering behind them and are discovering their own fullness again. I find that very sexy."

"Are you flirting with me, Marcus?"

"And if I was?"

"Then I would tell you that you and your Italian charm are barking up the wrong tree."

"I'm confused. Barking up a tree?"

She shook her head with patience. "It means to forget it. First, despite your great looks, I'm not attracted to you that way. I've always liked fair-haired men, *older* fair haired men with a bit of life behind them. Second, it's preposterous that a man like you would be with a . . . a woman my age."

"You're wrong, Carolyn, and perhaps I only wanted to make you smile and realize you are an attractive woman who—"

"And third," she interrupted. "you flat out lied to those people. Now, Ellen will be expecting me to call her about her party. Thank you, but no thanks."

"What if I found you a business partner? You could do her party and make a name for yourself with your old friends."

"Why in the world would I want to do that? It's bad

enough that everything has been taken from me, but now you expect me to go to my old friends and serve them, take money from them?"

"Why not?"

"Because it's embarrassing, that's why not. Look, I know you thought you were doing me a favor when you told them about this party planning madness, but I can't do it."

"Because you're embarrassed to take money from them for a service?"

"Yes. It's asking too much."

He sat for moment, thinking. "We don't know much about the other, do we?"

Carolyn shook her head, obviously upset.

"You just said you lost everything. What did you mean?"

She sighed with exasperation. "It means my husband took himself a younger woman and then put all our assets into her name and declared bankruptcy before I even knew of the affair. I lost my home, my car, my friends, my entire life."

"I am sorry you had to experience such a loss. There was nothing after thirty years of marriage?"

"Twenty-seven years. And no, nothing for me. Even my children are appalled by their father's behavior, but that doesn't change reality. I was traded in for a woman four years older than my daughter."

"The man was a fool," Marcus declared. "Believe me, one day in the future, and you may never know about it, he will come to his senses and his loss will overwhelm him. His foolishness will catch up with him. The wheel will turn and he will experience what he gave out. I wouldn't want to be in his shoes when it happens."

'That's all well and good, Marcus . . . and I hope you're right . . . but you can now see why I don't want to work for people in my old life."

"I will tell you something I learned many years ago. Most clichés hold a trace of truth within them, or they wouldn't endure time. Pride really does come before the fall. And as far as money is concerned . . . look around you, Carolyn. What do you see happening in this country? Very soon there will be little expendable income, save for those who are wealthy. Common sense tells you the way to make money will be in service to the poor or to the wealthy. You can open one of these Dollar Stores that keeps appearing in every town, or you can cater to the rich. If I were you, I'd pick the rich. You know them. You have years of research on them. Isn't it time you used it to your benefit?"

"Who *are* you?" She shook her head. "You're too intelligent to be seasonal help at Mitchell's. Why aren't you working in the city, at some investment firm or something? Why Mitchell's?"

Marcus smiled. "It seemed a good place to pick up extra money for Christmas. And I was right. Look at tonight. Fifty dollars."

"You should be using your intelligence somewhere else."

"So should you."

Carolyn grinned. "I walked right into that one, didn't I?"

Marcus laughed and the waitress brought their platters. The food was abundant and smelled delicious. When both of them were eating, Marcus paused to say, "Don't let pride or fear stop you, Carolyn. It's like when you put together a kite with the wind. The nature of both are meant for each other as they reach new heights. It's effortless; it's in harmony. You know, down deep, this is something you could do. The wind is filling your kite now. It's up to you to let out of the string so it can soar."

"Why do you care? Why are you pushing this?"

Marcus stopped eating. "I care because I recognize a kindred soul. The circumstances were different, but I, too, became disillusioned by life. Someone helped me to see it could be different, that perhaps, just perhaps, what we perceive as an injustice might well be what was needed to open the next door for us . . . to something better. If only we have the courage to walk through it."

She didn't say anything as she stared at him across the table.

"Just imagine this scene with me, Carolyn . . . you are excited again about life. You own your own business. You schedule your own time. You are successful because you know what you are doing. You are overflowing with clients who come to you because of your talent and because you love your work and it shows. And you don't mind putting in the time and effort because it's for you. You reap the rewards of your labor. Imagine being happy again because you feel in harmony with everything around you."

"You sound like one of those self-help gurus that make a fortune off of people's mixed up lives."

"My words come without a monetary payment. The cost is what you're willing to let go of, putting aside your negativity and starting to believe in yourself again."

"Sounds nice," she murmured, now staring down to her plate.

"It is possible, Carolyn. It can be your time again, if you don't let pride or fear hold you back. Try to think of it this way . . . what if the universe, or whatever you perceive as the source of intelligence on this planet, what if it has a plan for you? What if those twenty-seven years you spent entertaining were your preparation? What if you walked into Mitchell's, not just for the income to pay your rent, but it was there you were to discover your hidden talents? What if all this led up to Mrs. Hailey pleading with you to help her tonight and for us to be having this conversation? I don't believe in coincidences or luck. Your old friend Ellen might just be an angel in disguise, appearing at the right time and place with an opportunity. Now you have a decision to make. Do you call her tomorrow and plan her New Years' party, or do you not pay attention to the signs and miss the opportunity?"

Carolyn looked near tears. "How can I do it? Planning a party is one thing. Actually making it happen is another. I would need help, like tonight. I can't do it all myself."

"And who says you have to? Hire a few of the part-time teenagers from Mitchell's to help set up."

"I don't have the money for that, and what high school kid would be willing to give up their New Year's Eve?" She sniffled, as though determined not to shed a tear. "To be honest, Marcus, whatever Mrs. Hailey paid me tonight will be used toward my rent and electric bill. I'm living on the edge here, and I'm frightened. I can't gamble with money when my very survival is dependant on it."

Marcus sipped his wine and grinned. "What if you had a partner? A silent partner?"

"A partner?"

"Yes, someone who has the money to invest in a good business proposition."

"And who would that be?"

"Leave that to me." He began eating again, as though the subject were closed.

Obviously, Carolyn had more questions. "And what if I say yes, call Ellen tomorrow and take on this party? What if I can't get the help and I fail?"

Shaking his head, Marcus said, "Listen to yourself, Carolyn. You're setting yourself up for failure and you haven't even begun. How about this? If you find you need more help, I'll do it with you on New Year's Eve."

"You don't have plans?"

"No."

"No girlfriend?"

He thought of Deborah. "No, not in the way you mean it."

"I find that hard to believe."

'You do?"

"C'mon, Marcus, you could have any woman you wanted and you're going to be alone on New Year's?"

"But I won't be alone, will I? I'll be at a party."

"You're a very strange man, Marcus Bocelli."

"And you are not the first to have made that observation. Now finish your dinner and I will drive you home. You have a big day tomorrow."

"So now, let me get this straight . . ." D. said, narrowing her eyes at the paper in front of her. "Romano Construction is really owned by Gilbert Subsidiaries who is really owned down the paper trail by the Forsythe Group? And the Forsythe Group owns this network and pays our salary?"

"Yes, they're the parent company of Nova Communications," Tom Harris answered. "It isn't just our network either. You've seen what stories get attention across the networks, those that keep the public in fear, worried about their future, be it a terrorist threat or their Social Security. We feed the party line to the viewing audience and then they get to play out the rest of their coup. We're all pawns, right down to Norman Kove in the mayor's office. Kove has money invested in Cavelli Material Suppliers under his wife's name. The contract for the condos is given to Romano Construction, but Kove makes sure Romano uses Cavelli. He knows they use substandard material, pay off inspectors, and charge for the material they should have used in the first place. That gets added onto the price of the condos and they all make a nice profit, right back down the paper trail to the Forsythe Group. Everybody wins except the buyers, whose condos could tumble into the Delaware if hit by a hurricane. And it's not just happening right here in Philadelphia. It's all across the country, the world, using different subsidiaries."

"And you know for certain Norman Kove in the mayor's office is a part of it?"

Tom shuffled through his stack of papers. Pulling one out,

he handed it to D. "There. The corporation papers for Cavelli. Marion Kove. That's his wife. A friend of mine in records has been getting these copies for me."

D. stared at the papers in her hand. "Have you shown this to Dave or Mark?"

"I never got that far. The whole thing was shot down before I had the chance."

She let her breath out slowly. "Can you leave this with me? I'd like to go over it again and then decide what I want to do."

"What if I make you copies of everything? I really want to keep this file for myself."

"Copies are fine. Can you get them to me today?"

"I have to go out on a remote this afternoon. How about later in the day, or tomorrow morning at the latest?"

She nodded, picking up the rest of the manila folder and handing it to him. "Okay."

"Thanks, D.," Tom said earnestly. "I knew I was right to approach you."

He looked so eager, so relieved someone was listening to him, that D. smiled. "I didn't say I would take it on. I said I'd think about it."

"It's a step in the right direction."

D. opened a drawer and picked up her stop watch. "I have to meet Larry in editing in a few minutes to review some tapes. Somehow we have to cut them into minute and half slots and then do the voice overs. I'll be here until after seven. If I don't see you tonight I'll see you in the morning."

"Right. And thanks again, D."

"Don't get your hopes up, Tom. This may go nowhere."

"I have faith," the younger man said as he walked out of her office.

She fingered the silver watch in her hands, worn smooth over the years of use. It had been a gift to her by her mother many years ago when she'd first started editing her own work. She turned the watch over and read the inscription.

You must make tracks into the unknown. Thoreau

Whatever had made her mother inscribe those words? At the time she had thought it was for courage as she started her career, but now they seemed to be reminding her not to remain complacent and safe. She thought of Tom's file. This could be a major story involving not just city hall and the corruption in the building industry, but her own as well. She didn't trust any of the networks, not even CNN, and cable would bury it so deep it would never be heard of again. Maybe the BBC was the way to go, a network out of this country.

It was something to think about.

She spent the next three hours in editing, another forty-five minutes in makeup and was walking onto the set when Alan, the floor director pulled her aside.

"Did you hear yet?"

"Hear what?" she asked, blowing a wisp of hair away from her eyes. "I just got out of makeup."

"About three minutes ago, our remote van went off the expressway?"

A sudden rush of cold shivers ran down her back. "Are they okay?"

"Charlie and Tony had their seat belts on, but Tom Harris was in the back working and he's on his way to Einstein. The word isn't good on him."

"My God . . ." D. was so rattled that her hand holding her script began shaking. "How did it happen?"

"All I heard is that some car cut them off, forcing Charlie to the railing to avoid a collision and that's when the van rolled and went off the expressway. They don't call it the Schuykill for nothing. Mark's on his way to the hospital now. You're going to lead with it, so follow the prompter."

She nodded, making her way to the set. She had to calm down. She was going live in four minutes.

"Did you hear about the accident?" Matt, her co-anchor asked, looking shaken himself.

"Just now. Jesus, Matt, I was talking to Tom this afternoon." She put on her mic and ear piece. She could hear multiple conversations from the control room to Alan and to Andrea Miller, ready to go live at Einstein Medical Center.

A staffer hurried up to the news desk and placed a piece of paper before both her and Matt.

Alan, standing nearby, said, "There's your opening script. Read it and then follow the prompter."

D. picked up the paper and read the details of the accident, what they had so far. She wondered if anyone had notified Tom's family so they wouldn't hear the news like this.

"Okay, everything else is shuffled back, so we're flying by the seat of our pants on this one, folks," Alan said, moving away to stand next to the center camera.

They all listened to the signature theme music and D. stared at Alan for direction as his hand came up and fingers disappeared until only one was left, pointing at her.

"Good evening," she began. "We begin tonight's news with a report that hits close to home. Only moments ago we were informed Channel Four's remote van was involved in an accident on the Schuylkill Expressway. Right now details are sketchy, as the police are attempting to pull together information, but we'll go to Andrea Miller, standing outside Einstein Medical Center, for further news on Tom Harris, one of our valued team members. Andrea?"

"That's right, Deborah. I'm here at Einstein Medical Center where all three of Channel's Four's team were brought only moments ago. Two of our staff members, Charles Evert, who was driving the van, and Anthony Cox, in the passenger seat, seemed dazed, but unharmed. Unfortunately, Tom Harris, Channel Four's news reporter, was wheeled in with an oxygen mask and IV's inserted by the paramedics on the way to the hospital. I haven't been able to talk to anyone yet, but I'm standing by with positive thoughts and prayers until we receive more information. Back to you, Deborah."

"Yes . . . thoughts and prayers," she murmured, staring into the lens of the camera.

"D.! Read the prompter. Stick to the script," Alan directed into her ear.

She blinked to bring her back to reality. "We'll check in with Andrea later in the broadcast, and now on to other news affecting the Delaware Valley. Philadelphia's school board is back in court today to answer charges from the minority community that the No Child Left Behind law is being used to underfund schools in four of its districts . . ." She was on autopilot throughout the rest of the newscast and was grateful it was Matt who went back to Andrea for an update on the accident story. She waited through the weather, through the sports, and finally was able to sign off.

"And we're out," Alan declared from the floor.

She pulled off her mic and ear piece and pushed back her chair. "I'm going to the hospital," she announced, walking away from the set.

"Andrea is already there, D. She'll do an update on the eleven o'clock. We don't need you there."

"I'm not going there as a reporter, Alan," she said, passing him. "I'm going as a friend."

"Well, call us if you find out anything before Andrea, okay?"

Her back to the director, she simply waved her hand as she headed out of the dark studio. All of her spidey senses were telling her that this accident was just too coincidental. Sure there was fate, but what were the chances of her and Tom seriously discussing something that might be detrimental to the station, to the network, to the mayor's office and ultimately to whatever this Forsythe Group was? And then Tom gets into an accident? What did that mean? She had an urgent need to get to the bottom of it and, hopefully, put it down to chance, because if it wasn't . . . then that meant there was no accident. Tom had been watched and whoever was doing it knew she was now involved.

She wasn't heroic, but she was a survivor, and she needed to know what her next step should be. She went into the makeup room and began removing the orange pancake from her face. Glad to be alone, she hurried through the procedure until all traces of it were gone. She then applied a light dusting of color to her cheeks and a clear lip gloss. Just as she was leaving, she nearly bumped into Sheila and Gregg.

"Oh, D. This is terrible. Those poor guys," Sheila, the hairdresser cried.

"Yes, I know," D. said, trying to get past Gregg, the makeup artist.

"You never know from one day to the next, do you?"

She looked at Gregg and smiled tightly. "No, you don't. I . . . I have to go," she added, leaving them and hurrying to her office.

She picked up her coat and purse and rushed out, only to almost fall over Dan, her boss.

"Hold on there, lady," Dan said, steadying her shoulders. "Where are you off to in such a hurry?"

"Nowhere, not really. I . . . I just have plans and I'm going to be late."

Dan looked at her closely and said, "You did a good job tonight. We were all rattled by the news."

She tried to breathe steadily, to keep her gaze on him and not look away. "Terrible news," she said, clutching her purse to her stomach as if it might stop the tightening of her muscles, making her feel sick.

Dan nodded. "Now you watch yourself tonight out there. All kinds of crazies on the road."

"I will," she answered, moving away from him.

As she left the news department and made her way to the foyer entrance, she wondered if Dan's words might be interpreted as a threat. Did they know about Tom's conversation with her? Did Dan talk to Mark, the station manager, who had first turned down the story?

Was she becoming paranoid?

Nodding to the security man on duty, she walked out the station and into the cold winter night. If she was scared, imagine what Tom was feeling . . . that is if he was conscious enough to feel. Please, please, she mentally prayed, let him be all right.

She took a cab to the hospital, figuring it was easier than trying to find parking at night. Plus, she didn't want to drive her car until she'd talked to Tom.

Walking up to the emergency entrance, D. saw the other networks vans and a group of police officers standing around talking. She headed for them.

"Hi, I'm Deborah Stark from Channel Four. Any idea how this happened?"

She'd seen it before, that sudden dawning of recognition as eyes widen. The young cop blinked once, then said, "From what I hear it was a gray Chevy, nineteen seventy-five, seventy-six, pretty beat up, but it was like a tank hitting the side of your van. Lucky for the two who wore seatbelts."

"What about Tom Harris? He was working in the back of the van. Any word on him yet?"

The cop asked another if Harris was still in the ER.

"I think he's in surgery now."

"Okay, thanks. If you hear anything more about this Chevy you'll let me know?" She handed him her business card.

"Sure. I'll give this to the officer in charge."

"Thanks again."

She stood for a moment out of time. No sense going to the waiting room yet if Tom was in surgery. God, she wished she smoked. At the very least she could use a stiff drink. She started pacing in the night, her hands rolled into fists in her pockets. She needed to talk to someone, someone who could give her advice. Everybody at the station was suspect right now, so who did that leave?

She pictured Maggie's face. Julian was entering politics and Maggie's father was a United States senator. But did she really want to involve Maggie in something that could prove to be dangerous? And then she remembered Marcus telling her about his close relationship with Senator Gabriel Burke. Marcus. He was intelligent. He would tell her to stop being paranoid. It wasn't late, barely after seven. Pulling out her phone, she flipped it open and went through the directory until she found his name and cell number. He did leave it with her receptionist and she would never be calling him first after their night together if it wasn't for this emergency. She started to dial his number and then stopped herself.

Now she didn't even trust her cell phone. She really was getting paranoid. Better safe than sorry, she told herself as she headed for the emergency room and the bank of phones against the wall.

When the phone was ringing, she bit her bottom lip in apprehension waiting for him to pick up.

"Marcus Bocelli."

She let her breath out in a rush of gratitude.

"Hello?"

"Marcus, it's me, D., Deborah."

"*Ciao, bella mia.*"

"Listen, I'm sorry for calling you but I didn't know who else to talk to."

"What's wrong, Deborah?"

She could hear the concern in his voice. "Maybe I'm just paranoid, but things are happening here that I find just too coincidental."

"What are you talking about? What things?"

"Do you remember me telling you about this reporter friend of mine who I thought was chasing down a conspiracy theory?"

"Yes . . . what's happened?"

"Marcus, this afternoon he was in my office and he showed me some of his research and it was pretty damning, involving building contractors, material suppliers and a connection to city hall and something called the Forsythe Group. Have you ever heard of them?"

His answer was slow in coming. "Yes."

"What do you know about them?"

"Too much to discuss over the phone, Deborah. Where are you?"

"Einstein Medical Center. Tonight one of Channel Four's vans was forced off the road and rolled off the Schuykill Expressway. It was a hit-and-run. Tom Harris, the reporter who showed me his files this afternoon, is in surgery right now and I think I'm getting paranoid because he tried to get the story through the news department and was flatly turned down and then told to let it go. Tom says our network is owned by Nova Communications who in turn is owned by the Forsythe Group. I am paranoid, right? Tell me I am."

"Deborah, do you know where his research is?"

"No. He was going to make me copies. I was expecting them tomorrow."

"Perhaps it's best you don't have them right now. Look, it's going to take me about three hours to get there. Do you want to meet at the hospital or your apartment?"

A wave of relief washed over her. "You're coming here?"

"I have to make a few phone calls and rearrange some things, but I'll try to get to you before midnight."

"You don't know how much I appreciate this, Marcus. I didn't know who else to talk to about it."

"You did the right thing by calling. And listen, Deborah, try to speak with Tom's family. Find out if anything else suspicious has taken place. And if your network sends over a specialist, try to get the family to use their own doctor."

"Okay, this is really sounding sinister and scaring me even more."

"Just do it. I'll get to you tonight."

"Thank you, Marcus. You're a life saver, or at least a sanity saver."

"*Ciao*. And be careful, Deborah. I don't think you are paranoid."

She listened as the receiver went silent and then hung up the phone.

Now to find her way to the surgical waiting room.

14

D. made a pot of coffee and began pacing her living room, watching the clock, waiting for the phone to ring and announce Marcus' arrival. She kept going over everything in her head from the first lunch with Tom in the park to speaking with his fiancée in the waiting room of the hospital. There was really nothing to go on without Tom's file. She considered returning to the office and searching his desk, but she doubted he would keep anything so volatile at the station when both Dan and Mark had told him to drop it, and she didn't want to make anyone suspicious by searching another employee's filing cabinet. What else was she supposed to do? Was her own job safe?

She kept thinking about Arron Weiss found hanging in his apartment. Everyone in broadcasting had been shocked. Now, more than ever, she didn't believe it was suicide. He exposed the corruption, named names and was punished for it. Maybe just like they were punishing Tom. Who would be next?

When her phone rang she jumped like a startled rabbit and ran to the kitchen. "Yes."

"You have a visitor, Miss Stark. Marcus Bocelli."

"Send him right up. Thanks."

She hung up the phone and walked to her door. Opening it, she listened to the elevator, willing him to appear.

"Marcus!" she breathed in relief, walking out to meet him in the hallway.

He looked tired as he wrapped his arms around her and led her back to her apartment. "How are you?"

"Great, now that you're here. I'm so sorry to have put you through this tonight. I just didn't know who else to turn to. I can't go to the station for help."

"No, you did the right thing by calling me."

She closed the door and held out her hands for his leather bomber jacket. He was dressed in jeans and a white shirt and looked wonderful. Chiding herself for even thinking those thoughts at such a time, she said, "I made a pot of coffee. Do you want a cup?"

"Good idea," he answered, walking around the living room as though to stretch his legs after the long drive. "How is your friend?"

"He has some fractured ribs, a damaged spleen they operated on, but they're mostly concerned with the brain hemorrhage. They're putting him into a coma while they try and treat it."

"Sounds serious."

"It is," she said, bringing him the coffee. "Tom's poor fiancée was devastated. I told her what you said about bringing in their own doctor, someone she knew and trusted, but she wasn't convinced, I'm afraid. I didn't want to scare her too much, but asked her to contact me if there's any change of specialists. I also asked if she knew anything about Tom's file. She said she didn't. And I didn't want to push."

Marcus nodded as he sat next to her. He picked up his cup and took a drink. "Let's hope she stays in touch."

"I'm planning on going back to the hospital tomorrow morning," D. said, holding her mug in her hands.

"There's no point in going back until he awakens. If you keep appearing at his bedside, someone may get suspicious. All they know right now is that Tom talked to you about his research."

"Marcus, who are *they*, besides those who are running Channel Four? What do you know about this Forsythe Group?"

He sat back and blew his breath out in a tired rush. "I am not sure where to start."

"Start anywhere. I want to know."

"First of all they are very smart and, when crossed, they are very dangerous. They've had countless years to build their strength. It goes back a very long time ago, Deborah. Some say from the time of Christ. I, myself, think it's farther back than that."

"What?" she asked in disbelief. The reporter in her wanted to argue conspiracy theory again, but she bit her bottom lip and allowed him to continue . . . for now. She would wait and see what else he offered.

He nodded. "Yes, they've used different names for themselves down through the centuries and in this time it's the Forsythe Group. Powerful wealthy families believed they were special, their bloodlines were special. After they convinced themselves of their rights, they had to convince what they thought of as the common people such a drastically unbalanced distribution of wealth was divinely ordained. Think, Deborah . . . why when the unfortunate, who have always far outnumbered the fortunate, why have they not risen up for equality of wealth? There is more than enough on this planet for every single being to live happily."

She shrugged her shoulders, not having really thought about it that way. "Fear?"

"Yes, but fear of whom?"

"Wait a minute, wait a minute," she demanded. This was all becoming too surreal for her. What the hell had she stepped into? "How do you know all this?"

Marcus sighed deeply. "Deborah, I have been interested in the Forsythe Group nearly all of my adult life."

"Why?" she demanded, the reporter in her trying to surface.

"Fear," Marcus replied. "This group thrives on fear and I have spent most of my life trying to create a balance against it."

"How? What do you do?" She was staring at him as the questions raced through her brain. Who *was* this man seated next to her?

He looked down into his coffee cup, blinking, thinking.

"Marcus, who are you? What do you do?" she repeated.

"I've told you," he answered in a low voice. "I work to help balance out fear. What I am trying to explain to you is this fear you have named goes back before recorded history. Think of it this way . . . if you are programmed to believe the king is divine, god on earth, you don't question. You respect his bloodline and those he gives attention to, even if it is taking your property and handing it over to the king's family or friends. When man was convinced that kingship, leadership, equaled divine order, man gave up his freedom and allowed greed to flourish. People stopped thinking for themselves. They gave up their power and power is a very potent seduction. The more you have, the more you want, and the more willing you are to do anything to keep it, and the most effective way is to instill fear of God. You begin to believe you must be special and the common person is not your equal. They are beneath you, to be manipulated, to increase your coffers which increases your power. They are pawns in a game of greed."

Okay, it made sense so far. She give him this one, but she

was still skeptical. "So the powerful, like in the Forsythe Group, band together against the poor?"

Marcus nodded.

She still wasn't satisfied. "But we're not talking about ancient history here. This is the twenty-first century and my friend is in a coma. I want to know why."

"You have to understand this group is very old, very organized, very powerful, and to take root in America is a long time ambition."

"So you believe this has happened?"

"I know it's already happened," he answered. "Look, what I'm telling you is hard to understand. That's why I'm giving you this historical background. Just listen before you make up your mind."

"Okay, go ahead." She stated in a concerned voice, while trying to hide her impatience. "Give me the history."

Marcus nodded, closed his eyes for a moment, as though gathering his thoughts, and then began speaking. "When Rousseau wrote *The Social Contract* in the seventeen hundreds and directly challenged for the first time in nearly two thousand years the idea that people must be governed by a powerful father figure king, pope, or feudal lord, he stated truth. Man was born free, and he is everywhere in chains."

"You're still talking history here," she challenged, wanting to believe him, but needing him to get to the point. People's lives were at stake, maybe even her own.

"Be patient. You learn from studying the past. In the beginning of your own country, Jefferson, Madison, Washington, Franklin . . . they rejected the belief that society was weak and evil and would disintegrate without kings, popes or being ruled by a rich elite. Those men turned seven thousand years of history on its head by setting up a form of government where the people themselves rule through elected officials answerable to the voters, the people."

"But we don't have kings anymore, at least most coun-

tries have done away with royalty," D. said, needing to
counter his words with reality. Because if what he was saying was true, then this went beyond anything Tom Harris
had suspected. "No one looks at royalty any longer and
thinks they're divine. Read the headlines of the last twenty
years."

Again Marcus sighed. He finished the last of his coffee,
set the cup on the table and answered in a tired voice, "These
families have existed for thousands upon thousands of years.
Their bloodlines are meticulously maintained. What we see
today as the Forsythe Group began in the Middle East during its occupation by Rome. Select families were included as
it spread throughout the Roman Empire, from the Persian
Empire to the Ottoman Empire into what became Europe
and now here to the United States. There have been times
when the people are inspired by someone, and a rebellion
rises up against them. They appease the people and give up
their titles, move their families around the globe, adopt different religions or countries or names, but in actuality give
up little real power. They fabricate a crisis by blurring the
facts, then orchestrate chaos and profit from it. They are
diplomats, heads of State, reclusive munitions manufactur-
ers, natural resource pirates, banking thieves. They arrange
private treaties between themselves and are not concerned
with the aftermath of chaos as much as the profit. It's a very
exclusive group of families and most who belong are kept at
the fringes of the real power plays."

D. saw it all laid out before her and what he was saying
was overwhelming. Everything she had believed was being
challenged. Still, the reporter in her had to be appeased.
"What's the objective, besides money and power?"

"To create an elite ruling class, a one world order with
them pulling the strings behind the curtain."

"Oh my God . . ." D. remembered Tom had used that

phrase, a one world order, and she thought he was a nut case. What did that make the man next to her? Certifiable?

"Yes, exactly," Marcus murmured. "And they are gaining in power." He looked directly at her. "Can't you feel the shift? Don't you see it in people's eyes? People are frightened. Deborah, there is a battle taking place between those who believe that free people can govern themselves and have the right to keep out powerful interests that would corrupt government, and those who believe a powerful father figure is necessary and the people should be kept largely in ignorance . . . the rich know better, and We, The People, will only behave when there is a common power to keep them in awe. There seems no way to stop the corruption at all levels of government, up to the highest offices. Right here in your own country no longer is there transparency, with those in power answering to the people, the citizens who put them there. Many are falling asleep in their lives, giving up their most powerful rights for the illusion of security, promised by those who can't deliver. If anything, this group doesn't want security. They use any natural disaster to further their cause. Turmoil creates tension, and they count on tension to distract the people and fuel their objectives."

She was silent for a few moments, trying to digest all he was telling her. "So . . . this Forsythe Group is actually a conspiracy stretching back through time?" she asked, feeling that saying it aloud only made it more unbelievable. "To keep the poor people poor and the rich people rich?"

"Yes." Marcus closed his eyes briefly, then spoke. "Deborah, I know you're finding it hard to understand—"

"I *don't* understand." And she didn't. How could something like this exist?

"I know you don't, but keep in mind light is far more powerful than darkness. Light one candle and the darkness immediately recedes to the shadowy corners. That's what I do, try to keep it to the corners. You're going to have to trust me when I tell you that by following your instincts tonight in calling me, you are playing an important but dangerous role. Do you remember when I said I choose to remain invisible and you were filled with disbelief?"

She nodded.

"It is because the work I do is about balancing out the darkness with light. I know that must sound naïve to you, but there is much you can't possibly understand yet. Usually my work is on a one-to-one basis, helping one fear-filled person at a time. I think I told you I don't believe in coincidences. It is not by chance that all of this is happening at this time, nor that you and I have been brought together. I know how to remain invisible, Deborah. Unfortunately, you do not and I can't protect you around the clock. You have to be very, very careful how you proceed from here on. I made some calls before I left and there are now others who are aware of this situation."

"Others?" she asked, wondering how her fairly sane and predictable life had been turned upside down.

"Yes. People I have worked with in the past. Don't be surprised if there is a new doorman in your lobby, or a new cleaning person at your office. I will do all I can to prevent anything happening to you, but you must also be vigilant. Take nothing for granted. Be awake in your life, Deborah. It may save it."

"You're scaring me."

He reached out to take her into his arms. "Don't be afraid. That's what they want, what they thrive on. Instead, stay in the moment. It is, in truth, the only place you are alive, and watch for the signs to lead you. They'll be there, I promise."

She must be insane, because she was starting to believe him. Poor Tom had no idea what he was getting into, and now he was in a coma fighting for his life. "I don't know that I can do this, Marcus." It was the truth.

He squeezed her tighter. "Of course you can. You didn't just walk into this, Deborah. You made a choice by asking to see Tom's research again. You're a player in it now. You're a piece of the puzzle, and you have what is called street smarts, yes? You're also intelligent and you have finely honed instincts as a reporter. Use them. They won't fail you."

To hell with being a reporter. Right then she felt like a terrified kid! "But I don't know *what* to do!" she cried, clinging to his shirt. "If what you are telling me is the truth, I could be the next one they want to silence."

He didn't say anything for a few moments, so she took that opportunity to tell him about Arron Weiss. "He had just won the Pulitzer for an exposé on the drug wars. His wife had just given birth to twins. There was no logical reason for him to have committed suicide until that mistress showed up and everyone just accepted her story of a guilty conscience. It put to rest everyone's fears and the story was dropped in a week. But now I don't believe it. Not after talking to Tom, and especially not after what you've just told me about this Forsythe Group. For all I know they could be planning how to rid of me at this very moment."

He kissed her forehead and whispered against her skin, "Deborah, wake up. All you ever really had was this moment, and then the next. Nothing is real, save moment by moment. We flash into and out of existence beyond the speed of light. When you know nothing is real and plans are all illusions, you are free. You use your will and make your choices, not based on fear of the future, but on your own instincts and senses in the moment. There is something wondrous within you that has guided you this far. Trust that it is there now and will be there when you need it. In this moment you are safe. Fear not your death, Deborah. You will save yourself. There is nothing more threatening to the darkness than a person who doesn't fear death."

"How do you not fear death?" she asked in a tiny voice,

feeling like a child to put forth the question. But, seriously, how do you *not* fear death?

"Because it's not the end, *bella mia,* only the beginning of another adventure."

"How do you know that?"

"Someday, perhaps, I can tell you, but believe me when I say you take you with you. That same *you* within, who you were as a young child? And who is still there? Unchanged by time or circumstance?"

She simply nodded.

"*That* you begins a new adventure."

"But I was just starting to really like this one!"

He chuckled. "You will not go anywhere, Deborah, until you have fulfilled your purpose for being here. Now, stop your foolish talk and look at me."

She raised her head, desperately trying to keep the tears from running down her cheeks.

He was smiling into her eyes with such tenderness that her resolve broke and salty tears blurred her vision and trickled over her lids.

"Do you know the very best way to dissolve the fear of death?"

"Hm?" she asked, sniffling as he used his thumb to wipe away her tears.

"You celebrate your life with love."

"Yeah?"

He nodded. "Yeah."

She stared at him, his dark soulful eyes, his sensual mouth. She wanted all this crazy talk of conspiracies to go away, to recede, if only for tonight. "Then how do you say make love to me in Italian again?" she whispered.

Smiling with tenderness, he said, "*Facciamo l'amore.*"

"*Facciamo l'amore,* Marcus. Please . . ."

"Only this time, *tesaro mia,* we will take our time," he whispered, standing and pulling her up to him. His mouth against her lips, he breathed, "And before you ask, I called you my treasure. Let me show you how precious you really are."

He kissed her long and slow, tenderly biting her bottom lip and then teasing her with the tip of his tongue. His arms were encircling her, pulling her against him and she moaned as the length of him made contact with her.

When the kiss ended, she leaned her forehead against his chin and murmured, "Wow . . . this is gonna be intense, isn't it?"

He simply nodded as he took her hand and led her toward her bedroom.

Stopping at her bathroom, Marcus asked, "What about a warm shower?" He began unbuttoning her blouse and then smiled as he added, "It was a long drive for me and I'd like to join you, if I may."

Moments later, with warm soapy water covering their bodies and hands gliding over skin, D. had to admit it was working. The last thing she was thinking about was the Forsythe Group and any danger that might be coming her way. She didn't even want to think about the danger to her heart for, despite all reasoning, she really was falling in love with Marcus.

And who could blame her?

"Are you for real?" she whispered when he was holding her in his arms, running his hand ever so gently over her hip as they laid together in her bed. She could feel all that ice inside of her cracking a little at a time. She had spent so many years building it up around her heart and now it was slowly melting, softening her, making her vulnerable.

He smiled with tenderness. "I am, Deborah. I am as real as I know how to be."

She kissed him, breathing in the clean male scent of him as she ran her fingers through his soft curls. "I want to believe you."

"I have no reason to lie to you," he whispered back, bring his hand up to her breast and lowering his head. "Right here, right now, nothing exists but this moment we are sharing."

When he drew her nipple into his mouth, she gasped as the sudden pleasure raced down her body, infusing her with desire. He took his time, exploring her, adoring her, until she pulled him up and opened herself to accept him. All of him this time. This time she wasn't holding anything back. It was as if they were bonded together, fused into one being, and as the hunger grew in intensity, she looked up into his eyes and nearly cried out. He was staring at her in silence as he moved slowly, deliberately, looking deep into her soul, and she knew he knew.

He had to know.

God help her, even though her head told her she was going to get hurt, her heart was rejoicing. She was falling in love. For the first time in her carefully planned out life, she was falling without a net.

She was asleep in his arms, her limbs heavy, her mind punch-drunk with exhaustion after hours of exquisite love-making. She knew she was dreaming, but a part of her wished it wasn't a nightmare where some animal was growling. It was low and threatening and trying to take her away from the peace she had found in slumber.

In her dream she reached out for Marcus, but he wasn't there. Her hand felt the sheet, cool without the heat of his body. She tried to wake up, to lift her head, to find him. She tried to open her eyes, desperate to shake off the dream. Her lids felt like heavy weights were attached to them, forcing her to make more of an effort. She did, and then attempted to look around her darkened bedroom.

All she could see was a shadowy figure standing at the

door to her bedroom. In her sleepy fog, she felt that sudden jolt of heat in her chest, warning her of danger, but it was a dream . . . wasn't it?

And then she heard the growl again, low and threatening, backing the shadowy figure away from the doorway. She tried to call to Marcus, but his name stuck in her throat as though her voice were paralyzed. She heard the growl down her hallway until she was straining to listen and then she thought she heard the door open and close.

D. pushed herself up on her elbow and shook her head. She had to wake up. It was the only way to end this frightening dream. Dragging herself to the edge of the mattress, she swung her legs over the side and used the night table for support as she stood. Her legs felt like they might buckle under her and she forced herself to straighten, to pull together whatever strength she had to wake up and find Marcus. She made it to the doorway and held onto the molding as she stared down the hallway and beyond the dining table.

In the dim light from the street her eyes were able to focus and she felt her mouth dropping open in disbelief as she watched the image of a huge dog begin to swirl, dissolve, and then transform into a nude man.

Her nude man.

Marcus.

She blinked, willing her mind to wake up, to find herself in bed next to him, to touch him for reassurance and laugh at this bizarre nightmare. She was dreaming. She had to be dreaming . . . and then he turned to her and started walking in her direction.

She held up her trembling hand, as though to stop the apparition from coming closer to her. This shadowy specter could not be the same man who had made love to her tonight.

God, please, she mentally begged . . . *make me wake up! Make this go away!*

"Deborah."

He said her name! This thing, whatever it was, called out to her.

"No . . . please, no. Go away," she pleaded, forcing the words out of her dry throat.

"Deborah, calm down," he said, reaching out for her.

She backed up, holding onto the wall for support as she tried to retreat from this nightmare. It wasn't Marcus before her. It couldn't be. "I just want to wake up," she cried as the thing in Marcus' body closed the distance between them.

When it touched her, taking her wrist, she started screaming. She heard the sounds of her screams, but no one else could for it was a dream, a terrible, terrible dream . . .

She was trapped in the thing's arms, her back to it, a hand over her mouth to muffle her cries for help. Why couldn't she wake up and end this horror?

"Deborah," it whispered into her ear. "Stop it. Calm down. I am not going to hurt you."

She couldn't believe it, but she also felt as though she might be dying as her heart was slamming into the wall of her chest and her whole body felt on fire with fear as she tried to free her arms, to tear his hand away from her mouth.

"Breathe in through your nose. Deeply. Now. Do it!" he commanded, her body still trapped against his.

Not wanting to die, even in a dream, she did as she was directed, breathing in deeply through her nose . . . over and over again.

"Now listen to me," he said. "I'm going to remove my hand and you are not going to scream. You are all right. You're here in your apartment. You are safe." He waited a few moments as she continued to breathe.

"Are you all right now?" he asked in a soft voice that sounded just like Marcus.

She nodded, even though what she felt was the exact opposite.

His fingers loosened around her mouth and she gasped for a deeper breath. "Let me go," she said, her voice raspy with fear.

He continued to hold her tightly. "I'm sorry you saw that, Deborah."

She struggled against his hold. "Let me go. I want to wake up!"

"You are awake."

They were three common words, yet the sound of them breaking the silence, the meaning of them in the shadowy darkness of night, was chilling.

"I can't be awake," she whimpered, suddenly feeling like her world was reeling and she was fighting for her sanity. "This is a dream. It has to be a dream!"

"It's not a dream. Come back to bed with me, Deborah, and let me try to explain."

He must have felt all the fight drain from her muscles and he slowly released her, guiding her numb body to the bed. She allowed him to cover her, barely noticing how cold the sheets had become since she'd left it. She began to shake, not from the chill, but because she thought she was in the *Twilight Zone* . . . someplace surreal. Her mind wasn't fully functioning as he joined her in bed, gathering her into his arms and stroking the hair back from her face.

It couldn't have been real. What she saw . . .

"Deborah, I know you're frightened. I know you must feel as though you're in shock," he said while continuing to stroke her. "I wish the circumstances had been different, but I must now explain to you about myself."

"Yourself?" she mumbled stupidly, wondering if this too was a dream. All that stuff at her mother's house and now *this!* Surely she was losing her grip on reality.

She felt him nod above her head on his chest.

"I was asleep, holding you, when I was suddenly alerted to another presence in your apartment. A man came here tonight and his objective could only have been to search for a copy of that file and, if disturbed, to harm you or anyone else who might get in his way. Do you remember we discussed earlier that I preferred to go through life invisible to others who might not understand me?"

She could only nod, still not sure which was the dream and which was reality.

"I didn't tell you everything. In fact, I never would have revealed this part of me, if not for the urgency of the situation tonight . . . and what you saw."

She didn't respond. She had no words.

"I knew I had to protect you, both of us, tonight, but I didn't want whoever was in the apartment to see me, to be able to identify me at some later time. So I used the image of a guard dog to instill fear in the man."

She suddenly found the words. "You *used* the image of a guard dog? What the hell does that mean?"

She felt his hand tighten at her shoulder as he sighed deeply.

"In order to accomplish what I do in the world, sometimes I have to use methods not commonly known or accepted. It enables me to get into places, find out information, and get out again without revealing my identity. It has saved my life, and others, on more than one occasion."

She kept shaking her head. "But you said you used the image of a guard dog. How can *you* use the image of a dog? What do you do, transfer thoughts, or what?"

"No," he answered calmly. "I hold the image in my own mind," he paused. "And then I become what I've envisioned."

She found her strength and raised her head from his chest. Moving away so she could see his face, she sat up and pulled the covers over her breasts. "You are telling me you became that dog I saw?" Yes, heaven help her, those were the words that came out of her mouth.

When he nodded, she knew her trip to the *Twilight Zone* wasn't over. It was intensifying.

"Okay, this is insane," she declared, shaking her head again. "You're trying to tell me you're a . . . a . . . what?"

"The word you are searching for is shapeshifter. Yes, Deborah, I am a shapeshifter."

She had always known he was too good to be true.

He was delusional, a crazy man prone to hallucinations.

She was in bed with a lunatic. And what was worse, it was contagious . . . for she'd *seen* the very thing he had described.

'I can feel your fear."

She half laughed. "Well, good, because that means you aren't completely delusional. My fear is real. Marcus, what you're saying isn't possible. It simply isn't!"

"Then explain what you saw."

"I can't! I only know I had a nightmare that matched yours and now you're trying to get me to believe it's real. Maybe you need medication. Maybe I need medication. Ever since you came into my life all sorts of crazy things have been happening."

"It comes with the territory, Deborah. I tried to warn you off."

"What do you mean, it comes with the territory?"

Again, he sighed, as though very tired. She didn't care. She needed answers when she was fighting for her own sanity. "What did you mean?" she repeated in a stronger voice.

"Many times, when I enter someone's life, things start to happen. Unexplainable things. Fears come to the surface to be resolved. Their life is altered because I tend to vibrate on a slightly higher frequency than what is perceived as normal."

"Vibrate? What are you?" she demanded. "An alien?"

He cracked a slight smile. "No. Just a human being who

was fortunate to have had a mentor in life who could show me the possibilities. One of them being how to raise my vibration and manipulate matter. I apologize for the way you found out about me, but I don't apologize for who I am."

"But *who are you,* Marcus?" she demanded again. "You aren't normal!"

"I would hope not," he answered calmly. "Why would I want to be, when I'm unique? As are you and every other human being on this planet. Each of us comes into this life with gifts. I know what mine are, and I try to help others discover theirs."

"But you're saying your gift is being a . . ." She threw her head back and stared at the shadows on the ceiling. "I can't even say it."

"Shapeshifter." He said it for her. "Now, you can either slowly accept what I'm telling you or think I am unbalanced. I can't make that choice for you. But what we really should be discussing is the fact that you are in immediate danger here. You need to leave Philadelphia as quickly as possible."

Her head jerked back into place and she stared at his profile in the fading darkness. "I can't leave Philadelphia. I have a job. I can't simply walk out." He was crazy.

"Take a leave of absence. Do what you have to do, but you must leave this city."

"What you're asking is too much!" she protested. "I'm on television five nights a week. I have a high profile. No one is going kill me."

"Do I need to remind you of others with a much higher profile whose lives have been extinguished? If leaders of countries can be eliminated, you can too. You are nothing to them, Deborah, a nuisance, a minor move on a massive chess board. You need to take seriously what happened here tonight. Someone got into your apartment and they didn't break down the door. Besides searching for the file, they probably were going to set up listening devices. Whoever it was knew how to get to you. You were here and they were prepared to deal with you if they had to. Now you must make a choice. Your life or your career."

"You're trying to scare me into a decision," she complained, desperate for sanity. "How can I possibly make a sane decision after what I've seen tonight and what you've told me. And now you want me to jeopardize everything I've worked for because of it?"

"Did you see the man?"

"What?"

"I asked if you saw the man tonight."

She let her breath out slowly, deliberately. "I thought I saw the shadow of a man, but I also thought I was dreaming, having a nightmare."

"You know this is real. Don't listen to your fears of what will happen to your job. Your job is the least of your concerns right now. You wouldn't have called me if you already didn't know this possibility was real. What do your instincts tell you about this entire situation? About your safety?"

She hated that he was right. Everything inside of her was saying run away, hide. Find a safe place and figure out her next move. She knew he was waiting for her answer, yet her head with filled with so many thoughts flying around and bumping into each other, making no sense.

"Deborah?"

She swallowed. "I guess I could say I didn't take enough time to recover from my mother's death and I want to get away. I have vacation time coming. I could say I want to go some place warm. Maybe the islands."

"You would have to take a plane and they could easily find out whether or not you boarded."

"You think they'd check?"

"I don't take anything for granted, especially when it concerns this group."

"So what's your suggestion?"

He was silent for a few moments. "You go into work and tell them your story. Wear something casual, like jeans and a neutral raincoat. Have your bags with you. I'm sure you can convince your superiors that your emotional state is fragile. They won't want you on the air if they're not sure you can handle the pressure. Meanwhile I'll arrange for your trip. You go straight to the airport after you leave the television station. Check in, go through airport security and then use the nearest ladies room."

"Why?" she asked, amazed he could formulate a plan so easily that was going to throw her life into this madness that had descended upon her.

"Because you are going to switch places with someone. Give her your ticket and your passport. You'll get it back, I promise. Then you'll leave the ladies room, looking like you have just gotten off a plane. Go outside. I will meet you in a taxi cab and then we'll come back to the city and pick up my car."

"But how will this person get through security when she lands?"

"She will. Don't worry about it."

It might work, she thought, not quite believing she was having this conversation. It sounded so . . . so cloak and dagger. And crazy. Definitely crazy. "Who is this woman and how do you know she will do it?"

"You don't need to know that, Deborah. There are others, besides myself, who are aware of the Forsythe Group and who are doing their part to balance out the darkness."

"Is she like you? A . . . shapeshifter?" There. She said the word, making it almost real.

"I won't discuss another's assignment with you, so please don't ask any more. Just know I am trying to protect you, Deborah. I did it tonight and I will do it for as long as necessary, but you have to cooperate."

As crazy as it was, he did protect her tonight. She had

seen the shadowy figure and Marcus had warned her awake while making the intruder leave. A *shapeshifter?* Nothing in her logical reporter's life had prepared her to abandon hard reasoning and trust in what could only be termed the paranormal. But she had seen it all with her own eyes.

A tight lump formed in her throat, making it difficult to speak as her once rational world disintegrated and was replaced by stuff from a science fiction movie. But it had happened. She had seen it. And she knew she was in danger.

"Thank you, Marcus . . ." she said, forcing the words out. "Thank you for protecting me. I'm not sure of anything any longer, but I think I can trust you."

He brought her back into the circle of his arms and kissed her forehead with tenderness.

"Be brave, *bella mia.* You are not alone."

She closed her eyes in gratitude, exhaustion and, finally, surrender.

15

"Any news on Tom Harris?" she asked the security guard as she walked into work.

"Last I heard he's still in a coma. The cops found the car abandoned in North Philly. Clean as a whistle. No prints."

Dressed in jeans, flat shoes and sunglasses, D. simply nodded as she passed into the station, pulling her small black suitcase behind her. She couldn't look more nondescript and would blend into any crowd. She was even wearing a tan cashmere winter hat. That had been Marcus' idea. She would switch hats with the woman at the airport. D. wanted to be cool, collected, look like she knew what she was doing, but she was terrified. She had to keep reminding herself to breathe, Marcus' strong suggestion, for she found the muscles in her body in a perpetual state of tension.

It wouldn't be difficult to convince Dan and Mark she was teetering on the edge of self control. Considering that she may be the next target of an international cabal and her only ally at the moment was a shapeshifter, it was the truth. Now all she had to do was get into her office, take care of a few things, and then face her boss.

As she came into the news room, she called out to Pam, her P.A. "Good morning."

"You're here early."

"I know," she answered, stopping.

"What's with the suitcase? Are you going on assignment? I wasn't told."

"It's personal," she said, not lying. "Anything I need to see? Mail? Interoffice memos or files?"

Pam flipped through the paperwork on her desk. "Nothing unusual. You expecting something?"

"No, not really, just want to take care of anything that's outstanding. Will you find out if you can get me in to see Dan ASAP?"

"Sure, let me check with Marti and see what his schedule is today."

D. removed her sunglasses, knowing her face would show the effects of last night. "Tell Marti that I need to see her boss before eleven. It's important."

"Are you okay, D.? You look . . . I don't know . . . tried."

"That's putting it mildly," she said, walking toward her office. "Call Marti, okay?"

"I'm on it," Pam said, picking up the phone.

D. figured she was laying her groundwork. When Pam was questioned, as she would be, she could honestly say D. looked tired, maybe even terrible. An insane night and no makeup will do that to a woman. She paused at Tom Harris' desk, looked at the clutter, and casually opened the filing cabinet next to it.

"Looking for something, D.?" Mary, another researcher, asked.

D. shook her head and closed the cabinet. "Not really. Just wondering if anyone's going to the hospital today."

"I think Dan is going this afternoon. We're all still pretty shaken."

D. simply nodded as she moved away from the desk and

continued down the hallway. There was no way to check Tom's files without arousing suspicion, but she didn't think he would have left them in the office anyway. So what was she to do without them?

Walking into her office, she closed the door, put her suitcase in the corner and hung up her coat and hat. She looked around the space she had once thought was so glamorous, a private office away from the noisy cubicles outside. What if she lost it all? Everything she had worked so hard to achieve? What the hell would she do?"

Marcus' words echoed inside her head.

Her life or her career.

She'd made her choice last night when she had accepted her life was in danger. Now she just had to follow a plan. Get through today, she told herself. Take it one step at a time. Moment by moment . . .

The phone on her desk rang and D. was jolted back to the present. She picked up the receiver while sitting down. "Yes?"

"Marti said Dan can see you in a half hour."

D. found herself holding her breath again with tension and she silently exhaled. "Thanks, Pam."

"Anything else? Coffee? Massage? A week at a California spa?"

Despite the circumstances, D. smiled. "The spa sounds heavenly, but I'm making plans of my own, thanks. Remember I won that trip to Bermuda at the Dalton-Rhymes charity auction all those months ago?"

"Right. You did. You're going?"

"If I can clear it with Dan."

There was a pause.

"Well, good for you," Pam said, sounding like she really meant it. "So you won't be here for Christmas?"

She hadn't even thought of that. "No. I won't."

"I'll just give you your gift when you get back then."

Christmas presents. Usually a last-minute shopper, D. realized they were even lower on her priority list than before. "It's a deal. And I'll pick up something tropical for you. Now let me clear my desk before my meeting."

She hung up the receiver and started organizing her desk while looking around to see if Tom had dropped off the file for her. But he couldn't have . . . He never came back from the remote shoot. She got her purse and returned to the desk. Taking out a small card with a number on it, she called the hospital and waited until she was connected with intensive care.

No change. Tom Harris was still in a coma.

More determined than ever, D. cleared her clutter, checked her email, looked at her watch and began tapping her fingernail with impatience.

Ten minutes.

And then she would see how good an actress she was.

When the time came D. walked through the news room, acknowledging those she made eye contact with and took a deep steadying breath as she walked up to Marti's desk.

"He's expecting you," she said, waving her hand toward Dan's office.

"Thanks," D. answered, wishing that half of Dan's walls weren't glass. It would be so much easier if this were a private performance.

She knocked twice and opened the door.

"Dan?"

He was seated at his cluttered desk. Behind him was a huge chart, marking out assignments and schedules. In his fifties, Dan appeared older with the enormous responsibility of running a major broadcast newsroom weighing heavily on his shoulders. He always looked disheveled, like he had fallen into his clothes. And, despite the company policy on smoking, his office held the lingering acrid scent of room spray mixed with tobacco smoke. "Come in, come in."

"Hi, Dan," she said, closing the door behind her. "Thanks for seeing me on such short notice."

"Always have time for my star anchor, D. How are you? You look tired."

She half smiled. "I am tired, Dan. That's part of what I want to discuss with you. I have a huge request to make." Her heart started beating faster, harder, and she felt the adrenaline pumping through her veins. Her hands began shaking and she clasped them tightly together to get some control.

"What's up?"

Feeling suddenly that she couldn't trust anyone around her, D. experienced a tightness in her throat and a burning sensation gather at her eyes. She tried to control her emotions, wondered if it might be best if she really did cry, and then cleared her throat as her vision blurred with tears. "I . . . I need some time off, Dan," she began, not knowing if Dan was innocent of her suspicions. How much did he really know? She began wringing her hands. "You see, last night after I heard about the accident with our guys, I went home and . . . and all of a sudden it hits me . . . about my mother and . . . and it really slammed me hard. After the funeral I got right back to work, put it behind me and . . . and I guess I never really dealt with it."

Incredibly, D. realized she wasn't acting.

Everything she said *was* true, save the fact she didn't realize how true until it came out of her mouth. "I'm a mess, Dan. I don't feel like I can go on the air until I deal with this."

"God, I'm sorry, D. You're always so strong. I thought you were okay."

She couldn't look at him. Better to keep her eyes down as she wiped away a tear from her cheek. Shrugging, she said, "I thought so too. I . . . I've never missed work, except for the funeral, and I have vacation time I can use. I hate to drop all this in your lap, but I just don't know what else to do. I can't go on the air like this."

"You're right, of course. The timing isn't that bad. We'll manage. It's Christmas and there's no lack of features." He paused, as thought hesitating. "You know Mark is going to push for Andrea to fill in, don't you?"

Sniffling, she looked up at her boss. "I know she's ambitious, and I might as well tell you I know about the office gossip concerning Mark. I simply don't know what else to do, Dan. It's a gamble I have to take. I need to get away and . . . and get a grip on myself."

"I can see that. How long?"

"At least a week. Do you remember I won that getaway to Bermuda at the Dalton-Rhymes charity auction? I might as well use it."

"When are you leaving?"

"I have an early afternoon flight. I brought my bag to the office."

He looked behind him to the schedule and said, "I'll shuffle things around. We'll announce you're on vacation. Have you told Matt yet?"

She shook her head. "I wanted to talk to you first. I don't think he'll have a problem. He's co-anchored with Andrea before."

Dan nodded. "Well, get some rest and . . . and do whatever you have to," he added. "I don't know what else to tell you, D. Thirty years in hard news and I'm still at a loss about personal grief, but you know what I mean."

"I do," she said, standing up. "And thanks, Dan. I appreciate your understanding. I just need a little time."

"You've got it. Now let me get started on this."

She nodded, wanting to shake his hand, but he was already reaching for the telephone. "Thanks again."

It was done.

She was gambling everything on the advice of Marcus Bocelli, a man who had come into her life like a hurricane, sweeping away logic and making her consider things she would have laughed at had she not witnessed them with her own eyes.

He'd damn well better not be crazy.

The Philadelphia airport was bustling with activity. Commuters were rushing to or from their business or holiday destinations and D. found herself in the midst of it all, trying to keep composed, not look over her shoulder or think every single person who glanced at her was keeping tabs or talking into their wristwatches.

She had to keep the paranoia at bay.

Finally approaching the check-in counter, D. took out her passport and said, "I should have an e-ticket waiting for me."

The young woman smiled and asked, "Your name?"

"Deborah Stark," she answered, keeping her sunglasses in place as she found the paper she'd printed out on her home laptop with her confirmation number on it.

She watched as the ticket agent took the paper across the counter and started typing her name into her computer, then searching the monitor.

"Here we are. Deborah Stark. Flight 346. Destination Hamilton, Bermuda. Do you have luggage?"

"Just a carry-on."

"A preference for an aisle seat or window?"

"It doesn't matter." And it didn't. Not for the first time she was reminded that some other woman was going to be seated on this flight and spend time in a luxurious hotel overlooking that beautiful pink sandy beach where she and Marcus first made love. Well, it wasn't love. Not then. More like uncontrolled lust and—

"Your passport?" the woman asked, interrupting the totally inappropriate thoughts.

Sliding the dark blue booklet across the counter, D. chided herself. She simply had to keep her mind on her mission.

Dear God, she was even thinking about it as a mission. Like she was in a spy novel. Blowing her breath out in frustration, D. straightened her shoulders and waited for the woman to return her passport. That was another thing she wasn't thrilled about. Handing over her passport to a stranger in a bathroom had to be breaking some kind of law.

The agent gave her back the passport, then asked the standard questions about packing luggage.

"I did," D. answered. "No, no one has asked me to carry anything for them." She thought of the luggage she had dragged behind her all morning. Inside were clothes she no longer wore and had planned on giving away. But at least she'd told the truth. She had packed the bag.

D. heard the ticket being printed out and her shoulders dropped a good inch in relief.

"Your flight to Hamilton will be departing at Gate 5, Terminal C. That's up the escalator and to your right. You'll see the signs at the security check-in."

D. nodded as she accepted the formal airline ticket folder. "Thank you."

She put everything into her purse and was turning away when the woman called out her name again.

"Ms. Stark?"

D. thought she might be having a heart attack at her chest seemed to explode with the burning heat of fear. She turned back. "Yes?"

"I always watch you on the evening news. Channel Four is my favorite."

"Thanks . . ." she breathed in relief. "Thank you very much."

The younger woman smiled brightly and D. felt her stiff dry lips trying to return any form of a smile.

"Have a good flight."

"Thanks again," D. muttered and headed away from the counter. Okay, she'd made it through that. Now all she had to do was get through security and then meet up with a stranger in the ladies room, switch places and get the hell out of here. She simply couldn't wait to relax somewhere safe. And a big strong drink would be greatly appreciated.

Would her life ever be normal again?

She tried to keep her mind blank as she stepped onto the escalator, but found the paranoia returning with every stranger she passed. Keeping her gaze down to the ever shortening moving stairs before her, D. realized she would make a terrible spy. It was one thing to report on news, on terrible things happening around the world. It was quite another to find herself in danger. The only news she wanted to make concerned advancing her career . . . which might just be in shambles by the time she returned to it.

Andrea Miller was going to make as much of D.'s time away as she could. D. couldn't even blame her. In the same situation, D. knew she'd do the same. It was a chance she was just going to have to take.

The escalator deposited her fifty feet from the security check-in gate.

She walked toward it, joining the line already waiting to pass through. Staring ahead, she watched the procedure. There was no reason why she wouldn't pass easily. When she approached the gate, she put her suitcase on the conveyor belt, followed by her purse, and held her breath as she walked between the metal detectors.

Smooth. No alarm bells ringing, though she did have to show her ticket and answer a few questions. She was a simple holiday traveler to Bermuda. No suspicions aroused. She picked up her belongings from the belt and looked for the nearest ladies room.

She saw the universal sign for women and clenched her back teeth as she headed for it. Marcus had said the woman would recognize her. He said she would ask if Philadelphia had a train from the airport into the city.

D. walked into the ladies room. There were several women inside and she walked to the empty middle bank of sinks. Putting her purse on the counter, she looked at herself in the mirror and wondered what she should do. Deciding to wash her hands, she was about to pump soap into her palm when she saw a tall woman wearing almost the exact color of beige raincoat stop at the next sink. D. looked at the woman wearing sunglasses in the mirror. The woman caught her staring and smiled.

"Airports can be so tiring," she said, placing her rolling overnight case next to her and putting her purse on the counter.

D. nodded and started to wash her hands. Maybe it wasn't her. What did she know about Marcus' friends, others who worked to balance out darkness? But that did look like her luggage, only the bigger case.

"By any chance, would you know if there's an express train into Philadelphia?"

Startled, even though she was expecting that question, D. fought to find her voice. "Ah, yes, there is," she muttered. "I believe it's right before you go into baggage claim."

The woman nodded. "Thanks. Nice hat."

Her hat. She was supposed to give her the hat.

Slipping it off her head, D. handed it to her. "Try it on," she said.

She watched the woman take the hat and begin stuffing her longer brown hair into it, pulling out a few shorter strands to frame her pretty face. Smiling, the woman said, "It's lovely."

D. ran a hand through her own hair as the woman kept the hat on, then opened her wide shoulder bag. She withdrew a tan silk scarf. "For you," she said, handing it over.

Realizing she was supposed to wear it, D. wrapped it around her head and tied it in the back.

"I don't want to miss my plane."

The woman looked at D.'s suitcase.

"Right," D. murmured, handing it over to the pretty woman who now looked eerily like her with the sunglasses and hat. "Anything else?" And then she remembered. The ticket and passport. She opened her purse, revealing both.

The woman looked at herself in the mirror, stretched her left arm to adjust the sleeve of her raincoat and deftly picked up the documentation. Despite the situation, D. was impressed.

"Well, I'm off. Have a nice holiday."

"Yes, You too," D. answered, picturing this woman enjoying her prize in Bermuda. She felt as though she was losing a lot of things that she'd thought had been important to her. At the top of her list was losing her belief in a rational world. Last night's experience had spun her around so dramatically that she didn't knew if she'd ever recover.

"Don't look so sad." The stranger then smiled, almost kindly. "They say when you have no choice, it is best to mobilize the spirit of courage." She then slid her purse off the counter, took the suitcase and turned away.

What was that supposed to mean? The spirit of courage?

D. stood at the bank of sinks, staring after the woman until she disappeared from view. She then looked down to the suitcase a few feet away. She had packed that one too early this morning, this one containing the clothes she would need for the coming week. Somehow, Marcus had accomplished what he said he'd do. Now all that was remaining was to wait a few minutes more and then leave the airport.

It was done.

A strange woman would take the plane to Bermuda, check in under Deborah Stark, and spend Christmas on a tropical island.

She, on the other hand, was to spend the time in hiding with Marcus Bocelli . . . which should have made her heart leap with joy, save for the fact he was a shapeshifter with ties to some secret organization that sounded right out of the *Twilight Zone*.

Yes . . . most definitely she'd left the rational world behind her.

16

"Wow . . . I wouldn't have expected this. Very nice."

Exhausted, D. looked around the living room of Marcus' apartment.

"Thank you," he answered from across the room as he squatted in front of a fireplace.

In truth, she didn't know what she had expected, probably a bachelor's apartment, but this first floor of a brownstone was decorated with taste. She might not have the talent to do it, but she sure as hell could recognize it when she saw it. Reminded of quiet, European elegance, D. pulled off her glove and ran her hand over the buttery soft back of a dark leather wing chair that flanked the deep chocolate sofa. Everything was in shades of cream and mocha down to the richness of the sofa. It was a man's room, yet one in which a woman felt comfortable.

Walking over to the table behind the sofa, she gazed down to the a gallery of pictures, ranging from old black and whites to colorful ones of children, maybe nieces and nephews. "Family?" she asked, holding up a silver framed portrait. Don't let him say the adorable boy is his!

.Marcus looked up from building his fire and nodded. "Mario. My sister's son."

"He's cute. Great smile."

"He is a charmer, even at so young an age."

"Must run in the family," she murmured, placing the frame back.

Satisfied with his fire, Marcus rose. "I'm sorry. I didn't hear you," he said as he joined her.

"I said it must run in the family. The male charmers."

Marcus grinned. "There aren't that many of us, as you can tell by the photographs. We are outnumbered by females. Now, may I take your coat?" he asked, holding out his hands.

She slipped out of the raincoat and handed it over.

"We'll get you settled soon," he said, walking over to a closet by the front door. He hung up her coat and then re- moved his bomber jacket. "Then I'll think about food. You must be hungry."

Her stomach felt raw from nerves. "I don't know if I could eat," she called out, taking in the good furniture, the small dining room with tall windows. It really was a very nice place. She wondered if he'd had help decorating. Or was that another of his many talents? Like turning into animals. She still found it hard to believe and felt as though she were in some bizarre movie that just kept on running.

"You should eat, Deborah. We can order something in, if you like."

She smiled. "At least you don't expect me to cook. You know what a dismal failure I am in the kitchen."

"Come sit in front of the fire," he said, still grinning and not denying her last statement. "I will bring you some brandy."

Brandy in front of the fire . . . sounded real nice after the day she'd had.

She sat in the matching leather chair by the fire and stared into the building flames. Now what was she supposed to do? Stay here in New York City? Somehow, she had to get her life back, or at least her safety. Despite the heat now coming from the fire, D. shivered, seeing in her mind's eye that shadowy figure of a man at her bedroom door. What if Marcus hadn't spent the night? Would she even be here now? She had to do *something!*

A crystal glass appeared at her shoulder. "It's been a very long day for you, Deborah."

She smiled and accepted the brandy as he sat opposite her.

He crossed his legs and sipped, all the while staring across the space between them.

"I just want to thank you again . . . for last night and . . . and today. This is the first time in over twenty-four hours that I feel like I can breathe normally."

"You are safe here. No one will bother you. And you did very well today. I believe we accomplished our goal of secreting you out of Philadelphia. You can relax."

She simply nodded and studied the flames licking the charred wood. Always one to have a plan, she found herself lost.

"What are you thinking?" he asked in a soft voice.

She blinked and looked up. "I don't know what to do. With myself. The situation. My job. It feels like everything I once held so closely is slipping away."

"Perhaps you were holding on too tightly." He paused, sipped his brandy and then smiled again. There was kindness in his expression. "I have observed, throughout my years, that when a person begins to awake from the illusion of security, they are tested to bring the lesson home. With each loss you are given a choice of surrendering to anger and grief, or surrendering to a process that can lead to freedom. But in the end, it always comes down to surrender."

"Well, this doesn't feel like freedom."

"No, it doesn't, does it?"

"And I hate to surrender, to give up." She sipped her brandy and felt the heat of it warm her as it spread to her limbs.

"We all do, Deborah. We've built our lives around dearly held concepts and when those concepts are challenged, and we begin to sense cracks in the foundations supporting those concepts, the order of our lives is shaken. Nothing is as it seems. Treasured illusions begin to evaporate before our eyes. We are waking up to the true reality of life and it can be as frightening as any monster in a child's fairy tale. There is no long term safety. There never was, and that can be terrifying. We were programmed, as our parents were, and their parents, that if you follow the rules, behave yourself, do not question authority, be it a government or a church, you will increase your safety. It's a lie that millions of people are waking up to, just like you are. The only place you are safe, the only place safety is real, is in each moment. Today, right here, right now, you are safe." He paused, as though to allow that thought to take hold.

"So, it seems the logical conclusion is to learn to live moment by moment, holding nothing too closely for it can all disappear. When those things you held so closely begin slipping away, as you put it, in the end, stripped of all your labels that you thought you were, you realize you are left with you. Just you, Deborah, and that has to be enough, because nothing else ever really belonged to you."

She listened to his words, not liking what she was hearing. "So we're alone in life? Then why not just knock someone over the head if you like their car? Steal their money if you want to buy groceries?"

He grinned. "Because deep within each and every living organism is an animating force of energy, be it a flower, a man, a fish or a woman. Something, something more power-ful than we can fully comprehend, is shared by all of us . . . and deep down we know it. And we also instinctively know that to violate it in another violates it in ourselves. It is only when fear enters the equation that we forget who we are, and our connection to each other. Fear in the form of resentment or victim-hood would be at the core of stealing another's car. The fear that abundance is out of your reach would be behind someone stealing for groceries. It's always fear, Deborah, and forgetfulness, forgetting that we are all in this together."

Her brandy was nearly empty. "You sound like some New Age guru on PBS. If what you say is true then humanity is doomed, because very few people think like you, Marcus. Everyone's out to get what they can and to hell with the consequences."

"Not everyone, Deborah. You report the news. What makes your newscast isn't, for the most part, good news. You report the bad news. You are part of the programming. The media influences its viewers by a daily doze of despair."

"There's a lot of bad shit out there, Marcus," she said in defense.

"You are right. There is. But there is also a lot of good things that happen. Hopeful things, most will never hear about. Please don't think I am criticizing you or your pro-fession. Not many years ago your profession provided a great service in investigating reporting. You, yourself, have admitted that field is diminishing. Look at your friend, Tom Harris."

And Arron Weiss, she thought. "I can't think about this any more," she declared, placing her brandy glass on the in-laid wooden table at her side. "I don't see any way out."

Marcus leaned forward, resting his elbows on his knees. "What if," he said, "you don't have to think about it now, and you stop trying to figure out the future tonight? What if all you have to think about is what you want for dinner and a hot bath while you wait for it to be delivered?"

Despite everything, she found herself smiling. "Now that sounds heavenly."

"So what do you want? Chinese? American? Greek? We have it all here in the city."

"You know, I would really love a good American meal."

He grinned back at her. "And what would constitute a good American meal?"

"What else? A juicy cheeseburger and French fries."

"That I can do," he said, getting up and holding out his hand to her.

She rose and he led her from the living room to the stairs. He picked up her bag and proceeded her.

"I'll show you to the guest bedroom," he said, as they passed original artwork on the staircase. Everything had the feeling of old money, she thought as she followed him. Marcus Bocelli's home reflected who he was . . . a man of taste and money. She couldn't help thinking she was the exact opposite.

"Here we are," he said, leading her into a bedroom at the top of the stairs and turning on a light.

A high white wrought iron bed dominated the square room. It looked inviting with its cream silky bed skirt and matching matelasse bedding. A whitewashed dresser was against one wall and a comfy chair and small table were before the long window draped in a mossy green, silk material that complimented the lighter green walls.

Very nice, she thought, wondering where his bedroom was and too shy to ask to share it. "It's lovely, Marcus," she said, refusing to guess how many other women had used this room, because it was definitely a woman's room.

As though reading her mind, he replied, "My mother and sisters seem to like it on their rare visits."

She nodded. "You must miss them."

"I do," he said, placing her suitcase next to the dresser. "Especially now, during the holidays."

"That's right," she answered, running her hand over the curving metal at the foot of the bed. "I had almost forgotten Christmas is in days."

"It will be an unusual one for both of us, I'm afraid. Sorry."

"You mean my mother?"

He nodded. "You will miss her."

"Yes, I will," she answered, not realizing how true his statement was. She had always counted on her mother just *being there*. She really was all alone, no roots, no family. And now she was in a desperate situation, depending on a man. It was all depressing.

"And now you are sad. I shouldn't have brought it up. I apologize."

Forcing a smile, D. said, "That's all right. I have to face it, don't I? Now where's the bathroom?" she asked, to change the subject. "I haven't forgotten about that bath you offered."

"Coming right up, madam," he replied, heading for the door. "You can unpack and I'll call you when it's ready."

"Marcus, I didn't seriously think you were going to prepare my bath. I'll do it."

"You relax, and I'll draw your bath. After what you've been through you deserve some pampering and I happen to be just the man to provide it." There was a twinkle in his eye as he left her alone.

With nothing to do, save unpack, D. dragged her suitcase up to the mattress and opened it. Inside were clothes and things she thought she would need. No sexy nightgown or robe. She didn't want sex anyway. Feeling punch drunk, she was too exhausted to consider it. Besides, Marcus had installed her in his guest bedroom. She was a guest in his home, though he certainly knew how to be a good host, she thought as she heard water down the hallway. She took out a long sleeved pale yellow cotton nightgown, plain, but good quality. She wasn't one for fussiness, especially when she slept. Laying in on the bed, she opened the drawers behind her and began to unpack. How long would she be staying?

Don't think about it, she mentally commanded. If she believed half of Marcus' theories, she could only count on one day at a time. And right now, right here, she was grateful as hell to be hidden away with a very nice roof over her head, a warm bath being prepared and food on the way.

Right now, she was doing just fine.

The hot water soothed her aching muscles. The scent of almonds rising from the bubbles seemed to calm her chaotic thoughts. The scented candles had a tranquilizing effect, making her lids heavy with relaxation.

He was pampering her, all right. Like she'd never, ever, been pampered.

She had never wanted to be pampered, always preferring to project a strong personality and disposition, but this . . . was heavenly. What had she been missing?

When Marcus had arrived at her bedroom door to tell her the bath was ready, with towel over his arm, as though he were serving her, she'd laughed. Her mood had been light until she had seen his bathroom. She didn't expected a large square room with a marble platform surrounding a huge oval tub. Seeing the candles lit between leafy green foliage and the light playing with shadows on the walls, her throat had tightened with emotion. There was even a big fluffy white robe hanging on the back of the door for her. He had left her alone to call in their dinner and she'd had to bite the inside of her lip not to burst into tears.

The tears had come, slowly at first, trickling down her cheeks to land on the bubbles, and then in a steady stream as she laid back in the water. Her entire life was turned upside down and inside out. Nothing would ever again be the same.

And she was scared. For the first time in her life, she was truly frightened for her life.

Couldn't she take time out for herself, just this one night? Tomorrow she could figure out who was after her, how she could stop them from killing her, how she could expose them and whether or not Marcus was a functioning lunatic. Didn't she deserve one night?

Oh, she'd tried staying in the moment, but it was *hard*, like breaking a lifetime habit of worrying. And there was so much to worry about now. How could she just let it go and pretend everything was all right? It might never be right again.

And then the oddest thing happened.

It was as if a breeze entered the bathroom, making the candles flicker and wave to get her attention. She hadn't felt any wind. But then it passed through her mind that if she could, even for a moment, put her worries away, she might just find herself to be very happy.

She was with Marcus, and she knew she never could have arranged it on her own to find herself pampered in his bathroom. She was, in truth, exactly where she wanted to be.

Right here. Right now.

She could be happy, if she made the choice not to waste the moment.

She sat up in the tub and stared unseeing into the darkness beyond the candles.

It was so foreign to her, to not think about the future, her next move on the gigantic chess board of her life. What if she stopped playing, took a break, a time out for herself?

As the decision was made, she felt that fist unclench at her solar plexus, the muscles in her neck and shoulders unwind like a rubber band free of tension. She felt . . . lighter, happier.

Smiling, D. realized Marcus was right.

There were gifts to be found by staying in the moment. And in that moment, D. decided to try it Marcus' way. She would take this time away from work to live in the moment and see how it turned out.

Really . . . what did she have to lose?

He surprised her by ushering her into his bedroom after her bath. There a small table was set with food and soft classical music was playing in the background. Like the downstairs, his bedroom was decorated in shades of brown, only here the accent color was gold. It was very appealing, but not heavily masculine. And his bed was king-sized, hard to miss or not imagine tumbling around in with him.

Wrapped in the big fluffy cotton robe, D. almost giggled as Marcus pulled out a leather director's chair at the table.

"Your dinner, madam. Prepared, I hope, to your satisfaction."

"You didn't have to do this, Marcus," she said, sitting and inhaling her cheeseburger served on a good china plate, white with a simple thin rim of gold. Red wine was already poured and waiting. "We could have eaten downstairs."

"It seemed more convenient to eat here tonight. Besides, it wasn't all that difficult with our American meal being delivered to the front door."

"Well, this is certainly pampering," she said, sliding a white cloth napkin onto her lap as he sat down opposite her.

"You gave up your holiday of pampering in Bermuda and so it seemed only fair that I try to deliver what I promise."

"And you did," she answered as she picked up her wine glass. "To the moment," she proposed. "It can't get any better than this." Not even being in Bermuda could top being here with him like this.

Marcus raised his glass to hers. "A very good toast. To the moment then."

They each sipped wine and then sat back to enjoy their food.

Neither of them spoke, each murmuring their appreciation since neither one had eaten all day. After devouring the delicious cheeseburger and half her French fries, D. wiped her mouth, sat back and moaned. "Good God, this really is heavenly. I feel like a baby, bathed, fed and ready to be put to bed."

Marcus laughed. "Fortunately, madam, I won't have to carry you far." And he waved toward his huge bed.

She blinked. "I thought . . . well, you put my bag into the guest bedroom . . ."

"Yes, so you could put your clothes away. I'm afraid I don't have the room in here, but I didn't think you'd want to be alone tonight. If I am mistaken, then—"

"You're right," she interrupted. "I would like to fall asleep in your arms tonight." There. No point being coy.

"And so you shall," he murmured. "I'm afraid I have an early appointment in the morning, so I hope I won't awaken you."

She wanted to ask where he was going, but didn't dare pry. If it concerned her, he would tell her. She had to trust that.

"To use a cliché, I'm going to sleep like a babe. It feels like it's been days, instead of last night. So much has taken place."

Marcus pushed himself upright. "Don't think about it now. Come . . . if you're finished eating."

He held his hand out to her and led her to his bed.

"What about the dishes?" she asked, to be polite.

"I'll take care of them," he said, pulling back the thick silky cover. He stood her in front of him and untied the belt of her robe. Slipping it off her arms, he tossed it to the foot of the bed. He then tilted his head to the pillows, big square European pillows. "It is time for you to rest."

She sat on his bed and pulled her legs under the downy cover, shivering at the cold sheets.

"It will warm soon enough," Marcus said, pulling the cover to her chest and stroking the hair back from her forehead. "Would you like to read a book or magazine? I wouldn't suggest watching television, not tonight."

"I'm fine," she murmured, already beginning to feel warmer. "I don't know how long I'll be able to keep my eyes open anyway."

He nodded and went back to the table, gathering up their plates and putting them on a wide tray.

"I feel terrible, just lying in bed watching you do all the work."

She saw him smile. "You don't know how to be pampered, do you?"

"I will admit I haven't much experience with it, if that's what you mean."

"Pampering shouldn't have any guilt associated with it, so close your eyes and think of something wonderful."

She did as instructed, shutting out the sight of him cleaning up. The wonderful thing she concentrated on was the feeling she was going to have when he slid into bed next to her and held her in his arms.

Forty-five minutes later, Marcus came back into his bedroom and found her asleep. For a moment he was stunned and stood at his doorway, staring across the room to her. Two things hit him at once. She looked right in his bed, like she belonged there, and he knew, despite all his better judgements, he felt more than protective toward her.

He was falling in love with this beautiful, intelligent, strong-willed, funny and courageous woman. Yes. She was courageous, attempting to change her entire worldview to understand the things he had revealed to her. He knew she still had her doubts, but she was beginning to trust him and in that trust he was seeing into her soul.

Despite how tired he was, he felt his manhood stir with a desire for possession.

It never left . . . that desire. For him, Deborah was exactly the kind of woman he needed in his life, someone who would challenge him to be more of himself . . . but it could never be. She would never accept his life and especially his assignments. What woman could?

He came in the bedroom and began to unbutton his clothes, still watching her adorable face as she snuggled into a pillow. How had it all happened so quickly? The attraction had been there since the moment he'd met her with Maggie at an outdoor café in Philadelphia. Their coupling in Bermuda had been spontaneous combustion, and since then she had slowly crept under his skin with each encounter. He admired her zest for life, her ambition, her strong will, her intelligence, her fearlessness to confront him. He loved to see her laugh, to watch her eyes crinkle up in merriment, and tried to bring it out as often as he could, but his wit was no match for hers. And he loved to make love to her, to watch her body transform into an instrument of divine pleasure whose desire matched his own.

Deborah Stark was his equal in so many ways, but to think of a future was beyond foolish.

He then thought of Maggie as he dropped his clothes into a wicker basket in his closet. He'd told Maggie she had been foolish to think she could have a normal life. Neither of them would ever be considered normal. They were shapeshifters. They worked for a foundation whose business never eased. They were in service . . . but Maggie had found her happiness with Julian McDonald.

He wondered, for a timeless moment, what his life could be like if he were to make this his last assignment. Never before had the thought crossed his mind. Would he miss it? The excitement? That sense of accomplishment as another awakened into the reality of life? Could he be satisfied with one woman for the rest of his life?

As he approached the bed, he realized he didn't have time

to answer any of those questions. He set his vibrating alarm for four-thirty and slipped it under his pillow before getting under the covers. He moved toward Deborah and pulled her into his arms, wrapping his arm around her as she moved toward him, her back to his chest, her bottom cuddled against him as his knees sought the warmth of her legs. Spooned behind her, Marcus closed his eyes and prayed for the strength to get through whatever was coming.

It was enough to know tomorrow would be difficult. He would have to give his notice at Mitchell's Nursery. He didn't know how he could continue to work there and protect Deborah.

And that's when it hit him . . .

Deborah was more important to him than his assignment.

17

I t wasn't like she expected to find a bat cave . . .

D. awakened to a note from Marcus. He wrote that he hoped she had slept well and to have a restful day. He would return around seven in the evening.

Okay, what red-blooded American woman would not have looked?

Especially a reporter.

Her frustration was that Marcus Bocelli's home appeared to be normal, from the walk in closet where he meticulously kept his clothes to the kitchen where a pot of coffee was left warming for her. She wanted to find some information on this foundation he worked for, but there were no locked drawers, even at his bedroom desk, though she did find a few payroll stubs for a place called Mitchell's Nursery. It must be where he was doing his landscape studying. Though why he wanted to do that was a puzzle, for outside the back kitchen door was a small stone patio and not much room for gardening. There was one discovery. In a green marble bowl were an extra set of keys, to his car and the front door.

She wandered around the house in her robe, having her

coffee and trying to get to know who Marcus really was. His books were mainly about history, politics and philosophy, though there were some on art. Nothing on the Forsythe Group. His music was mostly classical with some jazz and a few U2 CDs. She took out her laptop and checked email and then did an extensive search on the Forsythe Group which only showed the usual boring corporate statements. There was one link that suggested something nefarious, but when D. clicked on it she was diverted to a page that wouldn't download. She tried again and again, but discovered nothing substantial. This group had hidden themselves very well and it appeared that any unwanted publicity was hacked out of existence. By eleven o'clock she gave up. She was frustrated and bored when she found his television in a bedroom cabinet, she drank her third cup of coffee in front of it while listening to CNN.

Not used to such rest and relaxation, she searched her mind for something to do.

Suddenly an idea came and she almost giggled as she hurried into the guest bedroom and pulled open drawers. She had a goal for the day. A plan. Since investigative reporting wasn't going to be on her agenda, she would try her hand at something entirely different.

Six hours later Marcus stopped on the second step leading to his front door. For a moment he thought he had gone to the wrong house. Single white candle lights were shining at each window. A huge Christmas wreath was hung on his front door.

It appeared Deborah had been busy.

As he continued to the door, he wasn't sure whether he was pleased or annoyed. He didn't do the commercial Christmas, hadn't since he'd left Italy and his family. He'd been a guest at Gabriel Burke's home for many years during the holidays and this year he had planned to stay at home. Quietly. No fuss.

He inserted his key into the lock and inhaled the scent of fresh pine. Truthfully, he was sick of the scent as his muscles ached with hauling trees to cars and securing them with rope. Thank heavens he only had one more day.

The front door opened to a scene right out of a Christmas card. A fire was lit and the mantle above it was decorated with a swag of pine and beaded fruit. Candles of varying size were placed on the mantle and around the room, all white and scented with spices. Soft jazz was playing on the stereo. No lights were turned on, only a soft, welcoming glow came from those at the windows and the lights from the fire and candles.

"Welcome home."

He turned his attention away from the room to see her standing in the dining room. He could also see the table had been set with more candles.

"Thank you," he said, recovering from the shock of his home transformed and the lovely woman who appeared to have prepared a meal.

"I hope you're not upset, Marcus," she said, coming into the living room and facing him. "I didn't know what to do with myself today. I tried to find out anything on the internet about the Forsythe Group and—"

"You won't find what you want there," he interrupted. "They are well fronted."

"I know. Nothing else would load except glowing mission statements and I had to keep busy. Just sitting around was driving me crazy, thinking about Tom in that hospital and the break-in at my apartment. Anyway, I thought . . . well, you've been so generous taking care of me that I might do this for you . . . Christmas . . . you know?"

He saw how fragile she was, how unsure of herself, and his heart melted. "It's lovely, Deborah. Thank you."

"You're not upset?"

He shook his head.

"I know it looks like I've taken over your home, but everything's been so serious lately and I just wanted to do something cheerful, and—"

"And I like it," he interrupted again. "How did you pay for all this?"

She shrugged. "Don't worry, I didn't use a credit card. I brought cash with me."

He took off his bomber jacket, hung it up, and walked back into the living room. When he came to her, he brushed a strand of hair behind her ear and said, "It really is lovely, and very cheerful. Thank you for your efforts."

"You really like it?"

"I just said I do."

"I tried to keep it tasteful, nothing over the top."

"It's very tasteful. I didn't know you were such a good decorator."

"I didn't either."

He could see a childlike quality in her, unsure and eager for praise. He grinned as he wrapped her in his arms and inhaled the warm and sensual scent of her. "A hidden talent then, and . . . judging by the aroma coming from the kitchen . . . another talent seems to be emerging also."

She pulled back and looked up at him, her dark eyes wide with wonder. "Really, Marcus . . . I can't believe it myself. I went to a small market around the corner and the butcher told me how to cook a perfect filet. We're having baked potatoes and asparagus spears with a Bearnaise sauce. You do like asparagus, don't you?"

He nodded. "I do. And you prepared all this yourself?"

"I did," she said proudly, then pulled out of his arms completely. "And you are to settle yourself in front of the fire while I pull it together. I hope you're hungry."

"I'm very hungry," he answered, and it was the truth.

"I'll get you a brandy," she said, going into the dining room. She stopped at the sideboard and lifted the crystal decanter. "Sit down, sit down . . . it's your turn to be pampered."

Amused by her enthusiasm, Marcus sat in the wing chair by the fire and waited.

"Here you are," she said, handing him a glass. "Now you just relax and we'll be having dinner soon."

"Thank you, Deborah," he answered. "This is a very nice surprise."

"Goody," she said with a big, pleased grin and then walked away, caught up in her own enthusiasm.

He was telling the truth. It was an nice surprise. So often he served others any way he could. It was his job. Being in service. Having the tables turned was very agreeable, even if it did mean Deborah was taking over his home. Sipping the brandy and staring into the fireplace, he wondered why he didn't mind it. An hour ago he would have. He didn't bring women to his home. It was his sanctuary, only to be invaded by the females of his family on visits. He hadn't wanted a female's influence here. It was his and his alone, a treasured retreat, a shelter from the outside world and its problems.

And now he found he liked having Deborah here and a part of him was waving a red flag. Don't get used to it, he told himself. Deborah was in trouble and the only reason she was here was for her safety. It was temporary. The feelings he had for her were inappropriate, considering the circumstances of both their lives. What had started as playmates, as she termed it, had escalated into something more because of the urgency and danger involved. That's all. He simply had to curb his feelings for nothing substantial could ever come of it.

He would never be normal. And even though Maggie was attempting to leave her life behind and begin anew with Julian, the fact remained that he liked his work. He was a shapeshifter in service to humanity. He didn't want to change that.

He simply had to be stronger. It would be better to stop any growing attachment now then risk a serious wound later that might take years to heal. Somehow, someway, he had to begin to detach.

"Dinner!"

Finishing off the remaining brandy, Marcus smiled sadly as he rose from the chair.

She wasn't going to understand.

When dinner was over, he sat back and smiled with contentment. "That was wonderful, Deborah. Thank you for all your efforts."

She looked so pleased with herself. "Listen, even I'm surprised how well it turned out." Sitting back, she shook her head. "Who would think, considering the last few days, that I'd enjoy doing girly things?"

"Girly things?" he asked, watching her expression become animated.

"You know, cooking for someone, putting up decorations. This is new territory for me, Marcus."

"And it appears you have a talent for girly things. I am glad you are exploring your more feminine side. It isn't weakness, you know."

She sighed, staring at the flame from a candle. "I guess I thought it was. Weakness. To compete in a man's world, I had to be strong, concentrate my efforts where they would pay off. Cooking, decorating, those things didn't interest me."

"You can have both, can't you?"

Nodded, D. murmured, "I'm learning that."

He pushed his chair away from the table. "Now I will clear the table and clean up. It's your turn to relax."

She reached out and stopped him from picking up his plate. "Please, Marcus, allow me to do this. Just this one night. I want you to be pampered. It's the least I can do after last night."

He saw how much it meant to her and nodded. "Then I thank you again. I have something I need to do and I'll be back later."

She appeared surprised as she stood. "You're going out?"

"Yes." He wasn't going to explain.

"Okay," she answered, gathering up the dishes and walking into the kitchen.

He wouldn't be drawn in by her hurt expression.

He left the dining room, the decorated living room, grabbed his coat from the hall closet and left his home that was now filled with her touches. She had moved in as quietly and as easily into his home as she had his heart.

He simply had to get away before he weakened and indulged himself, for they would both pay dearly later. Inhaling the cold December air, Marcus turned left and headed to the nearest bar.

Hopefully, she would be asleep when he returned.

Sleep was far from D.'s mind as she laid awake in bed, wondering where the hell he was. After one hour of waiting, ᴉe had turned off the stereo. After two hours, she had turned off the Christmas lights and had made sure the fire was out. After three hours she prepared for bed, was sitting up reading a magazine and wavering between worry and annoyance. Really, if he'd had plans he should have told her. Now her mind was racing with possibilities. Was it business, his secret foundation, something to do with the Forsythe Group, or was it another woman? How did she know if he was seeing someone here in New York City? She didn't. She had just assumed when he'd come to Philly and was kissing her off it was because he didn't want a serious relationship. And now she'd spooked him by doing all those girly things. He probably thought she was moving in on him, becoming so serious she was taking over.

Stupid. Stupid. Stupid.

She knew how a man's mind worked. And Marcus, above

all others, would see her girly efforts as a threat to his single lifestyle, no matter how he had denied it. He did seem detached during dinner, complimentary, but not at ease, not like last night. She'd been truly stupid spending her time fixing up his house when she should be finding out how to protect herself and expose what had happened to Tom Harris. She wasn't going to make that mistake again.

When she heard the front door opening, she brushed her hair into place, sat up straighter and waited for him to appear at the bedroom door.

"Good evening," he muttered, walking to his closet.

Good evening?!

"Excuse me, Marcus, but I think we have to talk."

He spun around unsteadily and grabbed the door molding to right himself. "It's too late to talk. I must sleep. So if you would postpone any discussion until tomorrow I would be most grateful." He then turned and entered his closet.

Marcus Bocelli was drunk. Maybe not falling down drunk, but tipsy to be sure.

He reappeared wearing blue pajamas with the top buttoned unevenly.

"You're drunk," she accused, glaring at him. What was with the pajamas? They looked like a Christmas present his mother had sent him.

"Madam, I beseech you to lower your voice," he said, pulling back the cover on his side of the bed. "I assure you I can hear your every word."

"I was not shouting," D. answered, getting more and more annoyed. Why did he leave her to get drunk? "I was making a statement. It's obvious you're drunk."

He waved his hand in dismissal. "All I need is sleep. I have an early appointment."

"Appointment?" she asked in amazement as he dropped to the mattress and pulled the cover over him, his back toward her.

"Yes. I work, Deborah. You . . . you don't know this," he slurred. "But I have to work tomorrow. So if we could just stop arguing . . ."

The Mitchell's Nursery? She knew from the pay stub that it was located in north Jersey, not all that far from Hadley. "We're not arguing," she stated.

"Good."

She stared at his back, resisting the urge to punch him into alertness. "So you couldn't stand being here with me to-night? Is that it? You had to go out and get drunk?" She knew she sounded like a harpy, but couldn't stop herself. "You *did* mind that I decorated your house, didn't you?"

"It's my house," he muttered sleepily.

"And you thought I was making myself a little too com-fortable, right?"

Nothing.

"Right?" she demanded, shaking his shoulder.

"What? Please, Deborah . . . I must sleep."

She folded her arms over her chest and scowled. "So what was I supposed to do all alone day and night? I gave up my work for this, whatever *this* is, and I can't stand not having anything to do. You go out. You have a life and I'm stuck here. I want you to take me to my mother's house. I can work from there. I'm not staying where I'm not wanted." She shook his shoulder again. "Do you hear me, Marcus?"

"Hear what?" he complained in a tired voice.

"I said I want you to take me to my mother's house to-morrow morning before you go to your mysterious work."

Nothing.

"Will you take me?" she demanded.

"Hmm . . . yes, Deborah, I will take you anywhere you want. Now can I sleep?"

"Fine," she declared as she turned off the bedside light. She punched her pillow and got ready for sleep. Who was she kidding? She couldn't sleep. Thankful there was a good three feet of space between them, D. stared out into the darkness and made her own plans.

No, she wouldn't stay where she wasn't wanted. To hell with him and all his plans and his secret organizations and the rest of his insanity. She mentally scolded herself. See what a momentary lapse into girliness will get you? Better to stay strong and figure a way back to her own life, her own job and forget Marcus Bocelli and his stupid theories about darkness and light and saving the world one soul at a time.

She'd spend Christmas at her mother's house. She'd wanted to go back and organize everything anyway. This was the perfect opportunity. And then she would return to Philadelphia and forget about Tom Harris' research and the big bad Forsythe Group.

Ignorance was bliss, and if she had to pretend to be ignorant to get her normal life back then she was going to do it come hell or high water. Tom would wake up from his coma and then she'd tell him to forget about it too. Enough of Marcus' craziness.

A shapeshifter.

Right.

She wanted out of the *Twilight Zone*.

D. was waiting for him when he awakened. Seated at the small table in front of the window, she was dressed, packed, and sipping her second cup of coffee.

He slammed off the alarm and appeared to be going back to sleep.

"You'll need to get up now, Marcus, to drive me to my mother's house before work." She poured another cup of coffee and brought it to his night table. "Rise and shine, Mr. Bocelli."

He opened one eye and squinted up at her. "What are you talking about? And why are you up this early?" His voice sounded gravelly and rough.

She smiled with satisfaction as she saw the effort of speaking caused his eyes to wince in pain. "You don't remember? Last night you said you would drive me to my mother's this morning. Drink your coffee and wake up."

She left him to sit down again at the table. Five a.m. couldn't have come soon enough for her. Unable to sleep, she had packed her suitcase and cleaned up a few other things while waiting for the morning to arrive. Now she was ready and she wasn't about to let his hangover stop her. "Marcus! Get up!"

"What?" he demanded, shifting into a sitting position. "What the hell are you talking about?" He shielded his eyes and asked, "Will you turn off some of these lights?"

Not completely without sympathy, D. did as he asked, leaving the light on his night stand on, and then resumed her place at the table, watching him bring the coffee to his mouth with a shaky hand. "Despite your hangover, you are going to take me to my mother's house before you go to your job, whatever that is, so pull your act together and get started."

He was shaking his head. "Deborah, we agreed the best place for you to be was here. No one would be looking for you here. You can't go to your mother's."

"And there you're wrong, my friend. *You* came up with this plan. I simply went along with it. And it's not working out. I want to get my life back and I don't want to stay here any longer. I am going to my mother's. If you won't take me, I'll get a cab."

"You're not making sense. Why are you so determined to do this? Because I went out last night?"

Her back teeth were grinding and she had to release the tension in her jaw. Instead of yelling at him, she sipped her coffee and then said, "What you do is your business, Marcus. I just don't like being idle all day and night. There are things I had planned to do at my mother's and this is the perfect opportunity."

"I can't protect you there."

She laughed. "I don't need your protection. In fact, I'm done with this whole bizarre nightmare of shapeshifters and mysterious foundations and elite, nefarious groups who want to rule the world. I'll spend a few days in Hadley and then I'm going back to Philly, back to work, and I'm not going to let this strange episode in my life have any more power over me. So stop staring at me and get up."

Despite the closed drapes, and the lack of brighter light, he was still squinting in pain. "Deborah . . . what you are saying is foolishness. You cannot make it all go away. It's already in motion."

"Can't I?" she challenged. "You just watch me. Now please take your shower so we can get on the road. I'm not going to discuss this again and waste time. I've made up my mind."

Sighing deeply, he rose from the bed and then stopped and looked down to the pajamas he was wearing. "I did this?" he muttered.

"Well, I didn't," she answered, watching him shake his head again as he headed for the bathroom. Her sympathy stretched only so far.

When she heard the water running in the bathroom, she got up and picked up the tray of coffee. Let him make up his own bed, she thought as she straightened her shoulders and left his bedroom. Now all she had to do was endure a car ride with him and then she could fall asleep in her mother's house. She'd figure out the rest of her plan after that.

Marcus came downstairs and stood for a moment in shock.

The pain in his head increased as he tried to make sense of it.

Gone were the lights in the windows. The pine garland had been removed, along with all the candles. The room felt empty of warmth in a way that was new to him. What had she done now?

"You have your home back," she said and he turned around to see her getting her coat from the hall closet. Her suitcase was placed by the front door.

"Why did you do this?" he demanded, anger starting to replace sadness.

"Because it wasn't appreciated and I apologize for over-stepping your hospitality. Now, can we get on the road?"

"So you threw away everything you bought? Is your ego that fragile?"

"It's all in two black garbage bags by your back door. I didn't know where your garbage was and, please, Marcus, after last night's drinking binge, let's not get into a discussion about fragile egos, okay?"

"Fine," he replied, walking past her to the closet and ripping down his jacket. "I can't believe you did that," he muttered, zipping up and pulling out his gloves from his pockets. "So childish."

She opened the front door and pulled her suitcase with her. "Like I said, let's not get into a discussion about egos or mature reactions, all right?"

Not staying around for an answer, she walked down the stairs and waited for him to lead her to the parking garage where he kept his car. Childish or not, she had no intention of invading his house ever again. Marcus Bocelli had been a big mistake, she thought as she watched him put on his sunglasses and turn to the right. Dragging her rolling suitcase she kept pace with him, feeling his anger as they walked in the crisp dawn of a winter morning. He may be a gorgeous mistake, but a mistake nonetheless. Just look at what had happened to her life since she'd hooked up with him. Her career was in jeopardy. Her life was in jeopardy. And her sanity had been in grave jeopardy too, until she'd been shaken awake from his spell last night.

All she wanted was her life back. No man, no matter how great he was in or out of bed, was worth risking it all. She shifted the strap of her purse on her shoulder and doggedly walked with him into the garage. What a fool she had been over this man, she thought, as they entered an elevator and Marcus punched in the third floor button. Riding up in silence, D. figured it was going to be one long ride into Jersey.

18

"You are sure you want to do this?"

Standing in her mother's driveway, she nodded as she looked down at him in the driver's seat of the Porsche. "Yes, I am. Like I said, thanks for all your help, but I can take it from here."

He stared out the windshield, not looking at her, his jaw clenched. "I hope you can, Deborah."

"Well, merry Christmas, Marcus. I'll see you around." What else was she supposed to say? *I'm all bravado, I have no plan and I'm scared?*

"Yes, I'll see you around," he repeated and shifted into reverse.

She was not going to stand in the driveway and watch him roar down the street. It was bad enough sitting next to him for forty-five minutes without speaking, just feeling him simmering in anger. Why was he so angry? Digging in her purse for her keys, she was thankful that she'd added her mother's to her own set last month. The only reason he could be angry was because she was rejecting him and his crazy ideas, in which case he was the one with the fragile ego. She entered the living room and felt how cold it was since she had turned down the heat after closing the house. She moved the thermostat setting up to seventy and blew her breath out, seeing a cloud of air before her lips.

Hot tea, she thought. Not coffee. Some of her mother's herbal tea.

Keeping her coat on, she walked into the kitchen and rummaged through the cabinets until she found a box of Tension Tamer. Perfect. Once the house warmed, she was going to take a nap and sleep as long as she wanted. Really. It had been years since she'd pulled an all nighter and her body was letting her know it. Still, it had been worth it. To see Marcus' face this morning when he'd awakened and then was told he was taking her to her mother's, and to have witnessed his reaction to her removing all her decorations was priceless.

First shock, then sadness, then anger.

She felt . . . vindicated. Maybe even for his behavior last night.

He didn't want her in his home, not really. And it had hurt. Deeply, cruelly. But now, here she was . . . alone in a freezing house, waiting for a pot of water to boil.

Alone. That was the key word, she reminded herself.

And, somehow, that had to be enough to get her life back in order. But first, sleep.

She awoke disoriented and cranky. Gazing up to the silk canopy above her mother's bed, D. experienced a moment of wonder. Who had her mother been, to have decorated her bedroom with swathes of colorful silk? It was stylish and . . . romantic. Her mother? Romantic? The two didn't fit in her mind. But then there had been that man, what was his name? Alex something . . . Finnley, Finney? He'd had picnics with her at the park. D. wished she had talked to him after the funeral, to find out more.

Pushing the comforter away from her, she swung her legs to the floor and sat on the edge of the mattress. It was now warm in the house and she took off her sweater as she glanced at the bedside clock and saw it was two-sixteen in the afternoon. She'd slept for almost six hours. She ran her hands over her eyes and scratched her scalp to wake up completely. There was no food in the house and she'd have to use her mother's car to go shopping before dark. Her funds were limited after her stupid decorating spree, so she'd have to be careful with the remaining money. Great. She had a checking account she couldn't use. Probably best to buy frozen dinners. To hell with cooking. That was another dumb move.

Stretching, she rose from the bed and headed to the bathroom. She'd wash her face and then get started. No sense procrastinating, she thought, making up a mental list of staples for the next few days. Within ten minutes she was out the door and sitting in her mother's car, turning the ignition. She listened as the engine strained to turn over.

"C'mon, c'mon . . ." she pleaded, realizing the battery might need to be charged after no one starting it for a month. She saw the pewter clip on the sun visor over her head. It was an angel. Now that was just like her mother. Believing in angels.

After the fifth try, she looked back up to the angel and said in frustration, "Okay, angel, Mom, whatever . . . you wanna give me a little help here?"

She tried again. No luck.

Then she was startled by a tapping on her window. She rolled it down and smiled. "Anna. Hi. I was just trying to start mom's car. It seems the battery is dead."

"Good to see you again, dear. Yes. I was coming home and heard it. You staying for awhile?"

"I have some days off and thought it might be the right time to come back and take care of a few things."

The kind neighbor nodded, her dark brown eyes showing compassion. "Well, you just wait right there. I'll give you a jump and you can get on your way."

"All right," D. answered, seeing Anna hurry across the lawn to her car.

She watched as Anna left her own driveway and then, startled, she saw Anna drive on her mother's lawn so her car was facing her mother's. Anna popped her hood and signaled D. to do the same. D. finally found the release lever and got out of the car as Anna was bringing cables from her trunk.

"You sure you know how to do this?" D. asked, sticking her hands into her pockets as she watched the older woman connect the cables.

Anna grinned. "You don't live with my boys without learning a thing or two about cars. Now you go on back and start this one."

D. obeyed and held her breath as she turned the key. To her amazement, the engine kicked over and began humming. "Wow, Anna! You did it!" D. got out of the car and saw the pleased expression on Anna's face.

"Course I did. This is small potatoes compared to changing tires or years of changing diapers and putting together meals from barely nothing or worrying about kids growing up to be decent and now there's the grandbabies. This was easy."

"You are one remarkable woman, Anna," D. said with sincerity. Anna truly was a strong intelligent woman and compared to her own bravado, D. felt dwarfed in comparison. Here was a real woman of strength, who didn't care what anyone thought as long as she did what needed to be done. "Thank you so much."

Anna removed the cables and began wrapping them up. "Sorry about your mother's lawn, but I couldn't think of another way."

"Don't worry about it," D. answered. "I'm just grateful you were home to help out."

"Now, you get on your way," she said, dropping the

jumper cables into her trunk. "You keep that engine running for a spell. Take a drive. And then come over for a visit before you leave this time."

"Yes, ma'am," D. answered obediently. "I will. I promise."

Anna waved and got back into her car, waiting for D. to move out of the way. D. returned to the driver's seat and pushed her foot down on the accelerator to give the engine more gas. She waited a few more moments and then put it into reverse. Waving to Anna as she pulled away, she glanced up to the angel over her head.

"Okay, thanks," she muttered, feeling foolish for talking out loud.

She didn't know if it was merely a coincidence, or not, but she was grateful for Anna's appearance at just the right time. Maybe Marcus had been right about one thing. Living in the moment she might be able to see the clues along the way.

And thinking about Marcus, D. knew exactly where she would go before shopping for food. A side trip to Mitchell's Nursery would give the battery the juice it needed, and it might also provide her with more clues.

Twenty minutes of driving and she was parked in the lot of a large shopping center. She'd had to stop at a gas station for directions to Mitchell's, but it was closer than she had thought. Marcus' Porsche was nowhere in sight. Maybe he didn't come here today. She was parked close enough to see customers going in and coming out with carts full of Christmas goodies. With the engine still running, she felt foolish sitting in the car, like she was stalking the man. At least she didn't wear a kerchief and sunglasses. If he caught her, she could simply say she was going to buy Christmas decorations for her mother's house.

Right . . . like that sounded credible.

Just when she was about to give up, she saw him and her jaw dropped in surprise.

Marcus, her suave, debonair Italian, was hauling a Christmas tree to the parking lot on his shoulder. D. put her head down and peeked out through strands of hair to watch him. He looked tired and cold, and she felt within her heart a pang of sympathy. What was he doing? Did he really *work* here? Like really *work?* None of it made sense. Where was his Porsche he had driven this morning? And how could he even afford the Porsche if he made his money like this? And what about that townhouse on the West Side of Manhattan? That had to have cost a fortune.

He wasn't studying landscaping. He was *doing* it as a job!

What the hell was going on?

She felt embarrassed for him when after he had tied the tree to the car, the man offered him money . . . and he took it, shoving it into the pocket of his jacket.

Wait a minute. That wasn't his bomber jacket he'd worn this morning. He was now wearing a thick tan parka. What did he do? Change clothes in a phone booth to become this mild mannered working stiff?

Something very, very suspicious was going on, she thought, as a blonde woman walked across the parking lot and called out Marcus' name. D. sat up straighter and watched the woman hurry up to where Marcus was standing. She looked pretty, animated, talking to him with gestures, until Marcus wrapped her in his arms and kissed her cheek.

D. felt her heart thudding and her breath stopped as a wave of jealousy washed over her. Who exactly *was* this chick? No, not a chick. Too old for that. Marcus was into older women? For the one who wrapped her arm inside his as they walked back into the nursery was definitely in her forties or maybe even fifties. She hadn't seen her face that well, but good enough to see she was older than Marcus. *A lot* older.

D.'s mind starting throwing out questions. Did he come back here to Jersey to see her last night? Is that why he was gone for three hours? How had he driven home if he was drinking? What was wrong with the man? Oh, and how like a man to keep someone on the side . . . but which one of them was supposed to be on the side? Her or the old lady?

She was spitting mad. At him. At herself. Mostly herself for falling for his line of bull. He probably had a whole script going . . . seduce the woman with your spiritual side, your theories about humanity, saving the world from the bad guys, apply heavy doses of your Italian charm, and then keep her in the dark, don't let her get too close and, god forbid, don't ever let her throw a Christmas wreath on your door or light a candle in your house.

Okay, she was done with spitting mad, now she was rambling.

Pull yourself together.

The mental command made her sit up straighter, inhale deeply and stare at the front of the nursery, decorated so prettily for the holidays. She should get out of the car and go right in there and confront him, ask him to explain himself and this . . . this double life he was leading. Who the hell *was* he?

Her hands were gripping the steering wheel so hard, they hurt as she tried to release them. Okay, okay . . . she needed to calm down. No point in confronting him and making a scene right now. No, she needed to get out of here. Get to the grocery store. Buy food. And then go back to her mother's house and formulate some plan to expose him for the liar he was.

He'd played her, getting what he wanted from her. Sex and an adoring fan to listen to his insane theories. And she'd almost believed him! She didn't know how he did that shapeshifting thing, but she wouldn't put it past him to use a hologram or something technical she would never discover. He played her like a damn fiddle and she'd fallen for it, hook, line and pathetic sinker.

Driving out of the parking lot onto the highway, D. felt

calm. Deadly calm. She wasn't even angry. But she was definitely going to get even with that delusional egomaniac if it was the last thing she ever did.

She sat on her mother's sofa, eating a frozen, but now cooked, dinner right out of the container, not really watching the movie on television. Her mind was trying to find a way to make Marcus Bocelli pay dearly for his deceptions.

What kind of sociopath played with people like that?

And every time she thought of that woman winding her arm through his so naturally, so comfortably, so damn intimately, her stomach curled into a fist of raw envy. It wasn't possession. She wasn't possessive of him. No one would possess Marcus Bocelli. Hadn't Maggie told her that over and over again? It was . . . she didn't know what it was, certainly not love. That had been another illusion. Still, it almost made her growl when she thought of that cozy scene between them. Who was that woman?

Marcus had a whole double life going. The thought sickened her and she dropped the plastic container to the coffee table, no longer hungry. Where was he now? With *her?* No longer having to worry about a gullible woman from Philly, was he now free to spend as much time with that woman as he wanted? How typical of an Italian to be stringing along two women. Hell, there could be more for all she knew.

It gave her a perverse gratification to imagine bringing Marcus down. She had to come up with a strategy. Should she embarrass him at work? Burst into Mitchell's nursery, announcing she was pregnant, loudly proclaiming him to be the father? She could use an Italian accent, begging him to come home and keep their little family together.

She would love to see Mr. Composure unravel.

But what galled her the most was that she had believed

him, believed in him . . . in his integrity. Now that image was wiped away and in its place was a deceiver, a liar, an actor.

Nothing between them had ever been real.

As that thought sunk in, she found her eyes burning and her throat tightening.

She would not cry. Not for him.

"Enough!" she muttered, getting up and taking her TV dinner into the kitchen. She threw it away and then headed straight for her mother's bedroom.

Taking a deep breath, she opened her mother's closet and looked up to the boxes neatly stored on the top shelf. Somebody had to do it, she thought, reaching up for the largest, and she was the only one. Time to get started clearing things out. She carried the box to the bed and sat down. Staring at the old dress box, D. felt a twinge of guilt for the invasion of her mother's privacy. She couldn't just throw it out, could she? Knowing she had to be an adult, she lifted the lid and the first thing she saw was her sixth grade class picture.

She picked it up and immediately was swept back in time to that afternoon when the photographer had come to the school. Quick shots. No time to run a comb through her hair. Sit down. Turn this way. Smile. Get up and go back to class. The funny looking girl staring back at her with big brown eyes, wild hair and a crooked smile evoked sympathy.

"Poor kid," she murmured, placing it on the mattress. She would make two piles. One to keep and one to throw out. She hadn't decided yet which pile to put the picture. She read through report cards, all with A's and B's, and put them on top of the picture. There were cards, mostly from her to her mother, and more pictures of Christmases, holidays and a trip to the Jersey shore with Aunt Tina, Uncle Joe and Rosemary.

She spent over an hour going down memory lane, making her way to the bottom of the box. Picking up a large brown legal envelope, D. untied the string at the back and pulled out a newspaper article. She blinked. Her mouth opened. She blinked again.

There was her mother, young, beautiful in a white gown and wearing short white gloves as she smiled for the photographer. And the headline read: *Philadelphia Socialite Debuts at Mandicott Ball.*

Her head began shaking a denial. Wait a minute! Wait a minute!

Her mother? A socialite? *Philadelphia* socialite?

She read the name under the picture. Emily Walden Morgan.

Morgan? Her mother's maiden name was Walden. She'd always said it was Walden. Who checks if their mother is telling the truth? D. began reading the short article. Her grandparents, Geoffrey and Lillian Morgan, the Main Line Morgans of Bryn Mawr, proudly presented their daughter last night at the annual Mandicott Ball held in the main ballroom of the Bellevue Stratford Hotel . . .

Grandparents? Main Line grandparents? Her heart was slamming against the wall of her chest and her breath was ragged.

She pulled everything out from the envelope with shaking hands. Cards. Letters. Another newspaper article announcing her mother's engagement to Alexander Arsnworth Finney.

Finney?

Alex Finney!

Jesus, her mother had been engaged to Finney and then married Danny Stark? She looked at the date. 1969. A year before she was born. None of this made sense. Finney said he met her mother while looking at furniture. Another lie to add to the mountain before her.

Stunned, D. picked up the folded pages of a letter, minus the envelope. It was written with a very proper penmanship.

Dear Emily,

It is with a heavy heart I put this in writing. Despite my efforts, your father remains unmoved in his position. He has forbidden me any further contact with you. You must know how you have wounded him by running away and marrying that man. The knowledge that you are pregnant almost killed him and he is now following his doctor's orders to remove all stress from his life. Unfortunately, that means you.

It truly breaks my heart, Emily, to tell you this will be my last letter to you. Your father, his health, is now my main concern. I agree with him that you are on your own, as he so crudely said, 'she made her bed and will now lie with the consequences.' Emily, you had every-thing any girl could ever desire and you threw it away on foolishness.

I do wish you find happiness, and I hope your child is born healthy, but for us, for now, you no longer are con-sidered our daughter.

God take care of you. I can not.

With a heavy heart,

Your mother

D. was beyond stunned. The page in her hand was shak-ing with outrage. Who did this to her mother? Geoffrey and Lillian Morgan? Who the hell did they think they were to cast out her mother like that? To let her live in poverty while they lived on the Main Line, pretending they never had a daughter?

Just then a strong whiff of honeydew melon drifted over her.

Stop it. Concentrate, she mentally commanded herself.

This, on top of everything at work? How much was a woman to take without going screaming mad?

D. got up and started pacing the bedroom, trying to release her anger with movement. Suddenly she knew what she had to do. She gathered everything back into the envelope and flipped off the bedroom light as she walked toward her coat. She was going to get some answers.

Fifteen minutes later she stood on her aunt's porch and banged on the front door. She was still furious when Aunt Tina's face appeared.

"Oh, Debbie! What a surprise! Come in, come in . . . Joe, you'll never guess who's here."

D. allowed herself to be wrapped in her aunt's embrace, inhaling the scent of perfume on her flowing purple caftan. Only then did D. realize how late it was and how she was imposing. "I'm sorry for not calling first. I have to talk to you two."

Uncle Joe walked into the living room from the kitchen. "Good to see you, Debbie. Come have a cup of tea. Your aunt's got me drinkin' green tea, but there's some real stuff you can have."

She kissed her uncle's cheek. "Tea sounds wonderful, thanks."

"So what brings you this way, honey? I just sent out my Christmas cards. Did you get yours yet?" her aunt asked, leading her into the kitchen.

D. sat down at the table and unbuttoned her coat. "No, not yet."

"Let me take that," Aunt Tina said, reaching for D's coat.

She had to stand up to take it off and D. smiled as she handed it over. "Thanks, Aunt Tina. I was wondering if I could talk to the two of you?"

"Sure enough, honey." Aunt Tina put her coat on the back of a dining room chair and then slid onto a kitchen chair opposite her. "Your Uncle Joe will have that tea ready soon enough. He bought one of those electric tea pots last week. Can you believe him? Ever since he's retired he thinks he knows best how to run my kitchen."

"Now, Tina, I never said I knew better, just pointed out ways to be more efficient, that's all." Uncle Joe brought the sugar bowl to the table, along with three cups.

Aunt Tina jumped up and opened a cabinet, bringing out four boxes of tea and then took a small container of half and half out of the refrigerator. D. took the opportunity to take the large envelope out of her purse and place it on the table.

"What's that, honey?" Uncle Joe asked as his kettle began to whistle.

D. placed her hand on the envelope. "Let's wait until we're all seated."

"Sounds serious," Aunt Tina said, handing D. a box.

"Maybe," D. murmured, taking out a tea bag and placing in her cup.

Uncle Joe poured the steaming water and then put his kettle back on its plate. "Okay, now what's the mystery?"

Just as D. was about to speak, Aunt Tina jumped up. "Oh, let me get some Christmas cookies."

D. reached over the table and grabbed her wrist. "We don't need cookies." She then looked at her relatives who were searching her face. "I'm sorry," she said, releasing her aunt. "I don't need cookies. What I do need is your attention."

"Sit down, Tina," Uncle Joe ordered. "The girl is troubled, can't you see that?"

Her aunt sat back down very slowly, still staring at D.

Taking a deep breath, D. began. "I'm staying at my mother's house for a few days, to clear out things and . . . and I came across this." She placed the old envelope in the center of the Formica table.

"What is it?" Aunt Tina asked, looking at the envelope as though it might explode.

D. turned it over and opened the flap. She pulled out the newspaper articles and placed them in front of her relatives. "What do you know about this?"

Aunt Tina seemed to grow smaller and Uncle Joe blew his breath out in a long exhale.

"'Bout time you knew everything," Uncle Joe said, turning the paper with a picture of her mother on it to better see.

"Oh, Debbie . . . I knew I should have gotten over there and . . . and . . ."

"And what?" D. demanded. "Took care of everything so I never found out about my mother?"

"She didn't want you to know," Uncle Joe answered for his wife. "She went through a lot of trouble so you wouldn't have to know."

"Didn't I have a right to know who my mother was?"

"Did you?" Uncle Joe asked. "Who says a child has to know everything about a parent? There are some things I wouldn't want my Rosemary to know about me when I was younger, and I bet there are some things you wouldn't want your kids to know about you when you have them. You protect kids, Debbie. You keep things from them that might hurt."

"So you knew all about this? The both of you?"

Aunt Tina was wringing her hands. "I didn't know where she had lived before Danny brought her home to meet us. I knew she was . . . well, different. She spoke so nicely and acted so proper. She wasn't stuck up, or anything, just different."

"And she laughed . . ." Uncle Joe murmured, still gazing at her mother's debut picture. "She kinda sparkled when she did that, right Tina?"

Her aunt was looking at her husband oddly. "I don't know if she sparkled." She turned her attention back to her niece. "But she did laugh a lot. In the beginning. She was happy, I thought."

D. took out the engagement picture. "Why did she marry my father if she was engaged to this man?"

Aunt Tina sat back and crossed her arms over her chest. Uncle Joe pursed his lips, as though biting back words.

"Was my mother pregnant with me when she married my father?" There. She said the words they couldn't.

"Honey, these things happen," Uncle Joe said in a conciliatory voice.

"I *know* they happen," D. answered, trying to keep her patience. "What I don't know is why the big secret . . . about all this?"

"It was different in those days, Debbie," Aunt Tina began. "A girl getting herself in trouble was a scandal, a terrible disappointment to her family. We never really talked about it with Emily. It wasn't something up for discussion. I do know her family wanted nothing to do with her after they found out. And, let's be honest, they weren't that thrilled with Danny either."

"Why? What was so wrong with your brother?"

She shook her head and shrugged her shoulders. "Danny wasn't like them, with their noses in the air. From what he told me, Emily had a big fight with that man she was engaged to and when he met her in a Philadelphia night club they hit it off right away. He loved her, Debbie. Your father loved your mother, you can believe that."

"So why did he leave, if he loved her so much?" D. couldn't stop the bitterness from coming out with her words.

"Danny started to feel real bad after you were born. Money problems. He couldn't keep a job. He had the worst luck. He'd start a good job and within weeks be let go. Then he started drinking. He'd come here and tell me how he'd ruined your mother's life and how he just wanted to make it right. So he left, thinking she would patch things up with her family and then the two of you would be taken care of. She didn't though. She never had anything to do with them again."

"Here's why," D. said, pulling out the letter.

She handed it to Uncle Joe, and Aunt Tina leaned in to read it with him.

"Oh my . . . poor Emily . . . what kind of people . . ." Aunt Tina had tears in her eyes as she sat back.

Uncle Joe slid the letter back across the table. "People sure can be stubborn fools."

Finally they all picked up their tea and drank in silence.

"Aunt Tina, I want to talk to my father."

Both Tina and Joe looked startled.

"Really?" Aunt Tina asked, her eyes once more filling with tears.

D. waved her hand. "Don't go thinking this is about a reunion. I don't even know the man. I just want some information about my mother. Will you tell him to call me at my mother's house?"

Tina nodded. "Absolutely. I can call him now if you want."

"No, not now. I've had enough today. Just tell him to call me at my mother's." She paused. "Is there anything else you can tell me, anything else I should know?"

Her uncle Joe reached for her hand. "Only that your mother loved you. You were everything to her and she did whatever she could to protect you and give you the best life possible."

D. bit the inside of her cheek. "I know she did. I just don't know why she lied about all this."

"What good would it have done if you knew?" he asked gently. "So your mother came from rich people who disowned her. What could you have done about that?" He hesitated. "She did the best she could for the two of you. You have to admire her for that. Even when things were really bad, she still put on a brave face. In my book, she was one hell of a woman." His voice sounded rough and emotional.

D. patted her uncle's hand, remembering their talk last month and how he had once had a crush on her mother. He said when he met her she sparkled.

"I know why she had an embolism," D. muttered, her own emotions coming close to the surface. "She worried and worried so damn much about money, about me, about everything, and her brain was overworked. It couldn't take any more. They could have helped her," she declared, sniffling back tears. "Those selfish bastards on the Main Line could have helped her."

"What's done is done," Aunt Tina answered. "there's no going back and changing things. I'm glad she was happy in the end."

D. pointed to the fading yellow newspaper cutting of her mother's engagement. "You want to know something weird? That man, Alexander Finney? I think he's the man my mother was seeing before she died. The man who came to her viewing."

Aunt Tina's jaw dropped. "No!"

D. nodded. "I think so."

Uncle Joe smiled sadly. "Now *that's* a love story. Her first love came back. Good for Emily."

D. couldn't agree. It would have been good if Emily lived long enough to enjoy it. In D.'s mind, her selfish grandparents had contributed to their daughter's early grave.

19

She was seated in a booth at the Red Lion Diner, sipping a cup of stale coffee when he walked in the door. Even though she had seen pictures of him before, and he looked much older, she knew it was her father by the nervous, guilty expression on his face as he scanned those already seated. Their gaze locked and he visibly swallowed as he came toward her.

At one time he must have been nice looking, but years of drinking had ravaged a handsome face and he seemed like a man beaten down by life. She straightened her shoulders as he approached.

"Debbie?"

She simply said, "Sit down, Danny. Thanks for meeting with me."

He nodded. "Was glad when Tina called. I've been wanting to tell you how sorry I am . . . about your mother, and all." He looked toward the waitress, as though the woman could rescue him. "Coffee, please."

He was dressed in a black wool jacket with a steel gray sweater underneath, almost the same color as his thinning hair. The whites of his eyes looked faintly yellow and watery and his nose and cheeks were tinged with red blotches. D. noticed his hand shaking as he reached into his jacket and brought out a pack of menthol cigarettes.

"Mind if I smoke?"

She wanted to say yes, but relented when she recognized his need. "Go ahead."

"Thanks," he muttered, sticking a cigarette into his mouth and lighting it with a match. He blew the smoke away from her and looked to the waitress who was bringing his coffee. "Thanks, hon," he said to the older woman.

"Anything else?" she asked, giving Danny the once over.

"Nah, I'm good," he answered, smiling back at the woman. "You want anything more, Debbie?"

"I'm fine," she said, watching all this with an observer's detachment. Danny Stark was past his prime, looking pretty bad as far as she was concerned, and yet he still thought he had *it*, that indefinable something that attracts the opposite sex. Men. Amazing. Age didn't matter.

The waitress left them alone and Danny picked up his coffee cup. Sipping, he kept his eyes down.

"I guess you're wondering why I asked to see you after so many years." Might as well get this thing started.

He dragged deeply on his cigarette. "Your Aunt Tina kinda told me."

D. nodded. "It was quite a shock to find that envelope. I didn't . . . know anything, it appears, about my mother's life."

"Aw, now don't go blamin' her for trying to protect you, Debbie, she was just doin' what she believed—"

"My name is Deborah," she interrupted. "Not Debbie." *And not coming from you,* she thought. He didn't earn that right, like Aunt Tina.

"All right . . . Deborah, then. I always thought of you as Debbie. Just don't blame your mother for anything."

"Who should I blame, Danny?"

He looked right into her eyes. "Life, kid. Blame life, if you gotta put blame somewhere. Life ain't fair."

Fatherly words of wisdom? Wow. She should have that on a plaque somewhere. "What about responsibility? Making choices?"

He exhaled deeply and D. watched a stream of gray smoke curl away from them. "Figured it would come to this. You got a right to be mad, I guess."

"You *guess?*"

"Okay, you do. But there were circumstances, reasons why things were the way the were, and you gotta let all this go. Believe me, you turned out a hell of a lot better without me being in your life, than if I'd stayed."

"You know, Danny, this really isn't about me. This is about my mother, a good woman, and all I remember growing up was watching her struggle and worry about keeping a roof over our heads, food on the table, water flushing the damn toilet. Where were you? Why couldn't you help her? That's the responsibility and choices I'm talking about."

He didn't say anything. He scratched the side of his head, looked out to the diner, and then turned to her. "I did help out, in the beginning, whenever I could. I . . . sent money. But the job scene wasn't consistent, you might say."

"Fine," she answered, feeling anger replace irritation. "And that really isn't what I want to talk about now. I'd like you to tell me about my mother. How did you meet her? What was she like?"

"Emily?" His expression softened.

D. nodded.

He stubbed out his cigarette and sat back, looking beyond her head, as though envisioning the past. "I was in Philly, working construction. I had a friend who got me into the union and I was makin' some good money. Dressed real nice on weekends. Me and Dave, that was his name, we went to this club where they had folk music, you know . . . Peter, Paul and Mary, Joanie Mitchell, Richie Havens and even Bob Dylan. Never saw Dylan, but that was the kind of place the Highpoint was. So we're sittin' there, takin' in the scene, and in walk these two girls. One short and blond and the other was tall with long dark hair that flipped up on the ends and she had the prettiest face. Like yours, Deborah. A real stunner."

D. felt her throat tighten with emotion as she listened.

"So I tell Dave, you see that girl over there? And I pointed her out. I tell him, I'm gonna marry her. Just like that. It hit me. *She* hit me like a bat to the back of the head. And I ain't even talked to her yet. But I knew, ya know? I just knew it in my gut."

D. smiled sadly, watching the memories play over his face. He did love her mother once. In his own irresponsible way.

"So me and Dave, we go over to their table. You may not believe this, but I could be a charmer when I wanted and they invite us to sit down. Right away I see Emily is way out of my league. Even though she laughed a lot, she had this refined way about her. And graceful . . . everything she did was like some damn ballet . . . the way her hands moved, the way she threw back her head and laughed. It was like I was hypnotized. And it may not be the right thing to say to you, but I wanted her. I wanted to sit and watch her, to listen to her. That night I felt on top of the world. We made plans for the next weekend and . . ."

"And . . . ?" D. prompted.

"And you gotta remember what the time was like. Summer of free love and all that. We fell in love fast and hard. She told me she'd broken off her engagement to someone else and her father was furious with her. Later I wondered if I was her way of rebelling against him, but hell, I didn't care then. All I knew was that Emily was like a breath of fresh air in my life and . . . and life seemed real good."

She felt her first pang of sympathy for him, watching his face, sensing his nostalgia for better times. "And then she became pregnant with me," D. said quietly.

Danny nodded. "Jesus, she was scared. Even said a girl-friend told her about a place in Puerto Rico to . . . to take care of things. You had to leave the country then. But she couldn't do it, didn't want to do it, and finally I said we should get married. To hell with her old man. She was twenty-one. She didn't need his blessing and her parents would come around. I thought they'd come around." He paused. "They didn't."

"Did you ever meet them? The Morgans?"

He shook his head. "No. Drove by the house once with her, a big old place in Bryn Mawr, outside Philly, but never did meet them." He lit another cigarette. "Met the old man's flunkie a couple of times."

D. jerked her head up from her coffee. "What do you mean?"

"See, me and Emily started out real good. Nice apartment and everything. You came along and then I lost my job. Got another one and lost that one too. Couldn't figure out the rea-son this wave of bad luck was hittin' me, until after the third job when this man in a slick suit comes up to me at my car and says every job I get I'll lose until I get out of Emily's life."

"Her father sent someone to threaten you?"

Danny shrugged. "I told the bastard to go to hell, but I saw him again after I lost the next job in two weeks. So I started drinking. Me and Emily fought. She was miserable with me. Couldn't blame her, either. I kept thinkin' about everything she gave up for me and I wasn't any good for her. I only brought her bad luck. She went from having it all to strug-gling to pay the rent and feed a baby. I swear when I left I thought she'd go back home to them. That you and her would be taken care of and it was best I get out of the way of that."

"But she didn't go home because they had disowned her. They let her live in poverty as some kind of punishment for not obeying their rules." D. wished the diner served alcohol. She would even buy Danny a drink.

"Look, I kept up with you through your Aunt Tina. You never knew I went to your grade school graduation and your high school one too. I was across the street when you left Tina and Joe's on Christmas. I saw you grow up from a distance. Whenever I could I gave Tina money to give your mom. I know it wasn't much. I was struggling to survive myself. And if you don't think I feel bad about you and your mother, you're wrong. I just did so much damage I didn't know how to fix it. And then . . . well, there's the drinking. Can't seem to stop. Went to AA, but I always go back to the bottle. Your mother wouldn't put up with that."

Remembering her mother, D. stared into her cold coffee cup and said, "No, she wouldn't have."

"Hey, but look at you now, right? All grown up and on the television. You did great, Deborah. Real good. She was proud of you. And, even though I ain't got the right, so am I."

D. slowly looked up and saw there were tears in her father's eyes.

That raw emotion she had been trying to keep in check threatened to bubble up even more. "Thanks."

Danny Stark nodded, sniffled, then cleared his throat. "Want somethin' to eat, Deborah? They got a good breakfast here."

She swallowed the tight lump in her throat and said, "Sure. I haven't eaten this morning."

He signaled the waitress to come back.

"And, Danny?"

"Hm?"

"It's okay if you call me Debbie. I can't seem to make Aunt Tina stop, so I've kind of given up." What the hell. She was fighting a losing battle where her relatives were concerned. And, like it or not, the man sitting across from her was more than a relative. She was a part of him, just as he was always a part of her. Without him, she wouldn't be alive.

"Nah . . . you're right. You're a Deborah now. Just like her. Pretty, graceful, intelligent. Deborah seems, what do they call it, appropriate. That's the word. Appropriate. It fits you now."

And in that moment, D. felt the hard shell around her beginning to crack. Just a little. She had spent so many years, from her earliest memories, building that protection it would take time and effort to repair her abandoned heart.

She wasn't proud of herself. In fact, ordinarily she would have little sympathy for someone who stopped at a liquor store on the way home to purchase a bottle of rum in order to drown their sorrows. But, come on, it had been one hell of a week so far.

She gulped her fourth rum and coke and then burped loudly. Who was going to hear her? It didn't matter any longer and she started counting on her fingers the reasons why. She might lose her job. A friend was run off the road and in a coma. She probably had lost her boyfriend. Okay, he wasn't exactly her boyfriend, but close enough. She may have people who wanted to harm her, maybe even kill her. Her mother had a whole identity she never knew about, had been disowned by rich parents, and her father's life had been systematically ruined by her evil grandfather.

Yeah . . . she deserved to get drunk.

She held up her glass to the room, empty of company save for her mother's Peter, Paul and Mary record she was playing in tribute to her parents ill-fated love affair.

"Like father, like daughter."

Drinking alone was not a good sign. She knew that, but

didn't care. This was one night to wallow in her miserable, screwed up life. Everything had been fine until she had met that damned Italian. Why hadn't she listened to Maggie and stayed clear of Marcus?

Because the moment she saw him she had wanted him, wanted to look at him, listen to him, watch the way he moved and laughed and—shit—she sounded just like her father when he'd seen her mother for the first time. Now that should be an omen, look how they had turned out. Still, somewhere in the back of her mind, D. had known Marcus Bocelli was the one. Just like her father had said, a bat to the back of the head.

She burst into laughter. Shows you how wrong that was. The damned bat probably was to knock some sense into them. She was more like Danny Stark than she wanted to admit. Neither one of them had any sense where love was concerned.

And yes . . . damn it . . . she had loved that lying Italian. For a little while anyway.

She sighed and then focused her attention on the song filling the room.

"Where have all the flowers gone," she began singing in a sad voice. "Gone to graveyards every one. When will they ever learn? When will they ever . . . learn?" She looked at the stereo while remembering her mother playing those old records and singing along. She'd liked to sing and D. had liked to listen to her. It meant her mother wasn't worrying.

As the refrain came back, she felt tears building up.

When *would* they ever learn?

When would she learn? Maybe what galled her the most was how stupid she had been. About everything. She had taken her mother's word that they had no extended family, save for Aunt Tina and Uncle Joe and Rosemary. It was easier to believe they were all alone, that the humiliation of their lives was limited. Or, maybe D. had just wanted it limited, kept a secret until she could escape it?

She noticed a spider that had come in from the cold and was crawling on the wall.

"You're not welcome, my friend," she called out, and then realized she really didn't have any friends, not real friends. Acquaintances. But not someone she could call and pour her heart out to . . . not like Maggie. Maggie would drop everything and leave the city and Julian and come over and then Marcus would get involved again and she was too embarrassed to even tell Maggie how screwed up everything had become. Nope. She was alone. Her and the spider. Too bad she had this stupid, childish aversion to insects, and spiders were at the top of her list.

"Look," she said, knowing she was well on her way to being drunk. She was speaking aloud. To an insect, no less. "You're going to have to get out, okay? I mean, I know it's cold out there, but the two of us can't inhabit the same space. I won't be able to sleep if you're here, ready to pounce on me." Shivering in horror at the thought of it, she added, "So, start crawling toward the door, or I've got this shoe, see? And I won't hesitate to use it."

It didn't move. Not that she thought it would move, but it was leaving her with no choice. She took off her shoe, a very nice black leather half boot with a good three inch heel.

"I don't want to hurt you," she said, standing up and feeling a bit woozy. Maybe it wasn't such a good idea to do battle with a big black spider when her reflexes weren't great. Still, she couldn't imagine trying to get to sleep with the thing crawling god knows where. And sleep sounded pretty good right now, she thought, coming closer to it. Just get rid of the thing and then crawl back into her mother's bed. No point wallowing any longer.

She was definitely drunk enough to sleep.

In fact, hobbling around with one boot on made it worse. She flopped back to the sofa and pulled off the other one. "Okay, now I'm ready," she muttered, heaving herself upright again. Steadier, she slowly moved toward it. "Ya didn't litsen, lit—*listen*," she slurred, trying to get her speech right. "I gave you fair warning, more than most would do. You coulda made it to the door, but nooooooooooo . . . you gotta make me into a spider killer."

Damn she was sounding crazy, talking like that to the wall. Where'd the thing go? There. She spotted it moving fast along the wall, closer to the carpet. She held the boot up by the heel, poised and ready to exterminate it when the thing hopped, actually hopped off the wall, and D. screamed, realizing the only things covering her feet were thin socks. Still screaming, she scrambled back to the sofa, jumping on it and then falling to her knees as she watched the thing grow bigger and then transform before her eyes into a sparkling dust cloud that swirled faster and faster and . . . "Oh, God . . ." she moaned, sinking back on her calves and clutching the arm of the sofa as though to keep upright.

He stood before her, looking angry. "You could have killed me!" he exclaimed.

She couldn't speak. In fact, although she knew her mouth was open, all thought escaped her.

"Deborah! Say something," he ordered in a quieter voice as he brushed the sleeve of his bomber jacket. "You certainly had enough to say a few moments ago."

Thoughts quickly returned with lightening speed. He heard her! Dear God, he not only heard everything she said, but he saw her getting drunk, feeling sorry for herself. Everything! What an invasion of privacy!

"How dare you?" she demanded, finding her voice somewhere in her humiliation and anger. "Who the hell do you think you are?" She held up her hand. "Oh, I know . . . a fucking shapeshifter, that's who, who comes into a person's home, uninvited, spies on them and then scares them half to death."

"Deborah, calm down and—"

"Do not tell me to calm down," she hotly interrupted. "*You* don't tell me to do anything anymore, you hear? I've *had it*, do you understand? Simply had it, with you and everything that's happened since I met you. Enough is enough. And I've had more than enough to last a lifetime. You're a liar, a deceiver and a damn good actor, and . . . and I can't take any more," she cried, feeling the tears rolling down her cheeks. "Between you, my career, poor Tom in that hospital, my mother and my father and . . . and everything else, I'm ready to surrender. The white flag is up. I can't take any more" She sniffled loudly and added through her tears, "I don't want to go crazy."

"You're not crazy, Deborah," Marcus said in a soft voice. "Granted, if I knew the way you felt about spiders, I would have shifted into something else, and then—"

"Why not use the fucking door!" she shouted at him. "Like a normal person."

"I didn't think you would let me in."

"Well, you're right. I would have slammed it in your face. What's wrong, Marcus? Your old lady need her sleep and you thought you'd try to patch things up with me? Is this my booty call?"

"What are you talking about? My old lady?"

Knowing she was getting foul and ugly, she pulled her legs out from under her and walked unsteadily back to the dining room where she poured herself another drink. What did she care what he thought? She'd get as foul and as ugly as she wanted. She had more than enough reason. "I meant that old lady part literally, not slang. I saw her. With you. Kissing and cuddling." She held her drink up to him in a toast. "Here's to you, Mrs. Robinson, wherever you are."

"Mrs. Robinson?"

She waved him off as she made her way back to the sofa, spilling some rum and coke on the way. "Didn't you hear, while you were playing Spiderman up there on the wall? It's my trip down memory lane night. Peter, Paul and Mary, and that, Mr. Bocelli, was my tribute to Simon and Garfunkel."

"Deborah, you're not making any sense," he said, coming closer to her.

She held up her hand like a traffic cop to stop him. "Excuse me, *I'm* not making any sense? This, coming from *you*, a—a shapeshifter and a phony and a liar."

"All right, exactly how am I a phony and a liar?"

She blew her breath out in a rush of exasperation. "How do I begin? The list is so long." She pretended like she was thinking, but in truth she was trying to think clearly. He was here now and never mind at the moment *how* he got in. Now was her opportunity to really let him have it. Ignoring the fact that he still looked just as handsome, maybe more since she was drunk, D. cleared her throat. "You lied to me when you said you didn't mind if I put up decorations."

"I didn't mind," he protested.

"Liar. And then you deceived me by leading a double life, keeping women on the side."

"What are you talking about?"

"I'll tell you what I'm talking about . . ." What was she talking about? Oh, right, right. "You may drive a Porsche and live on the West Side of Manhattan, but you work at Mitchell's Nursery and I saw you yesterday. You carried a tree to a car and then this woman, no young chippy either, comes across the parking lot and you kiss and she wraps her arm through yours and the two of you go skipping happily back into the nursery. *That's* what the hell I'm talking about."

She watched his jaw set and harden. "You saw me?"

Nodding, she said, "Yep . . . spied on you just like you did to me tonight. So now we both know the hard, cruel truth. I could one day perhaps become a lush, whereas you, Mr. Bocelli are a liar, a deceiver and a phony. Somehow I'd rather be a lush."

"I am not a liar, or a deceiver."

"Oh, but you are a phony?"

"If I understand your meaning, then no, I am not a phony either."

"Well, let me spell it out for you so we can be sure you get it. I trusted you. I trusted your integrity. And you have none. You pretend, Marcus. You aren't real. You go through life pretending to help people with all your phony spiritual talk, souls in need, and what you're really doing is satisfying your own need for attention. Oh you're good looking, maybe even great looking, and why your ego needs to be inflated is beyond me. So you string along women, so far there's me and Mrs. Robinson. How many others are out there? Maybe if you hurry you could still catch one of them awake." That was pretty good, she thought. That's what he was. A Pretender.

She saw his hands in the pockets of his jacket ball into fists.

Okay, he was angry.

Damn it, so was she!

"You do not know what you are talking about, Deborah. If you were sober, I would be highly insulted by your accusations."

She laughed. "Hah! Some comeback. Well, get insulted, Marcus, because the truth is the truth and the truth hurts when—"

She barely had time to register him coming up to her and grabbing her shoulders.

"You would not recognize the truth tonight, Deborah, if it slapped you in the face."

She stared right into his eyes. "I'm not afraid of you," she muttered. "I've had the truth slapped in my face all week, brutal truth, about how hurtful people can be, how they can ruin another's life and never think twice about the consequences. I've seen how cruel life can be growing up in this house and how a life wasted in worry will kill you. You know what Marie Pereggi and her band of tormentors used to call me? Dirty Socks. Poor Dirty Socks."

She knew she was drunk, but didn't care. She had never told another soul that, not even her mother. But it was out now, that horrible secret. "The water was shut off once for not paying the bill. It was winter and my mother boiled snow to flush the toilets. I tried to wash my socks to get them clean, but they were gray, not white. My mother handled it all with dignity and said we would survive because we were strong. She said one's surroundings don't have anything to do with character, but I watched her worry and I swore I would get out of this place and no one, not ever, would call me poor again."

He tried to touch her, but she pushed him away. "I'm not my mother and I'm not going to be my father. I'm me!" she said, not caring that tears were again sliding down her cheeks. "And I'm not going to let your lies hurt me anymore."

This time he pulled her into his arms and crushed her to his chest. "Deborah, you're wrong," he whispered into her hair. "What you have been thinking about me is not the truth."

"I'm tired, Marcus," she said through her tears, not holding on to him. "I'm tired of the lies about my family, about my career, about you."

"What about your family?"

She pulled away from him, wiped her eyes, and pointed to the brown envelope on the coffee table. "Read for yourself. I'm the daughter of a socialite, or I should say a fallen socialite. We lived this way because of my maternal grandparents. They helped kill their daughter with their cruelty. See for yourself what kind of people I come from."

He sat down and pulled the envelope to him. "Where did

you get this?" he asked, taking out the newspaper articles first.

"I figured since I was here I would start cleaning out things and . . . and there it was in the bottom of the box. I think she wanted me to find it."

"She was beautiful, your mother."

In spite of everything, D. leaned in closer to see the picture of her mother's debut again. "Yes, she was. I don't remember her like that. So young, so full of expectation. Little did she know she'd grow old fast in poverty. No wonder she decorated the house like this. And why she never wanted to visit me in Philly. It was too close to her family"

"What happened?" he asked gently.

She hesitated and then said it. "I did. I happened. My mother met my father in Philadelphia and got pregnant. Look at the other newspaper clipping. She was engaged to, get this, to Alexander Amsworth Finney, and broke it off. Her parents disowned her when she married my father. Does that name ring a bell? Alex Finney?"

Marcus scowled, thinking. "Why does it sound familiar?"

"Because he was at my mother's funeral. He told me they had picnics together at Rosemont Park."

Marcus whispered, "I remember now. Incredible, no?"

"Yes, incredible. I'm glad they found each other again," she added, watching as he read the letter. When he finished, he folded it and put it back in the envelope.

"Well? What kind of parent could write that letter?"

He didn't say anything for a few moments. "A frightened one. It sounds to me that your grandfather was not a man to be crossed, not even by his daughter or his wife."

"Bastard." Her jaw tightened.

Marcus turned to her and said, "Deborah, please, now that you've calmed down, please allow me to explain what you saw yesterday. If you still want me to leave after you have listened, then I will."

Her shoulders dropped in weariness. "Look, I'm drunk and I'm exhausted. Both mentally and physically. I don't want to listen to any more lies. Can't you see, I've had more than enough."

"I promise I will not lie to you. I never have."

Exhaling, D. closed her eyes in defeat. "Just say what you have to say then. I need to get to sleep. I'm too tired to fight anymore."

"Simply listen. Do you remember I told you that part of my job is to assist others who have lost their way and are falling into darkness? It's about balance, Deborah, shifting the energy toward harmony." He paused. "The woman you call Mrs. Robinson is my assignment. Her name is Carolyn Davies and she's the floral designer at Mitchell's Nursery. You are correct when you said she is no longer young. She's in her early fifties and last year her husband divorced her after nearly thirty years of marriage. He put all their holdings into his mistress' name and declared bankruptcy. Carolyn, who lived a privileged life, was left with nothing. It almost killed her. She lives in a small apartment, has no car and walks to work."

"God . . ."

"Yes, and the best way for me to make contact with her was to apply for seasonal work at the nursery. We became friends and she's turning her life around, believing in herself again, seeing the future holds hope. When you saw us yesterday, she had just accepted her first real job as a party planner for one of her old friends. A New Year's Eve party. And she had received a deposit. I was happy for her, seeing her come alive again, seeing her recognize her potential, and yes I hugged her and yes, she placed her arm inside mine as we both walked into work, but it was as friend, Deborah, nothing more."

"Your assignment?"

"I told you I work for a foundation and I receive the name of a person who has given up on life, who is sliding into a dark hole and can't find a way out. Carolyn was my assignment. There was nothing romantic about it."

"Nothing?" she asked, starting to believe him.

"Nothing, and that is the truth."

She felt a huge weight life from her shoulders. Wait. "But what about the other night? I put those decorations up and you bolted out of the house after dinner and then you come back drunk. What about that? You said you liked them."

"I did."

"Then what happened? Where did you go?"

He exhaled deeply. "I went to a bar and did just what you did tonight. A foolish answer to any problem."

"But why? I've got a whole list of reasons for tonight. What were yours?"

"I don't know how to answer you."

"Try, Marcus. I may be drunk and maybe I won't remember all this in the morning, but tell me why you had to get away from me, why you left me alone."

He didn't say anything for a few moments and D.'s stomach started to clench with dread. She closed her eyes, waiting for the words.

"Despite what you thought I really did like what you did to my house, maybe too much."

She opened her eyes and turned her head to see him. He was staring straight ahead. "Really?"

Nodding, he said, "It felt . . . right, somehow. You being there, making dinner, lighting candles, making my house a home. And it . . . it frightened me."

"Why?"

"Because I had told myself many years ago, such things would never be for me. I don't live the kind of life where that is possible."

"What does that mean?"

"It means I am not like most people. I will never have a normal life."

She sighed. "The shapeshifting thing."

"Yes."

"Well, you're right there," she said with a yawn she couldn't suppress. "You are not like most people."

"So now you see?" he asked, hopefully.

"I don't see anything," she answered. "Right now I'm too drained to see how I'm going to get into bed, let alone what you're telling me."

He looked at her and smiled sadly. "I'll help you."

"And I'll take you up on that. I don't know if my legs will hold me after everything that's happened."

He stood up and pulled her to her feet. "Lean on me. Are you sleeping in your mother's room?"

She clung to his waist as she tripped on one of her discarded boots. "Whoops. I'm okay, I'm okay . . ."

"Of course you are, *tesora mia*," he answered with a touch of humor in his voice as he held her more tightly.

"That's . . . what? Your treasure?" She leaned her head on his shoulder as he led her to the hallway.

"Yes, you have a good memory."

"See? I can't be that drunk, right?"

"Right, now let's get you to bed so you can sleep." He didn't bother to turn on the light. Pulling back the comforter, he placed her down. Covering her, he sat on the edge of the blanket and stroked her hair.

"Sleep, Deborah. You have had a very difficult time, but you are strong, perhaps one of the strongest women I have ever known. You will come through this challenge and be even more so."

"You think?" she mumbled sleepily, reveling in the soft touch of his hand on her skin, her hair. How she loved his touch.

"Oh yes. You are like a diamond. Do you know it takes years of stress and pressure to produce something so beautiful? That's what is happening to you now. A force is being applied to you and you will come through it even more beautiful. So sleep now," he whispered, hearing her deep steady breaths.

He rose and took off his jacket, then his shoes. Coming around to the other side of the bed, he laid down beside her and covered them both. He pulled her against him, spooning her to his body, wrapping his arm around her for protection.

Knowing she was asleep, he whispered the truth into her hair.

"Ti amo, amore mia. Sei la mia anima gemella."

And God help them both.

Tomorrow he would tell her Geoffrey Morgan, her grandfather, had been one of the main principals in establishing the Forsythe Group in the United States.

He had no idea how she would handle that, but he was convinced now that he and Deborah had been brought together for more than pleasure. Long ago he had learned that he was merely an actor on this stage of life.

Something else was pulling the strings.

20

Wearing her sunglasses, she stared through the wind-shield of the Porsche to the old brick house half hidden by tall trees and shrubs. "Wow. I didn't expect this," she murmured, that knot in her stomach tightening. It had become a familiar thing, ever since Marcus had told her this morning about her grandfather and the Forsythe Group.

She still couldn't fathom it. Her mother's father was part of this international cabal that has been ruling and controlling the world for thousands of years. No wonder he had disowned his daughter when he couldn't control her.

"Morgan certainly built a monument to himself." Marcus remarked as he looked up to the house.

Her jaw clenched in anger, once more remembering how they had abandoned her mother to live in poverty because she had tried to live her own life. And then they sabotaged that by making sure her husband would leave her. Too bad the old man was dead. She would have liked to have slapped him in his cruel face.

"You are sure you want to do this?"

"Absolutely," D. answered. "I have to, Marcus. She's the only one left. I want her to know just what she did to her daughter. I don't want her dying without realizing the consequences. Are you sure you're okay coming with me? It won't jeopardize anything with your . . . your foundation?"

He smiled in encouragement. "You aren't going in there alone."

"But you won't be invisible," she whispered with a smile.

He smiled back. "No, I won't."

"Okay, then let's do it," she answered and then took a deep breath.

They drove up the long winding drive to the main house and D. was astounded by the size of the place. They even had a long glass hot house attached to the main house and she could see it filled with large green trees.

"Are you ready?" Marcus asked, shutting off the engine and looking at her.

She let the tension out with a long sigh. "I wish I didn't have a hangover, but hey, stay in the moment, right?"

"Right. Just let things unfold, Deborah. Try to keep your anger under control and see what happens."

He opened his door and got out, then walked around the front of the car to her. Opening her door, he reached in to help her. They stood together for a moment and then she asked, "Were you talking to me last night in Italian when I was falling asleep?"

"Why?"

"I just remembered it when your hand touched mine. So, were you?"

"I was."

"You said nothing happened. I mean, both of us slept fully clothed."

"Nothing happened. Now, don't you think we should walk up to the front door?"

"Wait. What did you say?"

He reached out and took her hand in his. "I will tell you later."

"Promise?" she asked, holding on tightly.

"Yes, I promise."

"Okay then. Let's go meet my grandmother." She said the last word with all the distaste she felt.

They walked up to a large portico before the front doors and climbed the three brick steps to the oversized double wooden doors. Large Christmas wreaths were hung on them. Marcus rang the doorbell and she squeezed his hand even tighter.

"You will do well," he whispered. "Be the courageous woman you are."

She nodded, blowing out her breath in nervousness.

The door opened and a gray haired uniformed maid stood before them. "May I help you?"

"Yes," Deborah said, trying to keep her voice steady. "Would you please tell Mrs. Morgan that Deborah Stark is here to see her."

"Do you have an appointment?"

"No," Marcus answered, smiling at the woman. "Forgive our unannounced visit. If you could tell Mrs. Morgan that it is a family matter, I'm sure she will see us."

"Please come in," the woman said, opening the door wider. "If you'll wait here, I'll see if Mrs. Morgan is available to visitors today."

"Certainly," Marcus declared, ushering in D. "Thank you."

They stood in a foyer that was the size of her bedroom. A round center table with a huge arrangement of greens and white poinsettias was placed on top of a square Turkish rug. Hanging on the walls and up the wide curving staircase were paintings of male ancestors. Her ancestors, she realized with a jolt. None of them looked happy. Instead their faces were portrayed as stern images of power. Which one was her grandfather?

"Are you all right?" Marcus asked, still holding her hand.

"I guess. I was just wondering which of those men was Geoffrey."

Marcus looked. "There. That was him."

He pointed to a large painting, close to them. She dropped his hand and walked up to it. She couldn't see her mother in the man's steely blue eyes, but she did see that determined jaw he had passed on to his daughter.

"Excuse me."

She turned around to the maid. "Mrs. Morgan asks that you wait for her in the conservatory. She also asks if you wish something to drink."

D. joined Marcus. "Nothing, thank you."

"Please follow me."

Marcus took her hand again and they walked through a dining room with a table that must seat twelve. D. didn't recognize the type of furniture, but it looked antique, polished to a high gloss. Lots a shining silver was displayed. They proceeded down a long hallway with rooms on either side, an office, a book lined library with a television, a bath room and others with closed doors.

The older woman led them to double French doors and through the glass D. could see all those tall green trees. When the doors were opened, they were hit with a higher heat and humidity, almost tropical. They passed several flowering bushes and even orchids in white and yellow and purple. Despite her nervous resentment, D. was impressed.

The maid stopped at the seating of a cream sofa with green cording and two matching chairs. "May I take your coats? It can be oppressive in here when you're overdressed."

She looked at Marcus. "Thank you" And he handed her his jacket.

D. slipped out of her coat and did the same.

"Are you sure I can't get you something to drink? Perhaps something cool would be appropriate in here."

"Water?" D. asked, resisting the urge to pull on the neck of her cashmere sweater.

"And you, sir?"

"Water would be most welcome. Thank you."

D. had dressed in a her matching chocolate brown sweater set and gabardine slacks. It was the best she had brought with her on this bizarre trip from Philadelphia. When the woman left them alone, D. looked at Marcus. "Do you believe all this?"

"You have to admit, it is impressive," he said, touching the delicate petal of a white orchid that was placed on the metal and glass coffee table. "Either she has a gardener, or she has quite a green thumb."

"Thank you, young man, for your compliment. I take it that was a compliment."

They both turned to see an old woman dressed in black, walking toward them with the use of am ebony brass-handled cane. She had to be eighty. Maybe more, D. thought, as her heart jumped within her chest.

"Yes, madam. It was indeed a compliment," Marcus answered, showing his European charm. "Allow me to introduce myself. Marcus Bocelli."

"I am pleased to meet you."

Lillian Morgan looked to D. "I thought you would show up here one day soon, Deborah. Please, both of you, be seated. Suzanne will be here shortly with your water." She came closer, picking the nearest chair to sit down gingerly, as though it took an effort. "And please excuse the temperature in here. I'm afraid my old bones don't handle the cold winters well any longer."

Both D. and Marcus sat down on the sofa.

"You were expecting me?" D. asked, not wanting to have

polite chit chat with this woman. This was not a social call.

Lillian nodded and D. had to admit the old lady looked regal with her white hair wrapped in a loose bun, pearls at her neck and a diamond wedding band on her finger. "Ever since your mother died. Please accept my sympathies."

"Your sympathies?" D. asked in amazement.

"Yes, I know what it is like to lose a loved one."

"I think you would, and I'm not speaking about your husband."

"I know you weren't," Lillian replied evenly. "I was speaking of a loss we share."

"My mother?"

"Yes. Alexander Finney told me of her passing." Lillian seemed to shudder, then added, "I was there, you know, that day in the park when you released her ashes. Alex brought me, but I stayed in the car and we left before the rest of the mourners."

"You were there?" D. asked in disbelief and looked at Marcus. His face was expressionless. She turned back to Lillian. "Why did you come? To see that you had finally killed her?"

Lillian showed she was a woman of breeding by not flinching. She blinked several times, then said, "I'm sorry you feel that way."

"And what other way am I supposed to feel?" She opened her purse and took out that damn letter. "Remember this?" She handed it over.

The only clue as to the woman's reaction was her shaking hand as she read what she had written over thirty-five years ago. Just then, Suzanne brought a silver tray to the coffee table. Water was in a frosted crystal decanter, with matching frosted glasses. A fine china cup was filled with a dark amber tea.

Lillian's hand fell to her lap. "That will be all, Suzanne. Thank you."

When they were once more alone, D. asked, "I just want to know what kind of mother could write such a letter?"

"When did you find this?"

"Two days ago when I was cleaning out her things."

"I'm afraid there is no way I can give you an answer that will satisfy you."

"Try," D. nearly ordered, her back teeth clenching as she waited.

"There is no answer, Deborah. A mother should never write such a letter to her child, no matter the circumstances. I now that now. I have known it for many, many years."

"Then why did you do it? Do you have any idea what my mother's life was like? You sit here in this grand place and live like royalty and your daughter lived in poverty, worrying herself into an early grave trying to make ends meet. I came here to find out what kind of woman would allow her child to suffer because of stubborn pride."

"No, no . . . it wasn't pride," Lillian said, running her hands over her arms, as though cold. "you mustn't think that. Your grandfather . . . he was stubborn and willful, not me. I'm afraid, my dear, I was weak." She shivered slightly. "And frightened."

Marcus rose and handed Lillian her tea. "Perhaps this will warm you, madam."

Lillian smiled as she accepted the cup and saucer, her thin hands showing bones and veins and spots that marked her age. "Thank you, sir. You are very kind. I can see it in your eyes."

Great, he was charming her grandmother. Not exactly the right tact here, D. thought. "Getting back to the subject at hand. You were weak. Why were you frightened? Of him? Geoffrey?" And she said his name with unmasked distaste.

"You must try to understand the nature of things as they were then. Women were subservient to their husbands still, especially a woman who was brought up to marry for reasons other than wild infatuation. One married for the position of the family. If love came along then you were fortunate. If not," she shrugged, "you still had your position, your place in society."

"Excuse me, we're not talking about the middle ages. You disowned my mother in 1969. Surely you heard about women's liberation?" she asked incredulously. *This could not be the woman's defense.*

"The women's movement came in the next decade, if I remember correctly. During the time of Emily's difficulties, an independent woman was thought to be dangerous. Especially to a man like your grandfather."

"Why?" Marcus asked, his first venture into the conversation.

Lillian sipped her tea and then sat back, allowing the cup and saucer to rest on her lap. "Geoffrey Morgan was a difficult man under the best of circumstances. He didn't like to be challenged, particularly in his home. I tried to move his position on Emily. We fought terribly. And then he had a minor stroke. He demanded I write that letter and that he approve its wording. He then had it mailed. I felt so guilty. About Emily. About him."

"Did you love him, Mrs. Morgan?"

Even D. jerked her head to Marcus for asking that question.

"I'm afraid I don't know what love is, Mr. Bocelli," she said sadly, looking beyond them to her lush plants. "I didn't feel loved in my marriage. So I don't think I was loved by him. I was more of an acquisition, a successful merger of two families. He had other . . . interests, besides me, and we lived separate lives for the most part."

"Interests?" D. asked.

Lillian smiled. "Must I spell it out? He seemed to prefer a long succession of women. Of course his business always took priority, and I was the one on his arm at social functions, but long before Emily left it had become of marriage in name only."

"Why didn't you leave him?"

"You don't leave a Morgan," she said in a flat voice. "I brought it up many times, until it was implied that I would be destroyed if I filed for divorce. And Geoffrey could do that. He and his friends were very powerful men. So you see? I was a weak woman, a fact I must now face and ask your forgiveness, Deborah. I am only too aware of how your mother suffered and that I caused her great pain by my lack of courage."

D. shook her head, staring down to her untouched glass of water. "You can't ask that of me. Not now. All this is too new, too raw. I didn't even know you existed until the day before yesterday."

"But I knew about you," Lillian said. "Many times I tried to reconcile with your mother when you were growing up, but I wounded her so deeply and it was she who rejected me, and rightly so. She wouldn't accept anything from me. Letters were returned unopened. Offers of money were cast aside. I never spoke to her again, to tell her how sorry I was. I lost my daughter through my cowardice, and there is nothing you can do or say to me that will cause me greater pain. It is something I have lived with for decades and I shall die with it on my soul."

D. didn't say anything. She didn't know what to say.

"Mrs. Morgan, may I ask you a question?"

"Please, call me Lillian. You, sir, now know more about me than anyone alive. Let us dispense with formalities."

"Thank you, Lillian. You spoke about your husband's business dealings. Have you ever heard of the Forsythe Group?"

She seemed startled. "Why yes. That was his main interest. He and his business partners would sometimes meet here for weekends. I, of course, was purely a social hostess

at those times. Heaven forbid they discuss business in front
of a wife."

"Do you know what that group is?"

D. held her breath, glad it was Marcus who had taken over
this part of the discussion.

"Perhaps I should ask what you know, young man?"

"I only inquire because this group is threatening your
granddaughter."

Lillian sat up straighter and placed her cup and saucer
back on the table in front of her. "I beg your pardon?"

"The Forsythe Group is involved in criminal activity concerning the building of condominiums in Philadelphia. It
goes as high as individuals in the mayor's office and pay offs
to inspectors. These buildings are substandard and will be
dangerous to the future occupants. I'm sure you know Deborah is the anchor on Channel Four in Philadelphia. One of
her reporter friends brought her the story, after being turned
down by the station to pursue it. That man in now lying in a
coma in the hospital after a suspicious traffic accident. And
earlier in the week, Deborah's apartment was broken into,
probably someone searching for the files that lead from the
construction companies to the material suppliers to the
mayor's office. Her station is owned by Nova Communications and Nova is owned by the Forsythe Group." He paused
to allow the woman to digest what he was saying. "They
came after your granddaughter, Lillian, and I don't think
they're going to stop. I know we are placing our faith in you
now, by telling you all this, but I am hoping you will find
your courage and tell us what you know of them. Did your
husband have anything to do with Nova Communications?"

"I'm so sorry," she murmured, staring at D. "To think, after everything . . . they are trying to hurt Geoffrey's granddaughter. Have they no conscience at all?"

"And I am sorry, Lillian, but Geoffrey is dead. And they

don't have any conscience. Nothing matters to them, save accumulating power. What we need now is help."

"Yes, yes, of course. I don't know what to say."

Realizing she was old and she'd just had a shock, D. cleared her throat. "Did your husband ever say anything to you about Nova Communications, or television news, or manipulating the media? It's important." And her job might depend on it.

Lillian sat back in her chair and closed her eyes briefly. "There was a time, when he was dying upstairs and I was so upset about the news, our foreign policy, the state of the world, innocent children dying of hunger and disease, and I tried to talk to him about how I felt." She opened her eyes and smiled sadly. "I thought, near his end, he might have mellowed and we could finally share something. I didn't hope for peace, but maybe, perhaps, genuine conversation."

"What did he say?" Marcus asked gently.

"He ridiculed me, even as he was dying he was still disdainful of a woman's mind. He said the media was disciplined by corporate America and they finally were engineering conformity of supporting the party line. He bragged and said one political party's domination of the Federal Communications Commission eased decades long ownership restrictions. When that happened it allowed a single company or corporation to own television stations and newspapers in the same viewing area, encouraging mergers and stifling diversity of opinions. I believe I said it sounded like a repressive state regime and he laughed, saying they decided what the public will and won't be allowed to hear and see."

"And they punish anyone who tries to tell a different story." D. felt sick. Her grandfather, someone whose bloodline she carried, was a part of what she was fighting.

"Yes, I'm afraid that's true. He seemed almost gleeful when he said something to the effect that as these fantasies accumulate, the story told veers further and further from reality and anyone who tries to bring the viewers back to reality is denounced as a traitor and delusional. And he was very pleased to see this strategy unfolding here, in America."

"Did he ever mention Nova Communications?"

"I don't know," Lillian said. "I can't remember."

Marcus sighed. "I know this may seem rude, but could we look in his office?"

"It's been over four years since he died and his business partners came the very next day and took everything they said pertained to his business. I didn't object. At the time I was happy to have it done for me."

"So there's nothing." Marcus poured water into their glasses. "No personal papers?"

"No. Years ago I wiped this house clean of him, save for one thing. That portrait in the foyer. I've kept it there as a reminder of what he'd done to me and what I did to my daughter. Perhaps when you leave, Marcus, you might help Suzanne remove it."

She turned to D. "I know you are right. I can't ask you to forgive so many years of neglect. I take responsibility for not pushing harder to reunite with your mother. Perhaps the most distressing part was that Alex was talking to your mother about a meeting only a week before she died. I will always regret we didn't reconcile."

"Were they just friends, Alex and my mother?" D. asked. "I want to believe she was happy in the end."

Lillian smiled and nodded. "From what Alex has told me they were becoming more than friends. He's been a widower for many years and he is heartbroken to have lost Emily again."

"He seemed very nice," D. murmured.

"You should pay him a visit. He would welcome you."

"Maybe I will."

"And, perhaps, some day you will return and we can continue our discussion about your mother. I have pictures I would love to show you, things that belonged to your mother. You realize, Deborah, you are my only living relative. One day all this will be yours. You might spend some time here, if you think you could."

"I don't know, Lillian," she answered, flustered by the woman's statement, and by the realization that she was no longer angry with her. She actually felt sorry for the woman. A life spent without love seemed like a life sentence. "This is all overwhelming right now. I need to think about it."

"Of course. I'm not pressuring you, but time is moving quickly for me. And if it is possible, I would very much like to get to know you better. I watch you every night on the news. Lately I have thought of the irony of what Geoffrey said to me about the media and his granddaughter came to Philadelphia to report the news. You are very good at your job."

"Thank you," D. said while rising. "I will be in contact with you." Enough was enough. She simply had to get out of this heat and think about these new revelations.

Marcus quickly stood up and assisted Lillian in standing.

"Thank you, dear. I'm afraid my old bones lock up when I've been in one position too long." She looked back at D. "He's a very good man, Deborah. You've made a wise choice."

D. actually blushed. "I . . . I don't know that I've made—"

"Thank you, Lillian," Marcus interrupted as he offered the old woman his arm.

She walked behind them as they retraced their steps through the large house.

When they came to the foyer, Suzanne was standing there waiting for them, their coats over her arms.

"Suzanne, put the coats down and help Mr. Bocelli remove that picture," Lillian asked, using her cane to point to the large oil painting of her husband.

"Mr. Morgan?" Suzanne asked with surprise.

"That's right."

The maid put the coats on a nearby chair and joined Marcus at the foot of the staircase. In less than a minute the painting was removed. Marcus handed it to Suzanne.

"What should I do with it, ma'am?"

"Take it out back. Tell Charlie to make a fire."

"Burn the picture?" Suzanne asked in disbelief.

"Yes, and tell him to make sure I can see it from my bedroom window. Go ahead. Please get it out of here."

In a much lighter mood, Lillian turned to D. "Are you sure you don't want to stay and watch?"

D. smiled and shook her head. "As much as I'd like to, we have to leave. We have a long trip ahead of us."

"I understand completely," she said as Marcus held out D.'s coat.

She slipped her arms into the sleeves and smiled as she buttoned her coat. "I didn't think I would say this, but I'm glad we met." Her throat tightened with fresh emotion. "Thank you for everything you told me."

"Thank you for coming." Lillian reached out and then pulled back her hand. "Even though I haven't earned the right, may I just touch you?"

D. simply nodded.

For the first time, Lillian had tears in her eyes as she came forward and placed her thin hand on D.'s. "God protect you, Deborah. And I will be working on finding you help." She turned to Marcus. "Take care of my granddaughter, please."

"I will, madam. She's precious to me also."

He took D.'s hand and led her to the front door.

Once outside, D. was still reeling from the encounter and, truthfully, from Marcus' statement. Precious? She was precious to him? Or, was he just saying that for Lillian's benefit?

He wrapped his arm around her shoulders as he led her to the car.

"I am very proud of you," he murmured against her cheek. "You are an incredible lady."

D. laughed. "Hell, Marcus, it must be a recessive gene from the female side of my family. She was something, wasn't she?"

"*You* are something, Deborah. Something entirely wonderful. Now let's go home."

She felt that damn burning at her eyes again. "Whose home?"

"The one that needs a Christmas tree to go with the rest of your decorations."

Her heart burst open again with love. She couldn't help it. God help her, but she loved him. It was back, stronger than before.

21

Before returning to New York City, they stopped at her mother's house to pick up D.'s things. It was getting late and D. only planned to gather her clothes and shut the place down. When she turned the key, she tripped over mail and Marcus caught her from falling.

"Be careful, Deborah." He turned on the light switch. "Are you all right?"

She laughed. "Just a klutz." Unbuttoning her coat, she added, "Okay, give me a few minutes and then we're out of here. Too late to buy a Christmas tree tonight, right?"

"Yes, we'll do it tomorrow," he said, bending down and picking up the pieces of mail.

"I'm going to have to go to the post office and stop all that junk mail," she called out, hurrying into the bedroom to pack up. She didn't want to waste any time, picturing in her mind Marcus' warm cozy bed. She was way too tired for sex, but it would be heaven to cuddle in his arms and sleep together again. And for some reason the picture of the two of them buying and decorating a Christmas tree together warmed her

heart. She had never done that with a man, any man. And
she had never celebrated Christmas with a lover. *Was* he her
lover? All the signs were pointing in that direction, but she
suddenly felt as insecure as a teenager. Did she have a
boyfriend, or not?

"Deborah?"

She heard Marcus' voice from the living room. It sounded
strange, cautious. Her hand froze from picking up a pair of
jeans. "Yes?"

"Look at this," he said, now standing in the doorway. He
was holding out a thick white envelope.

"What is it?" In a flash her mind ran possibilities. Something about her mother's funeral? A bill?

She took it and saw her name neatly typed on the front of
the envelope.

"Look at the post mark."

Philadelphia? Mailed four days ago. There was no return
address. "Who would be sending me something here
from—"

Her jaw dropped and she stared at Marcus. "You think?"

He shrugged his shoulders. "Only one way to find out."

Her heart started beating faster and she could feel her
pulse throbbing in her fingertips as she ripped open the
back flap and pulled out folded papers. Slowly, she opened
them.

"Oh my God," she murmured. "It's from Tom," she added,
showing Marcus the cover note.

D.,
Sorry about this. Just a precaution. I know, conspiracy
nut, right?
  Got your mother's address from Pam's invoice when
she sent flowers after your mother died. Investigative re-

porters are like hound dogs and we don't give up easily.
So, just get rid of this if I've already given you the file
at work.
   Tom

"It must have been delayed because of the Christmas
rush," she whispered, looking at the next page. "It's all here,
Marcus." She flipped to the second page and the third.

"Okay, we need to get on the road, Deborah. And quickly.
I have to make a phone call."

"Call from here, or use your mobile."

"I want to use a pay phone on the turnpike. I need a secure
line."

"Who are you going to call?" she asked, handing him the
papers while throwing her clothes into her suitcase.

"Maggie's father."

D. stared at him. "Ga—"

He put his finger to her lips. "Let's get out of here.'

"Right." She closed her suitcase, stopped in the bathroom
to gather her make up bag, and followed him to the front
door. "I can come back in a couple of days and take care of
this place."

"We'll both do it," he said, taking her suitcase from her.
"Let's just go."

He walked out and she locked the front door. As they were
heading to his car in the driveway, they heard a voice.

"Merry Christmas, you two."

They stopped and looked toward Anna's house. She was
getting out of her car with a load of shopping bags.

"Merry Christmas," they each called back.

"When are you coming over for a visit?"

"Next week," D. said. "I promise. We'll both come."

Anna waved. "The two of you have a great holiday."

D. waved back. "You too, Anna. Give my best to your family."

Anna nodded and walked into her house.

Marcus opened the car door for her and put her bag into the back. "Let's go."

When he was seated next to her and turned over the engine, she blew her breath out and asked, "You're going to call Senator Burke?"

Nodding, he pulled out of the driveway saying, "He can put us in touch with a Federal prosecutor in Philadelphia, one we can trust. And he can make sure Tom Harris is guarded."

"Good idea." Thank God Marcus was with her. Feeling grateful, she shyly put her hand over his on the gear shift. "Thank you, Marcus. For everything. I really don't know what I would have done without you."

He shifted into third as they left Grandlake Estates behind them, then turned his hand over and squeezed hers. "You're going to be all right now, Deborah. We have what we need. And you'll get the exclusive story."

Her body froze and she looked at him. "Marcus, this isn't about an exclusive any more. This is about people lives, about trying to stop corruption and waking people up to see what's really happening to their country."

Marcus chuckled as they headed for the turnpike. "Welcome to my world, Deborah."

She collapsed against the leather headrest. "Your world . . . heaven help me," she muttered.

"Heaven already did," he answered, turning onto the entrance ramp.

It was the truth. Something, someone, was watching out for her.

* * *

"You put everything back?" she asked in amazement as she saw the wreath hanging on his front door.

He squeezed her shoulder while leading her up the steps. "Of course I did. Though when we get inside you'll want to give it your woman's touch. I'm afraid the garland over the fireplace looks a bit dilapidated. I couldn't get it hung correctly."

"Woman's touch?" she asked with a laugh of disbelief as he inserted his key.

"Absolutely, Deborah. You're just glimpsing the power of being feminine. It's not a weakness, you know. It is a blessing to be used wisely."

"I'll remember that," she answered, stepping over the threshold.

He turned on the light and D. saw he was right. The garland did look stuffed onto the mantle, not hanging gracefully. Did she actually have some latent talent with this girly stuff?

"Let's order dinner and eat in bed," Marcus suggested. "You've got to be exhausted."

"And tomorrow we'll buy a Christmas tree?"

"Yes," he said, taking her coat and hanging it up. "Where shall we put it?"

"You're asking me? This is your house."

He hung up his jacket and then put his arm over her shoulder as he turned her back to the living room. "I respect your opinion. Where do you see the tree?"

She surveyed the room. "How about in front of the windows? You could move that table over there temporarily and then you could see it from the street. I always loved to look into windows during the holidays and see decorated trees. I imagined happy people inside."

"Excellent suggestion. I hope we find a good one. Tomorrow is Christmas Eve, you know."

"Christmas Eve," she murmured. "Hard to believe. I haven't even sent out a single card."

He kissed her temple. "You've had other things on your mind. Now what shall we eat? I'm starved."

"You decide. I just want to get a shower and fall into bed."

He turned her to face him, wrapping both his arms around her. "Mind company? I could use a shower myself."

She smiled, staring into his beautiful dark eyes, eyes that showed a hint of teasing and something else . . . passion? No, something more tender. "I'd love company. You can wash my back."

"Always. We can begin with your back if you like."

Okay, he should stop talking like that, because it was making her think there was a future with him and she had told herself to stay in the moment and not torture herself with plans of happily ever after. If she loved him, and she did, she would be grateful for what was, not what might be. Now if she could only do that.

"Order dinner, Marcus," she said, then kissed him quickly on the mouth. "I'm going to go upstairs and get started."

He released her with a laugh. "Wait for me," he called out.

"Then hurry up. We probably only have a half hour to forty-five minutes to get the stink off us before the doorbell rings."

"You have such a way with words," he said with a wide grin as he headed for the phone.

"That's why I'm on TV," she called out, giggling as she dragged her suitcase up the stairs. This time she wasn't heading for the guest bedroom.

The next night she sat on the floor in front of the Christmas tree, adjusting the burgundy velvet tree skirt, making it flow in graceful waves of fabric on the hardwood floor. It was beautiful. And it was a bargain because of Christmas Eve. Retailers had slashed prices to get rid of stock and she and Marcus had landed a windfall of elegant, fragile crystal stars and hand blown burgundy glass ornaments. She had felt silly when they passed the flower market and she had bought armfuls of flowers and baby's breath. She'd used the baby's breath on the tree, making it look like delicate puffs of snow.

It was gorgeous, she thought, looking up at it. Not just a good tree, but really gorgeous. Soft Christmas music was playing in the background and D. had never felt this happy. Not even as a child. No gifts were under the tree, but that didn't matter. This wasn't about gifts, not the kind you could buy. This was about a feeling of coming home. A comfortable, relaxed and warm feeling of belonging.

"All right, you're going to have to be my critic," Marcus said, coming into the living room. "I followed the recipe, but I've never made eggnog before, so tell me the truth." He handed her a crystal glass half full with the creamy drink.

"I'm not a connoisseur of eggnog," she answered, reaching up for the glass.

"Go ahead. Taste it."

She could tell he was anxious to please her, wanting her to have all those things she thought others had been enjoying when she'd looked into Christmas windows. She sipped. "It's good," she said, taking another sip. "Really good."

"Truly?" he asked with a pleased expression.

"Truly, Marcus."

He handed her his glass. "Now wait here for me. I'll be right back."

"Yes, sir," she answered with a laugh. He seemed so happy. Maybe even excited.

He came back into the room with a large square box wrapped in red with a big white fabric bow on top.

"What did you do?" she demanded. "I don't have a gift for you." She felt disappointed that she'd been so busy with decorating she hadn't even bought him a card. "I feel bad."

He sat down on the floor with her and pushed the gift

closer to her. "This isn't to make you feel bad, Deborah. And it's a small gift, one I wanted to give you."

Her shoulders dropped. "But I don't have anything for you. And this isn't a small gift. It's heavy."

He stroked a strand of hair behind her ear and said, "Look around at the gifts you've given me. Do you know this is the first time I've had a Christmas tree here?"

"Really? You never put one up?"

"No. I didn't want to, until now. Open your present."

Feeling a bit better, she carefully untied the wide ribbon and pulled off the paper. It was a large box, looking like it came from a department store.

"Go ahead," he urged. "Open it."

She lifted the lid and pulled away the white tissue paper.

Her mind seemed to go blank for a moment as she stared into the box.

Inside were stacks and stacks of white socks. Short ones. Longer ones. Thick ones and fine cotton ones.

"Marcus . . . ?" Her throat closed with emotion as she touched a pair. A deep hot sensation filled her chest until she couldn't contain it. Feeling stupid, she burst into tears.

"Do what you want with them, my love. Use them to wipe your tears or dust the furniture." He kissed her temple. "But they are warm socks."

She sniffled and laughed. "I don't know what to say. I mean . . . I can't believe I told that to you, and now . . . this." She was shaking her head in disbelief. "You are the dearest man." And in that moment, after her dark humiliating secret had been exposed and accepted, she felt a lightness within her, a letting go of her past, leaving room to make new memories.

Hold on. He had called her his love. Not in Italian, but in good old American English. Could it be possible?

Suddenly she remembered he had never told her what he'd said to her the night she had drank too much. Last night after they made love in the shower they had eaten their dinner and had fallen asleep in each others arms. And today they had been so busy, she had forgotten.

"Marcus, you promised to tell me what you said to me that night at my mother's."

He smiled and drew her even closer. Sitting beside her, he turned and cupped her face in his hand. "I thought you had forgotten."

"No, but now I want to know."

He inhaled deeply and gazed into her eyes. "I have never said these words to another. I didn't think I ever would. But then you came into my life, Deborah Stark, and nothing has been the same. In such a short time, you've shown me a way I didn't think was possible."

"That's what you told me in Italian?" she asked in a whisper, trying not to cry again because this sounded important, real important, and she didn't want to screw up the moment by dissolving into tears and making some ugly face and—

"Shh, just listen to me," he murmured against her cheek. "*Sei la mia anima gemella.* You are my soul mate." His breath sent shivers of awe through her. "*Voglio passare il resto della mia vita con te.* And I want to spend the rest of my life with you."

Her breath left her body with the last of his words.

"I love you, Deborah," he said, taking her into his arms. "I didn't know someone like you would come into my life. I promise I will cherish you, not only your body, but also your mind and your heart."

"I love you too, Marcus," she managed to get out, clinging to him as her heart sang with joy. He loved her! He loved her! He wanted to spend his life with her! What a Christmas present! And what a way to begin a new year!

"This is the best Christmas of my whole life," she murmured, loving the feel of his heart beating against her breasts, his hands touching her body. She wanted to stand up, put on a new pair of socks and kick up her heels with happiness. She sniffled and wiped at her nose with the back of her hand. "Say, handsome, what are you doing New Years Eve? Wanna celebrate?"

His hand stroking her back stopped. "Ah . . . I may have a previous engagement."

She pulled back and looked into his eyes. "Wait a minute. Did we or did we not just declare our love like some Hallmark greeting card?"

He grinned. "It isn't what you think. Remember Carolyn? I said I would help her with her party. It's her first and she's nervous."

"You're going to be working on New Year's Eve?" Great.

"My love, our life is not going to follow normal society's dictates. My assignment with her is almost over. And I did promise." He paused. "But you could come and help too. We would be together."

"What, so now we're a team on these bizarre assignments?"

He squeezed her. "Look how well we've done so far. I think we make a great team."

"A team, huh? You help humanity by being a shapeshifter, and I help by finding out the truth and spreading it via the media?"

"Well, the only way it could work for us would be if we shared not only lives but also our occupations, no? We do make an excellent team."

"And we're going to do all this long distance? We live so far apart."

"You know, Deborah, when Gabriel Burke sets everything into motion and you are on hand with a television crew as Federal agents arrest Norman Kove at the mayor's office, I think you'll receive offers from the networks. Gabriel happens to be on very good terms with the BBC's news department, and I know for a fact they are looking for a new anchor for BBC America."

She blinked and then blinked again. Finding her voice, she said, "First of all this is Tom Harris' story and he will get due credit. And how do you know for a fact they are looking for a new anchor?"

"Gabriel told me. Three days from now we are all meeting here in the city. Then we go to Philadelphia."

"I have a contract with Channel Four. I can't break it."

"But you can be bought out of it. They are interested, Deborah. And I guess that means you would be living here."

"Here?" she asked hopefully, not quite believing all of it could be happening so quickly.

"Yes, my love. Here. With me. If you'll have me."

"Do you mean live together, or . . . are you proposing, Marcus? I mean, I just want to understand and—"

"You understand, Deborah," he said, reaching into his pocket. He held out a ring, a simple gold solitaire diamond that had to be two carats sparkled in the firelight.

D.'s jaw dropped. She was speechless.

"Will you marry me, Deborah? Will you share my life and my work?"

She kept staring at it.

"Deborah?"

She swallowed her disbelief. "Of course I'll marry you," she cried, throwing herself at him and kissing him until they both fell back onto the floor. She suddenly, pulled up and looked into his eyes. "But this BBC thing. What if it doesn't happen? I don't want to live apart. We can't count on it."

"You're right," he whispered into her mouth. "All we can count on is this moment. I love you and I will do whatever it takes to keep you happy and protected. Don't worry about the future. Stay here with me. Right now. In this moment."

He was right. "And what a moment it is," she whispered,

feeling at peace for the first time in her life. Nothing mattered, save being with him, seeing her love reflected back to her in his eyes. She belonged in his arms.

His smile was wide and filled with love. "Exactly. What a moment it is."

And then his mouth claimed her and she willingly surrendered to whatever force was directing her life.

Why not? It had gotten her precisely where she wanted to be.

Carnival Pride℠
April 2 - 9, 2006.

7 Day Exotic Mexican Riviera Itinerary

DAY	PORT	ARRIVE	DEPART
Sun	Los Angeles/Long Beach, CA		4:00 P.M.
Mon	"Book Lover's" Day at Sea		
Tue	"Book Lover's" Day at Sea		
Wed	Puerto Vallarta, Mexico	8:00 A.M.	10:00 P.M.
Thu	Mazatlan, Mexico	9:00 A.M.	6:00 P.M.
Fri	Cabo San Lucas, Mexico	7:00 A.M.	4:00 P.M.
Sat	"Book Lover's" Day at Sea		
Sun	Los Angeles/Long Beach, CA	9:00 A.M.	

ports of call subject to weather conditions

TERMS AND CONDITIONS

PAYMENT SCHEDULE:
50% due upon booking
Full and final payment due by February 10, 2006

Acceptable forms of payment are Visa, MasterCard, American Express, Discover and checks. The cardholder must be one of the passengers traveling. A fee of $25 will apply for all returned checks. Check payments must be made payable to **Advantage International, LLC** and sent to: **Advantage International, LLC, 195 North Harbor Drive, Suite 4206, Chicago, IL 60601**

CHANGE/CANCELLATION:
Notice of change/cancellation must be made in writing to Advantage International, LLC.

Change:
Changes in cabin category may be requested and can result in increased rate and penalties. A name change is permitted 60 days or more prior to departure and will incur a penalty of $50 per name change. Deviation from the group schedule and package is a cancellation.

Cancellation:

181 days or more prior to departure	$250 per person
121 - 180 days prior to departure	50% of the package price
120 - 61 days prior to departure	75% of the package price
60 days or less prior to departure	100% of the package price (nonrefundable)

US and Canadian citizens are required to present a valid passport or the original birth certificate and state issued photo ID (drivers license). All other nationalities must contact the consulate of the various ports that are visited for verification of documentation.

We strongly recommend trip cancellation insurance!

For complete details call 1-877-ADV-NTGE or visit www.AuthorsAtSea.com

---

This coupon does not constitute an offer from Tom Doherty Associates, LLC.

For booking form and complete information
go to **www.AuthorsAtSea.com** or call **1-877-ADV-NTGE**

Complete coupon and booking form and mail both to:
**Advantage International, LLC,
195 North Harbor Drive, Suite 4206, Chicago, IL 60601**